One Year's Time

ANGELA MILNE

First published in 1942

This edition published in 2023 by
The British Library
96 Euston Road
London NW1 2DB

Cataloguing in Publication Data
A catalogue record for this publication is available from the British Library

ISBN 978 0 7123 5457 8
e-ISBN 978 0 7123 6881 0

Text design and typesetting by JCS Publishing Services Ltd
Printed and bound by CPI Group (UK), Croydon, CR0 4YY

Contents

The 1940s

- **1940:** The average age of first marriage is 24.3 for men and 21.5 for women. Ninety-one per cent of marriages are the first for both parties – the highest this number reaches in modern records.

- Throughout the decade, only about 30 per cent of houses are owned by the people who live in them.

- **1942:** *One Year's Time* is published.

- **1942:** The average salary in 1942 is £320 – the equivalent of approximately £19,300 today.

- **1943:** In 1939, 5.1 million women are formerly employed; by 1943, this number has risen to 7.25 million (36 per cent of all women of working age).

- **1942:** All British men aged 18–51 and all unmarried British women aged 20–30 by 1942 are subject to conscription to National Service if they don't meet certain exemptions.

- **1944 (November):** On 25 November, 168 civilians are killed in a Woolworths department store in New Cross, London, in the worst V-2 attack of the Second World War.

- **1945 (May):** The War in Europe officially ends with the surrender of Germany on the 8th. The Second World War comes to an end with the surrender of Japan on 2 September.

❀ ❀ ❀

❀ **1947/8:** *Punch*, the humour and satire magazine for which Angela Milne wrote sketches, reaches its peak circulation at over 175,000.

❀ **1948:** The National Health Service is founded.

Angela Milne (1909 – 1990)

🌀

Angela Milne was born on 2 September 1909 to Ken and Maud Milne. She was the niece of writer A. A. Milne. Her childhood was spent in Croydon and she was best friends at school with Peggy Ashcroft, later to become a famed actor. She went on to attend Godolphin School, Salisbury.

Having initially found work as a secretary, and deciding she was 'the world's worst' at it, Angela decided to try a career in writing – helped by £50 from her uncle to give her a fair chance at it. She soon found some success and, from 1937, worked on the staff of the *Evening News*. During the War Angela undertook various forms of war work, first as part of the Land Army and later working in the Ministry of Information. She would describe her experiences as a 'land girl' in Dorset as 'living in quiet desperation, eating turnips and freezing in bed'.

Angela's sister had inspired a series of A. A. Milne's light-hearted sketches in *Punch*, and Angela would follow her uncle's footsteps there. She was the first woman to be invited to the hallowed *Punch* Table, although only on one occasion, at which she apparently took part in a heated discussion about Walt Disney's adaptation of *Winnie the Pooh*. This contretemps didn't stop her fulfilling her ambition to be a regular contributor to *Punch* and her pieces (under the pseudonym 'Ande') appeared through the late 1930s, 40s and 50s. Some years, her humorous sketches appeared in almost every issue. She selected her favourite pieces to include in the 1947 publication *Jam and Genius*, with topics including deck chairs, punctuality and cleaning your bicycle.

In the same year that *Jam and Genius* was published, she married Reginald Killey, a civil engineer and they had two children, Julia and Nigel. The family lived in London until 1958, when they moved to a neglected cottage in Breamore, Hampshire. Not a natural country-dweller but always a practical person, Angela became skilled at DIY and gardening. Her other writing activities included being a regular book reviewer for the *Observer* and working as an advertising copywriter. *One Year's Time* (1942) was her only published novel. In her last years she was severely disabled by rheumatoid arthritis, which her children remember her bearing bravely. Angela died on Christmas Eve in 1990.

Preface

New Year's Day – a time for new beginnings, for hopes, to re-evaluate and decide what it is that you really want from life. Two New Year's Days bookend Angela Milne's wonderful novel *One Year's Time*. At the start of the book we find the heroine, Liza, a secretary in her twenties, painting the floor of her Chelsea flat with sophisticated black gloss. Walter, a man she met the night before at a party, arrives unexpectedly and they start a sexual relationship. If this makes Liza sound a little like a passive hostage to fortune, this would not be totally unfair. She is an ostensibly modern woman, financially solvent with a job and a flat, but she is not confident or forthright enough to take the lead in this new relationship.

The novel takes us inside Liza's vivid inner life. We see through her eyes and experience her keen observations of people, clothes, places; Milne sketches these in deftly, avoiding the use of lengthy descriptions and yet without descending into caricature. Above all we feel Liza's pain, her joys and frustrations. We want more for her. Her growing love for Walter, although reciprocated, requires her to compromise her own happiness.

Published in 1942 and set in the late 30s, *One Year's Time* will surprise many readers with its frank depiction of an extramarital sexual liaison. And for Liza and Walter, this modern relationship outside of traditional social conventions does bring freedom – but this is not in any way experienced equally by the couple. Giving up much of her old life, Liza makes sacrifices that are not expected of Walter, and risks the loss of power, status and self-determination. As the New Year approaches again and Liza reassesses her life, will she regain control?

Tanya Kirk
Lead Curator, Printed Heritage Collections 1601–1900
British Library

Publisher's Note

The original novels reprinted in the British Library Women Writers series were written and published in a period ranging, for the most part, from the 1910s to the 1950s. There are many elements of these stories which continue to entertain modern readers, however in some cases there are also uses of language, instances of stereotyping and some attitudes expressed by narrators or characters which may not be endorsed by the publishing standards of today. We acknowledge therefore that some elements in the stories selected for reprinting may continue to make uncomfortable reading for some of our audience. With this series, British Library Publishing aims to offer a new readership a chance to read some of the rare books of the British Library's collections in an affordable paperback format, to enjoy their merits and to look back into the world of the twentieth century as portrayed by their writers. It is not possible to separate these stories from the history of their writing and as such the following novel is presented as it was originally published with one minor edit. We welcome feedback from our readers, which can be sent to the following address:

British Library Publishing
The British Library
96 Euston Road
London, NW1 2DB
United Kingdom

Part One

Spring

I

Liza stirred the brush into the black treacly depths of the tin and began to paint the floor round the carpet. She stopped to turn the carpet back farther, but it wouldn't stay there. She should have moved the furniture and folded it into the middle of the room; and she should have put on her overall instead of her pink chenille dressing-gown; and washed up the lunch things, and put a note in the laundry-box about the tablecloth. She thought, well, if I'd done all that first I should never have started the painting. She looked at the piece she had done. A rich and glossy black floor. A deep-piled carpet in softest plum. Gay, chintzy curtains. A cushion-heaped divan. Then she looked round the bed-sitting-room of her flat. There was a scrubby patch on the carpet where she had washed the ink out; and two cushions hardly counted as heaping a divan, and chintz curtains weren't necessarily chintzy, and they weren't gay, they were just curtains hanging up. She thought, oh, all those things the newspaper say about what they call Bachelor Girls.

Liza hated Saturday afternoons. The world went to football matches, it ate too much tea, it bought Sunday joints and packets of dull biscuits, it waited dumbly while its greengrocers squeezed cabbages into tight paper bags which would burst before it got them home; the wind blew round the street corners, and in Chelsea there were more street corners, and the wind blew more bitingly and dustily round them than anywhere else in

– 1 –

London; and Saturday evening blazed up along the King's Road and died into a shuttered Sunday. Sunday, in London, was dust and ashes. And Saturday afternoon, when you were alone, was dust and ashes too.

Liza had spread a newspaper for the paint-tin, and the date caught her eye. *Saturday, January 2.* She knew it already. Except for a fortnight every summer, Liza always knew the date. She was always typing it under the address on the office notepaper. But on January the first, the second and for a few more days you thought about the date more than usual. It was still the New Year. Liza turned back the carpet again, and tried to remember what she had been doing this time last year.

She thought, I was in this flat, I'd been here about three weeks. I've put off painting the floor for a year and three weeks. I wasn't wearing this dressing-gown, because it wouldn't be Saturday and I would be at the office; but I had it. It's funny how you never think you will have any of the same clothes this time next year. Or the same character. Well, and I was twenty-three, and I was at the same office. I always am. And whenever the telephone rang I thought it would be Hugh; and it wasn't often. And now, when it rings, I know it will be no one special.

Last year. She thought, this time last year the year that has just gone by was going to be the Future. Well, it didn't turn out to be. It's funny how the Future moves away as you move up to it; and how what you are going to do in it has no connexion with you as you are; always you as you might be, and won't.

Then Liza dug her paint-brush into the bottom of the tin and thought: I wonder where I shall be in one year's time. This time next year I shall think of this time last year and see where a year has taken me. I will be different, and so this year will be different. I'm painting the floor now, after putting it off so long. That's an omen that I can be different.

Liza had stopped stirring the paint. She knelt back. A taxi thrummed past, leaving the street quiet again. It was so quiet in the flat that she could hear the faint whirring she was never sure an electric clock should make. Twenty to four; a horrid time, nearly dark. She saw the invitation card, two days out of date, on the mantelpiece by the clock, and the ugly pink marbled ash-tray some one had given her; and, looking round the room, the divan on the right, the window at each end of the room, the net curtains which needed washing, the chintz curtains which needed the glaze putting back; and across the one armchair and the bookshelves to the mantelpiece again; and then ahead, past the four white-distempered walls of her little country to the world which waited outside.

And then, turning her heart over by its suddenness, the telephone rang.

It was a sort of omen. It was more than an omen, it was the Future, it was the world outside calling to her; and in a few seconds, when she had answered it, she would know it was none of these things. But Liza dropped the brush into the tin and jumped to her feet. She heard the dressing-gown tear somewhere, and the brush had sunk half-way up its handle. But the telephone was ringing, the Future was calling.

'Hullo?' she said.

'Hullo?' said a man's voice. And she didn't know whose.

'This is Walter,' said the voice. 'We met at that party no one had enough to drink at, so your mind can't be a blank about who you met, the way minds are sometimes at parties, don't you think?'

'Oh, no,' said Liza. 'I mean, yes, they are. I do remember you. How are you?'

'I'm fine,' said Walter. 'How are you?'

'I'm fine,' said Liza.

'That's fine,' said Walter. 'Isn't this a typical telephone conversation? How do you think I found your number?'

'Well, I don't know.' She thought, he might have asked some one at the party, or he might have looked me up in the book. If I say the wrong answer it will seem silly.

'Well, I looked you up in the book. Which I think is always so frightfully clever, don't you? Are you doing anything this evening?'

'Why no,' said Liza. 'I mean yes. I'm painting the floor. At least, the part that shows, round the carpet. If I stop it will go patchy. So I'm going on.'

'That's awfully diligent,' said Walter. 'I believe it's the secret of success, or something. Shall I come round and help you?'

Liza thought, it really is the Future. 'Oh, do,' she said. 'It would be such fun.'

'I'll bring a step-ladder and an overall,' said Walter. 'And I'll be round at half-past six, roughly. I've got to go out to tea, and they're always a bit keen on you being in time for the crumpets. So I will now stop and catch the post. Good-bye.'

'Good-bye,' said Liza. She went back and rescued her paint-brush, thinking, as she wiped it on the newspaper and made a black smear on her dressing-gown: this is the beginning of next year.

❀

Walter stood on the edge of the carpet and said, 'I can tell which bit you've done. I'd know it anywhere.'

Liza stood beside him. 'The tin said it would be black and glossy.'

'Well, you know what tins are. It's black, anyway. I think it's highly artistic.'

Liza found that she did and didn't like standing near him. She moved away and poured out the sherry.

'I thought you were going on till you'd finished it,' said Walter. He sounded absent. He had stepped on to the unpainted part and squatted down by the bookshelves.

'Well, I was,' said Liza. 'But I went and got something for dinner because I thought why didn't we have it here, and then I had to peel the potatoes, which I loathe, and one way and another the time sort of went.' She thought, and I spent an hour dressing and trying to make my hair go right. I don't seem to be being different from myself. I was going to wait till he said where shall we have dinner, and then sort of look as if I was whipping a meal together. Oh, it's no good trying to be different. She said, handing him his glass, 'I hope you like sherry.'

Walter put a book back and jumped to his feet. 'I adore it madly. And I'm dying of thirst.' He carried his glass to the divan. 'May I lie down on this? I hate sitting on chairs like ordinary people, don't you?'

'I hate it,' said Liza. 'I always sit on the floor.' She sat down by the armchair, watching Walter kick his shoes off. She said, 'Are you the kind of person who reads newspapers round haddocks?'

'Always. If there's one thing that makes a newspaper readable, even the Wanted, roll of wire netting, immediate, distance no object, bits, it's putting a damp haddock in it. And I think the bits that come off on the haddock are the most exciting of all, don't you?'

Liza was thinking, he has a quick, alive voice. I don't know if he's good-looking. Yes, I think he is. He's the sort of person you like going to a party with and knowing that people know you're with him. She thought of the party she had met him at, at the house of some strangers, and how she had nearly not gone there; and she decided that there was something in Fate after all. She said suddenly, 'What do you like best in the world?'

'Well,' said Walter, 'I'm not absolutely sure what plane we're on. I mean, I should like to say sex. It sprang to my mind. It's true, of course. I mean, who doesn't? But then it would be just as true to say Shakespeare. Or the Brandenburg Concertos. Or curried chicken. Or the moon on the sea. Or Groucho Marx. You see what I mean?'

'Oh, I do,' said Liza. 'I suppose it depends on who asks you.' And then she nearly blushed, and turned round and moved the telephone an inch from where it was before. But, when she turned back, she saw that Walter's head was hidden by a cushion, and she was very glad. She said, 'I think you said all the things I like too. Only not curried chicken. Perhaps kedgeree.' She thought, what fun it is getting to know some one. Everything either of you say is exciting, if the some one is a man. She said, 'Where's your glass?'

Walter rolled over and took it from the floor. Liza filled it and sat down on the floor by the divan. She hadn't really meant to. Walter said, wriggling round so that now she could see his face, 'Tell me about yourself. Your dreams, your hopes, your telephone number. That's not mine.'

'No,' said Liza. 'I have heard it. What shall I tell you?'

'Well, tell me all the things you hate.'

'I hate an awful lot of things. I hate church services on the wireless for any one to listen to. I hate cinema organs. And doggy ash-trays.' It was lovely to talk about yourself. 'And advertisements. And sort of coyness, if you know what I mean.'

'I know,' said Walter. 'What they call uproarious farces, with two people never quite in the same bed, and the audience being supposed to get a hell of a kick out of it. I suppose that sort of thing represents the lowest common factor of the estimated audience's mental age. You hate all my hates. I think you can summarize them as stupidity and vulgarity, don't you?'

'Yes, I think so,' said Liza. She was thinking, he has a quick, alive face to match his voice; and his hair isn't quite dark, it's dark brown, and his eyes are grey.

There was a silence. Then Walter said, 'Go on. Tell me some more. Are you alone in the world?'

'More or less,' said Liza. 'Why? Do I look it?'

'More or less.'

'Well. I've got a father. In India. And a brother. In Vancouver.'

'I say, that's a bit far-flung. Are they nice?'

'Yes,' said Liza. She thought, he's awfully interested in me. I feel sort of funny. Not exactly frightened. She said, 'Now it's your turn.'

'Oh, well. I've got a mother and father in Lincolnshire. And no little brothers and sisters, and a horrid selfish nature. What would happen if I took my tie off?'

'Everything.' And now she did blush. She hadn't meant it to mean what it sounded like; or to mean anything. It was just something to say. She saw that Walter was rather embarrassed too, and was a little surprised. He said, 'I don't think it need.' And then, 'Modern life's awfully trammelling, isn't it?'

'Yes. I should hate to wear a tie.'

'I didn't mean that.'

'Oh? What did you mean?' She wondered why she had said it.

'If you insist,' said Walter, undoing the top button of his shirt, 'I meant that there aren't any rules of conduct now. There probably weren't any ever. But people always say there were. So I suppose there were.'

Liza stood up and put her glass back on the tray. 'I think rules are rather silly. No, I don't, really.'

Walter stood up too. 'Nor do I, really.' Liza thought, we're just talking to keep ourselves from saying what we mean. She said, 'I think I'll go and see about the dinner. You would like us to have dinner here, wouldn't you? I always think it's so much nicer than going out.'

'I should just love it,' said Walter. 'Can I peel the potatoes?'

'Oh, no,' said Liza. She thought, I did tell you I peeled them; but I suppose you were reading.

They stood facing each other. Liza found that she couldn't look up and meet his eyes. She stared at the undone button on his collar and wondered if he got sunburnt in the summer; yes, she thought he did.

Walter said, 'Please. Would it be awful if I kissed you?'

Liza was suddenly very happy. They were friends, they were on the same side; all that he wanted was what she wanted—a flash of beauty in a dull world.

She said, 'No.'

'Do you mean no, it wouldn't be awful, or no, you mustn't?'

'No, it wouldn't be awful.' She shut her eyes; and, opening them what seemed a long time later, thought, it wasn't all we wanted, it was just the beginning, and we shall have to go on.

❦

Walter said, 'Do you have a perm? Or is it natural? Isn't perm a ghastly word?'

'Isn't it?' said Liza. 'It smells of cheap scent. No, it is natural. I think it's the only thing about me that isn't the same as every one else. Except that every one else is taller, but you sort of expect that.' She thought, this is a funny time to talk; me in bed with nothing on, and him kneeling there with only his socks. They had turned the light out; the gas-fire threw a pink glow on the ceiling. The clock said twenty past ten; in the silence she could hear its faint whirring. She thought, Walter and I are strangers again, and frightened, and that's why we're talking.

Walter said, 'I don't think you're like any one else. I've never seen a face like yours. It's—I don't know. Dreadfully unsullied.'

'It's not. I'm sullied.' She thought, that was a cheap come-back.

'You know I didn't mean that,' said Walter. She thought, his voice is different now; quiet, sort of damped down.

'I know,' she said. 'And I do know what you mean.'

'Do you mind things terribly?'

'Yes. I'm always so happy, or unhappy. It worries me.'

'I know,' said Walter. He took his socks off. 'I think your eyes are blue-grey. This light doesn't help much. Yes, blue-grey.'

'Yours are grey-grey,' said Liza. 'But I shall have forgotten them to-morrow.'

'Was that a flash of cynicism?'

'No, no. It's just that I never remember people's eyes.'

'Nor do I. I don't think observant people ever do.' He threw his socks across the carpet 'Liza. Do you think we shall be sorry?'

'I don't think people are sorry for the things they do. Only for the things they don't do.' She thought, yes, I know that's true.

'Yes,' said Walter. 'I think so too.' He got up.

Liza said, 'Could you give the kitchen door a bang?' She thought, I'm still frightened; no, I'm not.

Walter banged the door shut, and said, 'Damn! Oh, damn!' and hopped on to the carpet. 'I trod on where you painted the floor. Oh, darling, I'm awfully sorry.'

'Never mind,' said Liza. She thought, this is the first time he has called me darling. I don't think I can say it yet. 'It doesn't matter in the very least. Honestly.'

Walter rubbed his foot on a newspaper and said, as he got into bed, 'It was a accident. You aren't angry or anything, are you?'

'No, darling,' said Liza.

❀

Liza's office was in Chancery Lane. It had a staff of eight, if you counted Mr. Hill, the traveller, who appeared on two mornings a week, wearing a black hat which no one had ever seen him take off. The office had been the same eight people ever since Liza went there four years ago. When people at parties asked her what she was, if they went on after she said a secretary, she would tell them that her office had something to do with publishing music, but not much. No one in the office saw any music, published or not published, but that was what it led to, somewhere else.

The office was on the fourth floor of the usual sooty building, and it never looked quite dusted. It had olive-green paint, and boxes, and bundles of papers which no one was allowed to throw away, because no one asked to. There was a tray of papers outside the door which led from the passage to the main room. Liza had never seen any one go near these papers, and she had come to think that they might be a kind of mirage; she had read the top sheet, a list of things like FX/3/TC, but she had a funny feeling that if she looked at the next sheet the world would end. It would be like going into the flat above hers, instead of keeping it the mystery it was, thuds and creaks on her ceiling and the bass notes of a wireless set.

The door into the main room had a frosted glass top inset with an oblong of plain glass, with 'Enquiries' painted on it the wrong way round, so that it looked all right from inside, but from the passage you might have taken it for Greek, if you didn't know it so well that it was just Enquiries back to front. No one had ever said anything about it, and Liza had sometimes thought she imagined it, like the tray of papers.

The eight people in the office were Mr. Hollis, who was fat and pale and wore glasses and drank milk in the afternoon; Liza, his secretary, who typed most of the letters, some of them to quite exciting foreign addresses; Mr. Chiddock, whom Mr. Hollis called the Live Wire; Miss Netley and Miss Vane, his typists, whom Mr. Hollis was sometimes allowed to borrow; Partridge, the office-boy, who would be about seventeen now; Mr. Hill, and Miss Derry, who managed the telephone switchboard and did odd bits of typing on an old typewriter no one else could work.

There was a general feeling that the office was only there out of kindness. Liza never felt happy about turning the gas-fire full on, and if she asked Mr. Hollis for more money than her three pounds ten a week which had been her wages for the last two and a half years, Mr. Hollis would say that times had never been so bad as now, but perhaps a little later on. Liza never stopped feeling grateful to the office for paying her anything at all, especially as for the last eighteen months she had had a little money of her own—twenty-five pounds a quarter from a dead great-uncle; and she never stopped hating the office because it was an office. But it was really a very kind office, considering; and every afternoon Partridge brought her a cup of tea and two Thin Rich Tea Biscuits, soggy where the tea had slopped into the saucer, and sometimes Miss Derry handed round acid drops, and sometimes Mr. Chiddock would come into her room and lean on the mantelpiece, or walk angrily up and down with his hands in his trouser pockets, and talk about Life.

It was Monday morning, and raining. Liza thought, as she crossed the coconut matting in the doorway of the sooty building and changed from Liza to Miss Brett, the last time I trod on this mat was on Saturday morning. I suppose I was wondering what I should buy for lunch when I got home, and thinking about painting the floor. That was only two days ago. She went up in the lift, and the whirr was a new noise; the barrel-organ in the Strand had been a burst of splendour, all the world in a moment; she thought, I am alive, I have never been alive before. She opened the door and walked into Enquiries, as they called the main room.

'The better the day the better the deed,' Miss Derry was saying. Miss Derry sat at her switchboard in a bright pink jumper. Liza thought, she's washed the striped one. Oh, dear Miss Derry. She saw Miss Netley and Miss Vane, leaning against walls, and thought, dear Miss Vane, dear Miss Netley. Dear Partridge, with your silly collar. This is a lovely world.

Miss Derry liked to tell the office all about everything. The office knew what a trouble Miss Derry's striped jumper was; how, each time you washed it the stripes, which had once been white, got a little bluer from the navy background; and how, the jumper itself having shrunk as much as it would, the neck was the trouble, going out of shape immediately after every washing. Liza sometimes wondered what the office would do without Miss Derry, or Miss Derry without the office.

'So,' said Miss Derry, 'I laid it flat on Mum's biggest pastry-board and pulled that blasted neck up for all I was worth, and I don't think it's so bad. Give it another day to get it good and dry. Those blasted stripes are blue all over now, but who cares?' She snapped a peg down on the switchboard and her voice rose suddenly, losing its adenoids. '*I'll* tell them. *Righty*-ho!' She snapped the peg down and leant back, patting her greasy black sausage-curls. 'That's a pretty blouse, dear. I like green checks.'

'Think so?' said Miss Netley. 'I don't. Can't think why I bought it.' Miss Netley never liked anything. She leant against the switchboard and sucked a finger-nail; fairish, blobby-faced, gloomy. 'Hullo, Miss Brett.'

'Hullo,' said Liza. 'Hullo, Miss Derry. Hullo, Miss Vane. Hullo, Partridge.'

'Hullo, dear,' said Miss Derry. 'You're cheerful this morning.'

'Am I?' said Liza, blushing slightly. She thought, I want to kiss you all. I feel as happy as I did yesterday morning; it's seeing this poor dull office, which I haven't seen since last Saturday. Oh, lovely world.

Miss Vane blew her nose. Miss Vane was thin, dark and sallow, with very white teeth and lovely hands with square finger-nails which Miss Netley couldn't persuade her to varnish red. Miss Vane was as gloomy as Miss Netley, but sardonically so; and, poor girl, thought Liza, you've always got a cold and you live at home with a dreadful family; and I think you're a virgin. I don't think Miss Netley is, and I don't know about Miss Derry; but, oh, I'm so sorry for all of you.

Miss Derry held up a fountain-pen and said, 'Like it?' Liza went over to look. It was black vulcanite. It had a chromium lever, and a clip at the top. It was, in fact, a fountain-pen. Miss Vane and Miss Netley looked, and said nothing. Liza said, 'It's *heavenly*.' She saw Miss Vane's face. Miss Vane always made you think she knew all about you. Liza thought, she knows that I am so happy that everything is heavenly. So I am. So it is. She took Mr. Hollis's post from Partridge, thinking, dear, pale, dignified, funny Partridge, and went off to her room.

Liza's room was distempered a muddy green, it had brown curtains and a strip of brownish matting, a filing cabinet which either stuck or jerked its papers over you, a yellow oak desk and a revolving chair in brown leatherette. Miss Vane and Miss Netley had the same sort of room, but they had added a net curtain and a snapshot of Miss Netley's elder brother holding a fuzzy dog, and made the place rather a bower. Mr. Chiddock's room was all dusty papers and wire trays. Mr. Hollis, whose room joined

Liza's by another door with a frosted glass top, had the best room of all, but that was only fair; with an all-over carpet and waxed oak furniture. Liza arranged the letters on his glass-topped desk, and straightened his paper-knife parallel with the cigarette-box. Then she went back to her room and sat down, putting her chin on her typewriter.

She thought, I could sit here all day, just thinking. Every time I turn a corner of my mind I find something else I want to think about. I'm alive, I'm alive.

Liza thought about Saturday night; about Sunday morning, when they had sat at breakfast, Liza digging at the two charred sausages, Walter eating the nice brown bubbly ones; Walter, with his tie still off and his eyes laughing at her across the table; Walter dropping the *Observer* at a quarter to twelve and saying, 'Darling, I must go and shave'; Walter getting in his dark blue car, and Liza with him, and telling her about the uncle he was having lunch with, saying, 'The old boy's a bit dim on the facts of life, and he eats too much.' That was as the car turned the corner of her street. She could remember everything he said, and when and where he said it; Walter dropping her at the next corner by the delicatessen shop and saying, 'I'll ring you up to-morrow,' and making a face which meant, you and I have a secret.

Walter. Walter Latimer. Lovely name.

Liza thought, darling Walter, it isn't only that you're good-looking. You're so—I don't know. Elegant; that's a silly word. Graceful; that's silly too. But they're the best I can think of. Oh, Walter.

Liza lifted her chin from the typewriter and rubbed at where the typing ink would have left a mark. Mr. Hollis was in his room; you could see him against the frosted glass, like a tortoise in a tank. Soon the door would open, and his hateful, pale, fat face would come round it, saying, 'Well, Miss Brett?' and Liza would take her shorthand notebook and go to prison. She had been Mr. Hollis's secretary for four years, and she had never stopped being frightened of him because she was frightened of writing shorthand; afraid she wouldn't write it fast enough, wouldn't hear what he said, wouldn't be able to read it back. *Do you mind things terribly? Always so happy, or unhappy; you're never sorry for the things you do;* and the pink glow on the ceiling; *my true love hath my heart and I have his,* and we can never be strangers again.

The door-handle turned, and Liza snatched her shorthand notebook from the top drawer of her desk.

Mr. Hollis's telephone rang. The door closed. She was reprieved. She took the *Essays of Elia* from the drawer. Funny; Saturday morning had been so empty that she had shut herself in a book. She turned the pages. It was still lovely, but it was a book, and it was life that mattered.

🌀

Mr. Chiddock was dark and scraggy. He was different from the rest of the office, because he was interested in it; you felt that the others, except for Mr. Hollis, wouldn't care if it blew up; in fact they would like nothing better, because it would be so exciting, and they could all get jobs somewhere else. And Mr. Hollis, though it was his office, was too stupid to be interested in anything. But Mr. Chiddock was clever, which meant that he took life seriously enough not to believe in it. Liza was flattered because he argued with her; but she knew it was only because there was no one else he could talk to in the office.

This afternoon Mr. Chiddock leant on the mantelpiece, with his hands in his pockets, and said, 'Well, if you got any pleasure from giving twopence to a beggar pretending to play a fiddle and making not a sound, if you'd only listened, then your trouble is muddled thinking.' And he strode across the room and leant on the filing cabinet.

'I didn't say pleasure,' said Liza. 'It made me want to cry. Because you can get hardly any money in an Oxo tin, not counting notes, which he wouldn't have had, so he must only make about elevenpence a day.'

'He's got a biscuit-tin as a reserve,' said Mr. Chiddock. 'Those blighters are all the same. Anyway, you'—he took one hand from his pocket and pointed at her—'*you* gave him the twopence for the pleasure it gave *you.*'

'I did *not*,' said Liza, who had to take the opposite side of the argument. She wondered what Mr. Chiddock would say if she told him that she had to give a beggar twopence because she had a lover, and so she loved every one in the world. She said, 'Well, I suppose I did. It gave *him* pleasure too.'

'He's got a private income,' said Mr. Chiddock. 'Or he blew the lot on a drink. It probably ruined his life to have had twopence at that exact moment. How do you know?'

'I *don't* know,' said Liza. 'But his boots were coming off at the soles and it was raining. And I should only have spent the twopence on a bus-fare, or six-tenths of a cigarette or whatever it is—'

'Ten-thirds,' said Mr. Chiddock. 'Anyway, he changes to a perfectly good suit and shoes when he gets home. Those blighters all do. And, anyway, all *you* wanted was to see a smile of humble gratitude spread over his aged features.'

'Well, it didn't,' said Liza. 'A frightful muttering frown spread over it Because the tin wouldn't open.'

'Well,' Mr. Chiddock strode round the room, 'which would you rather have done, handed it out to him with visible generosity as you did, or dropped it anonymously out of Mr. Hollis's window?'

'Dropped it out of Mr. Hollis's window,' said Liza. 'It would have been such fun aiming at the tin.'

Mr. Chiddock leant on the mantelpiece and said, 'God defend me from arguing with a woman.'

Liza thought, well, I *am* a woman. Sometimes I can argue with you, Mr. Chiddock. Sometimes life is empty, and you are the only man in it, and I want to seem clever. But to-day I am alive. I love, I am loved; oh, darling Walter. She smiled. Dear Mr. Chiddock, I love you.

Mr. Chiddock actually blushed. He strode to the window and said, with his back to her, 'Anyway, you can't deny that every time people like you give a beggar twopence they're delaying the establishment of a decent social system.'

'They aren't like me,' said Liza. 'And I don't deny it, but it *was* only twopence. It can't delay it *much*, Mr. Chiddock.'

Mr. Chiddock strode to the mantelpiece, closed his eyes, opened them, said, 'Oh, well,' gave Liza a much nicer smile than usual and went out. Liza thought, I do love this office.

II

Going home in the evenings, Liza usually travelled by Underground, from the Temple to Sloane Square. A bus journey at night was as long and dull as it was swift and exciting in the morning; and at night tickets littered a dirty floor, and the other passengers were all elbows and evening papers. In the morning the left-hand front corner of a newly swept bus was a little world to think in. In the evening Liza preferred the Underground for that cosiness which reached its heights in the Inner Circle, which ran from nowhere to nowhere, just to please you. Even those bar-parlour mahogany coaches, kept by the management specially for Liza, were cosy. A stranger came in and shut or didn't shut the doors behind him, and he was some one, as he never could be on a bus. Every one stared; every one as good as asked him who he was, where he lived, why he lived, if he liked living, and what he had in that parcel.

And Liza would stare and stare, and the stranger might stare back, but sooner or later his eyes would wander off, leaving Liza the right to stare as much as she liked for the rest of their journey together. She would think, I can't stare at people I know; but I shall never see you again. Oh, I do want to know everything about you, because I shall never see you again.

But on this Monday evening Liza walked down Chancery Lane to get a bus at Temple Bar, thinking Walter is somewhere between here and the river. It was exciting that he should be so near; it was exciting just to know that he was in the world. She was taking a bus because she was going to a cocktail party in Bayswater, and a bus was slower. She would enjoy the party because everything was still rich and beautiful; but she wanted a little world to think in for another half-hour. The man next to her in the bus had bought an *Evening News,* the biggest paper he could find, the one he could spread farthest across Liza; but she didn't mind. She loved him because he was part of a lovely world.

There were two women's voices behind. One said to the other:

'Have you got two shillings for two shillings, dear?'

Lovely, lovely world.

The cocktail party was in the top flat of a tall yellow house near Lancaster Gate Station. It was being given by two friends of Liza's, Chloe and William Driffield, who had got married after living together for two years. Liza wondered, as she walked up the four flights of stairs, what had decided them. It wouldn't be anything as obvious as a baby. She thought, people are funny. No one knows what any one else is thinking. She reached the top flat and heard the party-murmur for a moment before Chloe opened the door and the murmur became a roar.

Chloe was dark and over-ripe, and probably older than William, and wore a fussy purple dress. She cried, in her opera-singer's voice, 'Why, if it isn't Liza!' There being nothing else to say, Liza said, 'Yes, it's me,' and left her coat in the bedroom and slipped back to the sitting-room. She stood at the edge of the crowd, wondering if she knew any one and why she had come. The world had stopped being rich and beautiful, it was loud, unfriendly and shutting-off. She stood outside it and thought, I don't care, I have Walter. But it didn't make it any better. Then William came up with a cocktail and a plate of biscuits.

Liza wondered if she ought to say anything about him being married now. She said, 'Hullo!'

'Hullo, Liza. How's things?' William was fair and narrow-eyed, and very quiet. Liza said, 'Lovely, thank you,' and thought, you're nice. I wonder if Chloe is anything like the woman you must once have imagined you would marry when you thought about the Future. I don't suppose so. People are funny.

William introduced her to a youngish man with a red face, brushed-back hair and fishy-blue eyes. Liza didn't hear his name. They stood together, an island of awkward silence in a sea of voices. Then Liza said:

'There are quite a lot of people here, aren't there?'

'Yes, aren't there?' He took out his cigarette-case. Well, he was trying.

Liza took a cigarette and wondered who he was, and why; but she hoped he wouldn't tell her. She saw his eyes wander across the room, and change, becoming fishily alive. She saw a fair girl smiling at him. Well, to some one he was some one. She felt a hand on her ankle, and looked down to see Frank and Molly, the link between her and this party, on the floor in the corner. She looked at the red-faced man; he smiled very nicely, meaning, that's that, so good-bye; and he moved over to the fair girl, while Liza sat on the floor with Frank and Molly, and felt happy. Molly was sweet and placid; Frank had red hair, a bony face and long bony wrists which made his sleeves seem too short. He cried, 'Oh, boy!' across the room, and sat back, with his bony hands round his knees. 'Hullo, Liza. How's life?'

'Lovely, thank you.' Lovely, lovely.

'So they say,' said Frank. He seemed a bit glassy. Liza saw the adoration in Molly's eyes, and thought, I suppose Frank is the only person in your world. That's funny. Well, he's awfully nice, but he *couldn't* be the only person; but I suppose when your telephone goes you feel sick, and if it's his voice the sun comes out, and if not then all your hope goes back on you, and you realize how much hope it was. Oh, Walter darling, soon I can go home and you will ring up.

Frank knocked his glass over, and Molly mopped it up with her printed silk scarf, and the colours ran. Liza thought, she'll keep that scarf to be happy over. No, perhaps she'll wash it and be annoyed if the colours don't go right again; because she is so placid and different from me. I don't think any one is the same as me.

The party wore on. Liza had drunk two cocktails and pleased Frank by telling him, when he asked her, that she thought he was the dangerous type. She thought, it's pleased Molly even more; but I can't think Frank's dangerous. Look at the way he goes on living at home. A strange young man with dancing blue eyes and a pink face dropped on his knees beside her and said, 'What do you think of the world?'

Every one seemed to want to know that this evening. She said, 'I think it's terrible,' because he seemed to want her to.

The strange young man patted her hand and said, 'Terrible it is. You know what? You remind me of some one.'

Liza did and didn't like to be told that. She said, 'Who?'

'I just can't think.' He had a faintly American accent.

There was something electric about him. Their eyes met, and they laughed. Liza said, 'It isn't really. It's a heavenly world.'

The strange young man shook his head and, finishing his cocktail, got up. A few minutes later Liza saw him saying good-bye to Chloe. She thought, I suppose I shall never see you again; oh, I would have liked to go on knowing you.

The clock said half-past seven. She had thought it was earlier. She said good-bye to Frank and Molly and found Chloe. Chloe said, 'Oh, now, do stay. It's just getting to be a party.'

Liza knew what kind of party it would get to be; it would go on till one in the morning, and every one would sit on the floor, and the gramophone would play, and the evening would have great dead patches when you knew drinking would do nothing but make you worse next morning. But it didn't matter what kind of a party it would be, she couldn't stay. She said, 'I really can't,' and then, thinking she should make some excuse, 'I've got to go out to dinner,' and believed it, as she always did when she told a lie.

Going back in the Underground, Liza thought, I *did* tell Walter I was going to this party. He can't ring up before half-past eight. No, eight. Oh, I must be back by eight. He may have rung up earlier, and not try again. And I can't ring him up. I mustn't.

Liza bought some steak and tinned carrots in the King's Road. She was empty, but not hungry. She wasn't happy now; drinking had squeezed the excitement from the world, which was now flat, dull, showing her such trivialities as the ladder the Underground had made in her stocking, the clothes she must wash and mend to-night; an empty evening in an empty flat, and the office to-morrow, and the next day, and the next day.

The flat was very empty indeed. She went over to the telephone. It showed no sign of having rung; but she didn't want it to yet; she wanted it to look as if it was just going to ring. No, it showed no sign of anything. She went across to the mantelpiece; there it was, a little white celluloid strut from Walter's collar. Perhaps she could ring up and tell him he'd left it and offer to post it on; but it wouldn't be necessary, he would ring. She crossed to the edge of the carpet.

There it was; the footmark on the black paint. It was dry. It was there for ever. If she pulled the carpet farther this way, it would hide what she had painted, so that she needn't go on; and it would hide the footmark. Walter might not want to see it again. With a lot of bumping of the furniture she got the carpet over it. There it was, safe, hers, for ever.

The flat was very quiet. She knelt there, her eyes on the bookshelves. One of those books he had put back when he said, 'I adore it madly,' and jumped up for his sherry; and he had clicked that lamp off, and the mantelpiece had thrown its shadow on a pink ceiling. She turned the carpet back. There it was; but if he didn't ring up to-night she would know that it was the end, and she would never be able to see this footmark again. She thought, I believe it is the end. Why didn't he want to ring up last night? Oh, I don't know. Men are different from women.

At nine Liza had had her dinner and was sitting on the floor by the gas-fire. She felt better. She was cutting up an old black dinner-dress she never wore now, making it into a skirt and a sort of bolero top, the gap to be filled in with a blouse she would buy later. A new evening dress for the cost of a blouse.

At ten Liza saw the time, and thought, it's extraordinary how it goes when you are sewing. She took the telephone down. She had found Walter's number yesterday in the directory. Yes, all the right letters and figures were on the dial. No; she would *not*. She would finish tacking the skirt first, anyway.

At half-past ten Liza was unhappier than she had ever been before. She had ruined a perfectly good dress; Walter wouldn't ring up now; and the wireless was playing what it had described as light music. Liza thought, I never told Walter I hated light music, and church bells; I'm sure he does too. Oh, darling, we were only at the beginning. She crawled over to the wireless and wrenched at the knob. She thought, if I had a hammer I would smash your silly wire-netting face.

At ten to eleven Liza wrote the laundry an angry postcard about the tablecloth and ran all the way to the letter-box and back. Now she could ring up. She could say, I've been out all the evening and just as I was coming upstairs I heard a telephone bell; and I thought it might be you, because you said you were ringing up.

A voice inside Liza said, *don't ring up*. It often said that sort of thing. Liza answered it; I don't care. Nothing matters now.

Burr–burr, said the receiver. She pressed it closer to her ear, imagining it ringing to a flat she had never seen. *Burr–burr.* Twice, three times. He was out. He was in another woman's flat, saying, tell me your dreams, your hopes, your telephone number; his voice and his face turned towards her.

Burr, said the receiver, and stopped with a click and a 'Hullo?'

Liza thought, you don't know it's me, and you sound so happy. She said, 'It's me.'

'Hullo, darling,' said Walter. 'I was just going to ring you. Aren't we psychic?'

'Were you really?' *We;* everything was all right again.

'Where are you?' said Walter.

'Why, I'm in the flat.'

'I mean, are you sitting on the floor?'

'Yes. How did you know? Where are you?'

'I know everything,' said Walter. 'I'm standing up. Dull, aren't I? Guess what I saw to-day.'

Liza thought for a moment. 'I can't.'

'Well, guess something, darling.'

'Well, a house on fire.'

'No, not exactly.'

'Please, please tell me.'

'Well,' said Walter, 'I'll give you a hint. It was in Northumberland Avenue.'

'One of those hotels there.'

'No, not exactly.'

'Oh, *please* tell me.' She was thinking what a lovely, funny face that wireless had.

'Well,' said Walter. 'A baby elephant holding a banana.'

'Oh, Walter. Are you sure?'

'Positive. I said to myself, there's a baby elephant. Afterwards you'll think, I didn't see a baby elephant. But you did. I mean I did. So I know I did.'

'What did you do?'

'Well, there wasn't anything much I could do. It had a big elephant with it. I should have told you that right away, but it would have spoilt the drama, don't you think?'

'I think it makes it even better,' said Liza. 'Two at once. Did people mind?'

'Considering what they were up against, no. There was a bit of cooing. I heard a woman say, the dear little mite, which I suppose is relativity. I expect it was saving the banana to eat in the train. Isn't it a lovely world?'

'Lovely,' said Liza. Lovely, lovely world.

'Shall I come round to-morrow night?' said Walter. 'Or why don't you come to sunny Hampstead, city of song and old romance?'

'Oh, no, you here,' said Liza, wondering why she should feel so shy of going there.

No, you here. Travel broadens the mind, dammit. And, darling, you can mend the margin thing on my typewriter.'

'Oh, I'd love to,' said Liza, wondering why she still found it so difficult to call him darling. 'What sort of time?'

'About seven. No, I'll tell you. You stand at the top of Temple Avenue, facing north, and hoping you don't look like a tart, and I'll swoop by and stop with a grinding of brakes. At six-thirty. Would that be nice? With suit-case.'

'Oh, darling,' said Liza. 'It would be lovely.'

Walter yawned. 'I shall now go to bed and read. What about you?'

'I think I shall too.'

'Good night, then, ducky. Sleep well.'

'And you. Good night, darling.' She suddenly remembered the two shillings on the bus. She said, with a rush, 'Oh, and darling, I must tell you—' but the receiver clicked and rattled. She rang off.

Liza knelt by the gas-fire. Oh, lovely world.

Then she rolled up the pieces of the dinner-dress and put them on the top shelf of the cupboard where she need never see them again. She brought out her black cocktail party dress from the cupboard. She had worn it on Saturday, but that didn't matter; Walter liked it. She thought, to-morrow I must have my hair set; and to-night I must do my nails. And before I iron the dress I must shorten the sleeves one inch. She began to unpick a hem with her nail-scissors.

Then she thought, no, I can't wear it at the office. I'll wear my grey flannel dress; it will be all right when it's brushed and ironed. And I'll leave my suit-case at the Temple station to-morrow morning and fetch it at six-twenty-five; and I shall have time to wash and do my face at the office; nearly an hour. She took out her grey flannel dress and the clothes-brush, and saw the clock. If she hurried she would be in bed in an hour and a half, because she would have to wash and iron a petticoat, and do her shoes, and mend the lining of her coat. Oh, darling Walter; all that mattered was that she would see him to-morrow.

❊

Liza opened her eyes and knew that she didn't know where she was. It was not light yet, but she could see a grey window, and a huge dark shape against a wall, which seemed very near the other walls. She was in Hampstead; it was like being abroad. And sleeping on the ground floor; that was exciting. She heard the clatter of a milk-cart. She turned towards Walter. There he was. She watched the back of his head, wondering if she could will him to wake up. Then, as it seemed that she couldn't, she moved her foot against his, telling her conscience you were always glad to be awake, when you were.

Walter grunted and turned over, curling up and settling his head against her shoulder. She didn't mind if he didn't wake up now. But she could feel his eyelashes moving. She said, 'Hullo, darling.'

Walter kissed her neck. 'Hullo, ducky. Another hopeless dawn.' Then there was a silence. Liza said, 'Are you still awake?'

'Yes,' said Walter through a yawn. 'I can't think why.'

'Well, then, please go on with your life-story.'

'I've forgotten where I was.'

'You'd been called to the Bar.'

'Oh, yes.' His voice was alive again. 'I remember. I was just about to be manacled to this frightful old boy and learn how to stick the stamps on straight so that I could be a real barrister with real briefs, though I can't think of any more ghastly prospect, can you?'

'I don't think I know any,' said Liza. 'What are they like?'

'Sort of kippered. You should see this one. But the point about the law, at least the only point I've found and I've gone into the question fairly thoroughly, is that you can always put off being a success and tell yourself you're gathering experience, and I suppose putting it off with this particular kipper is as good as with any one else. Well, there I was, a bright lad of rising twenty-eight. No, risen. It wasn't quite a year ago. God, I've been there nearly a year. I shall give notice.'

'What were you like when you were rising twenty-eight?'

'I was sweet. People patted me on the head and gave me chocolates with pink inside, and little tricycles to ride, and read me stories through and through. And even took me to the Zoo.'

'Oh, darling,' said Liza. She wanted to say how much she loved him, but it was no good trying. She said, 'Your hair's tickling my neck.'

'Change over.' He put his head back on the pillow, and Liza moved hers down so that against her forehead she could feel a pulse beating in his throat. Or was it in her forehead? It was lovely not to know. She could see the travelling clock by the bed; at least twenty minutes more. She said, 'I do love your wardrobe. Go on with the story.'

'It looms a bit, don't you think?' said Walter. 'I hate being loomed at. Well. Going back to where I was going back to, that's before that bit, I mean years before—I'll work along gradually, but I wanted to tell you about the nicest bit of my whole life, which was when I was a stripling of twenty-two, fresh from Oxford College, and went round lots of countries on the most appalling motor-bike. Every time I stopped it had to be mended, and I kept on stopping. So it took a year. About eleven months more than I'd meant. But before I tell you any more about that I must tell you about my typewriter.'

'Oh, darling,' said Liza. 'And I never mended the margin thing. Tell me all about it. Can you type fast? I can.' She was very glad that she could; after years and years of being rather ashamed.

'I sort of peck at it,' said Walter. 'I should be a bit shy of showing you. I write the sort of letters you let yourself go in, you know, the sort you hope people will publish when you're dead, and then you never post them. But what I got it for was to write a book on.'

'Are you writing a *book*? Oh, darling, you are clever.'

'Well, not exactly yet. But three weeks ago I found myself borrowing half a packet of quarto paper from my kipper. And a box of paper-clips, as new. I was sort of Guided. So, you see, it's coming to the boil.'

Liza suddenly didn't know what to say. Anything you said about writing and music and art, to the people they belonged to, sounded silly. But she must say something. She said, 'I know. It must take ages. I suppose—it sounds silly, but I suppose you have to suffer to create. Like—' she stopped. She had been going to say like having a baby, but it would have sounded too obvious. And then she knew that Walter knew she had been going to say it, and would think she had stopped because they were lovers; for policy. A shadow fell across her happiness.

So she kissed Walter's shoulder and said, 'Do you know you have a lovely side-face, at least from down here?'

'No.' Walter looked at his clock, gave her a quick kiss, wriggled himself free and climbed out of bed. Liza felt cheated.

Walter sat on the side of the bed and yawned. 'Ducky, remind me at breakfast to cut my toe-nails to-night.'

'You're like me,' said Liza. 'I always cut them as soon as possible after I think I must, but never when. I don't know why I can't. I just can't. And, darling, I can never not tear up my bus-ticket.'

'Precious. You have all the right faults.' He leant across and kissed her. 'I'm going to be lazy for five minutes more.'

'I do love your backbone,' said Liza. 'It's all lumps, one after the other.'

'Coo, fancy. I can't get at yours.'

'Now you can.' They lay together in each other's arms. Four minutes more; O time, stand still, and for ever.

Walter said, 'Have you ever been to bed with any one and just gone to sleep?'

'Well, no. It wasn't like that with Hugh. One of us always got up afterwards and went home.'

'Darling, don't be a waif and stray, or I shall cry. Well, we will to-night, shall we? Unless, of course, it happens to take us otherwise.'

Two minutes more; but Time was standing still; to-night, the next night, all the nights, just because we like to be together. 'Oh, darling. And I can remind you about your toe-nails. In sunny Chelsea?' It wasn't possible to be so happy.

'I think in sunny Chelsea,' and they lay there for another ten minutes.

※

While Walter sang and ran his bath-water, Liza, who had had her bath and dressed, turned on the light in the sitting-room and drew back the curtains. She looked round at the cream walls, panelled half-way up, the bookshelves, the blue armchairs, the brown carpet and the dead fire; thinking, when I first saw this yesterday I felt all funny and shy; now I don't. She tipped the ash-trays in the fireplace and took the tea-tray into the little yellow kitchen. Then she switched on the electric stove. The coffee was in the blue tin in the cupboard. The bread-bin was under the draining-board, and last night she had put the eggs on the window-sill. She thought, I know all about Walter's kitchen.

While she was arranging the bacon in the frying-pan, Walter came in, with his face all over shaving-soap, and said, putting his arm round her, 'Guess who I am. Roughly.'

'The Old Testament.'

'Near enough. Actually I'm my grandfather, who looks like this all day, on purpose. And wears green breeches and gaiters.' He sniffed at the frying-pan. 'Ducky, will you fry it till it just curls up, but doesn't frizzle?'

'Yes, darling.'

'I can't kiss you,' said Walter. 'But has any one ever called you a little woman?'

'Certainly not.'

'That's all right. I shan't, either.' He went back to the bathroom. Liza thought, he sings when he's soaping his face, and stops for the actual shaving. I know all about Walter. She cleared the books off the table, and laid the breakfast.

Walter said, as he put down his paper and took a mouthful of bacon, 'If we were a film, this is where I should lay my hand on yours and say, with a sort of hiccup in the middle, Happy?' He picked up the paper again and held his hand out. Liza took it and pinched his little finger. She was glad she didn't have to answer. It was possible to be too happy.

'Would you like to know what kind of a day the stars have planned for you?' said Walter, turning a page.

'Yes, please.'

'Well, darling, business prospects fair, if you take advantage of opportunities. That means, if you type a lot of letters you'll have to type a lot more. If not, not. Also, the evening has romantic tendencies. Well, it hasn't frightfully, has it? That's all. Lucky stone, topaz, which no one has ever been able to identify. Lucky colour, cinnamon. That's an innovation.'

'Dear stars,' said Liza. She was thinking, my birthday is on December the tenth; I wonder where Walter and I will be. No, it's too far ahead even to exist. But Walter's is on February the third; oh, darling Walter, we shall still be together then. She said, 'What's yours, darling?'

'Even duller. In the business world, uneventful. I could have told them. My evening's romantic too, though. Romance predominates, exclamation mark, the coy things. Well, you never know, do you? Coo, I say, here's a lovely human drama. Wait a minute.' He took a mouthful of fried egg and picked the paper up again.

'Please tell me,' said Liza.

'Well, in rather better English than the original, a Hornsey mother went to buy a pound of fancy biscuits and just as the man was going to weigh them out she thought I must get home, and so she made it a Swiss roll. And when she got back, there was her four-year-old tiny, Harold, lying on his back on the coal-house roof, having fallen twenty-five feet, and I should think bounced several times. Swiss roll saved child's life.

I don't see that it did, do you? I had a premonition, said Mrs. Smith, a widow. Well, then, it was the premonition. And what I say is, the grocer could have weighed out fancy biscuits till he bust and little Harold would have gone on lying there safe as safe, the horror. No, I don't think much of that. I do love this paper.'

'Read me some more, darling,' said Liza. 'First I must fetch the marmalade.' She got up and kissed his hair. Walter put his arm round her. 'No, no more. I never talk at breakfast. Did you know?'

'You are a darling,' said Liza. She pulled his hair and went into the kitchen. She had forgotten to draw the check curtains over the sink. She drew them back, and saw a grey sky and a greyer wall. Another hopeless dawn. Oh, darling Walter. Another lovely day.

III

The calendar on the wall in the bank said 22, very big and black. Liza thought, February the twenty-second; I've known Walter for a month and twenty days. She said to the sandy young man behind the bars, 'Please, have I got any money? I don't expect so.'

The sandy young man said, 'Miss Brett, isn't it? Just a minute,' and went behind the glass partition. He looked round it to say, 'Miss Elizabeth Brett, isn't it?'

'Yes,' said Liza; thinking, hurry, hurry, Walter's in the car outside. The young man came back and spread his stubby hands on the counter. The clock ticked; the bank was empty; it was only twenty past nine. Liza stood on one leg. The young man said:

'Well, this morning it really might be spring, mightn't it?'

'Yes, mightn't it?' Funny; it might have been spring for a month and twenty days. But it was a lovely day, clear, sunny, making you hate your clothes.

A hand came round the partition with a card. The sandy young man pushed it under the bars, its face discreetly downwards.

'Thank you,' said Liza. 15*s*. 10*d*. She gave the man a smile which meant that she only had a bank account for fun, and hurried out. She always felt guilty about the bank, and often had to tell herself that banks made money out of you, not lost it. She got in the car and Walter said, 'Well, ducky? Was it twopence or threepence?'

'Twopence,' said Liza. 'Sorry to keep you waiting, darling. I suddenly felt I had to know. I've got another month before the next cheque. I won't think about money. I do loathe it, don't you?'

'Absolutely loathe it,' said Walter absently, as the car threaded its way round Sloane Square. Liza was wondering exactly how much money

Walter had a year. She knew it was enough for him not to mind not earning anything to speak of; and she found that she would hate to know exactly how much.

'Go *away*,' said Walter, to the lorry ahead.

'It *is* rather a wardrobe, isn't it?'

Walter swung out and slipped past it, and Liza stole a proud glance. She loved to watch him driving; he drove negligently, gracefully, and impatiently. She thought, I am lucky. No one else in the world is so lucky.

Walter said, as they waited at a traffic light, 'Spring is in the air. I have an idea I'm being Guided.'

Liza was rather frightened. 'How, darling?'

'Well, to chuck everything up and go away. Fade far away, dissolve and quite forget. For the summer.'

There was a silly-looking woman standing on the pavement. Liza stared at her, hating her. She said:

'Oh.'

The traffic light changed, and they moved away. Walter said, 'It's only a sign of spring. I have it every year, and I suppose it's better than spots. Darling, look at that heavenly dog. Dogs *are* dogs, aren't they?'

Liza said, 'Yes.' She thought, it's only because of the spring. He has it every year. There was a barrow of waxy spring flowers by the kerb. The smell passed the car window. She put her hand out and saw the sun on it. Spring *was* in the air. She was suddenly happy again, and thought, I shall buy a new suit; I needn't pay till next month. She said, 'Darling, it is a lovely world. Is it my flat to-night?'

'If you like, ducky. It always seems to be yours.'

'Well, it's easier for cooking.' She thought, and I'm more myself; and I suppose my attitude is, you're in my flat, aren't you lucky and aren't I nice? And I'm horrid, I'm possessive; but then, I think every one is, just as every one is jealous, but not every one acts jealously.

'All right, darling,' said Walter;' and I'll bring you another lovely suit to iron on your beautiful ironing-board. Do you really like ironing my suits?'

'Yes, darling. You know I do.'

Walter took her hand. 'Precious. God damn and blast you, you pedestrian. Ducky, I must owe you ten bob by now.'

'I think it's only nine and threepence. I've got it all written down somewhere.'

'Well, it'll be more by the time you've bought our dinner.' He handed her his note-case. Liza took out a ten-shilling note.

'Darling, take a pound.'

'Oh, no,' said Liza. She put the case back in his pocket, and Walter moved it to the right pocket. 'You are heavenly, ducky. I mean, about money. I mean about everything else too. Shall I burst into song? Don't you think the Strand is the most hijjus street in London?'

'Absolutely frightful.' Lovely Strand, lovely world. 'I do love Monday mornings, don't you?'

'Love them,' said Walter. He drew the car up at the bottom of Chancery Lane, and Liza took her mackintosh from Walter's black hat on the back seat. 'Why did you make me bring a mackintosh, darling?'

'Because it's going to rain.'

'You always know.'

'I know everything.'

'I believe you do,' said Liza. She was thinking, oh, I wish some one from the office could see mc now. It's funny how no one ever seems to be passing just at this minute; oh, that might be Miss Derry; no, it's not. She said, 'Good-bye, darling. Be a good stamp sticker-on.'

'I'll try. But not too hard. Be a good secretary, darling.'

'As if I could. Or would. Good-bye, darling.'

Walter made his good-bye face and drove away. She watched him proudly; the only car in the world, with the only number-plate in the world.

At eleven the rain rattled Liza's window. She got up from her typewriter, thinking, I did know it would. But clever Walter, darling Walter, and lovely rain. She turned the gas-fire as high as it went and thought how at lunch-time she would see about a slate-blue suit, and have it ready for the first real day of spring.

The office was rather exciting to-day. First, Miss Derry had a new jumper. Last week she had dyed the navy one turquoise; or rather, as she had said, she had dyed the blasted stripes turquoise, you couldn't do anything with the navy part. It had made no difference that any one could see, and to-day Miss Derry had been saying, when Liza came in, 'So I gave it to Mum for polishing brass. What do you think of this one?' It was magenta, openwork, with very short puffed sleeves.

'Pretty hot,' Miss Netley had said gloomily.

But what was even more exciting was that Miss Derry's Ted, whom every one knew all about and who was in the motor business, was going to work in an agency in Burma; and either Miss Derry went too, or she never saw him again, or not for three years, which was the same thing. When Liza went into Enquiries at half-past eleven they were still talking about it; Miss Derry at her switchboard, Miss Netley and Miss Vane leaning against walls.

'Burma!' said Miss Derry, with a careless sniff. 'I didn't even know where it was. Catch *me* going there!'

'Do you really mean you're going to throw him over, just like that?' said Miss Netley, sucking a finger-nail.

'Throw him over nothing. The old boy could have stayed here if he wasn't so keen on his blasted cars.' She sniffed happily. 'Mum making him all those steak-and-kidney puddings, too.'

Partridge, who had stopped counting his twopenny stamps, gave a warning cough. 'It's between India and Australia.'

'What is?' said Miss Derry.

'Why, Burma.'

'Course it is, silly. I've seen it on the map. It looks horrid.'

'Probably is,' said Miss Netley. 'But, God! anything would be better than this office. Day after day after day after day.' She sighed wearily.

'I think you're mad, Miss Derry,' said Miss Vane suddenly. 'Stark staring'; and she walked out of the room.

'Now what's the matter with *her*?' said Miss Derry, arching her arched eyebrows further into her white, greasy forehead.

Miss Netley shrugged her shoulders. 'Probably the weather. What do *you* think, Miss Brett?'

Liza blushed. After all, she was practically a married woman, and had been considering the question as practically a married woman would. There was a world Miss Derry didn't know about, and didn't seem to want to know about. She thought, whatever I say will sound silly, but I must say it, it would be against truth and beauty not to. She looked round to see that Partridge had left the room, and said:

'Don't you *want* to get married, Miss Derry?'

'Not all that,' said Miss Derry, snapping a peg and turning the handle that rang the bell in Mr. Chiddock's room. She rang it triumphantly; Liza thought, she *is* enjoying this morning. She said, 'But, Miss Derry, do you *like* working that silly switchboard and sitting there every day with nothing to look forward to but going home so that you can get to bed in time to get up next day and get to this silly office and sit down at that silly switchboard again?'

'It's not silly,' said Miss Derry indignantly.

'But you'd be *alive.*'

'I'm alive all right. Might be dead if I went to Burma. Might be shipwrecked. Might be bitten by some blasted snake.'

'But, Miss Derry, it would all be *different.* It would be something you'd never have the chance of doing otherwise. Besides, which is more important than anything else, you'd be *married.* That's what I mean by being alive.'

'Mum'd miss me. I'd miss her. *Righty-ho,* Mr. Chiddock.' She snapped the peg up again and leant back, patting her sausage-curls.

Miss Netley stared gloomily out of the window. Liza, feeling warm and glad Miss Vane hadn't been there, went into her room to stare out of hers. Burma, for all Liza knew, might be dull and ugly. The lot Miss Derry had spurned might be a semi-detached villa in a road like a London suburb, only hotter; but it would have been a free world, all your own.

Liza thought, the people who have the chances don't take them. The people who want them don't have them. Look at Miss Netley and Miss Vane, just marking time. Look at me.

Liza leant her forehead on the rain-blurred window and felt very miserable indeed. She went on feeling miserable for half an hour. And then, when she was in Enquiries again, Mr. Hill put his head round the door and cried, 'Rotten morning, Miss Derry. But East West, Home's Best!' And he lifted his hat, and Liza saw, for the first time in all those years at the office, Mr. Hill's perfectly good hair. She thought, darling Mr. Hill; Walter will be so excited when I tell him.

Mr. Chiddock came into Liza's room. 'Hark at them,' he said, jerking a thumb over his shoulder. Liza listened, and heard Partridge reading Miss Derry a list of the principal exports of Burma. She laughed. And Mr. Chiddock did a thing he had never done before, in all those years. He asked her out to lunch.

Liza and Mr. Chiddock went down the side alley to the Bygone Days Tea Shop. Liza nearly always had lunch there, and didn't know what else to suggest. Mr. Chiddock politely hung her mackintosh on a peg with his, and they ate fish croquettes and mashed potatoes, and Liza felt very embarrassed. Because she knew Mr. Chiddock very well in the office, but not at all out of it.

Then they talked about Life, and content and discontent, and Liza stopped feeling embarrassed, because it was how they always talked. Mr. Chiddock said:

'My own belief is that every one's bloody miserable always.'

'Oh, no,' said Liza. 'You can't say that. Lots of people are happy. I am, all the time.'

Mr. Chiddock looked as if he didn't believe it. Liza thought, I must sound brave and pathetic. Because he thinks I go back every night to an empty flat, or sit on a camp-stool in a theatre queue with a girl-friend and argue over who owes who what. And, I suppose, as he asked me here, I don't say anything about paying for my lunch.

Mr. Chiddock paid the bill and they went back to the office, where, because she now knew Mr. Chiddock out of the office, Liza felt embarrassed all over again.

I am always happy, thought Liza a week later as she lay in her bath. But I know I'm not. I am now, because it's twenty-five past six, and in five minutes Walter will ring up, and in an hour he will be here; but sometimes I am un-happier than I was before I met him.

Liza soaped the sponge and washed her back; she was getting out of practice because Walter had done it so often. But, if she added up her solitary baths there would perhaps be quite a lot; no, not a lot, one here, and two there. It had not been to-night, and the next night, and all the nights; but three nights, and then Walter saying, 'Ducky, I've got to go out to dinner, so I'll stay in sunny Hampstead.' Not often; but any number of times was often. She thought, *I* never tell Walter I'm going out to dinner, so I'll stay in sunny Chelsea. I've rather given up my friends. But with my eyes open, because I would rather have Walter than a lot of silly dull parties; and if you have the unhappiness of love, the happiness is all the better.

A cracked and tinny clock, which struck from a church she had never traced because it was more fun not knowing, and which sometimes could be heard and sometimes couldn't, clanked a *ding-dong,* and another. Half-past six. Walter was to ring up at half-past six. Liza lay in her bath, ready to spring out and drip across the carpet to the telephone; she thought, how can I worry about unhappiness? Such very small clouds obscured happiness, such a bright sun waited behind them.

Liza lay there, thinking, I won't get out, because telephones always ring while you're in your bath; oh, darling Walter, it's not that I don't expect you to ring, but that I do so want you to.

It would be twenty to seven. Liza added more hot water and still lay there, more miserable than she had ever been before. She hadn't seen Walter since yesterday morning. He had rung up this morning; but since then he could have died; or last night, at the party he went to, he could have met a beautiful girl; *your dreams, your hopes, your telephone number.*

Liza sat up suddenly; she could have sworn she heard the telephone nearly ring. No, it was the ting of a taxi; she heard the whirr up the street. She lay back, her heart thumping. Some one had run from the taxi, up the two steps to the door. No one else in the world ran like that. Liza lay, clutching her sponge, and heard the footsteps running upstairs, the click of a latch-key; and the sun broke over the whole world; and Liza lifted her face to its light, thinking, I left my clothes all over the floor and the shopping on the bed. Oh, I wish I'd *known*.

Walter stood at the bathroom door, holding a square white box by a green tape. He knelt down by the bath. 'Guess what, darling.'

'Oh, darling.' If she said grapes, and it wasn't—she said, 'I can't guess.'

'Grapeses.' He kissed her over the rim of the bath. 'I carried them this side up with terrific care. Like visiting an invalid, taxi and all. Only you said you liked them. Don't you loathe visiting invalids, ducky?' He broke off a small bunch of grapes and shared them out.

'Oh, I loathe it. And you are an angel. Why a taxi?'

'The car's being mended. Mouse in the works. That reminds me.' He fished in his pocket and brought up a little paper bag.

'Oh, darling,' said Liza. Walter was holding up a pink sugar-mouse by its string tail. 'It's lovely. I really haven't seen one before. I'm sure now. Where did you get it?'

'Fleet Street. Very rare.' He took the sponge and began washing her back. 'Do you know what I nearly did to-day?'

'You nearly stuck a stamp on straight.'

'No. I wouldn't do a thing like that. No, I nearly broke our vow and rang you up and asked you out to lunch.'

'Oh, darling.' It had been his vow; he had said they'd have nothing to tell each other in the evenings, and she had thought, that's husbands and wives. 'Well, actually, darling,' she said, 'I went out to lunch. With a man.' She thought, I must make the most of this.

'What sort of a man?' He didn't sound jealous exactly, but interested.

'Well, only Mr. Chiddock.'

'Ha!' said Walter. 'He *has* got designs on you. I know his type.'

'Oh, no, darling. I think it's only because of asking me out last Monday and sort of breaking the ice of four years, and I think perhaps he feels if he didn't ask me again last Monday might mean something. Or he doesn't want to hurt my feelings. But, darling, what is awful is I'm terrified he'll think he has to ask me every Monday now; so next Monday, if he does,

I shall say some one else has and I couldn't say no. In fact, I shall ring up Pauline and ask her.'

Walter slapped her back with the sponge. 'You are heavenly.' He knelt down again, kissing her shoulder. Liza met his eyes. They were laughing at her. She thought, you know all about me. She said, 'What was the party like, darling?'

'So-so.'

'Were there—' their eyes met again, and laughed.

'No, darling. Some of them weren't bad-looking, and some were. I'm choosy.'

'Oh, darling.' And he had chosen her.

Walter squeezed the sponge over her shoulder. 'I'm going to tell you something, only you mustn't laugh. This morning, when I was cooking my own breakfast, I suddenly knew I was in love with you.'

Liza thought, Walter is a man. Men are different. She felt very humble. 'What was it like?'

'As if I'd swallowed a lot of sherbet dry,' said Walter, getting up. 'I did once. It was awful.' He pushed the sponge against her face. 'Get out, ducky. The big flick starts at eight-four.'

Liza made an omelette. She shook the frying-pan and stirred it, while Walter leant against the wall and watched her. She knew he was watching her. He said, rubbing his elbow, 'I've got pins and needles. I love you when you smile. I might say it's like the sun coming out, but I won't; I'll think of something better later. What were you smiling at, ducky?'

'I was thinking of my mouse. I'm going to frown now, because of the omelette. Give me that plate, darling.'

Walter handed it over. 'I love you when you frown.'

Liza thought, I feel different. I do love him as much as I did. Walter had picked up the Instructions for Use of Gas Cooker, and was lost in it. She thought, seeing his face, I love him more than ever. That was why I feel different.

Walter and Liza sat in the middle of the middle row of their cinema. In front of them sat a loving couple, sloping a little to the left, and behind them some one who clicked her tongue whenever anything happened in the film. Liza sat with her hand in Walter's. They always held hands in a cinema. It was a film they hadn't seen before, but, as Walter said, only just; soon it would pass from her mind and all she would remember was that to-night Walter had said he was in love with her, and to-night they had some Turkish cigarettes and she wore a new elastic roll-on belt which squeezed her together and would leave a pattern. But the funny bits of the film were exquisitely funny, the sad bits made her cry worse than ever before; and she always cried at films now. When the girl in the film told the man that she loved him, whatever happened she would always love him because he was a part of her and she wouldn't be alive if she didn't love him, the tears drowned Liza's eyes. And the man hadn't said he loved her. Oh, you poor girl; but he will. When they jacked the car up off the man and the girl took his head on her knee and he said he guessed he loved her, the tears ran right down Liza's face. Oh, he couldn't die, he couldn't. The man was in bed in a very shiny hospital. The woman behind them clicked her tongue and said, 'Look at his temperature!' but the doctor told the girl he was going to be all right. Liza thought, it's only a film I'm just watching, it has nothing to do with me, I'm not even interested. So she wasn't crying when the girl put her head down on the pillow by the man's and the music grew suddenly louder and the screen said *The End*. She took her hand from Walter's and they stood up while the gramophone played *God Save the King*. Liza saw, with great pleasure and great embarrassment, that Walter's eyes were almost pink; but that might just be from looking at the screen, or the smoke in the air. But she had never seen his eyes pink before. No, it would be the smoke; when other people looked as you felt, it didn't mean they felt the same. Other people. That was wrong.

Liza and Walter held hands as they made their way through the crowd, and in the King's Road he took her arm and linked her little finger with his. They walked slowly along.

'Well,' said Walter, 'what did you think of that?'

'Well. What did you?'

'Same again. Wouldn't it have been heavenly if the jack had slipped and bust his neck?'

'Heavenly,' said Liza. 'Some films *are* films, aren't they? But, darling, I cried dreadfully. I hope you didn't see me.'

'No, ducky. I was too busy not crying. Aren't we awful?' He squeezed her hand. Liza thought, we are in love. I did know, before, that I was more than he was. Now it will be different. I wish I didn't feel so sort of conceited.

At a Neon sign saying *Snax: Open*, Walter stopped, pulling her back. 'Let's have some coffee. No, tea.'

'We're having it when we get back, darling.'

'Well, what I really hanker for is a sausage roll.' He came back with a bag full, and they walked on, eating.

Liza said, 'Wouldn't it be awful to be the sort of person who couldn't eat things because of not sleeping?'

'Awful. I had a lovely night last night. I mean, I slept and slept. But when I woke up, you weren't there. Did you know? Darling, I did miss you.'

A wide-hatted man went past, carrying a cat and a pineapple.

Walter said, 'And I bet he slices the cat up and puts the pineapple out for the night.'

'Wasn't he heavenly?' Oh, lovely world. 'I do adore Chelsea.'

'Nowhere like it,' said Walter, with his mouth very full. He swallowed. 'I think next year I shall move here.'

'It would—' Liza was going to say, 'It would save trouble.' But she stopped in time. She was suddenly and deeply miserable. She swallowed her sausage roll, as if that had stopped the sentence. 'It would be nice. I mean, it *is* nice. You'd love it.'

'I know. I've lived here before, dammit.'

They neared the corner of Liza's street. Walter twiddled the bag up. 'No more till we get home.'

We and home; but still she wasn't happy.

At the corner Walter stopped under the lamp. 'Ducky.' He took her in his arms. 'Does this lamp make you feel like some one's cook?'

'Not really.'

'Then I'm not really some one's cook's policeman. Ducky, I do love you so much. Are you happy?'

'Yes, darling. You know I am.'

'I said that with all the implications implied.'

'Yes, darling, I know you did. I implicated them all.' The girl in the film had said, I love you, whatever happens I will always love you, because you are a part of me. And, only a few hundred feet of celluloid later, the man asked her to marry him.

'Bless you, ducky.' They kissed, and walked down the street, hand in hand.

'Here we are,' said Walter. 'There's that everlasting milk-bottle. One day I'm going up to the top flat disguised as a meter-reader. I've never seen a real Bohemian.'

Liza said, putting the bottle inside the door, 'I keep on thinking I can't be any happier. But I am, always.'

IV

One Sunday in March Walter and Liza, who spent most Sundays in the country now, went to Huntingdonshire. Liza said, as they studied the map after breakfast in Walter's flat:

'I don't really believe in Huntingdonshire. Like Russia. Because I've never been there.'

'Well, if you're sure you haven't,' said Walter. 'We shall only just get there and back, but if it broadens your mind, sweetheart, then all right. But I think you *have* been there, because you went to York.'

'It was a long time ago. I was sick.' She looked at the map. 'I suppose I did, then; and through Lincolnshire. Why, I went quite near you, darling. I wish I'd known.'

'You might have gone up that way though. By Sheffield. Then you'd have missed both. So it's all right, and we will go. I do love maps, don't you? Do you know, ducky, I haven't been home this year. Shall I go next week-end?'

Liza said, 'What about the theatre?' She thought of the black dinner-dress which Walter had never seen, because the cleaners had lost it for the fortnight when she could have worn it twice; and she thought, I might have known.

'Oh, well,' said Walter, 'I don't really want to. I'll go some time. It costs nineteen and sevenpence, and I like the Old Folks much better when I never see them, and I expect they feel the same.' He shut the atlas and opened a bigger-scale map.

Liza thought, that was him, not me. He doesn't *want* to go home; and I wish he didn't call it home.

In the car Liza said, 'When you went to bed with that tart that time, what was it like?'

Walter said, 'I felt awfully lonely.'

'I know. I felt like that about Hugh. He was just some one, I suppose. I can't think why I thought I was in love with him. I suppose you can make yourself in love with anybody.' She thought, we've said all this before; in those very words. And there was a silence, and she could think of nothing else to say till a gate appeared at the end of the road and Walter said, 'Ducky, look where you've map-read me.' He stopped the car and they read the map together, and kissed, and it was all right again.

Huntingdonshire, when you got there, was just like anywhere else in the country. They left the car by a gate and walked down a twisting lane. It was a day of mild sunshine; Liza wore the grey flannel suit she had bought instead of the slate-blue one, and said, taking her jacket off, and putting it on again, 'If you don't look up as far as the trees, but just get the hedge and the sky, it might be June. Oh, I wish it was June, and everything was all wild parsley and buttercups, and I lived in the country.' She thought, that isn't true; as if I would want to live in the country without Walter.

Walter said nothing. He had been very quiet since they got out of the car. They climbed a stile, and as Liza stood there he took her hand and said, 'Ducky.'

'Yes, darling?'

'I've been thinking. Voice from the back of the hall, how?'

Liza thought, he's sliding away from something he doesn't know how to say. But I know what it is. It didn't matter what they said next; just words to be gone through, and your own agony. She said, 'What have you been thinking, darling?'

'About going away,' said Walter. 'Till the end of the summer. I thought I could write my book, or even if I didn't I would be alive, not shut up in that damned cupboard all day. For a start, I've given my kipper notice. And was he pleased? As is consistent with a veneer of whatever kippers are kippered with.'

'Where would you go to?'

'I haven't thought yet.'

Well, it wasn't Australia yet; he hadn't bought a ticket. But that didn't make it any better. In the hot sunshine a bird whistled sharply. Hateful sun. Hateful bird. Hateful spring, and the summer would come after.

Walter was watching her. 'Darling, what would you do if I did?'

'I should go on living.' She thought, and doing all I did before I met you; sitting in an empty flat, with a summer evening over the chimney pots; thinking, when I met a man, that might be going to be the man, and knowing it wasn't. *Time passes, time passes, and I lie alone.* Her throat tightened. She wanted to get off the stile, but it meant a jump, and hitting the ground, and knowing that the world was round her, and she was in the world. So she went on standing there.

'Oh, precious,' said Walter suddenly; and he put his arms round her and lifted her down, saying:

'You come with me. Ducky, I didn't mean to hurt you. I wanted to ask you right away. But I didn't know how to.'

It was the most wonderful thing that had ever happened. It was the most surprising, and yet not in the least surprising. It was something that happened to other people, but when it happened to you you knew you had been certain of it all along; like winning a prize, or being run over.

Liza said, 'My petticoat feels awfully tight. Round the top. I think I may burst. Oh, listen to that lovely bird.'

Walter took her in his arms again. 'I do adore you. We'll have the most marvellous time any one ever had anywhere. Think of it, ducky, all the summer.'

Then Liza had a terrible thought. She didn't know why she hadn't thought of it at once. Walter would want to go abroad; they would go where people spoke a language she didn't know; where she would be a nuisance, some one who clung and couldn't do the shopping, or speak to any one but him. Even France would be awful, though she had been there for a fortnight, but she hadn't spoken any French. For a dreadful moment Liza thought, I shall have to say I can't leave my job. Then, before she could think that again, she said, 'Where do you think would be the nicest place to go?'

'Oh, sort of Sussex or Devonshire or somewhere. The duller the better.

Because of the book.' He took her hand. 'Ducky, you'll have to persuade me you want to and ought to and all that.'

'Oh, darling,' said Liza. 'Do I really have to?'

'No, precious, I don't think so. Oh, we will have fun. We'll rent a little lighthouse, to save you running up and down stairs.'

But nothing he said could make it any better.

Half an hour later they climbed back over the stile, Walter saying, 'Well, perhaps about the job. And perhaps about the flat, if you can let it.'

'Of course I can. And the lease is up in August. So it's sort of Fate.'

'Not very well-timed, ducky. But all right, it's Fate. But about the other—'

'I can't *help* feeling like that about money,' said Liza, as they walked up the lane to the car. 'You would if you'd always had to earn your own living. I mean all of it, till a year and a half ago.' She thought, that sounds like getting at Walter for not really earning his. And it makes me a Bachelor Girl; that's awful. Then she thought, if I didn't have that money of my own I couldn't go away with him. Uncle Alfred might not have died. Oh, poor Uncle Alfred; and selfish me.

'All right, ducky,' said Walter, getting in the car. 'You hand it over and I'll dole it out. But why I sound so rich and generous is because.' He started the car, and they drove off.

'Because why, darling?' said Liza, when she had realized he hadn't stopped because of starting the car.

'Because in the autumn, what shall I have but a job? I mean, more of one than this one.' Liza thought, then it really will be all the summer; and why haven't you told me all this? It's Sunday, you must have known yesterday. 'What job, darling?'

'Guess.'

She would guess something silly, and hurt him or annoy him. She said, 'Give me a hint.'

'Well. It's in Regent's Park. Oh, you angel. I really think you thought I was going to be a Zoo-keeper.'

'I was remembering the elephant.'

'Now, if I was going to be a Zoo-keeper I should be much more excited. I think I should keep the hippos. Why hippos, my man? Well, lady, any one can keep a hippo. The trouble is to get rid of it. I'm not going to be a park-keeper either, ducky. Too much chocolate-paper and immorality.'

He was sliding away again; he didn't want to tell her. 'Give me another hint.'

'Well. I'm going to be a sort of Evelyn Waugh character.'

'That's either a schoolmaster or a convict.' Walter was going to be a schoolmaster. Well, she thought, people never like to tell you when they are.

'You're right, ducky. I'm going to be a bit of both.'

'Are you going to live there?'

'No,' said Walter; and it was all right again. 'It's only for a term; I'm going to stop a gap.'

'What will you teach them, darling?'

'Latin and Greek. I shall keep one lesson ahead of the little perishers. Now, if it had been Eng. Lit. it would have been fun. However. And I shall have to help with the netball, or prisoners' base, or whatever they play nowadays.'

Liza said, 'I think it sounds lovely, darling,' and hoped he didn't think she wanted to be a schoolmaster's wife. Not because she didn't want to be one. She wondered if she did or didn't. You sat and watched cricket; well, that could be fun, you needn't look all the time, and Walter would be umpiring. Anyhow, it was all too far away to exist.

Walter drove on in silence. She wondered what he wanted to say.

'I've just thought, ducky. We shall be sort of living in sin.'

'Well, we are now, darling.'

'I know. But that's different. Will you begin imagining you're a fallen woman, darling, and be worried?'

'I don't think so. But it would be rather nice to be a fallen woman. I think sin is lovely.' It was funny; to-day she didn't really want in the least to marry Walter. And last Thursday they had been to dinner with some friends of his who had just got married; and when she saw the white satin bed Liza had been swept with a sick and terrible envy. But to-day all she had to do was wait, and let things happen. And anyway, for Walter to have pledged himself to her for six months was as good as being married.

Walter said, 'You've got something in your hair. Oh, I see, it's meant. All whimsical like.'

Liza took the daisy out. 'I know. I don't really like people who wear flowers in their hair. I was just feeling happy.'

'All right, ducky. As long as you don't stop in the middle of a walk with a glad cry, and sit down and make daisy-chains.'

Liza thought, I must remember not to make daisy-chains. I wouldn't want to make them, but it's just the sort of thing I might find myself doing because he doesn't like it.

They had tea in a place which Liza thought had sprung up for the afternoon. Not because it was beautiful; it was pink brick outside, and lined with what Walter called a wealth of new oak. But it belonged to the afternoon. She said, 'I don't think this place really exists.'

'It exists all right,' said Walter, putting a knife under a table-leg to stop the wobble. 'Though it may not for long. I've been here before.'

'With another woman?'

'Yes, darling. And we stayed in the most frightful pub. It had beetles. I'll show you on the way back.'

Liza thought, I'm glad he's had lots of women. It makes me somebody. She looked down at her left hand behind the teapot. Soon it would wear a wedding-ring. At least, she supposed so. A thin gold one; real gold; it was worth getting a good one for six months. Well, five, because they weren't starting till the end of April. Well, four and a half, because they would be back about September the seventh. She wondered how you bought a wedding-ring by yourself.

The next morning at the office the whole idea was wild and impossible. It had seemed so right yesterday; now she was back in the world she had known before she met him, and he seemed almost unreal; and she was a tram on nice safe tramlines, and to get out of them there were things like letting the flat, and telling Mr. Hollis, and facing his surprise—she would say she wanted to stay in the country with friends, but he would be surprised just because she wanted to leave; and getting some one to send on her letters, and arranging, arranging, arranging. It gave her a headache to think about it. She was glad she was having lunch with Pauline; she could sort of try it out on her. Pauline knew about Walter, but she hadn't met him. About six people knew about Walter; but you couldn't help it; and she knew she didn't want to help it, and was ashamed; but that didn't stop you telling some one else. And to tell Pauline about Walter was to have dragged Walter down to the level of Pauline's Carl, whom Liza had never met and didn't want to, but felt she knew very well indeed.

For once Pauline was early for lunch. She sat in the Bygone Days Tea Shop with her hands clasped under her chin, and her hat tipped back to show her very white forehead; small, pale, looking as if she was thinking hard about something a long way off; which was doubtful. Liza thought, I only like Pauline because I know her.

Pauline turned her eyes on Liza and said, 'Hullo, darling.'

Liza said, 'I'm so sorry I'm late.' Her voice sounded livelier than she had expected; she had come in feeling sulky.

'How's your boy friend?'

'Oh, he's all right.' Liza was as jarred as she had expected to be. She said, to oblige Pauline, 'How's yours?'

'Oh, Carl, my dear. I'm having scrambled eggs.'

'So am I.' You nearly always had scrambled eggs at the Bygone Days Tea Shop. Pauline went on, '*Carl*, my dear. I've had such a week.' And she plunged into the week she had had.

Liza listened. She had meant to think about Walter, but she found herself projected into Pauline's strange world, where any one who wanted to go to bed with you was therefore the sort of person you went to bed with. Carl sounded terrible, because Pauline seemed to want to make him sound terrible. He did something vague, prompting, Liza thought it was, at a small and furtive underground theatre. His real name was Charles, but you had more chance in the prompting world if you made it Carl; and he was rude, and bad-tempered, and borrowed half-crowns from Pauline, and once nearly bit her ear off. Liza's thoughts strayed to Walter, who was so different from Carl, and lingered there, as a fire draws you to its warmth and holds you.

'And *there* was Carl, my dear,' said Pauline, 'leaning against a table in the corner with a bowl of peppermint creams and dropping them on the floor. One by one. He wasn't tight. He just wanted to see people tread on them.'

Liza thought Carl might not be so bad. 'And what did you do?'

'My dear, I went up to him and I said, loud enough for this coffee-broking man to hear, because, my dear, he looked pretty hot, well, I said, Carl, I'm not going home with you. And he didn't look as if he'd heard, I mean Carl didn't, the coffee-broking man did all right, and so I said it again twice as loud.' The story flowed on, and Liza thought, I don't really want to tell Pauline about Walter. Oh, I don't know about going away. I'm a coward.

'And now tell me *your* news, darling,' said Pauline. They were drinking their coffee and eating rock-cakes studded with burnt currants looking, and tasting, like boot-buttons; and as she bit on a currant Liza's soul rose against the Bygone Days Tea Shop and all that it stood for. It stood for the office, and Pauline, and bus-fares, and an empty flat and a fine summer evening over the chimneys, no unladdered stockings and three and eightpence to last you till Friday. It was safe, that was all. Who wanted to be safe? She said, 'I'm going away.'

'Oh,' said Pauline. 'For the week-end, darling?' Liza thought, meaning you think I hardly ever go away for week-ends. You and Carl are always staying with terrible people, in illicit couples. Oh, you poor things. She said, 'No. For the whole summer. I'm leaving the office and going into the country. To—to stay with various people. I just want to get away from London for a bit.'

'What about the boy friend?'

'He'll be all right,' said Liza. She was feeling as Pauline always made her feel; under-sexed, cheerful to make up for it. Like Miss Derry. Perhaps Miss Derry only felt like that when Liza was there. Anyway, she had made up her mind now. She was going.

On the whole, Pauline was not so interested as she should have been; but then people never were. Pauline said that if only *she* had some money of her own, instead of having to work for that lousy man who looked at her worse than ever, she could go off and leave Carl to come to his senses. Then, when she heard that Liza was letting the flat, she was suddenly interested.

'How much?'

'Two and a half guineas a week with the furniture.' Walter had fixed it, though it sounded a lot to her.

Seventeen and six a week added to her income made her rich.

'Two and a half,' said Pauline thoughtfully. 'It seems an awful lot.' It isn't, thought Liza. 'How long for, my dear?'

'Till the middle of September. The lease is up then, anyway. She was thinking, it *is* Fate; I'm not meant to go back there after the summer.

Pauline looked at her watch and squeaked. 'I must get back to my lousy man.' The waitress gave them the bill; one bill for both lunches.

They went to the pay-desk and Liza said, 'I'll get change.' She gave the girl a ten-shilling note. She waited for Pauline to squeak and say, 'How much do I owe you?' But Pauline was staring into the street, looking quite surprisingly thoughtful. Liza told herself that it was only one and twopence extra, and nothing to be so angry about.

❧

Liza went back to the office and waited till Mr. Hollis appeared, an hour later, when she didn't feel quite so brave. But she went into his room and said:

'Can I speak to you for a minute, Mr. Hollis?' Mr. Hollis looked startled. Liza thought, I can't help it, there isn't any other way of telling people you want to speak to them for a minute. She said, 'Mr. Hollis,' a bit too dramatically.

'Yes, Miss Brett?'

'Well, it's only that I—would you mind if I—well, I suppose I want to give notice. I don't mean go at once. I just wanted to warn you.' She thought, no, I'm not doing it right.

Mr. Hollis put his elbows on his desk, took hold of the sides of his glasses and peered up at her. 'Aren't you happy with us, Miss Brett?' She had known he would look like that, and say exactly that.

'Oh, it isn't that, Mr. Hollis. I love it here.' She drew a chessboard pattern on her shorthand notebook, wondering why she had brought it in with her. She was a secretary, that was why; but she wasn't, she was Liza pretending to be one. Oh, but not for long. She said, 'I—I only want to be in the country for the summer.' It sounded pretty silly. 'I mean, I've got sort of tired of working in an office.' And that was rude. She said quickly:

'I don't mean I don't love it here, only I've never been in the country for a whole summer, and you know I've got a little money of my own, I mean enough to stay with friends with. So when they asked me it seemed an awfully good idea.' And that sounded rather pathetic and orphanish. She said, to make a good ending, 'Only I do hope you don't think I haven't been happy here. I have. I mean, I am.' They couldn't keep her there against her will; they couldn't. She waited anxiously, and felt as if she had passed an exam, when Mr. Hollis said:

'Well, Miss Brett, we shall be very sorry to lose you, you know.' She was out of the prison walls. 'I suppose you wouldn't like to come back in the autumn?' She was back in the prison walls. She said, so as not to give herself time to think it out, 'It's awfully kind of you, Mr. Hollis, but I don't know how long it's for, and you never know, I mean anything may happen.' Anything might happen.

Mr. Hollis said, 'Well, Miss Brett, you know best. We shall be sorry to lose you.'

She was out of the prison walls again. She would be here for another month, but it would be different; she would be gracious, some one staying on to help them; at one with the office instead of hiding her brain and her soul from it. And after that, the Future; no, before it; now was the Future.

Mr. Hollis clutched his glasses. 'Well, we'll talk about the details later, shall we? Plenty of time, isn't there?'

'Oh, yes. Weeks.' It was all suddenly very far away.

'Well, Miss Brett, if you've got your notebook there, there's just this one thing—' he cleared his throat and tipped his chair back, holding a paper on a level with his eyes. Liza sat down. That page was all shorthand, and that; she turned the book back to front and found a space half-way through. She would never find it again. She put a very black X at the top to mark it, and waited in dreadful suspense.

'*Dear* Sir,' Mr. Hollis began. 'In answer to yours to hand this morning, dated the twenty-somethingth—'

You didn't have to think about shorthand, when once you had started. The pencil slid across the page, and her mind off to the Future, outside the prison walls.

❀

The next day Miss Netley came into Liza's room and said, sucking a finger-nail, 'When you go can I have your typewriter? Mine jams if you type more than ten words a minute.'

'You can have everything in the room,' said Liza. On the whole, the office hadn't been surprised enough, as she might have expected; but Miss Vane had looked sardonically knowing, and said nothing.

Miss Netley looked round gloomily. 'I don't think I want anything else. Thanks a lot' She went out, her behind wiggling. Liza thought: provocatively, but I don't know who it would provoke to what. I must tell Walter. I don't know what I did with things before I told them to Walter. She lifted her arms and yawned till her knees tingled; and then her heart jumped, because the telephone rang on her desk.

'Hullo, my dear,' said a high voice, which sounded a long way from the mouthpiece at the other end, and would be; down below Pauline's chin, with Pauline clasping it exaggeratedly and gazing at the ceiling. Liza said, feeling sulky again, 'Hullo, Pauline.'

'My *dear*. I want to ask you about your flat. Not for me, my dear.'

'Oh?'

'*Carl*, my dear. He wants a little place not too far from his theatre.'

It wasn't a little place; it was her flat

'The *only* thing is, darling, he doesn't know that he wants to pay all that much. I mean, it is a bit much, isn't it?'

'Well, I don't think so. It was fixed for me by an estate agent.'

'Oh, *well*. Well, actually, I don't think he really thinks it is. I told him I'd *haggle* a bit. The pet's so unbusinesslike, bless his silly head. I told you how he paid eighteen pounds for a piano-accordion he can't play, didn't I?'

'Yes,' said Liza quickly, though Pauline hadn't.

'Well, now, my dear. Can I bring him round to-night? At six? We haven't got another free evening for *months*.'

Liza thought very fast. She didn't want Carl to have the flat. She wanted some one to have the flat. She didn't want to meet Carl, and there was hardly any sherry left, and she had promised herself not to buy another bottle this week. And she had been going round to Walter's flat at six. She said:

'Of course you can, my dear. Sharp at half-past six. It will be fun. We'll have a drink.' And then she rang up Walter, which she hardly ever did in the daytime, and said, 'Darling, will you mind if I don't come round to-night? I've got to have some people round about letting the flat. Isn't it a bore? At six.'

'Oh,' said Walter. He minded. 'Well, then, when they've gone.' Liza hadn't thought of that.

'Well, *I can*, darling, but I've got masses to do. And you're coming here to-morrow.'

'Oh, all right then. I'll ring you up to-night. Good-bye.'

Liza thought, the kipper must have been in the room; so he wasn't minding after all, it was just his kipper voice. I'll never ring him up at his office again. And now I've missed a night with him; I wonder how I made myself say it. I suppose because of the summer. It really is like being married.

❦

By six Liza had tidied the flat much harder than she thought she need have. At twenty-past she wanted to see Pauline and Carl more than anything else in the world. At twenty to seven the wrong door-bell rang. She went down to the flat below and found Pauline and Carl standing face to face on the doormat. Pauline looked pale and tense; so did Carl, but probably he always did.

Pauline stopped looking pale and tense and said, seizing Liza's hands, 'Darling, this is *Carl*,' as if Liza had thought it wasn't They went upstairs.

Liza had poured a new bottle of sherry into the decanter, making it very full. Now, at a quarter-past seven, it was more than half empty. Pauline was saying, 'You did, darling, you know you did.'

'I did *not*,' said Carl. 'You know perfectly well I did *not*.' He glared at Pauline, and glanced towards Liza.

'Isn't he sweet?' said Pauline. She darted at him and smoothed his hair back. 'Darling, you should *not* plaster your hair *sideways*. You might have been *swimming*, and you know you'd never do anything so hearty, you funny thing. Liza, darling, when I've finished this cigarette I must rush. I'll leave Carl with you.' Liza thought, Pauline is telling me how clever she is to have such a marvellous man to go to bed with. Carl is telling me what a marvellous man he is to have a woman in his power. Oh, darling Walter, we're not like that.

Carl without Pauline was almost a normal young man, only quieter. There was a nervous silence, and then Liza took him round the flat.

'This is the kitchen. You have to bang the door to shut it.' She thought, and that's Walter's footmark, under the carpet. All the summer. Oh, lovely world.

'Really, I say!' said Carl.

They went into the bathroom. 'This is the bathroom. I think the only nice thing about it is the towel-rail. That heater heats one big bathful of water, so you can only have one big bath at a time.'

'I say, y-yes!' said Carl. Without Pauline he stammered slightly.

They left the bathroom. 'And where it's distemper it's washable distemper, but I've never found it washes.' She thought, I'm not advertising this flat very well.

'Oh, yes,' said Carl. 'W-washable distemper.' He put a finger one inch from the wall, and drew it back. Liza thought, he really is rather nice.

Then they had another drink, and Carl said he would like to take the flat; and Liza was dreadfully worried till Walter rang up. She said, 'Darling, I suppose Carl won't break the flat up. He's what you'd call one of the sub-intelligentsia.'

'Ah,' said Walter. 'Sort of dank, is he?'

'Yes, a bit. And once he threw a lot of peppermint creams on a carpet for people to tread on. Do you think he'll throw them on mine?'

'Well, ducky, speaking as a lawyer, yes. As a student of human nature, N.W.3, no. It isn't the sort of thing you do twice. It loses its first fine careless rapture. Also you find you're treading on them yourself. So cheer up, ducky.'

'But, darling, do you mean as a lawyer you think he'll be a bad tenant?' She thought, please help me. Don't slide off.

'Oh, he'll be all right. As good as anything else. And you've cut out the middleman's profits, haven't you?'

Liza thought, you have helped. She said, 'I do love you.'

'Darling, I'm sorry I was so rude on the telephone. I was kipper-dogged, as I expect you guessed.'

'Oh, darling, I know. You weren't rude. Shall I come round after all?'

'Well, darling,' said Walter, 'I went and fixed to go out. Soon be to-morrow.'

Liza thought, I've slipped back a rung.

V

Walter took his tie and his shoes off and said, opening Liza's school atlas, 'Give me a pin, darling.' He dug it into the map of England. 'Well, we're spending the summer in Putney.'

'Oh, darling, let's. It would be such fun.'

'It's all uphill. You'd grow one leg shorter than the other. Like what they used to tell you about scooters.' He dug again. 'Stratford-on-Avon. We could see Henry Six, Part Two, every night, and go on the river all day.'

'Oh, darling, let's.' She couldn't think of anything better.

Walter had dug again. 'Swaffham, Norfolk.'

Liza thought of yachts, and said, 'Oh, darling, let's go there.'

Walter patted her head. 'You don't know what you're saying, my child.' His hand slid down to her neck again, and round to her ear. 'I've lost the pin. Never mind. We'll sit on it. Where shall we go?'

'We might go to Sussex.'

'Too many other people. I've got a terrible cousin with a glass eye in Lewes. He sort of permeates the whole county.' He sounded absent. He said suddenly, 'I know. Here. The New Forest.'

'But, darling, people don't live in the New Forest. It's all preserved, and the Rufus Stone, and litter-baskets and fire-brooms. We used to go for picnics there from school. In motor-coaches.' She was thinking, I might meet Miss Trafford. Or Miss Morton. She still felt rather sick when she thought of her divine Miss Morton. She thought, and Walter and I would be in an hotel in Lyndhurst, no, Brockenhurst, and having dinner, no, lunch, and I should be wearing a wedding-ring and a slate-blue suit, and into the dining-room who should walk but Miss Trafford and Miss Morton. And Mr. Hollis and Mr. Chiddock and Miss Netley and Miss

Vane and Miss Derry and Partridge and Mr. Hill with his hat on. She said, 'Darling, let's go to the New Forest.'

Walter said nothing; he was lost in the map. Liza watched his face, and put her hand to her throat and squeezed his fingers. He said, 'Look, ducky, this bit here. Not the Rufus Stone part. Up here. It's like Switzerland, and Scotland, and all sorts of places.' He put his finger on the map. 'Where that tongue of Wilts runs into Hants.'

'I do love maps,' said Liza. Wiltshire was pink, and Hampshire yellow; but Dorset was green, and the sea below blue as a summer's day. She thought, I shall buy a lot of cotton, checked, and make it into sun-suits and get brown all over.

Walter opened his suit-case. 'And here's a treat for you. Another lovely pair of trousers to be ironed! Don't delay! Write to-day!' And he shook them out. 'Two pairs.'

Liza thought of the dress she had to iron, and the underclothes, and the buttons to be sewn on two blouses, and the sleeves to be reset in another. She said, 'What fun. Look, this button is nearly off. And that one. I'll mend them first.'

'Thank you, darling,' said Walter, stretching himself on the divan. 'Can I do anything useful?'

'No, darling. I was just finishing making some of those rissole things.' She went back and floured them, and her head ached with thinking of all that she had to do in the next ten days. Besides all you had to do, anyhow, just to keep alive. She sat down on the divan. 'Only a week more. Are you excited?'

'Bursting,' said Walter. 'I must start throwing some things together soon.' He put his arm across her knees. Liza wanted more than anything in the world to take his hand, but her hands were floury.

Walter said, 'You've got a new overall on. Did you know?'

'Yes, I bought it to-day. I bought two.' And she felt silly, and nearly blushed.

'Ducky, are you sure you've never been called a little woman?'

'Certainly not.'

'No offence, darling. Nor have I. I was just asking because you never convinced me. And I still like to know things about you. After all these months. Have you ever been down a water-chute or had your corns cut?'

'Well, no.' It was lovely to talk about yourself. 'At least, I sort of fell off a very low spring-board once. I was trying to decide to learn to dive. I thought it was the end of the world. And I *have* got a corn. And I haven't been called a bachelor girl either. Not in so many words. I don't look like one, do I?'

'No, ducky. You have to wear a collar and tie and have square legs to be a bachelor girl.'

'It's awfully unfair that they don't call men spinster boys. I mean men who haven't married. Why do you think they don't?'

'I suppose they aren't a new enough invention,' said Walter. 'Have I read that *New Statesman*, do you think?'

'Yes,' said Liza. 'It's yours.'

So Walter went on reading it, and Liza went back to the kitchen, thinking, because her head had begun to ache again, whatever happens we shall be out of London in ten days. And then there will be time for everything.

❀

One week's time; and then, four days' time.

The restaurant was dark blue and chromium. People had said at first that it was very quick, even if it was a bit crowded. Now they said it was very crowded, but it had been quick once. Walter and Liza, Carl and Pauline, the limp and button-nosed girl called Poppet and the bullish-faced young man in the camelhair coat, with a name something like Goggy, stood by a corner table and watched a little man collect his bowler hat and his bill. He saw them watching him, grabbed everything and scuttled after his friends. Liza saw Walter's expression, and thought, Walter is as sorry for that poor little man as I am; and the others aren't anything, they didn't notice him. Oh, darling Walter.

Walter pulled out a chair for Pauline, and they all sat down. Liza was opposite Walter, which was nice; she felt gracious, and very married. She was fairly sure that Poppet and Goggy went to bed together sometimes; like Carl and Pauline. She was very sorry indeed for all four of them.

They ordered boiled beef, cabbage and dumplings for Goggy, a prawn salad for Poppet, a veal cutlet and spinach (which cost sixpence more than anything else) for Pauline, fish for Carl, and steak-and-kidney-pie for Walter and Liza; and chips for every one. The ordering went on and on, with arguments and sudden changes of mind. Liza thought, we shall be here for ever.

'No chips for me, Goggy,' said Poppet, in her small, strangled voice. She fiddled with one of her black curls and fixed her eyes on the door, lost in what Liza saw was meant to pass as thought. Liza had never met Poppet or Goggy before; they were friends of Carl and Pauline, and it was Goggy's car which was taking what Pauline called a few odds and ends of Carl's round to the flat after dinner. Liza thought, Poppet is dreadfully shy because of her nose; and it's not as bad as all that, and she has a very good figure. People are awfully sort of vulnerable.

Pauline said, 'Carl, darling, your *hair*. You do look sweet.' So Carl went out and bought an *Evening Standard* and put it up between himself and Pauline.

Pauline turned to Walter. 'Please talk to me, Walter.' Walter hadn't met her or Carl before this evening.

Walter took his eyes from the back of the paper. 'All right. What shall I talk about?' Liza watched rum happily.

Pauline clasped her hands under her chin. 'Your life-story.'

(Don't you touch that, thought Liza. It's mine. He gave it to me. He was born and bred in a nearly square house with a blobby stone lion on each side of the front door, and a greenhouse with grapes, and frogs in a tank smelling like a greenhouse.)

Walter leant back, and his eyes met Liza's across the table. Oh, darling Walter.

'Well,' said Walter, 'I haven't had a very happy life. I've been neglected right from the start. I was born in a little attic in London while my parents were on holiday in Brighton.'

Goggy made Carl jump with a sudden honking laugh.

'I say, it isn't true,' said Walter. 'I didn't even invent it. It's got whiskers all over.'

Pauline said, 'Oh, were you, Walter?' Liza thought, she doesn't belong. She can't play. She tried to make up for it by looking arch. Oh, darling Walter.

Pauline said, 'Give me a cigarette, please, Walter.' Liza turned to Poppet, who was still gazing at the door, 'Hasn't it been a lovely day?'

Poppet rolled up another curl. 'Yes, hasn't it?' Liza couldn't think of anything else to say.

Carl said from behind his paper, 'Does n-no one ever get any f-food in this place?'

'Precious,' said Pauline, 'you are the most *ghastly* pig. You ate a whole tin of twiglets before we left.'

'I did *not*.' Liza thought, he turns his stammer off for Pauline. Carl went back to his paper. Walter said:

'I should hazard a guess that no one *does* get any food in this place. Some of them have brought theirs in handkerchiefs, and the management has coughed up the plates. Others are toying with dummy food nailed to the tables. What do you think, ducky?'

'Well,' said Liza, 'I was thinking that all the people we can see eating are a mirage or a projection or whatever it is when you see a thing because you want to see it.'

'Yes,' said Walter. 'That's a much better theory.' They smiled across the table, and Liza thought, oh, darling Walter; you and me, talking the same language, and all the summer.

At ten they went back to Liza's flat in Goggy's car, and Goggy and Walter and Carl carried the odds and ends upstairs: the radiogram, the piano-accordion, a suit-case which fell open and scattered books all over the floor, some more books, a lamp with a pleated pink shade tied with a spotted ribbon, very Pauline, and, in a white flower-pot, the biggest cactus Liza had ever seen. She said, 'What do you call it?'

'F-Fitzpatrick,' said Carl eagerly. 'You know, the And So We Say F-Farewell Man. It's g-got it up that stick on the side.'

Liza thought, you really are rather nice.

Goggy, who was in the surveying business, whipped out a folding ruler and said that the box of tricks would go nicely next to the bookshelves. He and Walter edged it in; Liza thought, now it's not my fiat any more.

Pauline took her coffee and spilt some. She always did. She said, 'Thank you, Liza darling,' and turned back to Walter, who was sitting on the divan next to her. 'But, Walter, you *should* go and see it. It's so awfully true to life. What happens is this. There's a young man without any money, but who has a lot of friends who have, and he lives with his family in a dreadful home with sagging armchairs and the most ghastly patterned lino; that's the first scene when the curtain goes up. Well, *when* the curtain goes up—'

Liza thought, oh, poor Walter. If anything's more frightful than anything else, it's being told the plot of something. But Walter looked quite happy. But then he was so polite, he was so everything.

'And *then*, my dear,' said Pauline, 'George, that's the young man's name, *hangs* the telephone up, and there is this girl, not the girl I was telling you about before, but another girl who came on just before this first girl and went off again, so I'd better explain—'

'Honest, Poppet!' bellowed Goggy, and gave another honking laugh.

'*No*,' Carl cried across the room. 'You've got it all wrong. He *doesn't*, he goes very slowly downstage, keeping his eyes—'

'Be *quiet*, darling,' Pauline called back. 'Well, Walter, as I was saying—'

If you shut your eyes there might be twenty people in the room. Liza sat under the noise, thinking, this time in four days.

At eleven they began to dance to Carl's radiogram. Walter danced with Pauline, and Goggy with Poppet. Carl said he didn't dance. He sat on the floor beside the radiogram, and Liza sat by him and watched Walter. She had never danced with him; and he danced beautifully.

Liza watched Carl's face as he listened to the dance music, and was reminded of the people in the hard seats at the Queen's Hall. But then, dance music did stir your heart and your soul. She sat there, hoping the evening would go on for ever. Walter went into the kitchen to get Pauline a glass of water, and when he reappeared Liza thought, still, after nearly four months, whenever I see you I feel funny.

Liza danced with Walter, and could think of nothing to say. They were strangers, with their real selves, who knew each other so well, watching and embarrassing them.

'Been to any good theatres lately?' said Walter.

'Oo, not many. Are we just going to sleep to-night?'

'I say, you've skipped a conversational stage or two,' and they weren't strangers any more.

At one o'clock, when the party was really over, Goggy stepped back on to Fitzpatrick, breaking off one of his ears.

'His precious cactus!' said Pauline, with a squeak. Carl's eyes swung towards her, and away. 'It's all right, G-Goggy, old man.' Poor Carl; he minded dreadfully.

'Don't you worry,' said Walter. 'I had one once, not so good as this, and one of its ears broke off, and from that moment it never looked back. It grew ear after ear in mad profusion. I thought of pruning it, but that would have grown it more ears.' Liza thought, it isn't only that I love you; you're so *nice*.

❀

Walter gave the accordion a final squeeze and got up. He had taken his shoes off as soon as they were alone. He walked soundlessly to the bookshelves and squatted down.

When Liza got into bed he was still reading. He put the book back. 'What I'm really aiming at is the Stevenson. I was watching the patter of tiny feet in the Temple Gardens at lunch-time and it made me think of that essay on children. Something about seeing other children and getting towed away by a nursemaid. Why are children so nice in the abstract, and so bloody otherwise?'

'I know,' said Liza. 'I can never coo at prams.' She banged the pillows into the different shapes she and Walter liked, and scraped a speck of black paint from the ivory hand-mirror which her father had sent from India, with the brushes and the two little pots. She was glad she had never had them initialled, or she couldn't have taken them away. Liza Latimer, she thought. L.L. Lovely. I know Pauline will forget to put Mrs.

Latimer when she sends everything on in one envelope. She'll send them separately, just altering the address. I *won't* worry. And I won't think any more about the money; but a whole lump's gone from this twenty-five pounds. Well, there'll be seventeen and six a week from Carl.

Walter was still reading. He stood on one leg and threw his pants across the floor. When he had undressed Liza would get out of bed and pick all his clothes up. She thought, we are as good as married; and I love it when we just go to sleep. She watched Walter's face, willing him to stop reading and get into bed; when they would kiss, and he would roll over, and she would go to sleep with her chin by his shoulder, not touching him, but near him. She thought, I can't help being possessive, wanting to be near him; and that's because, whatever I tell myself, we're not married.

❦

On Liza's last day but one at the office a big fair girl turned up and Liza tried to explain the duties of Mr. Hollis's secretary. The girl was very shy. She wore a musquash coat and a green hat with an eye-veil, and said, 'Yes, I see,' to everything. She made Liza feel small and brisk. Liza said:

'And that's the filing cabinet, and everything in it is, well, it's like this, you see.' She pulled a drawer; it had stuck. She pulled it again, and a folder jerked out. 'It always does that.' She picked up the papers. 'Well, it's like this. This part is dates and this part is alphabetical, at least it would be if I'd put everything in the right places, which I will do. And you might think some of the date ones would go among the alphabetical ones, and the alphabetical ones among the date ones, but they don't, at least some of them do. It's rather difficult to explain.'

The fair girl said, 'Yes, I see.'

Liza got the drawer shut. 'Well, I don't think there's anything else. I mean, there will be, but you'll ask Miss Netley and Miss Vane absolutely everything, won't you? They're awfully helpful.' She wondered if she should warn her about Miss Netley's typewriter; but already the office, and the things that mattered to it, were in the Past.

The fair girl said, 'I see. Thank you.'

Liza showed her out of Enquiries and felt important. A business woman.

On Liza's last day at the office Mr. Hollis gave her the pay envelope and a cheque. Liza said, 'Oh, Mr. Hollis, thank you,' several times, and unfolded the cheque in her room, and didn't know if she was disappointed when she saw it was ten pounds. She hadn't expected anything; but seeing the cheque folded up for thirty seconds had made her think it might be for hundreds of pounds.

Liza thought, if I had had it before lunch I could have bought that lovely suit in Jaeger's window; my grey suit isn't new any more. But it's all right about the twenty-five pounds. Now I've got fifteen shillings too much. I'm rich. Then she remembered that on May the first she had to pay the rent money in advance, and Carl had promised to pay his rent in advance too, but probably wouldn't; and she was not rich now, but very poor indeed.

Liza looked round the room. She had been happy and unhappy here; nothing to do with the office—you could hardly count Mr. Chiddock— had affected her life, but this room had seen four years of living. That terrible club in Bloomsbury, with the orange blobs on the curtains, the wicker chairs, the cocoa, the old women with bulging feet; and the flat; and the flat before this one; and Hugh, and not Hugh. And Walter. Liza stared through the window and tried to remember what the dirty windows opposite might have reminded her of during the past four years. They, reminded her of Walter; nothing else now. There was a slate off the roof. That meant, this time in four hours.

🌀

Liza typed the last envelope and said good-bye to her typewriter. She took Mr. Hollis's post into Enquiries. There was Miss Derry, in her magenta jumper, which had been washed and stretched, plunging at her battered typewriter. Miss Derry's Ted had sailed to Burma, and for a few days Miss Derry was a heroine, and then it wore off. Liza thought, Miss Derry will buy a new jumper and I shall never see it. It was like being dead; your friends would tell each other they were sorry, and the next minute they would be crossing the street, or eating a meal, or answering the telephone; and the same sun would shine on them, and Tuesday would still come after Monday. Liza wondered if next Monday would be wet, when Mr. Hollis would hang his burberry in the cupboard and say that the weather didn't get any better; or fine, when he would say that it was fine at last; and Miss Vane would wear her new black straw hat and say she'd never had a cold last so long. Liza watched Partridge rubber-stamping a heap of papers. A smack on the ink-pad, a smack on the paper. Smack-smack, right through the heap, with his finger flipping up the papers, one by one. He was marvellous. But then he'd done it for so long. He was part of the office, and Liza had never belonged. But just at the moment she almost did.

Liza had said good-bye to Mr. Hollis when he left at four for the week-end. She would get Miss Netley and Miss Vane over. She knocked at their door and heard a scrambled rustle and Miss Netley's 'Come in.' When they saw Liza they both giggled.

'You must see Miss Netley's new evening dress,' said Miss Vane. Either Miss Vane didn't like it or she was jealous.

'It's nothing much,' said Miss Netley gloomily. But she pulled it out of its box. Liza thought, Miss Vane doesn't like it.

'I saw it advertised this morning,' said Miss Netley. 'So I rushed and got the last one.' It was pink net over blue taffeta. The advertisement would have called it a demure picture-frock; its skirt was rows of net frilling, its waist run through with blue ribbon, its sleeves hung in limp, gigantic puffs. Liza could see it on Miss Netley; it would struggle bravely to be demure, and lose.

'It's lovely,' said Liza. 'I think it's sweet.'

'Pretty waist, isn't it?' said Miss Netley. She patted it back in its box and took her comb from her handbag.

The snapshot of Miss Netley's elder brother had gone. Instead there was a close-up of a thin, haunted face with big ears. This would be Miss Netley's Geoff.

'Like him?' said Miss Netley, her mouth was full of hairpins.

'I think he looks *awfully* nice.'

Miss Vane was putting cold cream on her face. There was nothing else to say, so Liza said good-bye; and when it was over she knocked at the door leading to Mr. Chiddock's room. She felt funny. He had never asked her out to lunch since the second Monday; otherwise he had been just the same. Liza thought, I have not the least idea what Mr. Chiddock thinks of me. She knocked again. There was no answer.

'Oh, he's gone to the City,' said Miss Netley, winding an envelope into her typewriter. 'Blast! Blast this blasted machine!' She tore the envelope out.

Mr. Chiddock had suddenly become the only man in the world. Liza said, 'Well, good-bye again,' and Miss Vane and Miss Netley smiled and said they hoped they'd see her one day, and Liza went back to her room. She put her hat on and thought, Walter and I will be in this very nice hotel, at dinner this time, me wearing my black dinner-dress, and into the dining-room will walk Mr. Chiddock, and stop, stunned. And, because they've never seen me in evening dress either, Mr. Hollis and Miss Vane and Miss Netley and Miss Derry and Partridge and Mr. Hill with his hat on.

Liza said good-bye to her room and went back to Enquiries. Partridge dropped his rubber stamp and wrung her hand nearly off. Of course. He was a Boy Scout. Miss Derry twirled round in the new Tan-Sad chair which had appeared the day Ted sailed to Burma, and said:

'All the best. Probably turn up again, like a bad penny. Cheery-bye!'

Liza shut the glass door. There was Enquiries, finally and for ever back to front. There was the tray of papers on the window-sill. No one was watching.

Liza took the top sheet off the pile. The second sheet was a carbon copy of the top sheet. The third was another carbon copy. The fourth was another. The fifth was different, but still a list of things like FX/3/TC. The sixth was a carbon copy of the fifth.

Well, that was the end of the office. Liza put her gloves on her dusty hands and went down in the lift. One hour's time.

'Good night, Miss Brett,' said the baize-aproned old man who sometimes came out of the shadows and went back into them.

'Good night,' said Liza. She stood in the doorway. Behind her was Miss Brett, finally and for ever. Outside was Mrs. Latimer. She walked through the doorway, into the Future.

Part Two

Summer

VI

It had been dusk when they started, much later than they had meant to. Now it was dark. The car swept on and on, sending a shining, crumpled road before it. Walter burst into song.

> *Now Brian O'Lynn had no trousers to wear,*
> *So he got him a sheepskin and made him a pair,*
> *With the skinny side out and the woolly side in:*
> *That will do for the present, said Brian O'Lynn.*

Liza said, 'Dear Brian O'Lynn.'

'He is fun, isn't he? An epitome of life. I mean, you can see the old boy sweating away at making them, and saving about twopence, and never getting a proper pair and always meaning to. Not to speak of being dreadfully uncomfortable and totally unable to sit down or walk about. A typical bit of makeshift. Life all over.'

'I don't think he was an *old* boy,' said Liza. 'Brian is a young name.'

'Are you tired, ducky?'

When people said, are you tired, they meant, are you as cross as you sound? And her remark, which had only been said for something to say, *was* out of tune; it was, look at his temperature! with a click of the tongue.

Liza said, 'No, not at all,' and that did sound rather cross. She thought, we can't always be in tune if we're together all the time.

Walter said nothing. Walter liked thinking in cars at night; he had told Liza it was one of his Things; and Liza had meant to let him think to-night; and now he was, but it hadn't happened in the right way. Liza thought, and I should be so happy now, but all I can do is tell myself I should be; but I went to bed at four last night, and three the night before; so it's only that I'm tired. She thought of the monstrous white satin bed they would sleep in to-night, and said:

'Do you think we shall find a nice hotel?' She had said this earlier on to-night.

'Of course we will,' said Walter. 'Somewhere between here and Southampton will hove into view an old-world hostelry, faintly baronial, with antlers and pewter mugs. I can sort of see it. Where are we, ducky? You've got the map.'

Liza opened it. 'I'm not exactly sure.'

So at a wooden shack and two petrol pumps Walter stopped the car and worked out that they were getting on for Winchester; and asked for five gallons of Shell, and got out and walked up and down.

The pump ticked. The young man working it had a slow, rounded voice which reminded Liza of the clank of the milk-churns at the first small station. A bicycle-light wandered by. A moth danced before the headlights, throwing a hugely giddy shadow on the grass. Liza thought, it's begun. She took off her glove and put on the wedding-ring. It was a sixpenny one. She had been a coward, and economical, and gone to Woolworth's, and decided that it would have been less cowardly not to, because the fat, yellow-haired woman buying ear-rings and the Chelsea Pensioner staring so angrily at nothing in particular on the counter must have thought she was a tart. As for the girl behind the counter, she had worn a real wedding-ring, rounded inside as well as out, and she hadn't been specially pretty or specially anything.

Walter got back in the car, and Liza put her glove on. They drove through Winchester, and then there were no hotels any more. Liza said, 'Darling, let's stop anywhere for something to eat.'

'Well, here's a lorry-drivers' pull-up.'

'*I* don't mind.' She wasn't cross, only hungry.

'I didn't say you did,' Walter snapped. They went into the loudest and brightest room Liza had ever seen, with more men than she had known drove lorries. They found two places at a marble-topped table, and after a ham roll eaten in silence Liza said, she hoped not loud enough for the men opposite to hear:

'Isn't this fun?'

Walter took his eyes from a notice on the wall and said, 'Marvellous. I'm going to be a lorry-driver next.' And when they got back in the car they kissed.

Liza buttoned her camelhair coat up and wriggled herself comfortable as the car moved off. The car churred; the churr was suddenly faint and far away, and she was asleep. She opened her eyes to a bumping, and found that the car had stopped, and Walter was getting their suit-cases out. A tram clanged by. She said, 'Are we back in London?'

'Not exactly, ducky. We're on the verge of Southampton. Isn't this a lovely hotel?'

Liza looked, and saw a yellow brick wall and a swing-door.

'Lovely, darling.'

'That's the spirit,' said Walter. 'Do you want me to explain why we're here? You know how when you're on a picnic you start looking for somewhere really nice at twelve, and end up at two on a ribbon-developed by-pass? Well, roughly that has happened.'

'Fun,' said Liza, and followed him through the swing-door. She stood in a square brown hall, made of milk chocolate and brown paper, and said to the man in the booking-office, 'Good evening. Which room has my husband gone up to, please?' She wanted to see how she said it. No, it wasn't right yet, but it was fun.

The man put his overcoat on and said sleepily, 'Room 19. Would you like to sign the book now?'

Liza had known this would happen, which made it funny that it should. She took off both gloves and dipped the pen in the ink, removed an imaginary hair and dipped it again. The book was open at a nearly new page, the only other entry being *John Kirby, Cleethorpes*. There was a squiggle before the John; it might be Mr. or even Mrs. Liza's hands were sticky with fright. Did you write Mr. and Mrs. Latimer? Or Elizabeth Latimer and Walter Latimer, on the same line or on separate lines? Liza dug the pen at the paper and made a lovely blot. She was going to say, with a little-woman smile, I'm awfully bad at this sort of nib. Can I leave it for my husband? She smiled; and then she heard footsteps, and there was Walter on the stairs. It was the luckiest thing that had ever happened. She said, 'Darling, will you do this? I must fetch something from the car,' and pushed at the swing-door, and pulled it, and ran out. Well, that was all right; but it wouldn't be any easier next time.

Room 19 was rather like the hall. The mantelpiece and doors were made of milk chocolate, and the walls were brown paper with a wavy pattern, while the carpet was also brown and wavy. A dim sepia photograph of some low mountains hung over a grate stuffed with green crinkly paper. There was some pale brown furniture, and there were two narrow beds, separated by a rickety table.

'Isn't it heavenly?' said Walter. 'Sort of early Arnold Bennett. Or do I mean Wells? Early, anyway. I'm going to see about baths.' He went off, and Liza untied the Peter Jones bag and found her new face-flannel, among the shoulder-strap ribbon and the cellophaned stockings. Yes, it *was* fun; it was only for one night, and you couldn't see new stockings without being happy.

Walter came back. 'There isn't any bath-water. I met a chambermaid person with B.O. and she said they'd been having trouble with the cistern *all* day. Never before, though. I bet.' He took a towel off a jug. 'Uk. Tepid.'

'Never mind, darling,' said Liza.

Walter didn't answer. She didn't blame him. A little later he said, as he wuffled the soap over his face,' I keep thinking I'm in a house of ill-fame, don't you?'

Yes, it *was* fun.

Liza got into bed, and Walter emptied his pockets on the dressing-table and hung his coat over a chair. Liza moved her left hand under the sheet. She didn't think he had noticed the ring, and she didn't want him to. She lay there, thinking, hurry, darling, and move that horrid table away, or get into my bed, and then I can go to sleep with my chin by your shoulder.

Walter tied his pyjamas on and sat down on the other bed. 'Is that a lamp down there?' He took it off the floor.

'It doesn't look as if it worked,' said Liza. 'We shan't want it now, darling.'

'It's only the bulb.' He took his cigarette-lighter from the dressing-table. 'Ducky, be a plumber's mate and hold this.'

Liza climbed out of bed, and stood with the lighter while Walter stood on the end of the bed and reached for the green-shaded bulb which hung a few inches from the ceiling.

'Don't fall over, darling,' she said, thinking, I'm saying everything wrong to-night.

'Not?' said Walter. 'I was just thinking it would be rather fun. I suppose I mayn't now.' There was a tinkling crash. 'Damn and blast. Well, that's the end of that.' He jumped off the bed.

'Mind the glass,' said Liza.

'I was going to,' said Walter crossly, and drew back the curtains and got into his bed. Liza got into hers. A tram clanged past the window.

'Night falls in tropical suddenness in these parts,' said Walter. He yawned. 'Good night, ducky.'

'Good night, darling.'

Liza lay on the hardest bed she had had since school, and thought, well, it is fun. Or it will be. It's sort of life, and we're settled, and together for four months. If I tell myself we're married, then it will be all right; it was the sort of makeshift life we had in London, all suit-cases and having to get from Chelsea to Hampstead and to the office and back, that made everything such a strain. Oh, but it was so lovely; and her heart ached for the Past.

A strange clock struck twelve. This time yesterday she was packing. She would have been wrapping the shoes up; because she was holding a cork sandal as she watched the electric clock go by from a minute to twelve to a minute past, thinking, it's not to-morrow, it's to-day.

A railway line ran through the back of the hotel, just missing Room 19. Liza heard an express train roaring nearer, and clutched the bed; but it was all right. Lovely world, and everything was fun. She was thinking, if this time six months ago some one had said you will be in bed in an hotel in Southampton six months from to-day, wearing the pink satin nightdress you bought for Hugh, and with some one in the next bed called Walter Latimer, only you haven't met him yet, and you won't be at the office any more, and a man called Carl, you haven't met him either, will be living in your flat—well, but the Future was like that. You could always surprise yourself with it by imagining yourself in the Past.

Now Brian O'Lynn—

Go *away,* said Liza.

❀

Liza and Walter went to look at some more cottages; they had seen dozens. The estate agent they visited this morning gave them each a cigarette and called her Mrs. Latimer, just as if she was, and was a very nice man indeed. And the sun shone, and to-morrow they were leaving the hotel, after four days of brown paint, brown soup, tepid brown bath-water and a spinster in brown marocain who kept asking Walter to mend the hotel's wireless set. Liza had liked that part, because Walter had been so manly and helpful, and the spinster had fluttered coyly, saying, 'How very kind of your husband; *now* we'll have some *music,*' and had turned on a colliery prize band which had given Walter and Liza dreadful giggles. But on the whole the hotel had been awful; now it was over, and lovely.

Walter stopped the car at a hulk of a stone cottage with grass growing from the roof. 'This is the last but one on the list. Isn't it heavenly? Well, at least it's hollow.'

'Darling, this *can't* be it.'

'I'm beginning to think anything can be anything. For sale. Unfurnished. The chumps. Wll. nd. extsve. strctrl. alts. I should say it wll. The garden might be fun, though. I wonder what it'd cost to put the house right.'

So they went in, walking carefully where the floor might give way. Liza said, 'You know, this room is quite like a room. I mean, you can almost imagine it *as* a room.'

Walter stopped reading a newspaper up the chimney, and gave her a cigarette, and Liza picked three cowslips from the overgrown garden. When they got back in the car, she said, 'I sort of feel we've lived there.'

'You've taken the words from my mouth,' said Walter. Liza thought, we're in tune.

The next cottage was a semi-detached brick villa at one end of a long village. It didn't seem worth getting the keys from the grocer next door; but they did and went in. Liza lost Walter, and found him in the best bedroom, admiring the mahogany. 'There's a gas-stove,' she said. 'And a bath with taps. And a lav. called Windermere. Oh, darling, it's a real *house*.' They stood at the silk-curtained window. The house was right on the road, but over the grocer's van the beech-trees were opening.

'There's something about a beech-leaf,' said Walter. 'It doesn't take the light in. It gives it out. And it makes me dreadfully sad.'

'Me, too. I hate nearly summer evenings.'

Walter put his arm round her. Liza was thinking of the cottage she had planned and lived in for the past month. Oak beams, a thatched roof, currant-bushes, oak-trees all round, and the grass under them like a lawn. She thought, but I don't mind where I live, as long as I live with you. 'Do you think this house would do, darling?'

'No, ducky. I got ideals.' Perhaps he had dreamt a cottage like hers. She thought, no one knows about any one else.

'Look over there and cheer up,' said Walter. 'The Three Crows is or are open.' So they went across and drank flat beer from a barrel draped with a dish-cloth; and Walter and the man behind the counter discussed where the world was going, and the man called Liza missy, though she had her left hand on the counter. Liza listened to the talk, and thought happily of the flick to-night, and to-morrow the cottage with currant-bushes; and the new hotel.

Room 21 was on the second floor. There was a very big entrance hall, with two men at a counter, and rows of keys, and a mountain of red roses on a table. Liza and Walter walked up the wide stairs, because lifts made Walter's legs ache, and Liza said, 'Darling, you didn't choose here just because I was cross to-day? Because—' she couldn't say, I was only pretending to be because it was so nice when you kissed me and said you loved me, I didn't really mind about another day of horrid little villas.

'No, ducky. It was the only one I could think of. I've been here before.'

'With a woman?'

'Yes. One Christmas. It wasn't anything much. Except that the Christmas tree caught fire, which was heavenly.'

'Was the woman nice?'

'I suppose I thought so then. She didn't think much of me. I was but a lad. She was married to some one she didn't like.'

Liza was angry. This woman had a proper wedding-ring and a perfectly good husband; and Liza loved Walter, and her wedding-ring was flat inside, and she would have to keep her hand under the table in this kind of hotel. But when she saw Room 21 she was happy again; it had a thick blue carpet, and no pictures, and a huge double bed, and a basin with white tiles and chromium. She turned on the H tap. 'Oh, darling, the water's hot. Is it all frightfully expensive?'

'I don't mind if it is. We'll go a bust for a few days.' He took his tie off, and his shoes, and stretched himself on the bed. Liza lay down beside him. She saw the pink sheets and thought, this is the dream, and the Future. (And into the dining-room who should walk but Mr. Chiddock and stop, stunned by Liza in her black dinner-dress. And Mr. Hollis. And all the office. And Carl and Pauline, Goggy and Poppet, the spinster carrying the awful hotel's wireless set.) 'Darling, what do we wear for dinner?'

'Well, we're going to yet another flick. I shall brush my hair and put on my suit.'

So Liza went down to dinner in her black cocktail-party dress, thinking, I look just as nice in this, and oh, it is lovely to be some one's mistress. She thought it even more when they had had a gin and French and gone into the dining-room, a vast place hushing the hum and clatter.

She kept her eyes on the door, having seen a fat, pale man a bit like Mr. Hollis, and so perhaps an omen.

Walter said suddenly, 'Old Robert!' and got up. Liza watched him threading his way among the tables, smiling at the woman who moved her chair to let him past, and getting a smile back which meant, you're terribly attractive. Oh, darling Walter. Liza said to the waiter, 'My husband's just—oh well, *hors-d'oeuvres*. And thick soup. Yes, for both of us, please.' She sat, ready to put her hand under the table when Robert appeared. She should have ordered three *hors-d'oeuvres*. She couldn't hide her left hand all through a meal. Well, she was some one else's wife who had just met Walter for the evening. Fun. She didn't think much of Walter, and she was married to some one she didn't like.

Walter came back alone. 'Hullo, ducky. Robert's going to America to-night. Would you be dreadfully put out if I went down to the boat and mafficked? He's having quite a bender.' He stopped, and shook his napkin out. 'I mean, ducky, I don't think there'll be any women around—'

And if there were, thought Liza, you wouldn't want me. She twiddled her ring, which was getting to be a habit, and said, in a wifely voice, 'No, darling. You go. I'd like a nice quiet evening.'

The soup arrived, and Walter said, before the waiter had gone, 'Oh, ducky, I loathe thick soup. I mean, compared with thin.'

'Well, you like mulligatawny soup, darling, and oxtail.'

'Yes, precious, but this is whatever thick soup is when it isn't mulligatawny or oxtail.'

'Well, darling, do you hate every thick soup there is except those two?'

'Not really. I'm just making conversation. And this soup is lovely, so I take it all back.'

Liza thought, that sort of thing wouldn't matter if we were married; the trouble is, I'm not just up against the outside world, but against Walter too.

Liza sat in the hotel drawing-room, and, having knitted a row of the green jumper, glanced towards the tall, dark man of about forty. He had gone. She was quite extraordinarily disappointed. She went back to the knitting, and found she had done that row wrong. She unpicked it, and went a bit into the next row. By the time she had it all back on the needles she had lost three rows, and every one in the room would be watching. She knitted a row very slowly and carefully, and felt better. She hated knitting, really; she had wanted to sew her drawn-thread satin knickers, but that would be like combing your hair in a theatre. She thought, I wish I had some one to talk to.

The middle-aged woman in the next armchair put down her magazine. 'How tired one gets of silly photographs of silly society people.'

'Doesn't one?' said Liza.

The middle-aged woman was large, and quite handsome, and wore an expensive black lace dress with long sleeves, but she was shapeless, and probably wore layers of underclothes. Her hair was white and wispy, and she wore pince-nez on a chain. She took a square of embroidery from a vast cretonne bag, and said, 'And how do you like Southampton?'

That was being welcomed by the Mayoress. Liza said graciously, 'Oh, I like it very much, thank you,' and thought, I should have said we. I am a young wife whose husband has gone on a bender, and I am enjoying a nice quiet evening. She said, because the middle-aged woman seemed to have missed her turn, 'We're only here for a few days, though. And my husband's gone off on a bender.'

'I beg your pardon?'

'I mean, to a ship. I mean, he had to say good-bye to some one and I thought I'd rather have a nice quiet evening.' She had tangled the wool. She tugged, and it broke. She said, 'And do you know Southampton well, and are you staying here long?' Anyway, she would never wear the jersey, it had been lying round the flat since September.

'I live here,' said the middle-aged woman. 'I don't mean *here*, you know. I live with my daughter, but she's gone to Wensleydale for a fortnight. Her husband's an architect, you know. Such a clever boy.'

Liza thought, oh, darling Walter, you would enjoy this; I hope no one's listening; there's nothing sillier than two strangers starting a conversation.

'You must excuse me,' said the woman, 'but I don't think I know your name.'

'Latimer,' said Liza. 'Mrs. Latimer.' That would be a mistake. She blushed.

'Mine's Croft.' There was a silence. To fill it, Liza said, 'We're looking for a house for the summer. I mean a cottage. Somewhere in the New Forest. We want to live in the top left-hand bit, but it's awfully difficult to find anywhere.'

'How very nice!' said Mrs. Croft. 'And where did you live before?'

'Well, in London. In Chelsea.' It had slipped out; and Walter might have put Hampstead in the register, and Mr. Croft might see it. 'I mean, we *did* till a few weeks ago, and then we got a flat in Hampstead. I keep thinking we still live in Chelsea.' She gave a silly laugh. And Walter might have put Chelsea; no, she didn't think so.'

'So,' said Mrs. Croft to her embroidered canvas, 'you young people have a new flat and now you want a cottage! That sounds almost greedy.'

Liza laughed politely. 'Well, we had to put our furniture somewhere, and my husband has a lot of books, and this flat was empty and such a nice one.' She thought, well, we might be that sort of couple. In fact, if we were married, we would be.

'That's very nice, having a husband who can go off like that. My husband was a doctor, and terribly tied.'

'Was he really?' said Liza, meaning, I'm sorry he's dead, if you're sorry. Mrs. Croft didn't look sorry; Liza thought, every one gets over everything, and that's what's so awful. She went on, after a pause for the dead Dr. Croft, 'My husband's a barrister, which isn't so tying, at least not yet, and he hasn't been frightfully well, and he needed a rest, and he's—' but something stopped her from mentioning Walter's book. 'So we thought we'd have a few months' holiday.' Mrs. Croft dived into the cretonne bag and brought up some coconut-ice pink wool, and Liza said gratefully, 'What a pretty colour!'

'And how long have you been married?' said Mrs. Croft.

It was lovely talking about Walter. 'Oh, under a year. I think it's—yes, ten months.' She wondered what had made her choose ten.

'And did you work before your marriage, like so many of these modern young women?'

Liza wanted to say no, because she didn't think she had. She had been rather a butterfly, living in Sloane Street and buying everything at Harrods. But she heard herself saying, 'Well, I was a secretary, if you call that working.'

'Really? That must be most interesting.'

'Oh, no, it was awful. When I got married I thought how lovely, I need never type or shorthand another word.'

'And do you find you've forgotten it? My daughter took a course before she married, and she wonders if she'll take it up again.'

Liza thought about Mrs. Croft's daughter; well, some women must be like that. A collar and tie. She said, 'Oh, does she? What fun. Well, I find I've forgotten it completely. I mean, I would have, but sometimes I type for my husband.' That sounded convincing; a young barrister's wife.

'Well, now,' said Mrs. Croft, plunging in the bag again and looking over her pince-nez, 'I call that very good of you, if you dislike it so.'

'Oh, no,' said Liza, 'I love it. I mean, I love doing it for *him*.' She went on, wildly, 'He's got one of those portable typewriters that jump about if you type too fast, and it jumps when *I* type, but not when he does, though he says when he bought it last year he used to bang so hard it nearly shot off the table.'

'Then you haven't known each other long?'

Mrs. Croft was an inquisitive old woman. Liza said, 'Oh, no,' and stared at the door. 'Will you excuse me? I think I saw my husband.' She found the ball of wool under Mrs. Croft's chair. It was caught on the chair-leg. She broke it and said, 'Good night.'

'*Good* night,' said Mrs. Croft, smiling up over her pince-nez. 'You know, I saw your husband at dinner. Such a nice boy.'

Liza liked Mrs. Croft very much indeed.

'I'm *quite* sure I've seen him here before. Were you here four Christmases ago, when the tree caught fire? Oh, no, you couldn't have been. But I never forget a face. And he's just like the brave boy who threw the bucket of water.'

'Oh, no,' said Liza. 'I don't think so. I mean, we weren't. Good night.' And she hurried to her room, and, sitting miserably on the bed, thought, well, he's had time to get divorced and meet me and be married ten months. And I don't suppose the maids and porters and people would have been here four years, or remember so far back.

Then she thought, darling Walter. He threw a bucket of water, and he didn't tell me.

Then she thought, him having been here doesn't make it any righter for me to have talked about us. I don't think I said anything that mattered, or was against him. But I shouldn't have said anything; I should have let her talk about herself. Walter would have, because he would have known it was safer for him. And that's a horrid thought.

Liza was suddenly very desolate, alone in a world of strangers.

Then she thought, because it was fun to talk about him I shouldn't have. You should never do what's easy. I've always known that, but it hasn't made much difference.

It was half-past nine, and ten, and eleven, and Walter hadn't come back. He had fallen overboard, or gone to New York. Liza felt sick. But he had said he might be late; and that meant he would be.

Liza was dreadfully lonely. She had knitted several inches more, and might wear the jumper after all. She lay back on the bed, in her pink chenille dressing-gown, and studied the ribbing at the edge of the jumper, thinking, that must have been Hugh once. But I can't remember it. The top part is Walter being drowned, and the middle is Mrs. Croft. She was worried whenever she thought of Mrs. Croft. It would have been funny, when she began this silly jersey, to know what worries, happinesses and unhappinesses would go into it.

Liza dropped the knitting on the bed. She knew too much about what she thought; she had lived too much alone. It was dreadfully final to be able to blame a part of your life for something definite; it was like growing old.

Liza thought, if I have another bath now, with two cubes of bath-salts,

I shall be happy again. So she tied on her dressing-gown, and combing her hair and making up her face, admired herself in all the views given by the three dressing-table mirrors; and picked up her new sponge-bag and the two cubes of bath-salts, and was happy again.

❀

Walter woke up and said, from the other side of the bed, 'God. I'm lined with fur.'

'It's the champagne.'

'Mostly, but not only.'

'I know. It is unfair. Because, darling, I think the world is absolutely beautiful this morning.'

Walter groaned, and buried his face in his pillow. Liza remembered Mrs. Croft, and there was a small shadow over the beautiful morning. She would have to think of some reason for leaving. No, she would not. Walter had been divorced, poor Walter, and only to please his horrible first wife; and it was a beautiful morning. Liza felt serene and married, the sort of woman who had breakfast in bed. When Walter got up she said, 'Darling, I think I'll have breakfast in bed.'

'Good. I can sulk behind a paper. But don't be late, will you, ducky? To-day or never we find a cottage. And then I shall start woik.' He sat down on her side of the bed. 'I've got alcoholic remorse.'

Liza stroked his hair; she was an author's wife now, even better than a barrister's. Walter kissed her once more, and got up.

'I'll have coffee, and haddock if they've got any,' said Liza, 'and if not scrambled eggs and one sausage, and will you say brown rolls and if not toast, and honey and—'

'There's a bell behind you, ducky,' said Walter, as he put on his dressing-gown.

Liza sank inside. Did he mean order breakfast now? He had said she mustn't be late; and he had his dressing-gown on, so it would be all right if the chambermaid came in at once, but she might not, and Walter might have nothing on. Well, he would see her ring the bell; but he might not.

Why couldn't she say, do I ring it now or wait till you go downstairs? Because she couldn't. She was up against Walter, and the world.

Liza thought, I'll ring it very obviously. She said, 'Did you hear it ring?' and, anyway, it was all right, because the chambermaid appeared in a few seconds, while Walter was still scratching his hair and yawning. But it was like that awful hotel book, it wouldn't help for next time.

Liza walked down the sloping street which seemed the most important in Southampton. She wore her navy blue linen suit, and saw her reflection in all the available shop windows with the greatest pleasure, wishing at the same time that she had brought her camelhair coat; it was a fine day, pale blue and white, but you could tell the sea was near. Walter had gone off alone in the car, because, reading the paper while she had breakfast in bed, she had suddenly felt homesick for London; and shopping in Southampton would be as good. She went into a big store, wondering what she should buy, and ended up with a red and white cotton dress, which cost only fifteen and eleven, but she hadn't enough money with her.

'If you pay by cheque, madam,' said the girl, 'we can send it to your hotel.'

Liza had her cheque-book out of her bag before she remembered. 'I—I can't do that. I mean, I don't think I will. Would you keep it till to-morrow morning?' She put the cheque-book back and saw, on the counter, the only letter Walter had written her. *Miss Liza Brett.* The shop-girl would have seen it. Liza put it away and walked out. Well, she wouldn't see the girl again.

At the umbrellas Liza began to worry about spending fifteen and elevenpence. At the haberdashery she turned back, and found the girl. She said, 'I've just thought. Don't keep it for me. I'll come in to-morrow, and if I don't, don't keep it. In fact, I think I won't have it, definitely. I suddenly felt economical. I'm awfully sorry I gave you all that trouble.'

The shop-girl smiled. 'That's quite all right, madam.' She was a very nice shop-girl, and, as for the smile, all shop-girls smiled in the same way.

As Liza walked back to the hotel she thought, all these silly happenings affect me, but not Walter. He's still got his own surname; but it isn't only surnames, it's his attitude to us, and mine. I wish I could stop thinking he's my enemy. The trouble is, we're out of the true; in London we were illicit, and we are now, but we pretend not to be. And another trouble is that I *like* the pretence, I like the outward appearances of marriage; and they all come back on me to make me look silly. Well, it won't be for long. When we're in a cottage, and I'm doing the housework, I shall be established, and then I can be myself.

❁

In the car that afternoon Walter said, 'Wait till you've seen it. You may loathe it.'

'Oh, darling, you are clever. I know it will be heaven.'

'I wouldn't call it that. But it's a roof and four walls. No, more, there's a jutting out bit to hold the kitchen. The whole thing is rudely fashioned of grey plasticine. And the garden has fallen down the slope at the back. Leaving the most terrific view. Which is partly what decided me.'

It was funny to think that Walter had seen the Future, and she hadn't. She said, 'It sounds perfect. And where's the pub?'

'About two miles away; and in a week the Major will have taken himself to Ireland, and we shall move into our tiny home. He fishes like mad. I didn't tell you that. And he wears a heavenly plush hat which can only be described as battered. And a blue pullover. We had a long talk on fishing, and now I'm an expert. I think I might be a journalist next, ducky; I love interviewing people.'

Liza thought, Major Hobie and Walter will talk and I shall feel stupidly shy. The car left the main road and climbed a gravel track over heathland clumped with pines, nothing like a forest. The oak-trees and the currant-bushes had been only a dream.

'This is the sort of country I meant,' said Walter. 'Isn't it lovely, ducky?'

'Heavenly.' It was; but it would be too cold for sun-suits.

The cottage stood at the right of the gravel track, nearly at the top of the hill. It was a funny little stone box. Oyster shells edged the path, which turned past a green trellis-work porch to a creosoted shed. You couldn't see any garden at the back. Liza stood at the gate, glad she had brought her camelhair coat, and an old man, exactly the amiable walrus Walter had described, ambled down the path and called 'Morning! Morning!' Yes, and he said everything twice. Darling Walter.

'My wife, Major Hobie,' said Walter. Liza felt dreadfully embarrassed, and rather apologetic, as if she had somehow hurt Walter.

'Come in! Come in!' cried Major Hobie, and led the way. 'Step,' whispered Walter, just in time. They stood in a dark, oak-beamed room with mats and a lot of dark furniture, and Walter said, 'We're awfully sorry to bother you again.'

'That's all right,' said Major Hobie. 'That's all right.' He took a bundle of raffia from the bowl of oranges. 'Take a look round!' He ambled to the door and seemed to be wondering what to say. Liza could have told him. 'Take a look round!' he said, and ambled out.

Liza watched him go past, trundling a wheeled basket with a walking-stick handle. 'Isn't he heavenly, darling? I think I scared him off.'

'Yes, I imagine he mistrusts the fair sex. He's the sort of old bird who revels in fierce independence. The kitchen is a tangle of all the gadgets no one can cook with.' He opened a door at the back.

'Oh, darling, it's lovely,' said Liza, looking round at the saucepans, egg-whisks, sieves and mint-choppers. She saw herself at the back door which led out to the garden and the view, graciously ordering loaves from respectful tradesmen.

'Do you think it will do?' Walter sounded rather shy and proud; and as if it was to be Liza's cottage, not his. She kissed him and said, 'I think it will. And I can move all the clutter from the sitting-room to the shed.'

Walter smiled and patted her head. 'What did I nearly call you, ducky?'

'A little woman.'

'Sweetie, I didn't mean to annoy you.' He kissed her again. 'I love you.'

'I love you. And you wouldn't like me not to be domesticated?'

'I should simply hate it.' He took her into the dining-room, on the right of the sitting-room as you faced the front door. It was a surprise; the walls were papered a rough-cast peach, the furniture was waxed oak, like Mr. Hollis's.

'If you hadn't seen Major Hobie,' said Walter,' how would you deduce him from this room?'

'I think a young married couple, the hopes of the tennis-club.'

'Full marks,' said Walter, and they went through the door next to the dining-room door, up the stairs.

The bedrooms were nothing much. The stairs led straight into a bare, whitewashed room, with a splintery wooden floor, some more mats, a chest of drawers and a small wardrobe; beyond was a smaller room with a folding camp-bed and bamboo furniture, and beyond that a long and narrow bathroom. They looked out of the window. It was a lovely view; it lifted you up.

Liza said, 'Oh, darling, it is lovely.'

'It's a bit chaste and bleak, don't you think?' said Walter. 'I don't think his sex life is exactly riotous.' They went back to the first bedroom, and sat on the bed.

'It's sort of funny,' said Liza. 'It's got a sort of atmosphere. I don't mean it's funny so much as it's fun. Oh, darling, I do love you.' She sat on his lap, and they kissed. The sun shone through the little window, a bird whistled with an aching sweetness, and the summer stretched ahead, for as far as she could see.

VII

If you lay on the steepest slope of the lawn at the back of the cottage, about where the oyster-shells stopped and the path wanted weeding, you had either the sun or the wind on you. This morning the wind was at the top of the garden, and down here it was suddenly hot and still. Walter was lying on his front, reading; his shirt open at the neck, his sleeves rolled up, his bare feet rubbing the grass. Liza sat down next to him.

'Ullo,' said Walter, and went on reading. Well, she hadn't expected him to be exactly excited; only this was the first morning in five days that she had got as far as the garden; well, nothing clever in that, or in being there now, but she thought, you might have said *something*. Liza rolled over on to her front, and, propping her elbows on the prickly grass, began to read her book, Walter's Everyman copy of *Shakespeare's Historical Plays, Songs and Sonnets*. Walter moved nearer, so that their arms touched. Lovely sun, lovely day.

> *Live with me and be my love*
> *And we will all the pleasures prove—*

It danced, like the shallow river in the next verse. Her eyes went up to the opposite page.

> *If that the world and love were young*
> *And truth in every shepherd's tongue,*

and that danced even better.

Walter said, without looking up, 'What are you reading, ducky?'

'Shakespeare. Yours.'

He took her book. 'Not the bits you're reading. That bit's by I've forgotten who. And the live with me one is Marlowe. And the if that the world verse is Raleigh. And the thing after is a chap called Barnfield. End.'

'Thank you, darling. You are clever.'

Walter put his hand on her neck and went on reading. He took it off to turn a page. Liza waited, and then rolled over on to her back and shut her eyes. The sun was hot on her face, the world was the clear orange-red the other side of her eyelids, and a dancing summer. This was the first real day of summer.

Something tickled her chin. She opened her eyes and saw Walter, leaning on his elbow and playing with a piece of feathery grass. 'Hullo, ducky. What were you thinking?'

'Happy thoughts.'

'Such as?'

'Well, that poor Miss Netley and Miss Vane are banging away at their typewriters, with the same view, dirty windows with the sun on them to make them dirtier, and perhaps Miss Netley is a bit less gloomy because she has my typewriter now, and she's got my typewriter because I'm here, which is relativity again. And it's Tuesday, and all they've got to look forward to is pay-day on Friday.'

Walter kissed her. Liza pulled his hair and thought, sometimes I think that Walter is a house and I'm a lean-to shed; but just at this moment it's the other way round. She went on:

'And I can never stop being surprised that there are Tuesdays, Wednesdays and Thursdays all your own, not the office's.' She put her arms round his shoulders. 'And. And I love you.'

Walter ran the feathery grass over her face. 'Thank you, lady.' Liza released him and he went back to his book. She thought, if I'd said what I meant, that I wanted to thank him for letting me out of prison, he would have called me a waif and stray. Well, he did imply it; all the time undercurrents, and atmosphere, and knowing that what we say may not be what we mean, but that makes no difference. Sometimes I think we know each other too well. Already.

There was a welcome hammering at the back door. Liza scrambled to her feet and ran up the garden, meeting the wind. She held her hair down and stepped over a flowerbed towards the grocer's boy with the basket. He was not so much a boy as a youth, callow, dark and scowling, and Liza was dreadfully afraid of him. She said nervously:

'Good morning. Is your cold better?' The wind blew her voice away, and the youth said nothing. He searched in his basket and held out a white sandwich loaf.

'Haven't you got a small brown?' He had faithfully promised her one yesterday, and the wind was blowing her hair in her eyes. She was very angry. The youth shook his head.

'Oh, well. Can we have one to-morrow, please?'

He nodded sullenly.

'And have you got anything else to eat? I mean for us, me, to eat?' He had also promised to bring her a selection of groceries, and there were only loaves in the basket. He hitched his basket on his arm, saying, 'Got a few things in the van, miss,' and Liza followed him round to the little blue van and chose some tins and a pound of sausages. This was a difficult place to shop in, the village being a mile and a half away; well, Walter would motor her down to-night. She stared interestedly round the inside of the van, which she hadn't seen before, and said, 'What fun.'

The youth said nothing. Well, it wouldn't be fun for him. Liza wanted desperately to say something friendly; in London it was so easy, you had a ready-made angle on every one's life, but the country was a world of foreigners to whom the weather meant not football matches, umbrellas or Sunday in the Park, but dull, hard facts like the state of the ground and the crops. Oh, well. She said, 'Good-bye, and thank you,' and the van bumped away. Liza went back to her kitchen, with a glance down the garden. There was Walter. You only had to look and there he was. All the summer.

Liza was very proud of the kitchen. She had scrubbed the table and the floor, and cleaned the gas-cooker, which was now nearly as dirty again, and arranged everything differently, hoping she would be able afterwards to rearrange the kitchen and sitting-room as Major Hobie had them, but not minding much if she didn't; because it was not his cottage now. She began to line the larder shelves with newspaper. Monday, May 17; this Monday. Poor office.

Liza lined two shelves and went back to the garden. But Walter had gone. She found him in the shed, which smelt excitingly of creosote and string and was now stacked with Major Hobie's golf-clubs and clutter. Walter had pulled the lawnmower from a corner, and was gazing at it, rather wistfully. Then he said:

'Ducky, if I put lots of newspapers on the young married couple's waxed oak table, I don't suppose the typewriter will scratch it, do you?'

Liza was an author's wife again; she saw a scrubby linen-covered book with *For Liza* printed, one blank page, and *For Liza, with love from W.,* on another blank page. She said, 'No, darling, I'm sure it won't. Or you can have the table in the larder.'

'So I can,' said Walter. 'Thank you, ducky.' Then he kicked the lawnmower and said, 'I bet this is patent. If we take it out we can get at it.'

'Yes, and we shall have to mow the lawn one day. At least, I can. I love mowing lawns.'

'So do I,' said Walter. He carried the mower outside, and squatted down. So did Liza.

'It is,' said Walter. 'As patent as can be. I knew the old boy wouldn't let us down. We've got one of these at home. You move the blades high or low, and they sort of bend when they go over bumps or stones. As they'd have to on this lawn.'

'Oh, darling, what fun.'

Walter pulled at a lever which didn't move, and said, 'I think I shall oil it. I don't know. I must start work.'

Liza thought, this is a turning-point. Walter is being a lean-to shed, and he wants a house to lean on. She said, 'Yes, darling.'

'Well, ducky,' said Walter, 'find me an oil-can, because you're so clever.'

'There's one in the kitchen. And it's got oil in it. I know, because it blobbed on the floor.'

'Bless you. Just run and fetch it, there's a darling.'

So Liza ran and fetched it. The sun shone up from the crazy paving by the kitchen door, the wind had dropped. She thought, I couldn't have *forbidden* him. Anyway, there's plenty of time. She took the oil-can from the shelf, next to the paraffin bottle. She was a housewife, she knew where everything was. She put the can on a tray, with the bottle of Kia-Ora Lemon Squash and a jug of water and two glasses. They clinked as she walked, and Walter looked up and smiled. 'Marvellous, ducky. I don't know what I should do without you.'

❀

At six Liza walked down to the village, because Walter was mending his typewriter. It was a fine evening, but not hot. She put on her camelhair coat, which had been cleaned and relined and was like new, and walked down the gravel track, carrying the plaited straw bag. She was wearing socks and her white string sandals with cork soles, and as she went down the hill her toes pushed against the string, leaving the cork heels to flap on the gravel. She stopped to pick a gorse-flower, and wished she could decide on its smell. Perhaps almonds and honey. A little stream ran across the track, with a bridge at the side. When she had crossed it, she stood and listened to the silence.

The gravel track met the village at the road. There were some whitewashed cottages with no windows, and round the corner shops and more cottages. Liza went into the grocer's first. It was very dark after the sunlight, and smelt of corn and sweet biscuits. The grocer's shop was fun, with its tottering piles of biscuit-tins and cereal-packets; and the grocer wore a green rubber mat over his apron, his grey-brown hair stuck up like grass, and he wore a pencil behind one ear and a cigarette behind the other, making Liza wonder desperately, whenever she saw him, if it was always the same cigarette.

There was some one else in the shop. A girl, no, a woman of about thirty-something. She had a bright blue handkerchief round her head, tied in three little knots at the top. Liza moved to the back of the shop, where she could stare better, and saw she had dark hair with red lights, perhaps artificial, and she wore a teddy-bear swagger coat and grey flannel trousers. Liza undid the top button of her camelhair coat and told herself she must get some new buttons. She saw the woman's left hand on the counter; it had a narrow carved wedding-ring, platinum or white gold. Liza thought, for no reason at all I don't like you.

The grocer was saying, 'Well, Mrs. Dennison? Anything else we can get you?' in his funny, prim voice.

'I can't think,' said Mrs. Dennison. She spoke rather slowly, and her voice was not exactly deep, but full. 'One of those tins of cocktail biscuits, all different.'

'Now, now, you can't carry all those,' said the grocer.

'I've got the car.' She put everything down. 'And I think a jar of that galantine stuff, and a tin of those beans I had before.'

The grocer fetched them. 'Mr. Dennison well, Mrs. Dennison? Not still down here, I suppose?'

'No, he went back on Monday. How are you, Mr. Murdoch? How's the family?'

'All very well, thank you, Mrs. Dennison. How's yours?'

'All right if he hasn't got worms,' said Mrs. Dennison. 'He nearly always has.' She collected everything.

'Let me help you, Mrs. Dennison,' said the grocer, moving towards the flap in the counter.

'No,' said Mrs. Dennison. The grocer stopped moving. Liza watched her getting into a big grey car, and had a glimpse of a little black dog. The car slid away.

'Good evening, Mrs. Latimer,' said the grocer. 'What can we get you this evening?' But he said it in a different voice.

❧

Liza and Walter had supper under the window in the sitting-room, as the dining-room was Walter's study. They ate minced beef with triangles of toast, and cabbage and mashed potato. It was still light, but some of the colours had faded and some darkened, and the white arabis on the table glimmered. Liza said:

'And I saw two frightfully bored-looking cows standing side by side, having used up all their conversation. And I went to the grocer's and there was a woman there.'

Walter clicked his tongue and said, 'I don't know what the world is coming to.' He had been almost cross before supper; now he was nice again. 'What was she like?'

'Well, not pretty. I suppose more beautiful than pretty. Not exactly beautiful, though. Tall. And a bit sort of sulky. And she had a little black dog in a car. I can't think of anything else about her. And the dog had worms, or probably. She was telling the grocer.'

'People who have dogs with worms always do tell grocers.'

Liza felt rather smug. 'Well, she didn't say it quite like that. She wasn't doggy. And I don't mean exactly sulky, it was just her face.'

'You are a pet. I've never heard you be a cat.'

Liza thought she should have been more pleased than she was. Women who weren't cats were nice girls, and well-meaning, and knew they couldn't change the face of the world. But she did feel rather smug again. 'I do think catty thoughts, though. I think all women are Paulines, until I find they aren't.'

Walter came round and kissed her. 'Would I be very rude if I buried myself behind a bound volume of *The Field*? It's awfully mind-broadening.'

So Walter read, while Liza dished up the treacle-pudding, which stuck to the basin and came in half, but was otherwise a success. She sat, looking out of the window and thinking, I do feel settled, and a good housewife, and married; and I think I shall go to Salisbury and buy a real wedding-ring.

❦

Liza woke up two days later and saw the fretworked hair-tidy hanging by her shoulder-strap ribbon from the mirror. Walter had made it yesterday. He had said, 'All fretwork has to be useless. What's the most useless thing you know, ducky?'

Liza had said, 'A hair-tidy.'

'Well, I don't know. You can put hair in a hair-tidy.'

'Yes, but I wouldn't. And there's a waste-paper basket.' So Walter had made the hair-tidy. It had taken him all day, on and off, and after supper he had sat in his study and read Horace's *Odes* with the wireless full on. Liza had put her head round the door to say the tea was made, and had recognized the book, because she had dusted it. She only went in the study to dust it, and it was beginning to be like the flat above hers, not real; and she was rather surprised to find it had quite ordinary dust.

Liza lay and watched the rain, thinking, Walter read Horace to make up for the hair-tidy; and so I hate myself. But if he hadn't fretworked that he would have fretworked something else. She turned over and saw the back of Walter's head, in the next bed, which was a few inches higher than hers, and a good deal softer. Walter had said, 'I'll have the camp-bed, ducky. I can sleep on floors, and it wouldn't be much harder.'

Liza had said, 'No, darling, I'll have it. You're bigger and you kick more.' And now, whenever she saw the beds, she thought, Walter's got the best one. Yes, that sort of unselfishness was only cowardice, and selfishness, in about equal proportions; no, cowardice and selfishness were two words for the same thing.

It rained all through breakfast, and Walter put down the bound volume of *Fur and Feather*, which he had said knocked *The Field* sideways, and stretched and yawned. 'I'm going for what that sort of person calls a brisk walk, and then I shall begin to work.' He came round and kissed her head, putting his hand on her neck.

Liza looked up from her catalogue. 'What sort of person exactly, darling?'

'The sort of person who calls a brisk walk a brisk walk, of course, ducky.'

'Sorry. I thought you meant the sort of person who reads *Fur and Feather*.'

Walter flipped her neck with his finger-nail. Liza thought, I've slipped back a very small rung.

Walter drew a moustache on the man in pyjamas in the catalogue. 'I love those catalogue-men who do all their telephoning in immaculate pyjamas.' He turned a page, and drew a face on a hot-water bottle. 'And, ducky, when I was three I was carrying a hot-water bottle and I trod on it and fell downstairs.'

'Oh, darling,' said Liza; and she thought of the spring, and her heart ached. She said, 'Pauline sent all these on. I had to pay twopence.' The envelope said Mrs. Latimer; she turned it over. 'Darling, Pauline never sent the rent. Carl owes me three weeks.' The summer was three weeks less. 'What do I do?'

'I suppose write and ask him,' said Walter; and fetched his mackintosh, and went off. Liza was alone in the world.

After lunch, when he didn't say much, Walter went back to his study. Liza heard an occasional rattle from the typewriter, which was something. Perhaps he had been writing by hand all the morning. She did her hair a new way which looked the same as the old way, and began to wash up. There was a knock on the front door.

It was Mrs. Dennison. She had taken off the handkerchief and her hair was sleek and top-knotted and curled up the back, as if it had just been set. She said, 'Hullo! I'm Kate Dennison.'

'Hullo,' said Liza, and didn't know what to say next. The little black dog sniffed down the path. Liza said, 'Do come in out of that porch. It drips.' It had stopped raining, but the wind shook the wet leaves. Above a patter of drips she heard the purr of a car's engine at the gate.

'I can't,' said Kate. She looked like a Kate. 'I was just going by in the car, and I thought I'd say hullo. I live up the lane.' Liza had seen the cottage, about a quarter of a mile off; a bigger cottage than theirs, whitewashed, with red paint. She said, 'That was awfully nice of you. Our name's Latimer, and mine's Liza.'

'I know,' said Kate.

'Do come in for a minute.' The typewriter rattled. 'That's my husband, writing a book.'

'Good for him. Then I won't, or he might think he had to be polite. Hasty, come *off* that flower-bed.' The little black dog took no notice, so

– 93 –

Kate dived and picked him up. Liza walked with her through the gate, and Kate got in the car and switched the engine off. She said, sitting there, with her beautifully creased trouser-legs over the running-board, 'How do you like living here?'

'We love it. It's quiet for my husband.' She really was married now. 'Do you live here?'

'In the summer,' said Kate. 'My husband's in London, and he gets down for week-ends.' Liza thought, I suppose when you've been married a long time—or perhaps they're not happy; no, I don't know. They talked about Hasty, and Kate said his ears were too big to make him a good Cairn, and he had worms. Then it began to rain. Kate opened the door, and Liza got in the back seat.

'Well, we can't sit here,' said Kate. 'Let's go home.' And she turned the car and drove up the lane. The cottage inside reminded Liza of the ground floor of Peter Jones's, the bit between the carpets and the lift; the sitting-room had red and white striped arm-chairs and a white sheepskin rug by an open fireplace. Kate had said that in London they lived in a much too small house off Smith Square, and Maurice, her husband, was on the Stock Exchange. Liza imagined a thin, pale man who wore a bowler hat and looked as if he felt sick. That was a Maurice. No, it didn't fit the picture.

Liza took a cigarette from a white leather box and sat on the window-seat, and Kate said, 'Isn't everything frightful when it rains?' Kate wasn't a Pauline after all. Liza said, 'I always feel I've done something awful when it rains. Unless I'm happy, and then rain makes me happier.'

'Lucky you,' said Kate, and blew a smoke-ring. Liza thought, we haven't got the wave-length yet, and I'm having to do all the work. I always do. She wanted to ask why Kate was here when she might be in London with Maurice. She said, 'Do you like it here?'

'Yes.' Kate blew another smoke-ring. 'I loathe London in the summer.'

No, Kate wasn't a Pauline, or she wouldn't be missing what the papers and Society called The Season. 'It is lovely here,' said Liza, feeling more in tune. 'Walter says it's like Switzerland, or Scotland.' She put her right hand over her left, and told herself that to-morrow she would buy that wedding-ring.

'Yes, it is a bit. You must both come round soon. And when Maurice comes down we must go out in a car. You have got one, haven't you? Look at me knowing all about you.'

'Oh, yes, he has.' *He;* she blushed slightly.

'Does he play golf?'

Liza didn't know. She thought wildly; he had said something about it, and she thought he did; but if she said so and he didn't, it would be worse than saying he didn't if he did. She blushed again and said, 'Well, not really, you know. Is your husband awfully good?' That was quite subtle.

'Not bad. Not good either. At least, so he says. I wouldn't know. I sit in the car and read while he plays. We must get up a foursome or whatever they call it. I suppose I mean a twosome. You don't play, do you?'

'Oh, no.'

'That's all right, then.'

Liza thought, I suppose we shall go on knowing them all the summer. It will be an awful tight-rope. And oh, I wish I'd done my nails; Walter hates those long red nails, and I'm glad, and I'm a cat. She got up. 'I must fly. I was in the middle of washing up, and we aren't straight yet.' That gave her a status.

Kate got up too. 'Well, come to tea to-morrow.'

'Well, I don't know if my husband will be working.' She should have called him Walter.

'Tell him to take the afternoon off.' Liza tried to see herself saying it, just like that, and went back to make some scones for tea, because she had just found out how to make them.

Walter was almost in a bad temper at tea. Liza said, 'Darling, Kate Dennison called. She was the woman in the grocer's shop.'

'I saw her through the window.'

'What did you think of her?'

'Not much, if at all.'

'I went round to her cottage. It's lovely. And she asked us to tea to-morrow.'

'Well, I can't go,' said Walter. 'I'm not going to start mafficking.' He took another scone and went back to *Fur and Feather*, and Liza was alone in the world. She said, 'Well, why don't you take an afternoon off?'

'Because I haven't had an afternoon on yet. Not properly.' Well, at least Walter didn't run off after other women. But he would have to meet Kate, and she was the sort of woman men fell for. She said, 'Do you play golf?'

'Sort of,' said Walter. 'And isn't it a good floor? And a good band?' He was nice again.

'What's your handicap?'

'Ten. What's yours?'

'Oh, dear. I suppose that's dreadfully good. I told Kate you didn't play. No, I said not really. I could have been being modest.'

Walter got up and gave her his tea-cup. 'Darling, what have you been letting me in for?'

They were on the same side again. 'Well, darling, Kate said did you play and I said not really, and she said then you can make up a twosome with Maurice. That's her husband. He's on the Stock Exchange.' She was married again. She gave him his tea-cup, and a wifely smile.

'Well, that's all right,' said Walter. 'We shall play and I shall beat him. Or not. It's the game that matters, not who wins, dammit. I haven't brought my clubs, but I shall borrow the Major's, though he's taken his good ones.'

'Darling,' said Liza.

'Yes, ducky?'

'I was thinking. We ought to sort of make a list of all the things we did, or are supposed to have done before we—before we came here. I mean, all the things *you* did.' Why did she mean that? 'So that we can tally to the outside world. I always think I shall say something awful.' She hadn't told him about Mrs. Croft, but it didn't matter now.

'I shouldn't worry, ducky.'

Liza thought, that side of our relationship interests him about as much as the technical details of my clothes. Not his province, and that's that. 'Well, it *is* a worry, darling. I wish you'd type me a list of facts.'

'Ducky,' said Walter, 'as we trudge its thorny path, one of the things life insists on having a shot at teaching us is that other people never notice things. Not the way you do yourself.' He went back to *Fur and Feather*, and there was nothing more to say.

❀

Next morning Liza took a pleasantly reckless bus to Salisbury, and chose the nicest jeweller's shop, with iron bars and rows of wedding-rings on white velvet. The shop inside was blocked by a big grey man with a little black hat.

The jeweller, who was small and old, came out of a back room. 'Well, that's the best I can do for you.' He handed out a pound note and a card. Liza was dreadfully embarrassed. But the big grey man seemed quite happy; and out in the street again he would be any one; and lots of people used pawnshops as banks; and it was silly to be sorry for every one.

'Well, missy,' said the jeweller, 'what can I do for you?' Liza had taken her ring off with her glove. She said, 'I—I want a wedding-ring, please. I mean, I want to look at some. Then my fiancé can choose one.' She suddenly saw her fiancé; a young and successful doctor, who would be down here for a snatched week-end. And he wasn't Walter. But she put it down to the atmosphere here, all hushed and licit.

The jeweller reverently fetched a little black velvet cushion and a white velvet stand. It was like being in church; at a funeral. He said, 'Now, there's this one.'

It was four pounds. The one she had seen in the Regent Street window was twenty-three and sixpence. 'Isn't that a terrible lot for such a narrow one?'

'Hand-made. Look at it. A lovely piece of work.' He had stopped being reverent, and seemed rather surprised that you should have to sell any one a wedding-ring.

'I mean something rounded all over, not flat inside like this. I mean, it doesn't *look* expensive. Ought they to be flat inside?'

'Try it on.' She did, and for a dreadful moment it wouldn't come off. 'It was awfully tight. I should never be able to get it off.'

'Well,' said the jeweller, leering horribly, 'they aren't supposed to, you know. Ha! Ha!' Liza had never heard any one say Ha! Ha! before; she had thought only the comic papers did.

'What about the others?' she asked, thinking, they all look like Woolworth's.

'This is hand-made, too. Three thirteen six. And the rest—well, missy, they're all machine-made. All right, of course. But you want to get the best.'

'Well, it's an awful lot,' said Liza. She wasn't doing this right; but she was shopping, and she wasn't going to be cheated. 'Well,' she said, 'thank you very much for showing me. I'll bring my fiancé as soon as possible, but he's awfully busy. Thank you again, and I hope you didn't mind me just looking.'

'Quite all right, missy.' She hadn't used the black cushion, and he suspected. Liza put on her glove, and felt something hard in one finger. She went out and got the ring on, and went off to Woolworth's and bought another. It looked lovely; it had no green patch where the rolled gold had worn off, and it was as good as anything in the jeweller's.

※

Liza had been round the day before to tell Kate they were coming to tea, and Kate had said they'd go out in the car to a tea-place she knew; and at exactly four, an hour after Liza got back from Salisbury, she drove up to the gate. Liza heard the car from upstairs, and her lipstick smudged. She wiped it with a handkerchief and tried again, and finally had to wash her face and start again. It was like the dream when you were late for school. She could hear Kate and Walter talking outside, and when she went down they were by the rose-bushes, and Kate was pinching the buds off. She threw a handful in the hedge and said, 'And now you may get some roses. Hullo! Hasty, come *off* that flower-bed.'

Liza thought, already Walter knows Kate better than I do. She said, 'Hullo. I'm sorry I'm late, darling,' and wished she hadn't called him that. They got in Kate's car, Walter in the driving-seat, Liza at the back with Hasty because he was less likely to be sick there, and set off.

Liza had never sat behind Walter in a car. She thought, this is how he would look to any one sitting behind us. I would be Kate; only I suppose I would be nearer Walter. Kate had her shoulder against the door, and had half turned to talk to Walter. Liza wondered about Walter's other women. Perhaps the woman who hadn't liked her husband and didn't think much of Walter was something like Kate. She thought, I like to see Walter talking to other women and to think that they'd like to go to bed with him. Darling Walter.

Hasty put his head on Liza's foot. She was touched, and a bit nervous, in case he was sick. She leant forward and scratched behind his ear, and Hasty looked up blearily and wagged his tail. Liza thought, I am nice. She sat back and gave herself up to happy dreams.

Soon the bracken would be up to your waist and smell like bracken. The trees were all out now. They would be green for a long time, and then grey-green, and brown-green, and brown; months and months ahead; and when they were brown, Walter would be blowing a whistle in Regent's Park to a lot of little striped jerseys, and Liza would be on the touchline, or wherever you stood, in a grey squirrel coat, with, on her left hand, an antique emerald ring; Walter would have said, my mother gave it to me, it's been waiting for years till I found the right woman, and now it's yours. No, that didn't sound much like Walter. Well, he could say, here you are, ducky; or guess what. Liza went on dreaming; a rawhide case and a hatbox to match. With L. L. everywhere. She thought, I'm glad I didn't buy that wedding-ring; it would have been sort of unlucky.

Kate and Walter went on talking. Liza watched his animated face and thought, they'll be half an hour ahead of me when we stop. I wish I didn't feel sulky.

They had tea at a place called The Lupins; a cottage outside, inside the usual oak beams and warming-pans, with beyond a newer room with a skylight and pale green tables. Kate led the way to a pale green table by a window, and Walter sat down next to her. Liza decided that Kate was about thirty-five from her expression, but might be younger. She thought, her lipstick and her nails match exactly, and she looks so terribly sort of polished; and I wish I wasn't wearing my green linen trousers, because the creases have come out.

Hasty sat under the table, barking shrilly. Kate picked him up. 'You're going back in the car, you little brute.'

Walter got up. 'Shall I?'

'I don't think so. He'd bite you.' When she had gone, Walter said, 'Hullo, ducky.'

'Hullo, darling.'

Walter read the back of the menu, and Liza the front, wondering who paid for the tea. Well, anyhow, she didn't have to bother. She thought, I feel terribly unmarried this afternoon. If Kate asks us anything I shall hand it on to Walter; it's easy when we're together.

Kate came back, and Liza felt frightened. Walter ordered the tea, and, turning to Kate, said, 'What do you think of the world?'

'I don't,' said Kate. 'It wouldn't help if I did. Why?'

'I just wanted to know. It's one of those things you ask people when you meet them. Thank you, you've told me everything in a remarkably few well-chosen words.'

'Oh, well,' said Kate. 'Is there anything else you want to know?'

'Thank you, not for the moment. Shall I tell you my life-story?' He took a rock-cake from a left-over plate.

'I don't think so.'

'Ah, well,' said Walter. 'That takes care of that. I want an awkward pause now, please, while I suck a currant off a wisdom tooth.'

Liza thought, that's all right, I needn't think of anything to say. She was trying to see Walter's face as it had been when she first met him, and on the first evening in the flat; after that it had become Walter's face, his first face now was a stranger's, and sometimes she had tried to call it back; it wasn't memory so much as a flash which went again. No, this afternoon she couldn't get it.

Walter said, 'I'm back in circulation, every one,' and the tea arrived. Kate said, 'Who has milk and sugar?'

'Only milk for me, please,' said Liza. 'Both for him.' She watched Kate pour out Walter's tea, all wrong, and felt happy. She said, 'I do love those red tubs in your garden.'

'Don't talk to me about those tubs,' said Kate, and Liza was back in circulation too. 'Maurice painted them last weekend and Hasty leant against one and got the paint on his fur and his fur on the paint. You are going to play golf with Maurice, aren't you, Walter? And Liza and I can sit in the car. Can I call you by your names? I'm a bit old-fashioned.'

'Please do,' said Liza, and Walter said, 'I'd love to.' Liza thought, you might have said we. Then they talked about golf-courses, and the countryside, and Kate said, 'How long are you here for?'

'Oh, no exact time,' said Walter. Liza thought, oh, darling, and you've paid till September the fourth. You don't like to think of us as married. You shy off it. It's going to be awful knowing Kate and Maurice.

Kate stretched her left hand over the cake-plate. No, Liza had never liked platinum. 'Is any one putting in for that marzipan one?'

'Uk,' said Walter. ''Orrid.'

'Don't you like it, darling?' said Liza, glad he didn't, because she didn't.

'You know,' said Kate, 'I don't believe you two are married. But I'm a bit that way about life.'

'You old septic,' said Walter. 'Well. To tell you the honest truth, we're not.'

It was the end of the world.

But it wasn't really. In the front seat of the car, as they drove home, Liza tried to remember every word she had said to Kate, from the porch to the marzipan. No, she hadn't said anything silly. And Kate would have known one day, and Walter had saved her making up Mrs. Croft stories. And the tea had gone much better afterwards; Kate hadn't been surprised, and Walter had been himself, and as he paid the bill Liza had thought, all that matters is that I've got him. Maurice can't be so nice, and Kate must think I'm terribly lucky.

At their cottage Kate said, 'Well, good-bye, you sinners.' That didn't mean anything nowadays. But it meant something.

Walter said, as the car drove off, leaving them at the gate, 'Are you cross with me, ducky?'

'No, darling. Not in the very least. I'm very glad.'

'Precious.' He kissed her. 'I mean, it would have been awkward. Facts are facts.'

'Yes,' said Liza, and was unhappy; that was what it meant.

VIII

Liza dropped one of Major Hobie's best silver forks behind the gas-stove, and remembered it some days later, when they were washing up the breakfast things. Walter fished it out, with a dusty calendar called *Thoughts for the Day*. It had a big black 8, with a little *May* above it, and below, *He who hesitates is lost*.

'I do love this sort of calendar,' said Walter. 'But I don't call that much of a thought, do you?'

'Not much,' said Liza. Calendars not torn off always made you sad. She was thinking, on May the eighth we were in our lovely pub. I wish I could remember what we did; I think it rained, and we got lost in the car. I wonder if Walter is trying to remember too.

Walter tore off May 8. '*Look before you leap.* Well, they can't both be right.' He tore off the next day, and the next. 'I'm eating peeled shrimps.'

'That reminds me, darling. Mr. Murdoch has ordered about a gross of prawns, and we shall have to buy them all, I suppose.'

Walter patted her head and went on tearing the Past off, Thought by Thought. *Service is the true hall-mark of nobility. The daily round, the common task will furnish all we need to ask. Virtue is its own reward.* He tore them off in bundles. *Time flies. Backbone, not wishbone.* June 11. *That which is worth doing is worth doing well.* 'My God, why does he have to say That Which when he means What?' He hung the calendar up. 'I don't think the chap who compiled it had a very happy life. Or much between the ears.'

'I wonder if he's still alive and doing another. I hope they paid him enough. Darling, you mustn't look ahead. I'm sure it's bad luck, or something.'

'I thought you hadn't any superstitions,' said Walter.

'I haven't. At least, not other people's.' She had said that before.

Walter flattened the days down again. 'Well, ducky, I'm off. Next Thursday an honest man will be the noblest work of God.' He put his hand on her neck and kissed her hair.

'Where are you off to, darling?'

'Only the garden. If any one calls say I'm designing St. Paul's, will you?'

'Mr. Thorne is coming to mend the boiler at twelve.'

'Ducky,' said Walter, 'one day I shall say it.' And he flipped her neck.

'Well, darling, he has to mend it. And I do love your neck.'

'I love yours.' She had known he would say it. There was nothing else to say. Walter took a green Penguin and three digestive biscuits from the sitting-room and went off down the garden. Liza did the saucepans, which she always told Walter didn't count as washing up, and thought, I must get sunburnt. It's June the eleventh.

Mr. Thorne arrived at twelve, while Liza was turning out the kitchen drawer. He was a ponderous man with a little grey moustache; and he took the boiler to pieces and, spreading it freely over the kitchen floor, said, 'I was born, fifty-seven years ago to this very day, in Alberta.'

'Oh,' said Liza. 'Many happy returns.' It always embarrassed her to know people's ages.

'Thank you, missy.' He straightened himself, blew, and bent down again. 'Yes. It was fifty-seven years ago to this very day, it was. I'm not a Hampshire man, mind you.'

Liza said, 'Time flies, doesn't it?'

'That it does,' said Mr. Thorne. 'Yes. I was born in Alberta. In a little log-cabin. Like Abraham Lincoln.' He laughed. He had a ponderous laugh, to match.

'What fun,' said Liza.

'Fun you may call it, missy. But it wasn't fun for me, I can tell you. Snow thirteen feet deep in winter. Yes. Thirteen feet deep.' He clanked in his Gladstone bag and brought out a spanner.

Liza said, 'Would you like a cigarette?' It was a birthday present.

'Thank you, missy, but I don't smoke. No. And I never touch a drop of anything stronger than beer. Never a drop of anything stronger than beer.'

He blew again. 'Yes. And we went to school in snow-shoes. Snow-shoes. And if you uncovered your years they froze. Yes. Your years froze.'

It was going to be a life-story. Liza put the last tin-opener in the kitchen drawer and took the shoe-cleaning box from under the sink, and Walter's shoes, which she had just cleaned. But she had to do something quiet so as not to interrupt Mr. Thorne. She thought, I must tell it all to Walter. I wonder what Mr. Thorne would say if I told him *my* life-story.

At one o'clock Liza carried the lunch to the bottom of the garden, which they had found was sunnier and more sheltered than the lawn, and said, 'Mr. Thorne is having his in the shed.' She took off her green shirt and put it on again, because it was too cold for only a sun-top. 'I've got a sort of premonition the shed will catch fire, because when he was in Medicine Hat once singing hymns the hut caught fire under the floor, and before any one noticed it it was a charred heap. And in the war he fried an egg on a stone in the Sahara. And when the Armistice went he was in Manchester, and he and a Canadian and an American drank six bottles of champagne, and the American swallowed half a cork. And his wife is thirty years younger, and she made him swear off anything stronger than beer.'

'Ducky, you might have told me,' said Walter. 'I've been missing something.'

'I didn't want to disturb you.'

'Don't be a nasty.'

'I'm sorry, darling. I didn't mean it.' But she did; she had never hated herself more. And yesterday he had been typing in his study and she had stopped him to come and look at the boiler. He was only typing a letter, she thought, because she had seen two separate words at the top. But that hadn't made it any better.

Walter finished his cider and picked up his book. Liza said, 'Would you like some more, darling?'

'I don't want any more. If I do I can pour it out myself.'

Liza had a sudden pang for the office. It would be lunch-time, an hour of blessed freedom, blessed by the prison walls to its left and right. She thought, I shall cut out my cotton dress this afternoon.

Walter took her hand. 'Ducky, I've been Guided. Let's go for a brisk walk this afternoon.'

'Oh, darling, let's. I love your hand.'

'I love yours. And I love you without lipstick.'

'I never like it really. Only if you're dressed in clothes you have to be dressed all over. I don't like lipstick with no clothes.'

'Nor do I,' said Walter, and went back to his book. She knew what he was thinking: we've said that before. She said, 'Mr. Thorne calls ears years. And it's his birthday.'

Walter gave his reading grunt. Liza picked up the newspaper with the hand he wasn't holding and read about a plucky girl cashier who lived in Islington, N., and had hit a bank robber over the head.

❀

Liza and Walter walked down the gravel track. Liza stopped to tie her shoe-lace, and ran to catch him up. He smiled. 'Ducky, one day guess what. I shall throw you a stick to chase.'

And this afternoon she had been going to be different.

They left the track and walked across the heather. Liza said, 'To-morrow's Saturday. You haven't forgotten about the golf, have you?'

'No, ducky. It wouldn't have mattered if I had. I've got a whole ruddy day to remember.'

Liza thought, he's bored. Like me. Oh, no, no, I'm not. He's not. It's only June the eleventh. She said, 'Maurice reminds me of the statues in the British Museum.'

'Well, I wouldn't say that exactly.'

'But he does. The Greek ones. Only he's a bit fatter. I suppose it's the way his forehead goes into his nose, and his hair curling and being the same colour as his face.'

'Well, there may be something in it. I was thinking of those Easter Island things.'

Liza thought, we used to understand each other better.

Walter stopped, and Liza stopped too. He put his arms round her, and they kissed. She could feel a gorse-prickle through her sock, and smell the gorse-flowers behind her; honey, and almonds.

'Darling,' said Walter. 'You are a darling.'

Liza thought, don't look at me like that. I don't want to hear what you want to say.

Walter pinched her nose. 'Darling, are you sorry we're here?'

'Darling, how could I be?'

'Well, ducky,' said Walter, sliding his arms down to her waist, 'I'm having a nice lazy summer.'

'So am I. And I want to.'

'Yes, but I'm being lazier than you are.'

'Yes, but I like being domesticated. It's a change. Oh, darling, it's all such fun.'

'Well,' said Walter, squeezing her suddenly, 'the minute you think it isn't you've got to say so.'

'As if I would,' said Liza. They walked on, holding hands until the path was too narrow. She said, 'When shall we go to the Isle of Wight?'

'Yes. We simply must.'

'Because, darling, I've found you a yachting cap.'

'Ducky, you haven't. You are clever. Can I wear it if I promise not to bend it?'

'I should think you might. It was down between the coke and coal in the coke and coal shed. Darling, I do love our tiny home, don't you?'

Then, as they walked through the bracken, they talked about Life; about freedom, and progress, and the probable date of the war, and all the other things. Liza thought, I love talking to Walter, but I wish I didn't keep on hoping we'll start talking about each other. That is, I suppose, about me.

⚜

Kate and Liza sat in the car, and Maurice and Walter went off with their golf-bags. You could see the first tee, and some of the way to the first green, but after that the trees would hide them. Kate wore her teddy-bear swagger coat, and Liza her camelhair coat; she had bought some new leather buttons in Salisbury, and now they made the coat look old. She watched Walter as he took out a golf-club and dropped Major Hobie's bag. This was their second match. Last time Walter had lost, but only just.

Maurice drove his ball very high and a long way. Liza thought, desperately, oh, Walter darling. She crossed her thumbs, the way you did at school for a lacrosse match. Walter was rubbing his knee and talking to Maurice. Then he waggled his club and drove his ball even higher and farther than Maurice's. Oh, darling Walter, clever Walter.

Kate said suddenly, 'Why don't you two get married?'

'Well, I know it sounds silly, but I just don't know.'

'Oh, well,' said Kate. Liza didn't want it to stop there. She said, 'Do you think we ought to?'

'I don't know. I never know anything.'

'I suppose we haven't because we haven't wanted to yet,' said Liza. She hated Kate suddenly, because she was married. She wondered if Kate had lived with Maurice before their marriage. No, she didn't think so; or only because so many people did live together first.

'Oh, well,' said Kate, 'that's as good a reason as any.' She opened her book. Yes, thought Liza, as good as any you give to hide the real one. What is the real one? How would you say it to any one else? We can't get married because he hasn't asked me; yes, it couldn't sound much sillier.

But other people were never really interested in you, any more than you really were in other people; and the ones that gave most advice were the most interested in themselves of all. And Liza didn't hate Kate; it was funny that she had once been jealous of her. Things were not so simple as that in real life. And Kate thought they should be married; so they must look right for each other. Liza said:

'Kate, what do you think are the sort of essentials for married life?'

'Heavens,' said Kate, 'I'm one of those Aunt Somethings in Home Chat. I don't know. I suppose the usual ones, liking each other and thinking the same things are fun.'

'Yes. So do I.'

'I have a very simple mind,' said Kate. 'Everything comes out obvious.'

She opened the car door. '*Hasty!*' Hasty went on scratching up the grass; but it seemed to mean that Kate had finished with the conversation.

Kate went back to her book, and Liza opened Walter's green Penguin. A very old man, living in an overcrowded house, had been found dead in a water-butt, and the rest of the household turned to and in ten minutes had got hold of the police and a charming bachelor, very rich, who happened to be staying in the village and was good at finding out murderers; and every one in the book was strangely conscious of being a detective story. Liza had got to the third chapter. She gave a quick and guilty glance at the fifth, and turned back and began to read. It was difficult to care who had murdered a very old man, a corpse from the first page, when Walter was somewhere behind the trees, winning or losing.

Maurice and Walter came back a long time later, when Liza had finished the book, all but the last chapter, called *Explanations*, and hadn't guessed the murderer because he was a garage assistant she had hardly noticed. Maurice opened the car door. Whoever spoke first would have lost.

'Well, well,' said Walter. Liza gave him a look which meant, I love you even more.

Kate said, 'Did you let him beat you?' Walter was hunting on the floor by Kate's feet.

'It was damned close,' said Maurice. 'We had to play another hole.' He wiped his Greek forehead. Liza thought, you couldn't call Maurice intellectual. And I think he'll be really fat soon. But I suppose he's attractive; but Kate never calls him darling.

Walter said to Kate, 'It was your fault. I always play better when I'm watched.'

'You would,' said Kate.

'Your book, Mrs. Latimer,' said Maurice. 'Thank you,' said Liza. 'Thank you very much.' She didn't think she sounded very married, but it was difficult to pretend to Maurice when Kate and Walter knew.

Kate said, 'Walter, what does a reversionary annuity mean?'

Walter took Kate's book. 'This book talks about some one averring something. And, my God, there's a Yes, retorted that worthy. And, heaven help us all, a chap called Car-stairs.' He handed it back.

'Well, he had to be called something,' said Kate. 'But what does it mean?'

'I refuse to discuss such a book,' said Walter.

'You can't just refuse to tell me.'

'I utterly refuse. Any further communications will be placed in the hands of my solicitors. And if you lift your foot I can get at what you've left of my coat.'

Kate said, 'You're the most mentally intolerant man I ever met.'

'You ought to get about more. Take your foot off my coat for a start.'

Kate lifted her foot, and Walter shook his coat out.

Maurice said, as he shut himself in the driving-seat, 'Dammit, it's only an annuity you don't get till you get it.'

'Thank you, darling,' said Kate. 'Now I want my lunch.'

They had lunch at the same hotel as last time. Liza thought, I suppose it will be the same sort of lunch too. And it was.

❀

Liza and Walter went to a lantern lecture on Moths and Butterflies. Liza had seen the notice in the grocer's; it was to be given by a Mr. Hughes, F.Z.S. They had asked Kate if she would come too, but Kate said she was frightened of moths, and the hall smelt. Liza and Walter had supper early and motored down, and Liza said, as the car splashed across the little stream, 'Darling, if no one's there I shall go home.'

'So shall I, ducky,' said Walter. 'It makes me all hot and damp too. If there are more than twenty souls we'll brave it out.'

There were quite a lot of people in the village hall, so Walter handed over three shillings and they sat down, rather too near the front and on very hard chairs; Walter next to a fair girl holding the hand of a young man carved from raw beef, and Liza next to a fat woman; she could feel the heat coming out of her. She had seen Mr. Thorne at the back of the hall, with his wife, and felt embarrassed when they exchanged smiles; it was like meeting Mr. Chiddock out of the office. The grocer, the fishmonger and the young man with the squint, who sometimes helped at the local, also smiled. She said to Walter, 'I feel awfully gracious. And, darling, do you think all these people mind about moths and butterflies?'

'Not for a minute,' said Walter. 'Imagination boggles at their minding anything much. I suppose it's having no flicks. The lure of the magic lantern. And all they ever do here in the evenings is lean against the village and smoke.'

'Yes. I suppose it's relativity again.'

'Human nature is well-nigh inexplicable. Have we had that as a Thought for the Day?'

'Not yet. To-day it's—no, I forgot to tear it off.' It was rather sad to think that their lovely calendar had lost its newness. She sniffed. 'Would you say the smell was coffee and turpentine?'

'Yes, exactly. So far. Ducky, I'm getting all excited. I'm hoping great things of Slide Number One. It's going to be a butterfly standing on its head, gazing at the sky beneath it. Slide Number Two will be even more interesting. A plain background, and a close-up of a rustic thumb.'

Liza looked at him, and felt very loving and very proud. He had his tie on, and he was very sunburnt. She wore her blue-and-white printed crêpe de Chine dress and had wetted her hair and set it quite well. Lovely evening.

The vicar climbed the little ladder to the platform. Liza had seen him in the village and known he was the vicar by his collar. A tall grey-haired man in horn-rimmed glasses and a very baggy grey suit followed; Liza wondered what he was thinking of.

The vicar said, 'Well, ladies and gentlemen, I don't think I need to say that we've all been looking forward to having what I may call such a distinguished gentleman here tonight.' He sang it, holding on to 'distinguished gentleman' and letting go suddenly at 'here to-night.'

Walter whispered, 'Vicars *are* vicars. Like Indian Colonels.'

The vicar went on to make a vicar-speech. He told them how as a lad he'd collected birds' eggs, and how the screen had been repaired since last time through the generosity of certain ladies. There was a small stir; Liza decided that the ladies were somewhere at the back of the hall. Then the vicar said, 'Well, ladies and gentlemen, I won't keep you any longer from this very distinguished gentleman whom I am sure you're all waiting to hear with the most eager interest.' He held on a long time to 'eager' and let go very suddenly at 'interest.' The audience clapped dutifully, the lights went out, and Liza could hear him trying to find the ladder. Then the lantern clicked, and a shaft of light hit Mr. Hughes and moved to the screen. Liza thought, he isn't nervous. We're just another lot of faces in another hall. I shouldn't feel so sorry for people.

Then the lecture began, with a slide of tangled hay in bright sunlight, till you looked very hard, when you could see the chrysalis Mr. Hughes was pointing at with his pointer; at least, you could see where he was pointing, and knew that that must be the chrysalis.

Liza thought, lantern lectures *are* lantern lectures. She moved very slightly, and her shoulder touched Walter's. Walter moved very slightly, and now their arms were touching too.

Liza thought, we're back in London. Well, Southampton. I won't move my hand. But she moved it very slightly, and Walter took it and moved it down to the chair-edge between them. They sat there, holding hands in secret, with their eyes on the screen.

Mr. Hughes had a little clicker. Liza thought, it must be fun clicking it. I wonder if while he's talking he's thinking it may not go off all right next time, and if he suddenly wants to do it in the middle of a slide; like blowing the whistle in prep. Funny; that was the end of the world once. There were three chrysalises on the screen now, on a white background. They looked alike, but Mr. Hughes said they weren't. Liza thought, I must concentrate. Knowledge is power.

Walter squeezed Liza's hand; she squeezed his. She could feel his tweed coat against her arm, rough and lovely. She glanced at him; he was watching the screen, very serious. Darling Walter, he was so polite, so everything. She wondered how she would enjoy this lecture without him. She tried to imagine it, to imagine Walter suddenly taken from her now, leaving her in a strange village hall, with a butterfly sitting on a twig with its wings folded, and Mr. Hughes pointing out its antennae.

She thought, no, that's not quite fair; because if he went suddenly, now, I couldn't think of anything but that he had gone. I should look at the butterfly and it would be dreadful because it would be the same butterfly that Walter had seen.

The clicker clicked, and now it was a moth. Mr. Hughes said you could tell because it didn't fold its wings. Liza knew that. She went back to her thoughts. Well, I shall imagine myself in London; but then I would hardly be at a lecture on moths and butterflies. Well, here, and not having met Walter. I should be looking at this moth and thinking I was wearing a nice dress, and my hair looked all right. But I suppose I shouldn't have taken all that trouble over it. Well, and I should be interested in the moth; I know that. But I shouldn't know what to do with it afterwards. Well, I could tell Mr. Chiddock, at least I could sort of bring it into an argument. I could tell Funny. Liza looked at the moth, which was another moth now and wore glasses, and thought that perhaps her dear Funny, who had a funny pushed-in face and a dear, funny mind, would like it as much as Walter. But under everything you said to Funny was the feeling that you didn't want to touch him; that your minds went out and met, and drew back, and you thought, that was as if we'd kissed; and it spoilt it.

Liza squeezed Walter's hand, and he squeezed hers. It was lovely thinking he wasn't there when he was. Now she would watch the screen very hard and learn everything about moths and butterflies.

There were hundreds of moths and butterflies. Rows and rows of dead ones on a white background. Clumps of live ones on a brick wall. Liza wondered if it was Mr. Hughes's wall; it wanted mending. She thought, oh, Mr. Hughes, I hope you have a lot of money and do this for fun; and she tried to multiply one and sixpence by the possible number of people in the hall, and gave it up. More moths. More butterflies. More eggs and chrysalises. Liza was sure they'd had some of the slides before. She thought, please, Mr. Hughes, don't go on for ever. Walter and I are going to have a Night to-night.

The lecture went on and on. It had been on for ever, already.

Oh, Mr. Hughes, stop, *stop.*

Then Mr. Hughes clicked his clicker and said, 'Now, on this last slide.' It was a beautiful slide of a moth clinging to a stalk. It had been a lovely lecture.

Liza had taken the coffee up to their room. Walter had left half his. As they lay there, Liza imagined it. The milk would have risen to the top, and it would be cold and taste horrid, though she had made it rather well to-night. The moon shone on the chest of drawers. She thought, once that was Major Hobie's chest of drawers. Now it's ours. She said, wanting to move her arm, and not wanting to move it, because Walter was lying against it, 'I think to-night was better than it's ever been before.'

Walter said, and she could feel his chin moving against her shoulder, 'Yes. So do I. Is the coffee cold, do you think, ducky?'

'I expect so. Shall I hot it up?'

'No. I don't want any. It was a bit strong. I expect what I drank will keep me awake all night.'

'Well, darling, it was your idea.'

Walter put his hand up and flipped her neck. There was a silence. Then Liza said, 'What are you thinking of?'

'A lot of things. I was thinking I've nearly got cramp in one toe.'

'Well, wiggle it, darling. Or move your leg.'

'It's all right. Don't fuss, ducky.' There was another silence. Liza said, 'What else are you thinking of?'

'Potery.'

'What sort of potery?'

'All sorts. I was rooting in Memory's Garden. I was somewhere among Tennyson.'

Liza thought, please let me in. I love poetry as much as you do. But if I say anything I sound silly. She said, 'What do you like best in Tennyson?'

'I suppose *Ulysses*.'

'Please say it to me.'

'It takes a week.' But he began:

> *It little profits that an idle king,*
> *By this still hearth, among these barren crags,*
> *Matched with an aged wife, I mete and dole*

> *Unequal laws unto a savage race,*
> *That hoard, and sleep, and feed, and know not me.*
> *I cannot rest from travel: I will drink*
> *Life to the lees.*

He stopped. 'I'm Mr. Hughes.'

'Please go on.'

'I shall click my clicker and go on to the bit I like best.'

> *I am a part of all that I have met;*
> *Yet all experience is an arch wherethrough*
> *Gleams that untravelled world, whose margin fades*
> *For ever and for ever when I move.*

He stopped again. 'I think End. Your own voice sounds so damned silly if you listen to it. Good night, ducky.'

'May I stay here?'

'I think you might.' He kissed her, and went to sleep. Liza lay and watched the moonlight. Walter was still lying against her arm. Soon she would move it away, and hope she would be able to go to sleep in only half a bed. She put her arm across Walter and touched his shoulder-blade. She thought, I have him, here and now; and one day I won't. That's all it is. But then that's all anything is in life.

IX

Kate came round to the back door one morning at eleven, when Liza was cleaning the gas-oven and thinking happily that to-day she really would go for a long walk alone. Walter was sitting in the sun on the kitchen step with his typewriter, busy with a safety-pin, a bottle of benzine and some striped flannel which might once have been a part of Major Hobie's shirt. They hadn't seen Kate for a week; she turned up, or she didn't, and you didn't go there unless she asked you. This morning she was even sleeker and more polished, in a very tailored navy blue linen dress, and she was carrying something.

'*What*,' said Walter, looking up, 'is that strange growth?'

'It's a freak purple broccoli,' said Kate, stepping over the benzine. 'The last of the season. It goes green when you cook it.'

'Anti-climax,' said Walter, and rang the little bell on his typewriter. Liza said, 'Oh, thank you, Kate. You are nice,' and thought, Walter always brightens when he sees her.

'I had an idea,' said Kate. 'You two come to Salisbury with me in the car. I've got to shop. We can go to a flick.'

Walter uncorked the benzine. 'I've gotta woik.'

'Oh, go on,' said Kate. 'You never. I saw you in the front garden yesterday every time I looked through the hedge. You were tying up the clematis all wrong.'

'Well, I've still got to work,' said Walter, looking just a very little annoyed.

'Aren't you a ptarmigan?' said Kate. 'I say, Liza, you're being clever. I always think whatever it is that sticks to gas-ovens is the most frightful thing in the world.' Liza was flattered; she thought, more than I should be. But Kate doesn't often praise people.

Walter rang his little bell again. 'I've been Guided. I'm not going to woik.'

'Are you Guided every time you don't?' said Kate. 'You must be a record.'

Walter looked nearly annoyed again, but he put the lid on the typewriter, and half an hour later Liza had changed to a cotton dress, and they had had cocktails at Kate's cottage and started off.

Walter drove Kate's car. Liza heard him say, 'If I had this car I'd take it to bits and put it together again.'

'You wouldn't,' said Kate. 'You'd just take it to bits.' She turned round. 'Hullo, Liza. Is Hasty all right?'

'So far,' said Liza. Kate meant, are you all right? Walter half turned round. 'Hullo, ducky.'

'Hullo, darling,' said Liza. She was thinking, I like it when Kate and Walter sort of scrap; because it reminds me that he is my lover and no one else's. Then she thought, those red lights in Kate's hair are highly artificial; and I would like to tie my hair up in that sort of handkerchief, only it would be imitating her.

They parked the car in a street near the Market Square. Kate said, 'I know we shan't find it again.'

'I know we shall,' said Walter, and Kate said, 'You would,' and Walter made a grimace. Liza thought, when he's with Kate he's younger. Well, he is younger than she is; I wish I knew Kate's exact age. Perhaps thirty-four. They went past the jeweller's, and Liza felt suddenly dreadfully guilty, and into a grocer's, where Kate took them up the far end and said to the girl at the counter, 'I want a tin of Bow-Wow.'

'Kate, darling,' said Walter, 'you can't want a tin of Bow-Wow.'

'I can,' said Kate. 'It's Hasty's dinner. Hasty, come *off* that sack.' Liza thought, Hasty is the only person who takes no notice of Kate when she puts on that voice. She moved nearer to Walter, who was turning over the packets and boxes. He said, 'Hullo, ducky. Aren't they heavenly?' They were; they were called Pupsnak, and The Doggy Special, and No-Lice and Washaboy. Kate said to the shop-girl, 'And I think some Furtone.'

Walter leant on the packets. 'Madam, refuse it. It's a substitute. We don't know what for. But we strongly recommend our Doggy Special for quick-action results of every description.'

'Go away,' said Kate. The girl looked as if she knew every one in front of a counter was a bit queer, but nice; and Liza thought, you are a nice girl; and isn't he lovely? He's mine.

Kate said, 'Now, come along, children,' and led them outside.

'Please,' said Walter, 'can I have sixpence to buy some choc?'

'No, you may not. You'll spoil your lunch.' So Walter dived into a sweet-shop and came out with three Mars Bars, and he and Liza had one and a half each. They walked behind Kate and Hasty, and Liza said, 'I feel as if I'm back in London. Aren't the pavements hard?'

'Aren't they? And I always say that when you've seen the Chelsea Flower Show you've seen it.' Liza thought, we're on the same side; this is a lovely morning.

Kate took them to half a dozen shops, and then to the haberdashery counter of a draper's. Walter said, 'I'm quite horribly shy. Everywhere I look I see dress-shields.' Liza thought, oh, darling Walter, I think you are, a little.

'Never mind,' said Kate. 'Keep your eyes on the floor while I buy six yards of bright red ribbon,' and she did, just like that. Liza had wanted some green sewing cotton to begin making the dress she had cut out, but she hadn't brought a pattern, and it would have taken some time to choose the colour; only because Kate was there. But she thought she ought to buy something; so she bought a card of press-stud fasteners she didn't want.

'And I think some green buttons,' said Kate. The girl fetched a book with pages of buttons. Walter leant on the counter. 'You can't have that kind, or that, or that. You can only have that.'

'I was going to,' said Kate. 'I don't suppose I can now. Oh, well, I must. They're the only decent ones.' Liza thought, they are; clever Walter.

Then they went to an hotel for lunch, and Hasty wound his lead round their legs and barked at every one, and so Walter took him out to the office, where he had been put before. Kate said:

'I like your Walter.'

'Do you really?' said Liza. 'I am glad,' and she liked Kate very much indeed.

'No more Hasty,' said Walter, as he sat down again. 'Kate, darling, have you ever tried losing him instead of not losing him? I don't even know if you have tried not losing him. The whole thing's only an idea.'

'No,' said Kate, as she read the menu. Liza thought, well, that seems to count as a clever answer. Walter ordered the lunch, and Kate, who had been to London for a week, said, 'Well, has anything exciting happened?'

'Walter went for a ride in a train,' said Liza. 'All by himself.'

'He's growing up,' said Kate. 'Where did he go?' Liza thought, I didn't mean it like that; I've made him sound a little boy, or Kate has.

'If any one else calls me he,' said Walter, 'I shall froth and bite the table-leg.'

'You big bear,' said Kate. 'Tell me where you went.'

'I went to Beaulieu Road. And then I came back.'

'Is that all?'

'No. It's the barest outline. It took eight hours. Liza thought I was dead, and I knew I was. And yah, I shan't tell you any more. Not even about how I had tea with a station-master's wife and tinies, or how one side of a truck fell down and nine hundred logs shot out.'

'Never mind,' said Kate, and began to eat her lunch. Liza felt dreadfully unhappy, as if she had betrayed Walter; and dreadfully the third of the three, as Kate and Walter argued their way through lunch: about the car, and gardening, and which flick they should go to; and she thought, they aren't really arguments, they're just a chance for two people's personalities.

Kate put her cigarette out and said, 'I shall pay for the lunch, and any reason you can think of why I can't will have to be a frightfully good one.' She handed Walter a pound note.

Walter held it up. 'Well. This note might be a dud.'

'I don't think it is,' said Kate.

'Then it can't be. Well, Maurice might be a broken man, drummed off the Stock Exchange with all his buttons gone.'

'He wasn't up to this morning's post.'

'He might have been since. Always time.'

'I don't think so.'

'All right, then, Kate darling,' said Walter, and he paid the bill, and they went to put Hasty in the car. Walter said, 'I have lost the way,' and Liza loved him very much indeed. So Kate led them to the side street, and the carpark man, who seemed to know Kate quite well, said he would run Hasty up and down every five minutes. Then they went to the only film Kate didn't not want to see. Walter stopped to look at the stills outside. 'God! It will be even worse than I thought.' When they were settled in their places, first Kate, then Walter, then Liza, Walter trod gently on Liza's foot. That meant, we're not going to hold hands and I love you; and Liza was happy.

Liza carried the lunch down to the bottom of the garden, and Walter looked up from another green Penguin. 'Hullo, ducky. You're early.'

'I know. It's your lunch in advance.' She sat down and took one of his cigarettes. 'I'm going for a walk.'

'Not the same walk as what you were going for last time?'

'Yes, I really am. And will you listen for any hammering on the back door, darling? The fish is due. And I know what you're going to call me.'

'No, you don't,' said Walter, pinching her waist. 'I was going to call you a modern girl. Don't take any chocolates from strange gentlemen, and don't speak if you're spoken to, and you'll be all right.'

'It's funny,' said Liza. 'Housework does make you feel silly and sort of I don't know.' She wanted to say devoted. 'I think it diminishes the sex appeal.'

'No, ducky, that it doesn't. But why don't you get what they call a woman? Some one with a sniff and a husband a martyr to his lumbago, and a different life-story every day?'

'I don't know,' said Liza. They had discussed this before. 'Kate does all *her* housework.' She hadn't said that before; and now it was really only because she wanted to talk about Kate.

'Maurice wears a tie at supper. I don't.' She met his eyes, and they laughed. 'Darling, how much do you like Kate?'

'I think she's maddeningly finite, and as selfish as hell.'

That wasn't much of an answer. Liza said, without meaning to, 'Yes.

And she doesn't want to have a child, and I should think Maurice does, wouldn't you?'

'How awfully novelettish,' said Walter. 'Yes, I should think he'd be rather a good father. I can see him with a crowd of tinies, sort of Mickey's orphans, milling round his knees, with old Maurice proudly brushing them off, can't you?'

Liza was thinking, it's silly; Walter and I ought to be able to talk about anything, but I can tell he thinks I said that for a personal reason; and I can't say that *I* don't want a child either, at least not now, or he'll think I do, or I'm getting at him somehow. She said, 'Dear Maurice, he is rather sweet,' and they laughed again, and the tension had gone.

Walter yawned. 'Children or no children, ducky, may I ask Kate to tea, if you're really leaving me?'

'Yes, darling. I think you might.' She got up. 'And now I am going for my walk.'

'Mild sensation. Court cleared in forty minutes.'

'Talking of mild sensations, darling, I didn't tell you that Pauline sent me a cheque, I mean Carl actually wrote it, for all the rent money. I put it under the elephant's hoof, and I wrote my name on the back, so don't forget it.'

'You *are* a modern girl, ducky. Was it then that something snapped inside you and you decided to go for the walk?'

'Well, yes,' said Liza. 'I think you do know nearly everything. About me.'

Walter sat up and kissed her. 'I shall now have my lunch. It keeps looking at me.'

'Me, too. Shall I stay and have mine?'

'If you bring your own,' said Walter, pouring out his cider. 'This is Liberty Hall.' So Liza fetched a glass and some more bread-and-cheese, and didn't start the walk till half-past two.

It was a hot afternoon. Liza had told Walter she would walk about seven miles somewhere, have tea and take a bus back. She set off down the gravel track, and, out of the breeze, she was even hotter. She took her grey flannel jacket off, and lit a cigarette to keep the cloud of flies from her head; it didn't do much good. She had a new midge-bite on her wrist, and when she scratched it she dropped her cigarette in the stream. It was going to be that kind of walk.

Liza didn't know where she was walking to, so she chose a path which wandered narrowly among the high bracken, and followed it a little way, stopping to smell the bracken. The air quivered in the heat, the flies buzzed, a bee hummed past her ear, suddenly loud, and gone. It was beautiful, beautiful, and that didn't make you happy. She picked a piece of bracken and walked on, thinking about Kate.

She thought, I don't dislike Kate for any reason except that she's married and I'm not. And so I don't really dislike her at all; and I suppose that's typical jealousy. Kate isn't catty, and she never bores you with talking about Maurice and sort of showing him off, the way most women do their Men. And as for the way she treads on Walter's toes, that's a kind of exaggerated self-preservation; and besides, she's safe, she can get at Walter and all he feels is flattery. I don't mean just that she's got an income and a husband, she's mentally safe. She's everything I'm not.

Liza walked on through the bracken. Walter could seduce Kate this afternoon, or Kate Walter; and here was Liza wondering undramatically when was the earliest she could safely get home without Discovering. No, she thought, though it isn't in the least impossible, it is impossible; situations aren't often so definite as that; and I don't think Kate would have Walter. It's funny, that sort of hurts; I only think she wouldn't be unfaithful to Maurice. She only wants to possess Walter mentally, and be possessed; she wants to win over the ordinarinesses of life, and the un-ordinarinesses, like books or him being funny, she wants to lose. Oh, I don't know; now I shall enjoy my walk.

The path stopped at a gate and a plantation of pine-trees, tall, dark, straight, with the bracken showing in the sunlight on the other side. Liza climbed the gate and sat on a newly cut tree-trunk and sniffed the resinous air, and, kicking the brown pine-needles at her feet, pulled a tuft from the green but dying branches cut from the trunk. No; it was beautiful, and that was all. She climbed back over the gate and into the sunlight, along the path. She was thinking, when I was young I could have sat there for an hour, seeing and smelling and listening. I can't now; I wonder if you get it back. I suppose you do, but differently, like Wordsworth. I wonder what would happen to people if they never wanted to get things back. Well, wanting them doesn't give them to you, and I suppose that's part of the going forward.

Liza picked another piece of bracken and thought about the office. It was difficult to believe that it still carried on, that Life hadn't said, Liza's gone and you aren't needed any more, and closed it down. It might have gone bust, of course, but not now more than any other time. The office suddenly came back to her, frighteningly real; the soggy edges of the Thin Rich Tea biscuits, and their taste; the brown curtains that left your hands dusty; your knee-cap against the filing cabinet when it didn't shut; the smell of the varnished table-leg too near the gas-fire. It was all so itself; like the lovely pub she and Walter had spent their happy week in, with the white paint, the persisting smell of coffee, the Turkish carpet and the creak in the stairs. Dear, funny office. Just not being at the office ought to make her happy; and then she felt very unhappy, because just being with Walter should make her even happier.

Liza reached the gravel track again and walked to the village. It was half-past three, late enough for an early tea. She crossed the road to the brown house, saying *Teas, Accommodation*, with, on the gate, a wiggly *Dene View* on an oxydized bronze plate. Liza had often thought, as she passed it, I've never seen a dene. Looking across the road, she decided *Dene View* hadn't either.

The woman who opened the door was tall, limp and dejected. She was kept up by her hair, which was pinned very tightly in a twist at the top. Liza didn't want any tea now; but she said, 'Good afternoon. Can I have some tea, do you think?' The woman, who didn't look as if she did, kicked open a door and padded off, and Liza, hoping she hadn't turned the woman out of her best drawing-room, sat on a chair with a red wool seat and was reminded of vicars and Indian colonels. This room *was* a room. A piano with a pile of tattered music, and on the music-rest a piece called Fairy Footsteps, with the letters made of pink twigs; velvet-framed photographs, a crowded mantelpiece, and two petrified hedgehogs on the window-sill. Liza sat there, longing for a closer view of the photographs, but not wanting to be caught out by that melancholy woman. The tea was a long time coming. She went on thinking about Kate, and every road of thought reached the same ending: if I could be like Kate, or something like her, Walter would want to marry me; and you can't be what you aren't, and the further Walter and I go as we are the more difficult it will be for me to be different.

The tea arrived. Liza tried to think of something kind to cheer her up. She said, 'What nice photographs.' The woman glanced at her, and padded off. Liza had a sudden fear that *Teas, Accommodation* belonged to the next house; no, it was all right. She turned from the window and sat down to her melancholy tea; three thick pieces of bread-and-butter and a slice of yellow felt cake. She was a bachelor girl again. And then she decided: she would go to London, and come back being different, with her hair different, and her mind newly angled. She had considered it before, but there was always a moment when you knew you had decided.

Liza ate two pieces of bread-and-butter and the cake, and hoped the woman wouldn't be angry that she couldn't eat everything. It was twenty-past four. If she went home now, walking very slowly, she would be back at five, and Kate and Walter would think she didn't want to leave them alone; no, not quite that, but they would know they were entitled to; and she only wanted to go home because she was bored. She wandered round the room, storing up the photographs to tell Walter. Janet Frisby, in brown sloping writing, had won the Primary Division Certificate of the Association of the Royal Academy and the Royal College of Music. Liza longed fiercely to know if Janet Frisby was the little girl in pigtails with a very small and widely meshed tennis-racket, and the Girl Guide, and the bride in the short dress and a kind of bathing-cap down to her eyes, and finally the Young Mother on the sands with a cross baby. It would be such a happy ending. But you couldn't ask that limp woman anything. The woman came back, and Liza said, 'How much, please?'

'Eightpence,' said the woman, in a rusty voice.

Liza had guessed tenpence; she was rich. She bought a Mars Bar at the grocer's and walked slowly up the hill.

Kate and Walter were reading, one at each end of the sofa. Walter, looked rather sulky, Kate as calm as usual. She said, 'Hullo, Liza. I'm afraid I ate most of the cake.'

Liza was being roped in on Kate's side; but she was on Walter's. So, instead of telling Kate that Walter had put the wrong cake out, a very stale one, she said, 'That's all right. We wanted to finish it.'

'Oh, well,' said Kate, standing up, 'I've done some good. Come *on*, Hasty; I must get you your dinner. When do we all see each other again?'

'I—I think I'm going to London for a few days,' said Liza, wishing she could see Walter's face, but he was behind her, still reading.

'If you wait till Monday,' said Kate, 'there'll be two cars going up. We've got some people for the week-end.'

Liza thought, then I won't wait till Monday and go up with a lot of society women; and I suppose Walter and I will get asked to the cottage to meet them. She said quickly, 'No, it's awfully nice of you, but I'd decided to go on about Friday.' She hadn't, she didn't know if she meant to go at all, but now it seemed settled.

'Oh, well,' said Kate. 'Good-bye. Thank you for my tea, Walter.'

'Good-bye, Kate,' said Walter, very politely. When she had gone he put down *Fur and. Feather*. 'Hullo, ducky. Did you have a nice walk?'

'Yes, lovely,' said Liza. 'I mean, frightful. Did you have a nice quarrel?'

'Not bad,' said Walter, putting an arm round her as she sat down on the sofa. 'I wasn't really trying. I told her she was an Old Bossy and she ought to take up good works to keep her quiet, but I don't think that was awfully clever, do you?'

Liza thought, she's been telling him he's lazy and ought to marry me. And she doesn't really mind in the least if he marries me or not; she just wants to bully him.

'Cheer up, ducky,' said Walter. 'If I'd moved up to my own level, or down, but I prefer to call it up, I could have retaliated. But I was too much of a gempleman. Or lazy.' He yawned and undid his sand-shoes.

'Well, yes,' said Liza. 'But I suppose the trouble is that all the people on Kate's level think theirs is the only one that matters, and the people on your level know that *theirs* is a sort of luxury, if you know what I mean.' She thought, your level and mine.

'I do.' Walter kissed her neck and, kicking his shoes off, wandered round the room in his bare feet. 'Damn. This floor is all splinters. Please, does any one want that orange?'

'No, darling. I don't like oranges.'

Walter sat down and began to peel it. 'Well, I think that's true. I've never seen you eat one.'

Yes, thought Liza, I know all the things Kate said to you.

'There's something keen about oranges, isn't there?' said Walter. 'The colour and the smell and the taste. Even the way they take aim and hit you plumb in the eye.'

'I know,' said Liza. 'Once I saw a cabbage with snow on top and the cabbage underneath sort of looking at me, dreadfully pathetic and yet dignified. Did you get that splinter out, darling?'

'I didn't get it in,' and he flipped her neck. Liza thought, I know; don't be unselfish, don't fuss, don't love me, don't make me think I ought to marry you; all because of Kate; and yet I know it isn't all because of her. She rubbed her neck with her handkerchief. 'I hate the smell of oranges.'

'Well, you'll have to do any moving there is. I can't. I'm all wedged up.'

Liza moved to the other end of the sofa.

'There's to be mafficking up at the Hall this week-end,' said Walter.

'No, I heard Kate telling you, so I needn't.'

Liza thought, that's about the first time you've ever admitted to hearing anything when you're reading. She said, 'I really do want to go to London. I mean, alone. I mean, I've got lots of things to do. I might see if the flat's awfully bent, and I must do some shopping.'

'All very nice. And you can get my golf-clubs, ducky, and eat up the tins before my Mrs. Something succumbs to their lure, and you can check up on the layers of dust on the books and tell the porter man to tick her off, and you can tell *him* to send on all the letters he keeps from me, and not to read the postcards, and to cheer up. What fun you can have. No, darling, don't bother about the clubs. They weigh a ton.'

'No, that'll be all right, darling,' said Liza. 'I can put them in a taxi.' She was thinking, he takes it for granted that I shall stay in his flat, and I'm grateful; after all these months I'm grateful.

Walter swallowed his last piece of orange and shook the juice from his fingers. 'Kate hurled at me, among all the other insults, that I was a spoilt tot. Do you think I am? I do, of course. But it would be sort of fun to find some one who didn't.'

'I think you're lovely, darling,' said Liza, and was very unhappy indeed; but the day after to-morrow she was going to London, and she would be different, and everything would be different.

X

As he soaped his face, Walter lifted his chin and burst into one of his shaving-songs.

> *The bear went over the mountain,*
> *The bear went over the mountain,*
> *The bear went over the mou-oun-tain,*
> *To see what he could see,*
> *To see what he could see,*
> *To see what he could see—*

He put the shaving-brush down. Now he was his grand-father, who wore green breeches and gaiters. He twiddled his razor.

> *And the other side of the mountain,*
> *The other side of the mountain,*
> *The other side of the mou-oun-tain*
> *Was all that he could see.*

Liza finished washing as much of her back as she could reach, and lay down in the bath again. 'Dear bear.'

'He is fun, isn't he?' Walter had to stop his shaving to say it.

Liza saw the blue sky through the window; London at a week-end would be horrible. She said, 'Darling, I really only want two pounds. Because I can go to the bank when I get there.'

There was a silence. Then she said, 'Well, no. I suppose all my money is in your bank.'

Walter stopped shaving again. 'Dear Sir, please reserve two seats in the dress circle for Tuesday night. PS.—I've just remembered I've got to go out that night, so please don't reserve them after all. I have now wobbled my Adam's apple all I want to for the next ten seconds.'

Liza thought, well, you needn't have answered; and she managed not to tell him that it would be all right because she could overdraw and he could pay it back.

The train went at eleven-fifteen. Walter stood on the platform and said, 'Drop me a dirty postcard and give my love to Aunt Ethel. I say, that was funny, wasn't it?'

'Marvellous,' said Liza. 'I will.' She managed not to say, take care of yourself and eat a lot, and remember about the bread and make the boiler up every night with the damper just turned on. She said, 'Have a nice time.'

'And you, ducky. Isn't this damned train ever going to start? We might be in Sofia and points east.'

'You don't have to wait.'

'I'll brave it out. Why aren't I coming with you?'

Half of Liza thought, please, please, do; jump in, I've got enough money for your ticket. The other half thought, go away, let me be different and myself, not the self I am with you. She said, 'You can go to Beaulieu Road again.'

'It's an idea. I might see the abbey. Only the mafficking starts in nine hours, which doesn't leave much margin. You do look nice, ducky.'

'Do I?' said Liza, who hadn't thought so. She wore her grey flannel suit and no hat, and her hair was a mess.

'I love your hair like that.'

'It wants doing. I'll get it done.'

There was a silence. An Airedale sniffed at Walter's ankles. He patted it. 'He can smell *my* little doggie. I think dog-keeping is a bit of a mystery, don't you? The owners wonder why they have the dogs, and the dogs wonder why they have the owners. The whole thing's an *impasse*.'

The Airedale's mistress, a tweedy woman with pearl earrings, looked at Walter as if she didn't like him. Walter gave her a smile which Liza knew meant, sorry, I didn't see you there, and I was only being not very funny;

and the tweedy woman looked at him as if she liked him very much indeed. Walter glanced past her up the platform and seized Liza's hand. 'The engine-driver is buttoning his sou'wester! The great locomotive is gathering steam! We're off!'

Liza thought, you needn't be so happy. But you're holding my hand. She said, 'Good-bye, darling.'

'Good-bye, ducky.' He kissed her. Liza watched him through *Booking Office and Way Out* and sat back in her corner, thinking, Walter is the best-looking man I have ever seen. She stared happily at the only other man in the carriage, a whiskered farmer in a very white shirt, but no collar; and then at the two women with Hats, and wondered about them all the way to Salisbury, when she changed to a real train.

Liza decided to have lunch on the train, after the usual struggle with her conscience; and then she went through the usual stages of excitement that she was having lunch on a train, and disappointment when she sat down to it and found that it was only lunch. On a train. As it always was.

She sat opposite a big brown man. They caught each other's eyes, and then stared out of the window next to them, and the window opposite. Liza thought it should make some difference wearing a wedding-ring; but no, the tension was acute, cross-currents hummed. Liza thought, I'd better make some sort of conversation; what is so silly is that he doesn't want to talk to me any more than I do to him. She stared at a cow, and a white house, and a dull ploughed field; and the big brown man loomed, like Walter's wardrobe.

The train ran slowly through a large station. Liza leant to see the clock, which said twelve minutes past one. 'What do you think the time is, please?'

The big brown man said, looking at his watch, 'Twelve past one.'

'Thank you. When do you think we shall get to Waterloo?'

The big brown man wiped his mouth on his napkin. 'It *should* be in at two-fourteen. But we might be a minute or two late, I suppose. But we might not.'

Liza said, 'How nice,' and they went on eating. Well, she had tried. She took up her book, and gave the man a look which meant, do you mind if I read? I should be awfully surprised if you said yes. The big brown man seemed to have got the message, and Liza read and wrote shopping-lists till the train ran into Waterloo, a vast, slamming, echoing cavern.

London was as unfamiliar as Waterloo; the buses were very red, the trees bushy with tired leaves; there were sun-blinds and the smell of tar, and London had never been so stiflingly hot; and the roar was everywhere. It followed her into the hairdresser's, meeting a wave of hot scent which made her very homesick for the spring.

The girl combed a piece out of the front of Liza's hair and said, 'Well, what about curls on the top? I could cut this piece to a few inches.'

Liza thought, I mustn't look like Kate; like every one else too, of course, but that would make no difference. She said, 'Well, I don't know, if it means cutting.'

'Well,' said the girl, running her comb over Liza's head, 'we could wave it at the top and curl it closer at the sides and back. I don't know what else we could do, do you?' She sounded very languid and mid-July; Liza thought, poor you, poor every one who's had the summer here; and oh, lucky me.

'We could have the wave *here* to begin with,' said the girl, bending the front piece. 'That's where it seems to want to go.'

Yes, thought Liza, that's where it always does. Oh, well, I suppose the way I have it is best. She said, 'I think it will be very nice,' and read the shiny magazines, and then all the magazines written for modern women. She read an article, printed diagonally, called 'Lovely, for Him.' How to show you're enjoying your evening without losing that elusiveness which is a part of your essential charm; and how to brace sagging chin muscles. What a world for love!

❊

Hot and polished from the hairdresser's, Liza took a bus to Pauline's flat and rang the bottom door-bell. She was staying in Pauline's flat, Pauline apparently living in hers now; and she was angry with herself for having said she would; she had had a sudden idea that it would be good policy, because Walter would ring up on at least one of the three evenings, and by not going to his flat till Monday morning, she would be unattainable.

Liza rang the bottom door-bell again, and the bottom but two, and, after a wait, the top; then, finding the outer door was open after all, she walked up to the top floor, where she found a door called *Madame West, Clairvoyante*, 10-3. If no one else had Pauline's key, Madame West would; Pauline's flat was like that. Madame West's door opened, and a small wispy woman in a kimono peered out, and fluttered with surprise when Liza explained that she wanted the key. Liza thought, if you could really see the future you'd have known; and oh, do I look as if I'm just going to be married? This wedding-ring doesn't count. She took the key and made her way down the dark stairs to Pauline's flat, thinking, as she always did when she saw it, Pauline is a tart.

Pauline's bed-sitting-room was a litter of clothes and magazines, bottles of face-lotion, jars of face-cream, and a vase of dead roses. Liza stepped over a lamp-shade which Pauline had apparently begun to re-thong and got tired of, into the bathroom, which Pauline had repainted apricot, and, putting the jars and bottles back too soon on the window-sill, had left a network of rings. A muddle. Everything was a muddle as soon as you stepped into this flat; life was a muddle, and you were the muddle which caused it. Liza's heart ached suddenly for the cottage; the moths bumping at night on the bedroom walls, the creaking floorboards, the lavender bushes, the supper-table by the window; and Walter, darling Walter, making life funny, and silly, and gay, and beautiful.

Well, it would soon be Monday. Liza nerved herself to light the geyser, and had a bath and changed to her black dress because she wanted to look a young matron, and went round to see Carl and Pauline.

There was a notice on the outer door. 'No Milk To-Day,' typed in purple. That was the man in the flat above, Walter's Bohemian. It was funny to think that he was the flat above Carl and Pauline now. Liza rang the bell, and Carl flumped down, with his hair over one eye, and said, 'Hullo. It's v-very nice to see you,' and Liza thought, you *are* nice, and followed him upstairs. She was going to see her flat suddenly as it was;

as she had last year, when she came back from staying at the seaside with Aunt Vi and Uncle George.

The flat sprang at her; whiter than she had imagined, the carpet a deeper plum, the curtains with more white in the pattern, the mantelpiece with a new chip in it; but her flat, terribly hers, reproaching her, as it lost its strangeness, for having abandoned it to foreigners. Pauline came out of the kitchen, swinging the door so that it didn't shut, crying, 'Darling! My dear, you *do* look well.' Meaning, thought Liza, you're fatter; it always means that when women say it. And I think I've all frozen up inside, the way you do at the wrong kind of party. She said, 'Hullo, Pauline,' and knew, by her voice, that she had. She looked round for something else to say. 'Where's Fitzpatrick?'

'My dear, he died,' said Pauline. '*I mean*, we pawned him.'

'I did *not*,' said Carl angrily. 'He died because his ear broke off.'

'*All* right, darling,' said Pauline, straightening his tie, 'he died.'

Liza saw that the radiogram had gone; so Carl would have pawned that; she felt ashamed of having taken the rent money. She sat down on the divan, and Pauline, handing her a glass of gin and French, either all gin or all French, said, 'Well, my dear. Tell us your news.'

'I don't think there is any,' said Liza. 'Much.' There was nothing she could tell them; it was another world. So she said, 'It's all very nice, and the weather's been mostly lovely.'

'I wish sunburn suited *me*, my dear,' said Pauline. Liza thought, I'm glad it doesn't. She glanced down at her left hand; no, there was no mark where the ring had been, because the last one, bought three weeks ago, was loose and slipped about. She moved away from the gas-fire.

'My dear, are you too hot? I thought it was a bit cold this evening. Carl, turn it out.'

'No, don't bother,' said Liza. 'It's only that I've got sort of tough, living in the country.' She thought, I feel like some one's dull cousin, up for the day.

'I *know*, my dear. Carl, darling, why did you have to turn it out?'

'Well, Liza didn't w-want it.'

'No, really, I don't mind,' said Liza, 'let's have it on again.' So Carl turned it up again, and it back-fired, and Pauline said, with her squeak, 'You are the *most*.'

'I always do that,' said Liza. 'It's something to do with the fire.' She was feeling awkward, in her own flat and yet in some one else's. She was longing to be back in her own world, with Walter and Kate; then she thought of the mafficking, and of Walter, and felt rather sick.

'My dear,' said Pauline, 'do you know the man in the flat above?'

'I've sort of seen him,' said Liza. Pauline was the kind of person who knew all the flats, above and below, anywhere she lived.

'My *dear*, we went to a party there. Because we had a party here once, I mean about six of us, not *him*, and, my dear, he came down and said would we make not so much noise as he was writing a *play*, as if you could disturb any one in the flat *above* you, and so we asked him in and he did some awfully feeble conjuring tricks.'

'They weren't,' said Carl. 'They were jolly good.'

'They were feeble, darling. Well, and we went up to a party in *his* flat, my dear, and he's borrowed your biggest saucepan and I don't think we shall ever get it back. Because he only gets up at *night*, being artistic.'

Yes, it was another world, lived in a few cubic feet, a world of small ideas and small happenings, with sooty chimney pots through the windows and a summer sky waiting for you. Liza thought, I've grown out of it.

'—and he'd have hung by his *toes* to your curtains if we'd let him, wouldn't he, darling?'

Liza went on listening to Pauline's strange world, and left at half-past seven, after ten minutes of excuses and untruths about having been asked out to dinner, and took the bus back to Pauline's flat. Pauline had given her a letter which she said had come that very morning, but was postmarked three days ago. Liza thought, almost no one writes to me now, and I write to almost no one. This letter was from Aunt Vi, and so it hardly counted. It said, in its large, generous handwriting:

Darling Liza, We have taken another house by the seaside, near Poole this time, for August, we all hope very much you will stay with us for your fortnight. I had meant to have written months ago but have been very busy with the W.I.

– 133 –

and one thing and another, your Uncle George sends his love and so does Betty
and we all hope to see you, how the summer has flown, well, write and tell me
you are coming, your loving aunt Vi.

Liza put the letter in her bag; she would write an awfully nice one back,
all apologies, from the cottage, and say she was staying with friends. She
counted up her money. She had four pounds seven and eightpence at
half-past three, and now she had two pounds fourteen and ninepence. But
money didn't seem to matter in the same way; because there was another
half to Liza, and he didn't worry.

Liza thought, Walter is the other half of me; and her eyes filled with
tears, and she tore her bus ticket into very small pieces. She got out at
the delicatessen and bought, to be economical, a quarter of a pound
of corned beef, a loaf, some milk and butter and coffee. As she went
up the stairs to Pauline's flat the corned beef, damply cold through its
greaseproof paper, reminded her suddenly of all the lonely meals she
had had in a lonely flat. She sat on the divan, watching the sunshine on
the curtains, the sad evening tree outside, and was unhappier than she
had ever been before. And perhaps Walter's telephone was ringing to
the panelled walls and the blue armchairs, and he would think she was
dead, or didn't love him; but she did, more than ever; and she had spoilt
his week-end.

Then Liza got up and thought, I shall have my dinner, and alter the
sleeves of the cotton dress I've bought on Pauline's sewing-machine; and
was perfectly happy again, as she had known she would be.

❧

Liza moved from Pauline's flat to Walter's on Saturday afternoon. Pauline
had been round in the morning to wash her clothes, and Liza had
explained why she had to go, inventing an important telephone message;
and then she had had to sit on the edge of the bath while Pauline talked
about Carl, and had scrambled some eggs and they had had lunch on the
floor, Liza thinking, well, that got the morning over, and I do like Pauline

really. She came out of the Underground to a Hampstead she had never seen in full leaf, at least not since she had known Walter, and therefore not at all, and, crossing to the shade, turned into Walter's street and was almost as excited as if she was seeing Walter again.

The porter man lived in the basement; he was a tall, sad man who didn't even laugh at Walter's little jokes. Liza rang his bell, and waited, not expecting to see him, and went into Walter's flat. It sprang at her, as hers had; she was suddenly as shy as the first evening she had seen it. She crossed to the telephone and ran her finger over the dust. It might have rung; and it might not have. She heard the porter man in the hall, and went out. 'Did Mr. Latimer ring up last night, do you happen to know?'

'Couldn't say, miss.' He seemed to think it a silly question to bring any one up for. Liza said, 'No, I suppose not. I thought you might perhaps have been in the flat, or the hall.' She wanted to tell him to ask Mrs. Something to dust the books; and, looking at his sad face, knew that it was hopeless. Any one else could; she could never tell any one anything. She said:

'Mr. Latimer wanted me to collect his golf-clubs. Do you know where they would be?'

'Couldn't say, miss.' Well, it didn't matter; she knew. She said, 'Thank you,' wondering what the porter thought of her, because he must have known about her and Walter; and the porter went sadly back to his dim basement, and Liza to the hearthrug by the summer grate. Here she and Walter had listened to Bach and old dance records by the fire, and talked about themselves and each other, and Life; and said nothing because there was nothing to say.

Liza thought, we can't go on if we're not married. We're marking time. When we were in London and he went out in the evenings I was jealous if it was a woman, and if it was a man I was resentful, and I thought, he doesn't want me to meet his friends. And when I did, either I was his girl friend or some one he had known a long time and would never be in love with, according to the occasion. And all the time I was waiting to be me.

Liza sat on an armchair, and got up, and walked round the room. She could never be herself till she was married. When they were married she could be nasty to Walter when it was necessary, because she wouldn't be afraid of losing him. She could tell him he was lazy, she could make him a proper barrister and bully him to write his book. And all she did now was stop him working; not by saying anything, by saying nothing; because she was afraid, because at the heart of their relationship, instead of the courage to take each other for life, was a blank, a fear on her side, on his—she sat down again and thought, trying to put herself in Walter's place. Yes, he was being perfectly reasonable; he had always told her what he wanted, she had always said she wanted it too, because she was afraid.

Walter's clock threw out its handful of bright silver tings. Four o'clock. Liza went into the kitchen and made some tea. Afterwards she would read, or find a shirt to mend, because there was nothing you could do on a Saturday evening alone, except go to the pictures; and after seven the telephone would ring. Well, let it, she would go out.

So after tea Liza rang up John, and found he had gone away for the week-end; and Norman, and found he didn't live there now, and found where he lived and that he was just going down to Marlow for the night; and Funny, and he was out. So she ended by ringing Geraldine, and fixing dinner for to-morrow night, and sat down to mend Walter's shirts and listen to the wireless, and hope that the telephone would ring, and realize, at eleven, that it wouldn't.

❦

On Sunday evening Liza sat in the lounge of a women's club in Bloomsbury. At least, the management called it a club, which made it even more of a hostel. Liza had lived here once, and made friends with Geraldine, who was dull and kind. Liza sat in a wicker chair which creaked horribly, and waited for Geraldine to come back from playing tennis. She was thinking, darling Walter, you would define this evening as relativity; and you will laugh when I tell you that I meant to have dinner with John to make you jealous, and so I'm having it with Geraldine, who is secretary of a social centre in Peckham and has never been in love, and makes cocoa on a gas-ring. Oh, darling Walter, I wanted to make you jealous; I was feeling cheap and retrogressive.

The lounge was nearly empty. Liza looked round at the orange-blobbed curtains and tried to evoke three rather drab years of the Past. No, it had been a very dim section of her life. She must have been happy sometimes; now she couldn't think why. A wicker chair in the corner creaked as a faded spinster bent to untangle her knitting-wool from a table-leg. Liza was reminded of that evening with Mrs. Croft; that had been dreadful then, but now it was drama, and Life; some-thing these poor creatures here had never known;

A square woman with short dark bobbed hair and a tie strode through the lounge, crying a hearty 'Evening!' to the spinster. Liza thought, oh, you poor thing, you are a bachelor girl. Walter said I wasn't one. I am the mistress of Walter Latimer, whose golf handicap is ten and who is the best-looking man I have ever seen.

Another spinster shuffled across the lounge, in plaid felt slippers, a jumper like a grey sack, a skirt like another grey sack; flat-chested, with a pink face, white hair and pathetically twinkling eyes. Liza denned her as not a poor thing but a poor soul.

'Well, Russell!' said the poor soul, beaming valiantly, 'I thought I'd missed you. I looked *everywhere* in the upstairs drawing-room.'

Russell laid her knitting down and peered up over her spectacles. '*There now!* You didn't! And all the time I was down here!'

'Well!' said the poor soul, lowering herself with a creak into another wicker chair, 'and there was I, waiting and waiting! And you were down here!'

'*There* now!' said Russell, clicking her tongue, 'and you were up there. I'm so *vexed* you should have sat in that uncomfortable room!'

The gong boomed from a side passage, and both the poor souls looked up, and at each other, and creaked to their feet and shuffled happily to the swing-doors of the dining-room, Russell wrapping her knitting round its needles and peering over her glasses.

Liza watched them, thinking, I shouldn't *exult* over other people. They weren't here when I was. I suppose they lived in another hostel just like this, and waited for each other in the wrong rooms, and got all excited about it, and even more excited over meals; and nothing has happened to either of them, ever.

The bachelor girl strode back, with another bachelor girl, but a different sort; with a narrow, long-nosed face and hair like straw thatch, and a palely striped cotton dress which fell away at her sloping shoulders. Liza thought, you could be almost pretty if you made your face up and had your hair set and your shoulders disguised. The fair girl smiled shyly at the door; she could be quite pretty. A pale young man approached them; Liza had forgotten you were allowed to ask men here, if they didn't go up to your room. The young man shook hands with the fair girl, and was introduced to the dark girl, and they all looked ill at ease and much too animated, and passed awkwardly through the swing-doors of the dining-room.

The lounge was empty now. From the dining-room came the usual clatter of happy eaters, loud or fainter as the swing-doors swung or shut. Liza thought, oh, I am lucky. I live with the best-looking man in the world. He loved me enough to ask me to spend the summer with him. His mistress; beautiful word. And we live in a heavenly cottage, with, as our nearest neighbours, a charming youngish married couple who speak our language. Oh, I am so happy; and, darling Walter, all I want in the world is you, and I have you.

❀

Liza jumped on to the platform and took her suit-case, the parcel of books and Walter's golf-bag from the nice woman she had travelled with from Salisbury; she wore a velour hat with tucks radiating from a rosette in the front, and a brown coat, and had a shining, weather-beaten face, and had told Liza about her son in the motor-works, and her three budgerigars all the wrong colour; and Liza had said she was shopping in London, and hoped her husband would be there to meet her; and they said good-bye like friends, and would never see each other again.

Walter wasn't on the platform. He might have been the man in the distance, but he wasn't; and he wasn't outside. Liza put the luggage in the cloakroom and set off to walk the mile. She was walking nearer Walter, nearer his car, which would be whining up the hill she had just achieved; no, turning the corner past Kate's cottage; no, backing out of the garage. Darling Walter, he would be sorry he was late, and she would forgive him.

Liza walked past Kate's cottage, which looked empty, and down the hill and round the corner, and there was the car outside the cottage, with Walter with his head in the bonnet. Nothing else mattered; here was Walter.

'Hullo, ducky!' said Walter, shaking out his dirty hands and kissing her. 'Another mouse in the works. It developed on Saturday, and I kept meaning. So please forgive me.'

Liza thought, you had two days to mend it, and gave him what must have seemed like a rather sulky kiss. Walter flipped her neck. 'Did you have a good time, ducky? I don't call Trooping the Colour a very dirty postcard.'

Liza said, 'It was meant to be funny,' and thought, you're out of tune sometimes. But I always have to feel as if I am. She followed him into the sitting-room.

'I'll get your luggage after lunch,' said Walter, stretching himself on the sofa, 'or shall I get it now?'

'No, darling,' said Liza. 'Any time will do.' Well, it would. 'Did you have a nice time?'

'I'm dead,' said Walter, untying his shoes. 'I've got an accumulated hangover, and I've spent the whole morning weeding the path and computing how many dozen oysters Major Hobie has eaten in his life. Or gone round with his little basket, collecting from his friends. I have missed you, ducky.'

Liza sat on the floor, and kissed his hair. 'I've missed you.'

'What was London like? Tell me everything.'

'Hot. Nothing happened. I did some shopping and got my hair set. Darling, did you ring up? I was in Pauline's flat on Friday night, and out on Sunday.'

'Well, ducky, Kate's cottage was full of the most ghastly people. So I thought not.'

'Did you maffick?'

Walter kicked his shoes off. 'Mafficking you may call it. Yes. Mafficking. We met Mr. Thorne yesterday, in the pub. Which is why I talk like this. He had his Sunday suit on.'

Liza felt frightened. Walter flipped her neck. 'Darling, don't look at me. No one seduced me. I told you they were all ghastly.'

Liza thought, he always knows what I think. Now I'm in the wrong. She said, 'I didn't suppose any one did. I only looked annoyed because you sort of slid away from what you were saying. Never mind what I was thinking. Tell me what sort of people, and what you did, and everything.'

'Well, there were only four extra, really. It seemed more. One Mayfair bitch. One real Chelsea bitch, very rare, and I think even worse, don't you? One Stock Exchange man, the husband of the Mayfair bitch. And a rather heavenly near-pansy, who very properly lives in St. John's Wood, nothing so obvious as Bloomsbury, and wears a lovely plum-coloured shirt. I said coo, I wish I had a shirt like yours, and he bridled beautifully. Aren't people typical?'

'Aren't they?' said Liza. 'Oh, darling, I wish I hadn't missed it. No, I'm glad I did. I always feel so silly with society people.' Walter didn't. 'Did you go there for lots of meals? I hope you did, darling, and didn't starve.'

'Well, I went to supper on Friday night, and was made what you might call much of, being a romantic grass widower run away from by his wife.' Liza's heart sang. 'And then Kate said there was an attic I could sleep in. So I did.'

He would, because Kate said so.

Walter pulled her ear. 'Cheer up, ducky. It was ghastly. Bats winged their eerie way through the rafters. I've hardly slept for three nights. There was a spring like a gasworks in the middle of the mattress. The first night I curled myself round it and thought, this is the first strange bed I haven't slept in for over two months.'

Liza thought, he's tired of being here. 'Well, darling, why did you stay for the other two?'

'It was a change,' said Walter. 'And they turned the mattress next day and the gasworks went. Another one came up somewhere under the pillow, but that didn't matter. I stuck it out. And this morning I came back here thinking I'd wasted three days and drunk too much. So I weeded the path, which I suppose counts as not wasting time.'

There was a silence. Liza thought, this is the end of the summer. I should have known. I haven't answered Aunt Vi's letter; I suppose that's lucky.

Walter got up and walked round the room. '*I* don't know.'

Liza thought, I do, now. For certain. 'What don't you know?'

Walter drew back his bare foot to luck an armchair. Liza said, 'Mind your foot.'

'Walter put his foot down and stood with his back to her for a second. Then he sat on the sofa, and took hold of her chin. 'Darling. If I had kicked it and bust my damned toe, what would it have mattered? I mean, not counting the damage to me, which would have been considerable, but temporary.'

'I only wanted to remind you,' said Liza.

Walter stared into her eyes. 'You should leave me to make my own mistakes. A Thought for the Day.'

Liza said, 'Kate doesn't leave you to make your own mistakes. She makes you make them.' She met his eyes again and thought, I know now that your eyes are grey. 'I want my chin back.'

Walter dropped his hand. She said, 'I'm sorry. I didn't mean to be catty. I only meant she was different from me.'

'Yes, she is. I don't suppose any two people could be more different.'

Liza said, desperately, 'I could say all the things Kate says to you. They're not clever. They're not even funny. They're just rude. Any one can be rude.'

Liza was very angry. She got up and pulled the dead roses from the bowl on the table, dropping them in the waste-paper basket. Walter said, 'I'm sorry, ducky. I haven't done a thing to the house since you left. Wherefore I hate myself.'

Liza went back to the floor and kissed him. 'It doesn't matter. Honestly.'

– 141 –

'I still hate myself. I hate myself for hanging about and reading a lot of bloody books I forget the next minute, and thinking to-morrow I shall be different. And to-morrow I'm not. I'm the same damned me.'

Liza thought, I don't want to know that you have faults. She said, 'I think you're lovely, darling.'

Walter's eyes were laughing at her. 'Ducky, any minute now you really may be a little woman. A hundred-percenter. You're in the finals.'

Liza was very angry indeed. 'I can't help being whatever you think I am. I've got to be me. And I do know what you're like. I know all about you. And if I don't tell you you're lazy it's because—' she stopped and thought, it's because anything I say you may hold against me as a reason for not marrying me. 'It's because.'

Walter stroked her throat. 'Darling, have you been happy here?'

It was in the Past. She said, 'I wish you wouldn't say that.'

'Why, ducky?'

'Because it makes me want to cry.' The plush of the sofa blurred suddenly. Walter knelt down beside her. 'Ducky, oh, sweetheart.' Liza put her face against his, thinking, I don't ever really have to cry. I don't have to now. But I could if I thought how sorry I am for myself. Oh, I am sorry for myself. And she began to cry. She was in his arms, crying all over his shirt, thinking, you don't know that the real reason I'm crying is that it makes me important, and you nice.

Liza blew her nose and sniffed. 'I've finished. Don't look so unhappy, darling.'

Walter twiddled the top button of her grey jacket. 'I am unhappy. You know I want to go abroad for a bit, don't you? No, I don't see why you should know. Oh, darling, I do hate telling you. I wish you weren't so hurtable. And what would you do if I do?'

'I'm *not* hurtable. And I'm not a waif and stray, I've been asked away to the seaside for August. Only with those awful relations. And I did know.'

'Yes, you are hurtable, ducky. You've just made me feel I'm a murderer. When I think about us, I'm always a murderer. I was one that first night.'

'You insult me.'

'I'm sorry, darling. I know you wanted to as much as I did. And I stopped being one pretty soon, because we were so happy. And all the other women I've had to do with have been sort of Kates and nagged me and made fun of the things I liked. And you haven't. And you always said you liked it as we were.'

Liza thought, yes, I've always been a coward. And because I like the things he likes he wanted us to live together; and because I'm not a Kate he doesn't want to marry me. She said, 'Darling, I did like it this way, and I do.'

Walter kissed the top of her head. 'I'm still unhappy.'

'Well, you mustn't be.' Here she was arguing against herself. 'I haven't said anything I didn't mean. I don't think people should be afraid of consequences. And what you put into life you get back. We had that as a Thought last Wednesday.'

Walter said, 'Darling, I do love you.' Liza thought, that's all that matters. I must put the summer behind me, and learn from my mistakes, and when we meet in London, in the autumn, it will be different. It would only have got worse if we had gone on here.

'If you're really going to the seaside, ducky,' said Walter, 'I'll buy you a bucket and a wooden spade. The iron sort are for cads, like iron hoops. Is it with the aunt and uncle from Wilts?'

'Yes,' said Liza, feeling very desolate. 'Darling, when do you want to go? I mean, will it be before August? I suppose I can go to Wilts first.'

'No, don't let's go till August.' Liza stopped feeling desolate.

'And I've got some good news for you,' said Walter, sitting back against the sofa. 'Kate's going away next week. All the way to Norway with the Mayfair bitch. And Maurice will go there in August, and keep fit running up and down the mountains.'

'Oh.'

'And I'm not going to Norway, I'm going to France, which doesn't join anywhere. So don't look at me like that, darling.'

'I wasn't,' said Liza. She had been thinking, he's not going away because of Kate, and yet he is, really, because of the week-end. I wonder what the summer would have been like without Kate; perhaps it would have stopped sooner.

Walter got up. 'Lunch, lunch.'

'Yes,' said Liza and went into the kitchen. Walter followed, and, fetching the patent tin-opener, began to open a tin of soup.

'It never works, darling,' said Liza, and fetched the ordinary one. Walter kissed her. 'Shall I light the fire in the parlour, ducky?'

'Yes, that would be lovely. I like winter in summer, don't you?' She looked at the grey sky; soon it would be autumn. Lovely.

'We'll do all the things we've meant to,' said Walter. 'We've got twelve days. I won't say but what we mightn't get to the Isle of Wight after all.'

'Oh, darling, that would be fun.' Everything was fun.

❧

For most of the last week it rained. On the last whole day Walter said at lunch, 'Well, we never got to the Isle of Wight. Fate ruled otherwise. Do we want to now?'

'I don't think so. We've got to put the sitting-room back in the right places.'

'What a bore. Let's get up early and do it to-morrow.'

Liza thought of to-morrow, and was rather frightened. But it was to-morrow, and not to be thought about.

'Let's go to a flick in Salisbury,' said Walter. 'And eat too much tea. And go on somewhere and have dinner in a pub. Would that be nice?'

'Lovely.'

So they drove to Salisbury, and parked the car in the side-street off the Market Square. Walter said, 'I know what you're thinking. Because so am I.'

Liza thought, we're on the same side. We have been for eleven days. To-day it's almost like knowing you have so many more hours to live. She said, 'There are an awful lot of memories everywhere.'

'Roses in December; only I don't remember that it ever rained so hard before.' He put his arm round her, and they ran across the road.

The film they wanted to see was at the same cinema as last time. Liza thought, we sat over there, and the seats have been there ever since, empty, or with other people on them, working out their own lives. The big film hadn't begun yet; it was one of the And So We Say Farewell series. Liza thought, well, I suppose there is such a place, with people there who have never lived anywhere else. Her mind slid off. Walter wasn't holding her hand. She was glad; this afternoon she wanted to be herself, because they had the evening, and the night, and the morning ahead of them. And after that the autumn.

Liza thought, we've got somewhere this summer. We know each other terribly well. And I have stopped thinking we're not married. That's not true. I think it all the time. But I've got a long way from the Mrs. Croft stage. It was funny how that worried me once.

On the screen an almond-tree shivered against a fleecy cloud. It might be England; and the wind would blow your hair there, and people would leave cigarette-packets, printed with strange names, but no less ugly, on the grass. Soon Walter would be across the sea. She thought, I wish I could tell him about the part of France I went to; but he makes me feel untravelled and shy and silly. Oh, Walter, all the time you stop me from being myself.

And so we say farewell. The lights went up and changed from pink to blue, to a wobble of sound. The air dripped thickly. Walter clutched his hair. 'Priestley called that noise treacle. My God, treacle it is.'

'Never mind, darling,' said Liza. 'Soon be over.' She thought, it hurts my ears as much as yours, but because you loathe it I think it's rather fun. I wonder if you do too. Walter took her hand; she was a helpmeet. Walter let go of her hand and gave her a cigarette. The organ began to play *In a Persian Market.*

'Cor,' said Walter. 'What a melody.'

Liza thought with a sudden and terrible pang that this time to-morrow he would be gone; no longer wherever she looked, no longer a dark head or a bare arm and a shirt-sleeve to be seen from the kitchen window and turned away from because she knew he was still there; or a voice on the stairs, a clatter at the door and that sudden leap and kindling of her soul; still, whenever she saw him, after three months together.

The music wallowed on. *If you were the only girl in the world*. It swooped and tore at her heart. She looked away, at a blur of changing lights; and as they melted into darkness, thought, I won't let myself think that he's going till we're in the car to-morrow. Till then he isn't.

The big film began. It was a back-stage drama, with a young man who had written a great song number and a girl who wanted to sing it, but had refused the attentions of the show's producer, an evil man with a triumphant moustache. Walter murmured, 'Same again,' and sat back. Liza wondered why they weren't holding hands; perhaps he was being kind. The misery of their present relationship swept over her; you can make me happy, I am happy if you make me; if you make me too happy I shall suffer, and so will you, but differently; because I have only to say *let's end it* and you would, however much you love me. Because you are a man and I am a woman.

The young man on the screen played a surprisingly resonant chord on the piano in his humble attic, and launched into his big song number, with full orchestra; and Liza's heart rose and sang with it. The world was before her, the whole beautiful world. She was herself. To-morrow she went back to the world, after three months of another world; she had let her life go off its course to please him, no, to please herself; but she was no less herself, and to-morrow her life was her own. She thought, I shall read all the Shakespeare I haven't read. Beginning with *Titus Andronicus*, because Walter said Shakespeare only just wrote it, and you only read it to show off.

A lot of things had happened on the screen since Liza had last noticed it. There was a baby. She didn't think it was the girl's, or even the man's; but they were both cooing at it, and perhaps it would bring them to the point of declaring their love, which was quite dreadfully obvious already. Liza thought, I should simply hate to have *that* baby. But I suppose I would love to have one that looked like Walter. Not because I *want* it; it's something you can't help, like being thirsty.

The baby had disappeared, and the man and the girl were singing a

– 146 –

duet at each other. Walter moved his arm and put his hand on her wrist. Liza took his hand, and Walter put it down on the chair-edge between them. They sat, hand in hand, while on the screen life danced and sang, sweeping an hour nearer to the death that came to everything.

Part Three

Autumn

XI

The seaside house was like every other seaside house; pink brick, with nautical white woodwork, and separated from the village by an unmade road and a string of kiosks, bungalows and asbestos cafés. It was almost exactly the same as the house Aunt Vi and Uncle George had taken last year for August

Liza had never before spent the whole month with her aunt and uncle and cousins, but she knew it would be the same as a fortnight, only twice as long. Arriving a few days after the month had begun, she found that you plodded every morning round a hill and down a cliff path to reach the bathing-place, a bay of rocks and shingle; and two days later they were all plodding up a hill and down another and longer cliff path to a bay with less rocks but sharper shingle, while there was one more carrier-bag now, with Aunt Vi's rug-making outfit and six oranges.

Liza walked at the back of the procession, carrying her bathing-towel, two mackintoshes and *Shakespeare's Tragedies*. She would have carried more, but there had been so much arguing and sharing out that it seemed easier, and perhaps kinder, not to. It was a cool but sunny day; she wore her bathing-suit under her blue shirt and trousers, and was too hot and too cold. She crunched over the shingle to a place not too near to have to join in the chatter, and perhaps not too far to seem rude. She wanted to be alone, and so with Walter, in the real world. But, after only two days, the outside and unreal world had stolen something from it; had put it in the Past. She spread her bathing-towel on the shingle, and Betty called out, 'Want a ginger-nut?'

Liza went over to the group. James was doing an easy crossword; she gave him two words. Margaret said, 'You *are* brown, Liza.' Liza had told them she had been staying with some friends she'd met in the spring, and wondered how likely it sounded. But then no one cared what you did; you wasted a lot of worry. She thought, I tell myself I'm a married woman whose husband is abroad for August; and I tell them I've had three months in the country, and in September I go back to London and get another job; and I know which is right. Aunt Vi brought out some coconut-ice pink wool. Liza admired it, with a small ache, and went back to her bathing-towel. She lay down and opened the book at *Titus Andronicus*, holding it uncomfortably above her head.

> Sat. *Noble patricians, patrons of my right,*
> *Defend the justice of my cause with arms;*
> *And, countrymen, my loving followers,*
> *Plead my successive title with your swords.*

She referred to the Dramatis Personae. Sat. was Saturninus, son to the late Emperor of Rome, afterwards Emperor. He wanted to be made Emperor, and he was saying it twice; no, perhaps patricians were different from countrymen, who had swords. But the patricians were armed too. Oh, well. She read on. Now Bassianus wanted to be Emperor; and so did Marcus Andronicus. No, he wanted Pius Andronicus to be; and Pius was Titus. Liza thought, I shall just about get the plot of this; but I *will* read it. She turned the pages. *Enter a Messenger, with two heads and a hand.* She turned on: *Macbeth, Hamlet, Antony and Cleopatra.*

> *I dream'd there was an emperor Antony:*
> *O, such another sleep, that I might see*
> *But such another man!*

The tears ran out of the corners of Liza's eyes. She shut them and put the book down. The sun struck her face. From the other side of the clear orange-red came the swish and murmur of a calm sea. The shingle was hot under her hands. She clutched it and thought, if Walter died I should be Cleopatra. I am all the lovers in the world.

Walter hadn't written. He had said—he was tying up the clematis, and Liza was polishing the brass on the front door—'Don't write, ducky. I'll send what they call an occasional postcard. But I don't know where I'll be, and getting letters from home rather breaks the spell. Have you read *An Inland Voyage*?'

Liza had said yes, and it was lovely. 'The best book ever written,' Walter had said. All the books he liked were. 'Then you know what it says and what I mean, don't you?' Liza had said, 'I suppose I do,' and he had kissed her. But each morning she waited for the postcard giving her an address to write to; how could you not want to be written to by some one you loved? She put her book under the bathing-towel out of the sun, and went on imagining the letter she would write down later.

Uncle George is heavenly. He has a flat face and a grey-brown moustache, a bit like Mr. Thorne's, and an inferiority complex which comes out in facts and fussing. This morning at breakfast he said that by getting up an hour earlier every day you saved over a fortnight a year. He is very keen on dew rising, not falling, but thinks that if a penny comes down heads fifty-nine times the odds are fifty-nine to one against it being tails next time. I'm glad he's only a relation by marriage, because that sort of mind spreads over a family. Aunt Vi is an aunt, and that's all you need know about her. Betty is even more pear-shaped than last year, because she does her hair in a roll on top and hanging down each side, and she is sunburnt to match it. She really is a pear, ripe and placid and aged twenty, well perhaps not ripe because I suppose she's a virgin. James is gruffer and keener on cars because he is allowed to drive now. Margaret is the pride of the Upper Fourth, not the Lower, and I expect I was like that at fourteen, which makes me very smug. I love you with all my heart, and everything is unreal. When I think about the summer it has a terrific itselfness. I think about it all the time, and, darling, did we bolt the back door? Not that we can do much about it, unless I write to Mr. Murdoch. I've got 17 and 32 of Builders of the Empire, so I could send them to Jim. It's funny how frightened I used to be of him and his van. There is a thrown-away caravan on the cliff, I saw it this morning, with 'Alleluia! Praise Him Evermore!' and so on painted on it, but I don't suppose the others think it is so funny and sad. I am lying on a sharp beach, and when I put my hand up the sun shines off my fingernails, but you are not here and all is dust and ashes.

Liza picked up her book again.

> *Princes, that strive by factions and by friends*
> *Ambitiously for rule and empery,*
> *Know that the people of Rome, for whom we stand*
> *A special party, have by common voice,*
> *In election for the Roman empery,*
> *Chosen Andronicus, surnamed Pius.*

But they hadn't, because Saturninus was afterwards Emperor. Liza put the book down, and, shutting her eyes, thought about the summer.

❀

On the fourth day Liza came down to breakfast to find a biscuit-coloured postcard on her side-plate. All the beauty of life in a postcard, with lines drawn for the address, in the only handwriting in the world.

A marvellous time so far, said the handwriting on the left. *I wasn't sick; every one else was, so I felt rather rugged. I have been on a train or platform for the past five years, but now I am in a rude hostelry. Why is a French railway station not a bit like an English railway station? Because of the sand which is not there, thank God. I only put this in to fill up the space, which I have, so all my love, ducky. W.* Liza turned it over and saw a row of sepia houses and a statue, and went on eating her breakfast. Cornflakes stuck in your throat.

'Well, well, well,' said Uncle George, rubbing his hands. 'What are we going to do to-day?'

'Don't *eat* like that,' said Betty to Margaret, who answered, 'You've got a blob of powder this side of your nose.'

Hateful family; foreign, unreal world.

After breakfast Liza went up to her room and tore up her letter to Walter, now six pages long. Then she looked out of the window. The sea was a blue-grey, holding the colours of the sky as it danced. Uncle George's voice, slowly pompous, came up from the verandah:

'Now if you *four*—'

'We're only three,' said Margaret's voice with a giggle.

'Counting Liza, four. Now if you four hold the three carrier-bags between you, keeping step alternately—'

'Why?' from Betty.

'Because, you chump,' said James's gruff voice, 'your arms would swing all over the place. And why the hell do you need that bath-coat thing and that coat thing as well?'

Liza thought, only three weeks and a few days. I can measure it in days. All his love. It's a lovely morning. And it's fun. She put the bits of the letter in her suit-case, where no one would see them, and hurried downstairs to take her place in the row.

❀

When you did the same thing every day, and spent most of each day wishing it behind you, time didn't drag, as you would expect, it slipped by very quickly. But it didn't leave much to be remembered by. The month became a procession, with two landmarks to each day, the morning and the afternoon post; two rising curves of hope, mounting steadily against reason, dropping suddenly to sick despair as the postman came and went, sliding to a more gradual despair as he didn't come and Liza knew he wouldn't. But that kind of despair didn't last long, because it was only the bottom of the next slope upwards. There were two mornings when the world crystallized again into a biscuit-coloured postcard which lit up the rest of the day. But in retrospect each day was a pattern of carrier bags, wet bathing-suits, rum-and-butter toffee, endless games of rummy; and each day put the summer further in the Past, and was more the real world; and it was perfectly possible to be happy in the real world, and that hurt.

There had been several rainy days, and towards the end came one that made you think of winter. Liza put on her grey suit and stockings and sat in the drawing-room, reading *Titus Andronicus*. She had reached Act IV, and the characters were old friends. She stopped reading to glance round the room. Betty, James and Margaret were deep in magazines, round the crackling fire. Uncle George was on the verandah, hammering new staples into the wall. Liza watched him against the dripping apple-trees and the faint grey line of the sea, interrupted by the white rails of the balcony. Uncle George was frowning, and he wheezed tunelessly, which meant he was concentrating. Liza heard the tap of the hammer, high as it hit the staple, low as it got the wall, and thought, dear Uncle George. She tried to imagine him in the Indian Civil Service. When she was a child and had first heard of red tape, she had associated it with Uncle George; he would be sitting at a school-desk, wearing a pith helmet and winding the tape on cards. She found that that, to her, was still red tape. Betty was frowning over some woman's magazine; she had dark eyebrows and fair hair, which made her nearly pretty. Dear family, absorbed in their funny lives; James leaning forward on the sofa, his soul in *The Motor;* Margaret fidgeting behind a copy of *Vogue* that she couldn't really appreciate. In five days' time the month would be over, and it would have an itselfness. She heard Aunt Vi's voice through the door:

'Liza dear, come and tell me what you think of this.'

Liza went out to the kitchen and found Aunt Vi holding a dead hen up by the string round its legs. She said, 'I think it looks lovely,' and wondered why Aunt Vi should suddenly want an amateur's advice.

'I suppose it will do,' said Aunt Vi, handing it back to the boy on the doorstep. The boy dropped the chicken in his basket. 'Now by three o'clock, mind.' The boy nodded and went off whistling as only boys with baskets can whistle. Aunt Vi put her hands to her head, and Liza decided that she was rather a dear, and could be quite handsome; only she had straight black hair combed back and cut in a dull bob, and she was rather thick, though not fat. But she had nice dark eyes, perhaps too dark, and she was cheerful. Liza thought, I wonder at what age you lose your waistline, and ran her hand under her pink jersey round her skirt, and found it encouragingly loose.

'You'd better do Mr. Shaw's room, Brenda,' said Aunt Vi to the maid they had rented with the house. Liza thought, Aunt Vi wants to Talk to me; I wonder what I've done wrong. She sat down opposite Aunt Vi, who was stringing the runner beans, and took a knife from the kitchen drawer. Aunt Vi couldn't know about Walter.

'Liza dear,' said Aunt Vi, 'why don't you come and stay with us instead of going back to London?'

So it was only that, all over again. Liza said, once more, 'It's awfully sweet of you, but I had definitely decided to go back.' She strung a bean very carefully, to make up for perhaps sounding ungrateful.

'But you haven't still got your post, you know.' Aunt Vi always called a job a post.

'No, but I can always get another,' said Liza, thinking how unreal all this was, trying to imagine the effect on Aunt Vi if told what was pulling Liza back to London. 'I can spend a week looking for one, you see, or longer; jobs are awfully easy to find.'

'But you know you've got nowhere to live. Your flat's gone.' She made it sound as if it had been blown away.

'Well, there are plenty more.' Liza knew her way of life sounded funny to Aunt Vi, who went on and on living in the same house. She didn't want to talk about her flat; she had an idea she had been silly to give it up; and there it was, empty, with Carl and Pauline in Brittany with what sounded like an awful party of toughs. No, she hadn't been silly to decide to give it up. When a phase of your life changed, you should change your background. She sliced down another bean, trying to cut as little off as Aunt Vi did, and said, 'It's awfully sweet of you, but you know I must *work*. I couldn't just do nothing.'

'You could help Uncle George in his office,' said Aunt Vi. Uncle George, who missed his red tape, put in two days a week with some agricultural committee. With a delighted horror, Liza imagined herself typing about cows and turnips, and said, 'I mean real *work*, Aunt Vi. I didn't mean that

that wouldn't be, but you know how it is when you've lived in London and gone to an office every day.' And she felt very homesick for the office and the Bygone Days Tea Shop.

Aunt Vi, who certainly didn't, said, 'I know, dear. But Uncle George and I think you're much too thin'—Liza was flattered—' and a month or two in the country would do you good, you know. And I'm sure your father would like to think you were having a rest.'

'It's awfully sweet of you,' said Liza, 'but really I don't think I *could*. You see—' and it would have gone on indefinitely if James hadn't put his head round the kitchen door and said, 'Are there any ginger-nuts?'

In the afternoon the rain stopped, and Liza took the bus to Poole. In the bus she went on with the letter which she didn't write down now.

I went to Poole this afternoon on a green and beige bus on the front left-hand seat with a hippopotamus bulging into me as well as into the aisle. I always get them, I never have more than a third of a seat. I thought happy bus-thoughts about you and the autumn, and behind me were two women's voices. I tried to deduce them but got nowhere. One turned out to be the felt hat kind, the other had a small triangular face, the wide bit at the top of course, and looked and talked like a good wife, standard model. We passed a biscuit-tin. I don't know why a biscuit-tin should be more exciting on the road than in a grocer's shop. Yes, I do really, but I like to tell you what I see and think.

She went on with it in the old world tea-shop, where a resourceful Aberdeen terrier called Hamish frightened a waitress into dropping a meringue, and then ate it. She came out to a dull grey evening, with some of the shops lit up. They shone into an unnatural dusk. Walking along the crowded pavement, hearing the motor-horns, the shouts of the newsboys, she was suddenly given the sense of a London night. She thought of Charles Lamb, crying for joy in the Strand at the fullness of life, and was rather pleased to find tears in her own eyes.

🌀

Betty had come to London with Liza, to buy a suit. Liza felt she was letting the family down by saying she would be too busy to help Betty with her shopping, and couldn't put her up for the night. Well, there was a good excuse, because the furniture van was taking the furniture to-morrow and keeping it till she found a permanent flat. But ordinarily she and Betty could have divided the bed into two mattresses. But Liza would be in Walter's flat to-night. Betty had said placidly that she would stay with the Listers, and Aunt Vi had looked anxious and motherly at Betty being alone in wicked London. Liza thought, as she dropped Betty at Oxford Street and directed the taxi-driver to her flat, my life is a guilty muddle. But I shall get it straight, because I must.

Hyde Park was sad and faded, as empty as the rest of London. It was neither summer nor autumn. Liza was conscious of her stockings and all her extra underclothes. She thought, I'm beginning a new chapter, but first there's all the muddle of finding a flat and a job. It's like walking a tightrope; but there is a net underneath. She remembered Aunt Vi: 'Now, dear, you're to tell us if you want *any* money. You must *promise*. And if anything happens you must stay with us for as long as you want to. Now *promise*.' It was easy to promise, and to tell Aunt Vi she was a darling.

Liza thought, my life has gone a little off the true. I haven't put into it what I've taken out. Walter really paid for the summer. I shouldn't have anything in the bank and I've got ten pounds thirteen and fourpence, and on the twenty-first I get the next twenty-five pounds; and I haven't had a job for five months. Well, if I haven't paid for that bit of my life now, I shall; you always do. Perhaps I paid for it last year; but then Hugh made me more or less happy, at least I thought so then, and the unhappiness afterwards paid for that.

The taxi-man bumped the trunk upstairs. Liza gave him a shilling extra and her best smile, and shut the door and hurried to the telephone. The flat was different again; very white, and her hand very brown against the bookshelves.

Burr-burr, said the receiver. *Burr-burr*. Twice, three times, four times. Liza had untwisted the flex and turned two books the right way round; and still it burred. She rang off.

Walter had said, on the third postcard, that he would be back early to-day. Perhaps he was out. How could she tell? Perhaps the boat was late.

Perhaps he had drowned. Perhaps he wanted to stay in France. Perhaps he had met some marvellous woman there; or on the boat. Liza sat on the edge of her bath, which had shrunk terribly, and thought with an ache of the carrier-bags, the wet bathing-suits, the canvas shoes with sandy rope soles, the rummy; a sunlit haven with no ups and so no downs. All that hoping for the post had been a happy game of make-believe. This was the real agony.

It was a Thought for the Day that when you were busy you forgot the time. Liza began to pack the flat up. Carl and Pauline had, probably by mistake, left a useful pile of newspapers in the cupboard under the sink. Liza took them out and began to read them. They stabbed at you. July, and June, and even May. On about July the tenth Walter had read her a bit about a 38-year-old Wallasey, Cheshire, widow, being found dead under a bath, and had objected that no bath had a space for being dead under; and they had gone up to look at their bath. Liza searched through two papers; yes, there it was, July the seventh. It didn't seem possible that the same print, on the same page, should have been pushed through a letter-box on a London summer morning and flumped downstairs for by a sleepy Carl. Liza wrapped the teapot in the newspaper and put it in a drawer she had emptied.

It was two hours later; she went across to the telephone and dialled Walter's number. This was the third time; the last was nearly an hour ago. She listened, and rang off. Well, no one could get back from France in under an hour. She went back to the cupboard under the sink, and her thoughts.

She was packing her life up. It was wrong to be afraid of change, and she didn't think she was; but you couldn't sidestep being reminded. She took out a claret bottle. That was the evening Walter had been playing tennis at some club, and arrived in his flannels, and her heart had turned over, because he had looked so lovely; and he had said claret ought to have the chill off, dammit, and she had stood it in the bathroom basin while he splashed in the bath; that was April, and the spring. A sleepy fly crawled up the window and fell down, buzzing Donald Duckishly. All the summer had gone.

It's funny, thought Liza a little later, I used to belong to this sort of life. She had her head in another cupboard and was separating the paper-clips from the pile of linen. Carl and Pauline had upset the box, as she used to. This sort of life was a makeshift, an apology, to you and by you, for not being the life of the ordinary world which kept its furniture in different rooms, its linen in a linen-cupboard, and in its pocket a plan of living for this year, next year, some time and as far as never. Liza had once been, not a Bachelor Girl, but some one happening to live the life of one; now she knew she had been as much a Bachelor Girl as the rest of them. She thought, oh, I'm hot and I didn't have enough lunch. She dumped the small pile of linen on the armchair and put the kettle on; and while it boiled she dialled Walter's number, and told herself she wouldn't mind so much when she'd had some tea; and, when she had, she didn't.

As she washed the tea-cup afterwards Liza remembered about her biggest saucepan. She went up the stairs, feeling excited and very nervous, and rang the bell of the man in the flat above. He was sure to be in bed; she had better creep downstairs and he would think she had been a meter-reader.

But he was up, and dressed in his usual grey tweed jacket and flannel trousers. Liza said, 'Good afternoon, Mr. North.' She knew his name from the downstairs doorbell, and the post. She was dreadfully ashamed to think she had read his postcards and knew his girl friend was called Hannah.

Mr. North was a rabbit. He had a long face, and long teeth and long hair, brushed back and reminding you of a rabbit's ears. He smiled toothily. 'Oh, yes. The saucepan. Do come in.'

Liza stepped in, like Alice going through the looking-glass. It was her fiat, and it wasn't. It had been divided into two little rooms; this one was the sitting-room, papered with a faint pattern, and with an unframed picture, in coloured chalks, of what looked like marigolds so would be something else. She sat down on the sofa, which had spindly legs and its upholstery built into a wooden back, and wondered what to say. Mr. North fetched the saucepan and said, staring toothily into it, 'I'm afraid it's a bit messy.'

'Oh, that's quite all right,' said Liza. 'I'm awfully sorry to bother you.' She felt very mean, taking poor Mr. North's best saucepan. She stared round the room again and said, 'What a nice typewriter.' It stood on a card-table, with crumpled typing paper all over the floor.

'Not bad, is it?' said Mr. North going over. He took one hand from his pocket and struck a few keys. Liza remembered the tap-dancing noise which had once puzzled her and Walter. She wondered if he knew that they used to hear Hannah shouting at him when the windows were open; and if he could hear Walter singing when he shaved. He must know about Walter. She sat there, feeling horribly embarrassed; she and Mr. North had lived twelve feet apart for months, and had never said more than a 'Sorry' or 'Thank you' over the milk-bottles and the post. And to-day they were more strangers than if they had never met.

Mr. North offered her a cigarette; so she would have to stay while she smoked it. He said, as he struck a match, 'I see they've begun to paint the house opposite at last.'

'I know,' said Liza. 'Isn't it fun?'

Mr. North smiled toothily. 'I was beginning to think they'd never do it.' Liza thought, we have the same view; that's funny. She saw that the sun had come out, and hated all sunny evenings with a miserable pang.

Below the floor a telephone bell rang faintly. Liza suddenly knew that it was hers. She said, 'Oh, my telephone! Oh, will you excuse me?' and seized the saucepan, and ran. The telephone would stop ringing. No, it mustn't, it couldn't. It cried its shrill anguish to a heartlessly empty flat. She lifted the receiver in the middle of its ring and said, 'Hullo?' and there was Walter's voice, after more than a month. What she had forgotten was that the despair and the agony ended in this.

Liza stood at the tall window of Walter's sitting-room in the evening sunlight. *Most she loathed the hour when the thick-moted sunbeam lay:* that was for the lonely. In one minute Walter would be back. He had left the outer door open, and pinned on his front door, *bak in 1 min.* Liza watched an old man pathetically happy over a barrowful of rags, and wondered why she should be so shy of seeing Walter again. No, she wasn't, she hungered and thirsted for him; but she was. She watched the old man past the window, and heard the outer door bang, and footsteps in the hall, and turned to see Walter at the door. He stood there, with a bottle under his arm; and Liza stood by the window. She said:

'You are brown.'

Walter threw the bottle on the armchair and strode to the window. She was in his arms; he was here; here and now, saying, 'Hullo, ducky. So are you.' Liza thought, we're strangers; and, as they kissed, oh, but we're not. This is the end of a month that didn't happen, except to bring us to this.

'Sweetheart,' said Walter, and kissed her again. Liza said, 'Oh.'

'Oh what?'

'Oh, I do love you.' Walter flipped her neck. She lifted her head and said, 'You've got a tie on.'

'So I have. Thank you, lady.' He took it off and threw it behind him. Liza thought, I won't pick it up; I can't. It wouldn't be right now. She looked up and saw his eyes laughing at her.

'Now or then?' said Walter.

'Now,' said Liza, and thought, we're illicit again. She followed him into the bedroom. 'You've still got your shoes on.'

'Give me time, ducky,' said Walter, taking his coat off. Liza thought, I've nearly annoyed him; I've harked back. I suppose I knew we couldn't go on from where we stopped. Because, by trying to, you only show up the gap. Oh, and I was going to be different. But even in her unhappiness she was happy; that was what was so wrong, so falsifying; she thought, how can I be myself with you, when because I am with you everything is real, or not real, I don't know which, but different, so that I can't judge anything? And how can I be something for you to win, when you've won me? But the me you have is not the real me.

Liza sat on the bed and thought, as she took off her stockings: if only we could begin again. And eight months of the Past rose, crying, unlive us if you can.

Walter sat down next to her, and said, 'You look lovely with nothing on.'

'So do you. And you've been wearing shorts. I've never seen you in shorts.'

'I know. I wouldn't wish it on any one I minded about. I look a bit of a cubmaster.'

'But, darling, you've got lovely legs.'

'So have you, ducky.' She had known he would say it. Then she was in his arms, thinking, I can feel your heart beating. She said, 'Your heart's beating.'

'I know,' said Walter. 'It does sometimes.' Liza thought, never mind about the other me. Here I am.

🌀

Walter was singing in his bath. Soon Liza would get up; but she lay there, watching the wardrobe. Soon the street-lamp in the mews at the back of the flat would be lit, and one small ray would shine on the far door of the wardrobe; sometimes in the country the night was so dark that you woke up and thought you had gone blind. But to-night they would go to bed in the friendly half-dark, and she would wake to hear the milk-cart's rattle. They were beginning again, in London, and in the autumn. She got up and put on her house-coat, and went into the bathroom. Walter said, 'I love you when you've just woken up.'

'I wasn't asleep. It's the light. It's so sudden.' Walter stood up and shook himself, and she said, 'Darling, you've washed your hair.'

'So I have,' said Walter. 'I had a sort of dim idea, and now I know.' Liza thought, I seem to be saying a lot of silly things to-night. We haven't seen each other for a month; and this is how we talk. And it's my fault. It always is.

Walter dried himself and turned Liza's bath on. He said, through his towel and the noise of the running water, 'Have you seen Kate?'

Liza thought, as if I'd had time. Or wanted to. She said, 'No.' Well, you couldn't really talk above that noise. She turned the taps off and got into the bath. 'Have you?'

'No, ducky. I know I wasn't being very bright. But I want my dinner.

We've got a dozen eggs and everything else is tins, so you can nearly be a little woman and cook us something that seems frightfully clever but isn't in the least. Give me my sponge and I'll wash your back. Aren't you brown?'

'Darling. It hasn't been washed for a month.'

'So I see. What I thought was brown isn't.' She was happy again.

They lit the fire and ate their dinner on the floor; it was very uncomfortable and reminded Liza of the only picnic they had ever had, when she had seen the adder and knocked the beer over Walter's special sandwiches. Once that was now; and she was looking at it, from another now.

Walter said, 'Well, and so I got on the boat and we weighed anchor and struck across the foam, and no one was sick but me. End. To be amplified later. I hate talking like a travel book, or Mr. Hughes. I've got lots of photographs, but, cameras facing the way they do, I don't seem to appear in any of them. Now, darling, tell me everything.'

'There isn't anything,' said Liza. 'Not unless you put it under a microscope. We did the same things every day, and I don't remember now what they were.'

Walter put his plate down, and she could feel his eyes on her. He said, 'All right, ducky. If you left your music in the taxi, you left it.' And he leant across and flipped her neck.

Liza thought, it isn't always my fault. Perhaps it is. She kissed him. 'We kept on playing rummy. And no one could see that this man's father is my father's son is his son, not him. And Uncle George found the front half of a cuttlefish, and sort of dined out on it for the rest of the time. Now you know what kind of a time it was.'

'Oh, I do,' said Walter, settling himself by the armchair again. 'It rises before the stricken vision. But it was fun, wasn't it?'

Liza thought, you want me to say yes. Because you were happy alone, you want me to have been. She said, 'It was heavenly,' and looked up and saw the laugh in his eyes. He knew everything. About her.

Walter put the plates in the sink and said, 'Watch and tell me if you notice anything.'

'Yes. You're washing up. I'll dry.'

'No. You go and have what they call a nice sit-down with your feet up, ducky.'

'You are a darling. But I want to.' She took the drying-up cloth. Walter caught hold of her wrist and hung it up again. She said, 'All right. Only tell me when the kettle boils,' and went back to the hearthrug, and wondered what Kate would have done.

Walter came in with the coffee, and Liza put her book down. 'Darling, are you going to see Kate?'

'I don't know. Anyway she's still away. No, I don't suppose I am. Not specially on purpose.'

'So she is,' said Liza, and, as she poured the coffee out, 'Darling, you've made it beautifully. I felt very lazy.'

Walter sat down on the hearthrug and took his shoes off. 'Ducky, tell me about yourself.'

'You know all about me.' She thought, if you've got a conscience about us, it's my fault.

'I mean the flat and the job.'

'Oh,' said Liza. That side of life rose up suddenly, a sooty brick wall; and with it a small surge of ridiculous hope. 'I don't know. I packed the flat up to-day, or very nearly. Tomorrow a van's coming to take it away.'

'Where to?'

'Wherever you take furniture to. Till I get another flat.'

'Bending my brain to cracking point,' said Walter, 'I see a few snags.' Her heart thudded. 'They've got to put it in and take it out and put it somewhere else. Ducky, why didn't you renew the lease? You could of.'

'I don't want to go on living there. It's dead. I hate a place when it's finished with.'

'Well, all the best people do,' said Walter. 'But you could have gone on with it for a few more weeks, same like you had already. And you can't find a flat in one day. At least you can, but then the mills of God get going and it's weeks.' He handed her his cup. Liza thought, I know by your voice it's no good; but I don't know. She said, 'Well I can find somewhere frightful to live meanwhile. It's my life. I can do what I want to.' She was thinking,

please, please say come and live here; *Come live with me and be my love.*
She handed over his cup, and it rattled slightly.

'Well, ducky,' said Walter, 'I suppose you can. But I was only trying to be helpful. I was just giving you the sort of advice you must have given yourself. Now can I stop and play the gramophone, please?'

'Yes, darling,' said Liza. She thought, I know two people couldn't really live in this flat. And it's funny; I'd invented a whole piece of our lives for us, with me mending his clothes and cooking and not bothering about flats or jobs till he went to his school, and, now it can't happen, I feel as if it has. And it slid through her mind, in bright, unreal pictures; mushrooms for breakfast, bus-rides to Richmond, dinner by the fire on the table she would have cleared the books from, and, afterwards, the firelight, the hearthrug, the gramophone, Walter lying with his head on her knees, saying, I love you, I don't want anything but you. Something acted by two strangers. She turned her head to the fire. She wouldn't be sorry for herself. It was her life.

'What shall we have?'

'I don't know. Something like Delius.'

'Well, the nearest we can get to Delius is Delius. What?'

'I think the *Hassan* music.' She thought, I can't bear anything too absolute or impersonal. Yes, I want to wallow in self-pity.

The gramophone hummed and clicked, and Walter lay down by the hearthrug and rolled over on his face, rubbing his bare feet against the carpet. He took her hand. The music strayed through the room, a wandering sweetness, and through it came his voice:

> *And one night or the other night*
> *Will come the Gardener in white, and gathered flowers are dead,*
> *Yasmin.*

She said, 'And what does that mean?'

Walter took his hand away. 'It means that it's lovely, and the first bit to spring to my head.' She thought, you know exactly why I said that. You know I thought you were aiming at me. It hit me, anyway.

The music stopped. The gramophone clicked again. Walter didn't move. She said, lying down beside him, 'Tell me something.'

Walter pinched her nose. 'It's my mother's birthday to-day.'

'What fun.'

'And I'm on my way with a lovely bokay.' Liza was frightened; no, it didn't mean anything. She said, 'Well, darling, you'll have to hurry.'

Walter kissed her neck. 'You are a pet. It isn't really, and she wouldn't get a bokay either. But, ducky, a hell of a lot of water has flowed under London Bridge, and I must fetch my footer togs and my Hornby signal-box. Crikey, it's a topper.'

Liza thought, I might have known. A fortnight in London, with neither of us working; no, it couldn't have happened. She said, to get it over, 'How long will you be away?'

'About ten days, I think,' said Walter, and got up and switched the gramophone off. 'Beginning to-morrow.'

Liza thought, Kate would have been angry. She would have said, you've brought me back to London, she would have said all the things I want to say and can't; no, she would have said, oh, never mind, and made you feel like a little boy running home to his parents; and you would have stayed. She heard her own voice. 'Well, it's not very nice for me.'

Walter turned round.

'I mean, I've come back to London, and you had a fortnight before the school. We had a fortnight. We arranged it at the cottage. Well, no, I know we didn't arrange it. But you knew I was coming back.' Her voice was sulky and miserable, like a disappointed child.

Walter said, after a pause, 'I think that entitles me to be very angry.'

'I'm sorry. It was silly.'

'And, my God, it entitles you to be even angrier.' She had never heard his voice quite like that; tense, and frightening. She said, desperately, 'Well, I am. But I don't have to get up and bite the furniture.' She thought, and why not? Because I'm a coward.

Walter said suddenly, 'Oh, damn and blast everything'; and he walked across the room and kicked the table-leg with his bare foot. Liza said:

'I hope you hurt your toe.'

Walter stopped rubbing his toe. He had his back to her; Liza wondered if he was trying not to laugh. Then he turned round, and she saw his face, and was very frightened indeed.

Walter knelt on the hearthrug and said, 'Listen, ducky. If you don't stop making a murderer of me, I shall—I shall resign from the murder business. Or do I mean go in for it? I don't know what I'm saying.'

Liza thought, yes, you do, and so do I. She stared at his eyes; they didn't belong to her now. They were saying, *leave me alone.* She thought, this wasn't going to happen; where are we? We must get back. She said, 'We're being very silly.'

'One of us is.' He got up and sat in the armchair. She thought, you must be very angry to sit in a chair like an ordinary person. She felt sick. 'Can I have a cigarette?'

Walter took the packet from the mantelpiece and threw it at her. It hit her arm. He dropped on his knee by her, saying, 'I'm sorry, darling, I didn't hurt you, did I?' and she wanted, more than anything in the world, to say, no, darling, of course you didn't, and oh, I hope you didn't hurt your toe. But she said, 'No,' and lit her cigarette from his lighter, and thought, I shouldn't enjoy quarrelling. Oh, darling, in a minute I'll stop and everything will be all right. You want it to be; that's all that matters.

Walter took his hand from her arm and, walking over to the bookshelves, squatted down and began to read. Liza thought, I won't speak till he does. I won't. She smoked most of her cigarette, and threw it in the fire. Then she said:

'Well, I'm going back to the country.'

'Where?' said Walter, without looking up.

Liza thought, I don't have to tell you. She said, 'To the aunt and uncle. They're going home to-morrow morning.'

Walter put the book away. 'Well, ducky, that's very sensible.' He yawned. 'Let's go to bed. I'm so tired.' And he came back to the hearthrug, and lay down with his head on her knee. 'And let's have some tea first.'

Liza thought, I can't, I can't; I was going to say no, I'm going home to-night. How can I? More than anything in the world she wanted to go to sleep next to him, to wake thinking, I am waking to you, and we shall have breakfast together. And, even more than that, she wanted now to put her hand on his hair. She clasped her hands in her lap, and thought, no, I'm still angry. I haven't said anything to show I'm not. *Very sensible*; she was very angry indeed. That was, you've chosen the best way to pass the time without me. She said:

'I think I shall go home to-night.' Dying a day sooner; and this time without knowing how much longer there was to live.

Walter sat up and said to the fire, 'All right. If you want to.'

'I *don't* want to.' That had burst out of her. She thought fast. 'Only I'm tired too, and you'll want a good night with a bed to yourself.'

'Well, it's a point,' said Walter, getting to his feet and stretching. 'For the last month I've been sharing beds with all sorts of things, none of them with less than six legs.' She thought, you're trying to get us back to normal, but you know you can't. She got up, without meeting his eyes, and went into the bedroom to dress. That was life all over; you wanted to make a good exit, and you remembered you were still in your house-coat. She dressed miserably, while Walter, out of sight in the next room, read; she heard the pages turning and saw the smoke from his cigarette.

She finished dressing and went back. Walter jumped up and put his arms round her. 'Ducky. I don't know what's happened to us.'

'Nothing has,' said Liza. 'Nothing. I'm only going home for the night instead of staying here.'

Walter flipped her neck and walked away. Liza put her house-coat in the suit-case and shut it. They stood staring at each other, with the suit-case between them.

Liza said, 'Oh, I forgot.' She opened the suit-case. 'Your shaving-brush and a tie, and odds and ends. I didn't think you'd want them stored.' She searched. 'No, not the shaving-brush. I must have packed it up.'

'Never mind, ducky. Give it to me when you unpack it up. I mean, don't give it to me. Keep it. I shall still want it.'

The evening was cancelled out; she was in his arms, saying, 'I do love you. I hope you sleep terribly well; it's only so that you will, and because of that horrid furniture van'; and believing it.

'I'll be back in ten days promp, ducky. And give me your address. I shall take my typewriter.'

Liza wrote it down. She knew his. She said, 'Well, I'll be back in about ten days. I wouldn't go if they hadn't been so keen. Aunt Vi's running a sale of work.' She was happy again.

'You lucky,' said Walter, taking her in his arms again and squeezing her very tightly. 'I went to a sale of work once.'

'Oh, darling. What happened?'

'I won the most paralysing *objet*, something like a small umbrella-holder, appleekied here and there with cherry-blossom.'

'Oh, darling. What did you do with it?'

'I threw it at my favourite lion, the one with the chip off his ear. I think it was the greatest moment of my life.'

'Precious. Put your head round.'

'Why, ducky?'

'Because I want to see how your hair grows down the back of your neck. I couldn't remember for certain. Will you get me a taxi, darling?' She thought, I am myself. I've broken away from the chain. When I get back to London, I believe everything will be all right.

❀

Liza's flat looked very bare and white and empty, with a grey toothed line where the books had been, and dark, naked windows; it reminded her of the end of term. She took the curtains from the chest of drawers and hung them over the pelmets, and went to bed between blankets. She thought, it doesn't matter if he doesn't ring up to-night; I shall know why. We are on the same side again. She woke up when it was still dark, but the street-lamp had gone out, so it would be nearly morning; and it was the end of the world; till she told herself he would to-morrow.

At twelve the furniture van squeezed itself into the street, and at half-past lumbered off, with Liza's furniture and half a crown to buy a drink for the two nice men who had told her their life-stories. Liza looked at the telephone. She thought, I don't know why you didn't ring up; you might have caught an earlier train, or rung when I was out. But I'm glad I didn't ring you up. It was worth it, in self-respect. Then she rang for a taxi and went off to Paddington, where the placid Betty, who hadn't sounded at all surprised on the telephone, was waiting in a new tweed suit which meant that it would soon be autumn.

XII

Aunt Vi was as surprised to Liza as Betty hadn't been. Liza had expected it; and she hated surprise. All the way from the station in the hired car she rehearsed a short, bright explanation, peppered with apologies, and thought about the telegram she would see on the hall table. Then, when Aunt Vi opened the door and said, '*Well!*' Liza looked past her and the dull and trivial world rose up again, and she knew how passionately she had counted on the telegram; which would have said, *sorry didn't ring up love you very much love W.*

Aunt Vi's surprise was really only a way of greeting you. Liza said, 'I hope you don't mind, Aunt Vi, but there was a muddle about flats and I shan't have anywhere to live for ten days. I mean—' she was sounding rather rude, and as if she took Aunt Vi for granted. Well, she did; relations were like that, and it was their fault. 'And I hope I'm not a nuisance arriving the day you get back and everything.'

'I'm very glad you have, dear,' said Aunt Vi. 'You must stay a long time and have a nice rest.' It was funny how relations always wanted to see you; no one else did. Liza said, as she followed her into the drawing-room, 'It's awfully sweet of you, Aunt Vi, but truly only for ten days. I have to get back then.' She felt suddenly rather hopeless. No, they couldn't stop her, she could explain about another job awaiting her, and having to arrange about a flat she had nearly taken. It was this atmosphere, where women who earned their own living were a bit queer, and if you didn't eat four huge meals a day and wear layers of clothes you were frozen and starving. Liza sat on the pale chintz sofa and had tea with Aunt Vi and Betty; Uncle George had motored off to his committee, and James and Margaret were out playing tennis. That would mean more surprise. She ate a scone, and another to save arguing, and thought, I must remember that this is only an interval, and I shall hear from Walter to-morrow. It was going to be rather a nice interval.

❁

The next morning Liza woke up in half a double bed and found, with a sudden ache, that she knew where she was; she hadn't been expecting to see the back of Walter's head. She looked at the empty pillow and turned over. *Time passes, time passes, and I lie alone,* and I am used to it now. Then she thought about the typed envelope she would see on her plate; sometimes you knew when a thing would happen. She was happy again; she would mend and alter all her clothes, and go for walks, and read. She had never told Walter about *Titus Andronicus;* she could write it to him. That was something new and exciting, almost like first being in love.

Betty brought her a cup of tea. Liza said, 'Oh, you are nice. You shouldn't.'

'It's all right,' said Betty, staring at her chin in the mirror. 'Mummy says we can't get any maids now. Only a frightful daily.' Liza had heard this yesterday. She said, 'Well, I can sort of help.'

'Oh, that's all right. You know what Mummy is. She likes work. Funny.' Betty yawned and wrapped her purple dressing-gown closer. Liza thought, Betty has a dreadful tummy and she's only twenty.

Betty yawned again, said, 'Mummy says breakfast's at half-past eight now, but it isn't really,' and drifted out. Liza wondered if she would find herself telling Betty about Walter; she didn't want to, and perhaps she could hold off for another ten days. She heard James crooning passionately from the bathroom. Perhaps he was shaving; oh, darling Walter.

Liza went in to breakfast and saw a typed envelope on her plate. The world was a lovely place, smelling of coffee and bacon. She kissed Aunt Vi, and said, 'Hullo, Uncle George. Isn't it a heavenly day?'

'Well, well, not bad,' said Uncle George, who rather owned the weather. 'But I wouldn't call it good. The glass is going down. James, I've told you before that hitting it like that upsets the mechanism.'

James went on reading the sporting page of the newspaper; it was doled out to him or Betty, whichever got down to breakfast first; Betty wanted it for the Woman's Page on the back. Liza remembered how yesterday evening Uncle George had cut some white cardboard into little rectangles, and bound them with red sticky paper, and no one had asked why, and thought, oh, darling Walter, I can write and tell you all about this silly family; I hardly told you anything. She pinched the letter; it would be pages long.

'Aren't you going to open your letter, Liza?' said Margaret, picking up her hair-slide from the floor. Margaret had dreadful trouble with her hair.

'It's not very exciting,' said Liza. 'I know what it's about.' And she managed not to till after breakfast, when she took it to the far corner of the tennis-court, where you could see no one and only faintly hear James crooning about his heart from the garage.

Darling love, said the letter, typed in Walter's very small type, with a new ribbon. (Darling love; dear darling love.) *I thought about us last night and this morning over the cigarette ends. I mean over the c.e.'s last night, before I threw them in the fire with a fine wolitary oh what a heavenly word solitary gesture.* Liza was frightened. *I what they call Faced Up.* She was very frightened indeed. *I don't know what to do, darling. If you want to stop, then we must. That sounds dreadfully abrupt. I'll start again and lead up to it if you like. But, darling, I suppose it isn't fair to say so, but I don't want to stop if you don't½ I mean.* Liza's heart rose and sang; it was all right. *I'm perfectly xertain it wasn't fair to say it, but if I put a row of /s you could still read it. Dammit, why am I being so chivalrous and Anglo)Indian? That's the worst of love, all the rules have been laid down for you.* Oh, I know, darling; that's just what I always think. *My sweet, I shall now stop talking about us, because we seem to do nothing else, and tell youhow I reached this God-forsaken outpost. I am typing this in a tinny I mean tiny it's wooden, did you know the ancients sometimes wrote wodden, and they called birds brids, summerhouse. Pause while you collect that sentence. There is a hole in the floor what a rat came out of about twenty years ago and I'm still frightened it will again. I tell myself DON't worry It May Never Happen. I wonder if the Major is tearing off our thoughts for the day and plodding round with his little basket, bless him.*

Liza had a sudden wave of the Past. But it was the Past for him too; the oyster-shells, the sound of the lawnmower, the smell of the lavender; the same rush of memory to the senses. She went on reading; four pages, and single spacing. Oh, darling Walter, you must love me if you love writing to me; as if I could want us to stop.

That afternoon Liza sat in her bedroom by the window and wrote to Walter. It was cold, but she didn't like to light the gas-fire because it wasn't hers. She put on her camelhair coat and sat for a minute before she could decide how to begin. Then she wrote, *Darling love.* She sat and thought again. *I did love getting your letter, and you type beautifully. I do know what you mean about Us. I—*

Liza stopped again. Then she wrote: *I think it will be better if we never see each other again.*

Liza sat and stared at these terrible words as a walker gazes down a cliff he has no intention of falling over. Then she tore the sheet off, and, folding it very small, put a match to it and dropped it in the grate. When finally it had burnt away she crumbled the ash to a black powder and went back to the letter.

Darling love, thank you for your lovely letter, and you type beautifully. Darling, I do love you. Don't think of how silly I was, because we are so happy together. Perhaps that wasn't definite enough. *I mean, you know I don't want us to stop. I've always told you I Went Into This knowing all the possible consequences, and so far they've been lovely.* That was rather good; sort of detached and independent, and almost selfish. Now she would go on to impersonalities, and back to Us later, as Walter had. *I must tell you about the furniture van. No, first about this house, which is grey, all the village is grey, but it is up the exclusive end with the vicarage and the church and one other house and then fields. I'd forgotten how nice the garden is; it has a wall covered with plums and, darling, there is a tank in the greenhouse with frogs.* She wrote on until James shouted 'Teeea!' up the stairs. Well, she would wash up the tea-things and help with the dinner; only Aunt Vi really did like housework.

Liza went down to tea feeling as if she had done a day's work at the office. Lovely; and soon it would be autumn, and in nine days she would be back in London. She sat under the family cross-talk, planning her new clothes; no, first the clothes she would wear in nine days' time. She would make a skirt to wear with the jacket of her grey flannel suit. She sat there, eating another rock-cake to save arguing, and thought about striped flannel, grey and dusty pink with a thin navy blue line, and was completely happy.

Aunt Vi's sale of work was held every year at about the same time as the Harvest Festival, and for the same main reasons. The village collected its fruit and vegetables and sold them to itself at more than you would pay in the shops, and every one seemed to like it. Liza worked it out as the equivalent of a house-to-house collection, but more fun. Besides, it wasn't only a sale of what the poster on the vicarage garden wall called Produce; there were Confectionery, Grocery, and Etc. Liza was to help at the needlework stall, and her conscience had driven her to line a padded tea-cosy. The sale began at two-thirty, and Liza put on her grey flannel suit, thinking, it was cleaned a fortnight ago and I've hardly worn it, but it must look like new in three days' time; so she would get some aviation spirit and do it herself. She arrived at the hall feeling quite extraordinarily nervous, as if Mr. Hollis was just going to dictate a lot of shorthand, but telling herself that things were never so bad as you expected, and got behind her allotted table, which was spread with table-runners and mats, little blue bootees, lace bonnets and cretonne aprons; all, as Aunt Vi had said, with the prices clearly marked. A pig-faced woman held a pair of bootees very close to her eyes, put them down, moved a few yards off, came back and handed them to Liza. 'How much, miss?'

The label said either one and sixpence or nine and a penny. Liza said 'One and six,' and felt dreadfully brisk. The woman paid and trotted off.

Sales of work weren't frightening at all. Liza sold a padded coat-hanger and a set of hand-painted mats; at least the woman buying them said, 'Are they reely hand-painted, miss?' and Liza said, 'Oh, yes, that's what sort of makes them. Aren't they fun?' Well, they could hardly be machine-painted. She thought, I wouldn't mind working in a shop, one of those small exclusive ones that go bust in a year. There was the vicar; she had missed his speech. This was a lovely world, and she would write it all down to Walter to-night. The vicar's wife was raffling an iced cake and a cushion; Liza took a ticket, but won nothing. That was something else to tell Walter. It was lovely not winning a raffle, when Walter had won an *objet*.

Betty was at the grocery stall. Liza watched her, when the needlework business went suddenly slack, and wondered what Betty wanted from life. She looked quite different this afternoon; her eyes shone, and her honey-coloured face had some pink in it; she was really pretty. Poor Betty, she hated living at home, she hated her mother and father just because they were her parents, and treated her like a child pretending to be grown up; and so she couldn't grow up, and knew it. Liza watched Betty weighing a pound of dried apricots and counting out the change. Poor, pathetic humanity, playing at being important.

A woman came up to Liza's stall. 'Please, miss, could you tell me who Mrs. Shaw is?'

Mrs. Shaw was Aunt Vi. Liza said, 'Why, yes. Over there, with the dark hair and the red dress.'

'Oh, thank you, miss,' said the woman. 'It is Mrs. Shaw who's running this, isn't it?'

'Why, yes,' said Liza proudly; and when the woman had gone, she thought, I'm proud of being Aunt Vi's niece. Poor, pathetic me.

The sale dragged on. Liza's stall wore down to a hard core of table-runners no one would ever buy. She was bored. She was tired. She stared at the silly women eddying round all the other stalls, willing them to come and buy a table-runner. No one did. She thought, watching the clock, this is like the office again. Only half-past four. Some one brought her a cup of tea. Twenty-five to five; that was better, the sale would be over at five. Ten to five. A small woman picked up a table-runner and said timidly, 'Do you think this would make a nice present, miss?'

'Oh, a lovely present,' said Liza. 'It's awfully pretty, don't you think? I mean, I always think ships look awfully nice.'

'Not bad. Do you think it would look all right on a sideboard, miss?'

Liza was important. She was deciding some one's life. Well, it would look as all right as whatever else would get put on the sideboard if that didn't. And anyway the woman wanted to buy it. She said, 'Oh, I think it would look lovely.'

So the woman paid four shillings, and Liza counted out ninepence change, and thought, looking in the notepaper box, I've made all that money to help mend the roof of a tin hall. I've done some good in the world.

It was five o'clock. Betty came up and said, 'We've got to clear things away.' Liza thought, all right, just because you had a bigger stall you needn't boss me. Then Aunt Vi came up and said, 'Liza dear, do come and help me here for a minute, will you?' and Liza was important again.

At half-past six it was all over, and a Miss Stevens had given her a glass of the nicest sherry she had ever tasted. Liza walked out of the hall, carrying a giant marrow, and met James with the car. He reddened and said eagerly, holding the door open, 'Hop in.'

'It's awfully sweet of you, James,' said Liza graciously, 'but I would really rather walk, if you don't mind.'

'Well, let me take that stupendous marrow.'

Liza handed it over. 'It's quite tame.' James gave a snort of delight. It was awfully easy to make him laugh; she had an idea he had fallen for her. She gave him her best smile and walked away.

It was a lovely evening; not so much the beginning of autumn as the end of summer. The horse-chestnuts were still in leaf, but the gravel road was strewn with glossy red conkers and green prickly shells. A cow mooed a long way off. The light was beginning to fade. Walter had once said, 'Light thickens, and I don't think Shakespeare ever hit a better word.' And she would see Walter in three days. She had done a day's work at the office, and after supper the light would have thickened to a cold dusk, and she would put on her camelhair coat and go for a walk in the big field past the church; and go to bed early, and write to Walter. He had written to her five times in seven days; and she had lived another week away from him, and had been happy. That was somehow wrong; but you could never tell with, happiness.

Liza took a basin into the yard, and tipped in the aviation spirit and swished the grey flannel jacket round. She had enough to do the skirt as well; she hadn't made the striped skirt, but a whole suit looked smarter.

James had smelt the petrol. She might have guessed. He appeared through the door which led to the garage and sat down on a slatted wooden box; and Liza felt dreadfully silly, being watched like that.

'Aviation, isn't it?' said James.

'Yes,' said Liza, adding, to spread the subject out, 'That's right. Aviation.' She never knew what to say to James when they were alone.

'Thought so,' said James. 'Ordinary petrol's too oily. Aviation's more volatile.'

'Yes, isn't it?' She wrung the coat out and saw that the petrol was still as clear as water; and probably the smell would never come out of the suit. She had wasted five and threepence. And she would have to do the skirt as well, because James was still watching, with his hands on his knees, and his mouth half open with the effort of thinking of something to say. Poor James, she would help him if she could; but all she could think of was, 'Are you looking forward to going back to school?' That was what aunts asked you.

'Mmmm,' said James. 'It's not bad.' He looked at his finger-nails, chronically rimmed with something off cars, and crooned softly.

Liza thought, oh, I wonder what you're really like; what you want in the world, what you think you've been born for. I suppose cars. But you can't be born for things like cars. But people are funny.

James said suddenly, lifting his chin to the sky, 'It might—' he cleared his throat. 'It might rain.'

Liza stared up at the clouds. 'Yes, it does look like it.' They brought their faces down, by some telepathic agreement, at the same moment. James said, even more suddenly:

'You never realize it's not raining till it is.'

'Oh, but that's exactly what *I* always think,' said Liza. James was a real person. He had thoughts. She must follow the discovery up; she was wondering exactly how when there was a sharp crack. One of the slats had gone. She gave the polite half-laugh this called for, and James said, shifting slightly, 'Sounds as if it's broken.' There was another crack. He stood up. There was nowhere else to sit. He turned towards the door, and stopped to say:

'Do you like blackberries?'

'I adore them.'

'Well, if you go to the left when you get out of the front gate, and down the first lane past the shoemender's, there are some pretty good ones. About three hundred yards along. Only not the side facing the lane, because of the dust You try the field behind.' And, crooning loudly, he disappeared.

Liza hung her skirt on the line; yes, definitely James was in love, or what went for it when you were seventeen. And she thought, I could tell Walter in my letter to-day; not make it definitely James, just say some one. I suppose I *ought* to make him jealous. It's so cheap, and so going back on where we've got to. But then sex relations *are* cheap; the rules are. Dishonesty is honesty. Oh, why can't we be ourselves?

Liza went in to lay lunch, thinking, we *are* ourselves, and that's the trouble. And I know what's the matter with us. Nothing outside us is keeping us from marriage, and we try to behave as if it is. We think it's fun to be illicit, at least he does; and that's terribly second-hand, Romeo and Juliet without the stars. No, that's not quite fair to him; *he* takes our relationship at the value we first gave it; I've imagined it to be what it isn't. But what I mean is that we can't get any further like this; nothing in his mind will change him, and nothing outside it keeps us apart. That is, nothing outside *him*; here am I, putting the plates round a table in a dull house I never wanted to be in, hundreds of miles from Walter and longing to be near him. I suppose if I could make him long to be near me, it would be all right.

❀

Only one more day. Liza came back from Swindon, where she had had her hair set not very well and bought some stockings and a blue jersey which had cost too much, and put her parcels on the hall table while she looked at her face in the glass. Her skin was pink and white from the rain, and her hair, when she untied the scarf, looked much better; and she hadn't got that spot on her chin after all. There was such a thing as perfect happiness. She stood, living it, and then went into the drawing-room; and, from the way Uncle George and Betty turned towards her, saw that something had happened.

Uncle George said, 'Your aunt's had to go away. Your Uncle Bernard is very ill.'

'Dying,' said Margaret, and hitched desperately at her stockings. Margaret had dreadful trouble with her stockings.

'Don't be a ghoul, Margaret,' said Betty. 'You don't know he's dying.'

'Well, he *is*,' said James, who usually took the side Betty didn't; 'the man's a goner.'

'Be quiet, all of you,' said Uncle George. Liza decided they had been at it all the afternoon. She said, 'Oh, poor Uncle Bernard,' and escaped to her room. Uncle Bernard was a dim figure, married to another aunt and living in Herefordshire; he had been something in a bank till he bought a small farm, which he hadn't liked, and had sold a year later when he went to live in the next village. He was a very dim figure indeed, and had always been rather a joke. But now he was dying. Liza thought, I'm dreadfully sorry for any one who dies; that's all. I wonder why relations have to gather round and watch you die; it's horrible; but I think Aunt Vi enjoys it.

Liza sat down at the dressing-table. She wouldn't comb her hair out all day, it would call for terrible strength of mind, but it was worth it for to-morrow. Oh, poor Uncle Bernard; the sun would rise to-morrow, and the next day, and one day he wouldn't see it, and the sun would rise just the same, and set at night. She thought, I hate people dying. *There but for the grace of God;* it's a kind of cowardice, and selfishness.

Betty put her head round the door. 'I say. Liza.'

Liza was rather frightened. Death, and the outside world.

Betty shut the door and sat on the bed. 'Isn't everything a bore?'

'I know. Have a cigarette.' Liza had grown to like Betty very much; she had told her about Walter, but found that whenever she mentioned him Betty had to tell her about Edward, whom Betty had met in Frankfurt last winter and had a short and, it seemed, terribly passionate affair with, and this had finally decided Liza that every one had had an affair with some one, if you only knew.

Betty lit her cigarette. 'Daddy's been being a frightful nuisance. Mummy began to fuss about who would mend all the school clothes for next week, and Daddy fussed back to stop her fussing and said, well, Liza's here, isn't she?' Betty blew out a cloud of smoke and gazed across the room at the mirror, fiddling with her curls.

Liza was trapped. She said, 'Why yes, of course. I mean—'

'Oh, it's all right,' said Betty. 'You needn't. I'll manage. Margaret can mend her own blasted clothes. I'll mess us along somehow.' She rolled up a back curl and tucked her chin in. Before long it would be a double chin. Liza told herself that Betty liked being important; but it was no good. She said, 'No, Betty. I will stay.'

'*No,*' said Betty, in her bossy voice. 'I just thought I'd tell you, that's all. I must fly.' Liza watched her along the passage, with her knock-kneed, bus-catching run, and shut the door. She looked round the room: at the new stockings in their cellophane, the new jersey on the chair, the picture over the mantelpiece, Hope despairing on an empty world. She thought, no, it's no good; it's only selfishness again, or cowardice, but I shall have to stay; oh, darling, and we were going to the Zoo, and Southend. And the next four days, which would never happen, slid through her mind and took their place among the other dreams.

❦

At eight the telephone rang. Liza said, 'It's my trunk call,' and dropped her fruit-knife. James picked it up, saying gruffly, 'Pears go brown when you leave them. I'll put a plate over it.'

'Silly,' said Margaret, 'that won't make any difference.' Liza left them to their quarrels and ran to the drawing-room; and at Walter's 'Hullo?' she felt sick. 'Hullo, darling.'

'Hullo, ducky. What a nice surprise.'

'It isn't. It's a horrid surprise. Something awful's happened.'

'Don't frighten me,' said Walter. 'You aren't dead, are you?'

'No, I'm all right'; she thought, he would mind terribly if I was.

'Not even ill?'

'Not even ill. It's only that I can't come to London tomorrow.' It was rather an anti-climax.

'What a pity, darling,' said Walter. He didn't sound very disappointed. But then he never did. She said, 'Isn't it awful?'

'Cheer up, ducky. Not as bad as all that.'

'I think it is.' He was doing the cheering up; that was all wrong. 'Oh, darling, I am *angry*. I've got to stay and mend James's clothes and Margaret's and wash up, and—oh, I hate everything.'

'Now, ducky. Take a grip on things. Backbone, not wishbone. Aren't I maddening? Darling, I *am* sorry, frightfully. But it's not the end of the world.'

Liza thought, you haven't even asked why I'm staying. She said, 'No, I know it isn't. But it's annoying. And it's because some uncle's dying, and Aunt Vi's gone to see him die.'

'Oh, I am sorry.'

'Well, he's not even an uncle really. He's married to an aunt.'

'Oh, well,' said Walter, 'I suppose that makes it all right for him.'

'I'm sorry, darling. I know I sound heartless. But I do feel so miserable.'

'Now, ducky. Take a—no, I've said that bit. Look for the silver lining, and when you do come up I shall be a prep. schoolmaster and even funnier. And we'll have a lovely time, and go to Southend on a Sunday, also even funnier. I say, can you hear me?'

'Yes, darling. Why?'

'Only because it's a trunk call, and you have to say that at least once.'

'Well, can you hear me?'

'Yes, ducky. Isn't nature wonderful?'

There was a silence. Then Walter said, 'Well, tell me something.'

'There isn't anything.' She sounded dreadfully sulky. 'I went to Swindon to-day.'

'I say, did you really? Isn't it fun? Give me your impressions, will you? Just something we can tell our readers.'

'It was grey and pink.' She sounded even more miserable; and he would know she was trying to be cheerful, which made it worse. 'And I saw a train.'

'Now, I want that confirmed,' said Walter. 'Did you say a *train*?' The pips went. 'Coo, I say, listen to them. I'll ring off.'

'No, don't,' said Liza. And there was another silence. She said, 'Darling, I do love you.'

'Bless you. I love you.'

'I love you more than ever.'

'Do you now?' His voice had changed. Liza said, 'Is the room full of people?'

'Silting up. Well, darling, I'll write and so must you. Thank you for yours of yesterday's date. I think and so we say farewell, don't you?'

'Yes,' said Liza. 'Good-bye, darling.'

'Good-bye, darling.' The receiver clicked and rattled, and she rang off. She sat there, thinking, I was going to be so different. I was going to make him say, please, please come up, never mind about anything; and I would have answered, no, darling, I must stay here. I love you but that doesn't make me go against my conscience; and cheer up, I'll see you soon; and he wouldn't have cheered up till I said, I love you.

There was a scuffle outside, and James and Margaret burst in, fighting. Margaret screamed, and sank on the sofa, giggling. Liza smiled palely; it quite hurt. She thought, James has forgotten about my pear. I'm alone in the world.

'I say, everybody!' said Margaret. Uncle George and Betty had come in, and the drawing-room seemed very hot and bright and full. 'I say! Let's play rummy!'

'We've got to wash up,' said Betty. 'At least, I have.'

'Oh, I will,' said Liza.

'Oh, not this *minute*,' said Margaret, tugging at her stockings. 'Daddy! Let's play rummy.'

'Well, well,' said Uncle George, folding the local evening paper with his usual hideous precision, 'I wouldn't mind a little game, now you mention it.'

James dived at the wireless. Margaret unflapped the card-table. A wave of thrumming sound broke over the room, and James drew a deep breath, shut his eyes and crooned as he had never crooned before:

> *Fish gotta swim—and—birds gotta fly—*
> *I gotta love—that—man till I die—*
> *Can't—help—*
> *Loving that ma-an of mi-ine.*

Liza clutched the sofa-arm.

'Bet!' cried James. 'Don't let's have the pink cards. They stick.'

'The which cards?' Betty called back.

'Turn that thing down,' boomed Uncle George. Betty turned the knob, and the music sank into the background. Liza listened; that was her world, and perhaps in Lincolnshire, in a room crowded with beautiful women, Walter was listening too.

'They're not *pink* cards, they're *red* cards,' said Betty.

'They're not, they're pink,' said Margaret.

'They're not,' said Uncle George. 'They're a red and white pattern which *looks* pink.'

Liza thought, it's a dream. She pulled her chair up to a corner of the card-table. There was a jag in the green baize; she stared at it; it was something real. Why should she be so miserable? What had she expected? Hadn't she said what she had to say, hadn't he answered as she had known he would?

'Don't you like rummy, Liza?' said Margaret.

'I love it,' said Liza thinly.

'Would you like one of Father's very special cigarettes?' said James. Uncle George, flipping the cards round, shot an unhappy glance at the box. Three left. Betty frowned at James.

'No, truly,' said Liza. 'I don't want one.'

'Go on,' said James. 'Father doesn't mind, do you, Father?'

'Eh?' said Uncle George. 'No, help yourself.'

Either way the complications were enormous. But these were very special Turkish cigarettes, fat, smooth, fragrant. Liza took one.

'Well, well, *well!*' said Uncle George to the hand he had dealt himself. 'Gosh!' said Margaret to hers. Liza picked up her cards. Quite a lot of them matched, or joined together, or nearly. What did a few more days matter? The fire crackled behind her. Soon it would be autumn. Autumn was fun. Rummy was sort of fun, too; sort of cosy. It was strange what one Turkish cigarette could do for you.

Poor Uncle Bernard died obediently, and Aunt Vi stayed for the funeral; and Liza scored a mild triumph in turning James's shirt-cuffs. It annoyed her that James would now put his shirts on and think, Liza turned my cuffs; getting out of them a devotion she had never put in. James's gruff face, reddening when she spoke to him, haunted her. She went to some lengths not to speak to him. Every one in the house was quite extraordinarily busy; Margaret was told she must mend her own clothes, and there was a dreadful moral compulsion not to have any time to yourself.

'Only one more day,' said James, with a sigh which blew an envelope off the mantelpiece.

The day after to-morrow Liza would see Walter. She looked at the clock. Ten-past three. In fifty-two hours. The Zoo and Southend had given place to theatres, long evenings in Walter's flat, and football matches where every one cheered a brilliant bit of refereeing by Walter, and Liza, standing on the touchline or wherever you stood, took the credit with her usual charm. The emerald ring was a sapphire now, because it went better with her eyes and a new wine-coloured suit. Among these bright pictures was a less definite one to be filled in later; of a frightfully important job which left her not much time for Walter, and yet a lot. The pictures went as far as Christmas, and blazed up into an everlasting splendour. For at Christmas they would be married. They could be married sooner, but then she would be a prep. schoolmaster's wife, and though she had tried hard, she couldn't make a picture of that. Liza threaded her needle and thought of Christmas; the Chelsea Town Hall register office; and firelight in an hotel bedroom, playing on a wealth of old oak, with carol-singers outside while they dressed for dinner.

The telephone bell was in the hall, and the telephone behind Liza's chair. The bell rang, and Liza turned to answer it; her heart had jumped, only because it did now whenever a telephone rang anywhere.

'It won't be for me,' said Margaret. 'Whoever said it would?' said James. 'Telephone!' Uncle George shouted from the fruit-trees. Betty was running downstairs. Dear, funny family. It was a trunk call.

'Hullo?' said the only voice in the world.

'Why, darling,' said Liza, thinking, it's only a quarter-past three. 'Just a minute.' She put her hand over the mouthpiece. 'I say, every one, would you mind? This line is terrible.'

'We won't make a sound,' said Margaret. But James pushed her out. Darling James.

'Sorry, darling,' she said to the telephone. 'The room was seething. Darling, why are you being so extravagant?'

'I had a big lunch,' said Walter. 'Everything is lovely, and in about an hour it will be ghastly. Hullo, ducky. How are you? Guess what.'

'Darling, I can't. I know it's something dreadful.'

'No, it's not, ducky. It's only about the school. I went there to-day, and wodger think?'

Liza thought, he isn't going there after all; and I don't know if I'm glad. She said, 'I don't think anything, darling. I mean, tell me quickly.'

'Well,' said Walter, 'I'm going to have to sleep there. I've got an attic with green casement cloth curtains and a gas-ring, but what though?'

'What though what?' said Liza, clutching at something she could say.

'What though nothing, ducky. Just what though. I was being Elizabethan. Darling—'

'Yes?'

'I don't know. I just wanted to tell you. Oh, damn.'

Liza thought, I mustn't make him a murderer. That's all that matters. She said quickly, 'Never mind, darling. I expect it will be fun. Why so suddenly, though?'

'Well, they haven't got a quorum. Some one has to put the little perishers to bed, or teach them to make bead purses after supper, or something. I don't absolutely have to, ducky. But that which is not worth doing is worth doing well, dammit. And they want some one to play the hymns. I think I'd be rather good at hymns.'

'I've never heard you play the piano.'

'I can't really. But, ducky, that doesn't mean I mayn't play it if you've never heard me, does it?'

'No,' said Liza. She felt very angry.

'Sorry, ducky.'

'It's all right, I'm sorry.'

'We're a sorry lot,' said Walter. 'But, ducky, it will be sort of atmosphere. I shall write a powerful novel and make cocoa on the gas-ring. Listen to all those pips. I mean, I shall write the powerful novel in about six years' time, and the cocoa will be the atmosphere.'

Behind his voice Liza could hear music, the faint, tinny waves of an orchestra. She said, 'You sound very cheerful. Where are you?'

'In Robert's flat. We had a party. I'm in the hall. Can you hear the gramophone? It's deafening?'

'It's what?' said Liza. 'Oh, deafening. I thought you said who it was by.' She was being dreadfully dull.

'No, it's not by deafening, though it's a bit like his earlier vein. It's the Seventh. Ducky, are you terribly unhappy?'

'No, darling.'

'But you sound it.'

'I can't help my voice.'

'Well, there's probably a nice platitudinous answer to that, but I can't think of it. Ducky, I can't *help* it. And we'll have lots of fun. I'll get a Saturday night off about once a month.'

'Once a month,' said Liza.

'Darling,' said Walter. 'If I could gnash my teeth I would.'

Liza felt frightened. 'I'm sorry, darling. I didn't mean to sound like that. Truly.'

'Sorry, ducky. Everything is all right, isn't it? We can't help the forces of circumstances. In fact, I think they're rather fun. We haven't had enough of them, really.'

So he knew about that too. Yes, they were rather fun; she and Walter were star-crossed at last. She said, 'I know, darling. I think so too. I do, really.'

'Precious.' The faint, tinny waves swelled, and Walter's voice went far away. 'All right, you old Scotchman. I'm paying.' The music died down again. 'Ducky, I must get. We're going to a flick. When shall I see you? I suppose even this place has a half-term. We'll have a long week-end in the nicest pub in the whole of England. You shall choose. Would that be nice?'

'Oh, darling. It would be heavenly.' Already her wine-coloured suit was the smartest in the hotel dining-room; already the door swung to let in Mrs. Croft, Kate and Maurice, James, the vicar, Miss Stevens who had given her the sherry. 'Darling, wouldn't it be fun? How long are half-term week-ends?'

'At least four days. Look, ducky, I must ring off. Good-bye, darling.'

'Good-bye, darling.' She rang off.

Margaret came in with a pile of blue blouses, stiffly laundered. 'Miss Heather got in an awful bait because she couldn't read some of our names. She said we must all use Cash's.' And she unrolled a hank of name-tapes and looked wistfully at Liza.

'I must just post a letter,' said Liza, and ran up to her room. It was true, her to-day's letter to Walter lay on the window-sill; a happy letter, full of this time the day after to-morrow.

Oh, *Walter*. She would post it. Serve him right.

This resolution carried her out of the house and as far as the front gate; and then she stopped, and walked on very fast.

First, the facts as they were. Walter was to be shut away in Regent's Park, where there might be a pretty matron or a Headmaster's daughter; but it was funny, Walter didn't run after other women; as far as any one could know about any one else she knew he had been faithful to her from the first day they met. She didn't even have to worry about Kate. Darling Walter.

Well, thought Liza, and here am I living in a comfortable house for nothing, and when James and Margaret go there won't be much work. I can go for walks and read and sew, and make my face and my figure different and beautiful, and alter all my clothes and make new ones, and have the money to buy a lot more. I would *ask* Aunt Vi if I could pay so much a week. But I know they wouldn't let me.

And then, at the half-term week-end, I shall burst upon Walter; all different and beautiful, with new clothes; and independent. I *am* independent here; I like going for walks alone, and being alone all the time. I shall let my independence grow into me.

Then Liza thought about London; one Saturday a month, a strange and lonely fiat, a telephone that didn't ring more often than it did; letters on the mat, or not. And she would have to get a job, to be another secretary; and she'd grown out of that, after such a summer. It took time to grow out of wanting to be a slave just so that you could enjoy your evenings; but she had done it.

Then she thought, Walter and I could have gone on like this for ever. It *needed* something sudden; it's Fate.

Liza reached the vicarage wall. And if it was too awful, she could always go back to London any time. And, of course, after the half-term week-end she would. Because Walter would say, ducky, I can't be without you even till Christmas; let's get married this minute. And she would say—no, she wouldn't say, yes, let's, she would say, well, darling, I've got to fix up about some clothes, and if we did get married now where would I sleep? and Walter, putting his head back on her lap—well, they would have to be in their bedroom, but there would be a fire—would say, all right, darling, I can just about hang on, but if you come up to London with me in the car and live in my flat I'll be round every evening, and get all the week-ends off; and she would say, well, darling, I must go back and pack, but I'll come up by train to-morrow, and that will be just as good, won't it; and he would say, well, nearly. And there couldn't very well be a gramophone in a hotel bedroom, but she had heard it wandering through their voices; the *Hassan* music; all the sweetness in the world, all for her, for ever.

Liza was standing by the letter-box in the vicarage wall. She had been standing there for some time. Two little boys with a soap-box on wheels approached and stood beside her.

Liza held the letter up and turned it over. No, she couldn't post it now. It was petty to want to hurt Walter. Besides, he might think when he read it, I've been a murderer.

Liza had put the letter in the slit, but she was still holding it. The little boys pressed closer. It would be the most exciting thing that had ever happened to them.

So Liza dropped it in and went home. It didn't matter; she had posted it before he rang up; yes, and she would write another this evening and use this first happy letter to her advantage; saying, *Darling love, in case the last letter made you a murderer, here is another which won't; I don't want to cancel it because I was all excited about seeing you, but now I'm all excited about staying here for a bit and reading and sort of taking in the autumn. Not sulking, darling, but recognizing the forces of circumstances, like what you said, and taking time by the fetlock, and doing all the other philosophical things you and I know to be right.* They were on the same side again.

When Liza got back to the drawing-room, Margaret was reading the paper, with a blouse on her knees. When she saw Liza she blushed and dropped the paper, and the blouse. Liza was a prefect taking prep.; she took another blouse from the pile.

'Oo, I say,' said Margaret. 'Thanks awfully.'

And now, thought Liza, I shall throw myself into life. Other people's lives. That's how you get poise, and independence. She said, cutting off a name-tape:

'Do you like being at school?'

'It's all right,' said Margaret defensively.

'How much free time do they give you?'

Margaret warmed up. 'An hour after tea. Only half an hour in the summer, though. But we have tea half an hour later then, you see.'

'I see,' said Liza. *O love! O fire! once he drew With one long kiss my whole soul through My lips as sunlight drinketh dew.* And *I will possess him, or will die.* But once, in the Past, she had possessed him, had opened her eyes to him every morning, had closed them on him every night.

'But in the *winter* we have tea half an hour earlier. At half-past four. In the summer, you see, games go on longer because it's light and we have it at five.'

We, that did nothing study but the way To love each other, with which thoughts the day Rose with delight to us and with them set, Must learn the hateful art, how to forget. No, no. The beautiful, the inevitable art how to be certain of each other, to take for granted what has been the most important part of our relationship, make it the least important and go on, not stay as we are now with me afraid to go forward or I may lose you.

'Of course after supper doesn't count as free time.'

'No,' said Liza. 'We used to have darning after supper. It seems like every night now, but it can't have been.'

'Oh, so do we,' said Margaret. 'But only on Mondays and Thursdays. Tuesday and Friday are reading, Wednesday is hobbies, Saturday is the dance and Sunday is Sunday.'

'Yes,' said Liza. 'I think so did we.' Girls' schools were lovely; all the same. Oh, darling Walter, with his little perishers; clever Walter, who was going to play the hymns. 'What's your hobby, Margaret?'

'Leatherwork. Three of us share a puncher. But this term I *think* one of them is swopping to lettering, you know, Herrick's poems on really good drawing-paper. Mainly because she's keen on Indian ink. Then there'll be only Cynthia and me using the puncher. We shall do blotters. It will be jolly fine. Last term—'

Liza thought, I've struck what Walter would call a rich vein of anecdote. She listened; she didn't want to think about anything. A shadow had fallen, a truth. *The hateful art, how to forget.* Last summer, three nights away from Walter was a separation; now she had spent six weeks without him and could face another six weeks.

That was what was so dreadful; being able to face it. It was like not minding any more after some one had died.

XIII

Liza put four telephone directories on the chair and sat down. Not being London directories, they raised her only two inches, not enough for a typewriter as high as an old-fashioned taxi. But after a month of Wednesday and Friday mornings she was getting used to it. She rolled a foolscap sheet into the typewriter and, as she was alone, sat back and yawned.

The Wiltshire and Dorset Committee for the Improvement of Agricultural Conditions and Output had a small room over a small outfitter's shop in a small town five miles from Uncle George's village. Downstairs, porridge-coloured woollen pants and striped pyjamas deadened your voice; up here, through the door at the back of the shop, it was bare and brown, and the gas-fire whistled to the empty air. There were two posters on the walls, one a very yellow cornfield, one the face of a carthorse, taken from the ground so that it was all teeth and nostrils; and some curling notices in pale mauve type with a lot of mistakes and no space between the full stop and the next sentence; but they had been typed a long time ago by some one else.

Liza moved her chair to the fire. She had come here at the end of September to type for two mornings a week, unpaid; and she was practically a married woman whose husband was at a prep. school, and that would give her the necessary poise for dealing with all the tweed-suited young men, as militantly handsome as the lime juice advertisements, who would crowd Uncle George's office to improve the agriculture of Wiltshire and Dorset.

Liza suddenly scraped her chair back to the table and grabbed a sheet of handwriting. She had hardly typed *Hiefers* when the door opened on two elderly men. They were both short and thick, and they both wore plus-fours and expressions of set chivalry, as if they had stopped half-way through a dirty story; but one was clean-shaven and the other had a white convex moustache, edged with brown. This was Mr. Duffey, the honorary secretary. His companion was Mr. Wyatt, whom the alphabet had doomed to the bottom of the list, and no one took any notice of him.

Mr. Duffey ambled across and laid what looked like a huge and complicated hotel bill by Liza's typewriter. Liza had turned *Hiefers* down into the works of the typewriter, but she put her arm across the paper to make sure.

'Well, Miss Brett,' said Mr. Duffey, 'what do you think of us here, eh? Not like London! Ha!' He must have said this every morning Liza had been here; eight, no, nine times.

'I think it's very nice,' said Liza, blushing slightly.

'Ha!' said Mr. Duffey. It was not so much a laugh as a questing bark, showing that Mr. Duffey had taken an idea in or given one out. 'Well, well, we're very quiet down here. But here's something to give you a headache. Ha! Think you can manage it?'

Liza leant sideways over the bill. 'I think I can, Mr. Duffey. Shall I do four copies?'

Mr. Duffey pressed his hands on the table edge. 'We want six.' It was one of his Moments; he paused. 'Think you can manage six? Ha?'

'I think I can,' said Liza, her heart sinking.

'Ha!' said Mr. Duffey, stepping back and feeling in his pocket for his pipe. 'That's the stuff. And look here, Miss Brett, don't you work too hard. We'll be leaving you alone for the morning.' He struck a match and sucked at his pipe. 'Ha! But don't you stay a minute after one o'clock.'

'Oh, thank you, Mr. Duffey,' said Liza, who so far hadn't gone later than twenty to. 'Thank you very much.' That meant half-past twelve this morning; plenty of time to buy the handkerchiefs and the double satin ribbon before the shops shut.

'Ha!' said Mr. Duffey, sucking at his pipe again. 'Well, good morning, Miss Brett.'

'Good morning, Miss Brett,' said poor Mr. Wyatt from the door.

'Good morning,' said Liza in one voice, and '*Good* morning,' in another, for Mr. Wyatt. The door shut. When she had watched them down the street, Liza went back to the fire. Mr. Duffey's typing, two lots of three copies, would take an hour; the rest she could do any time. She would sit and think. She lit a cigarette.

It was only three days to Saturday; the Day, November the sixth. It had been worth six weeks. Six weeks achieved, telescoped and put behind her. Liza looked back at them. They had been nice, they had won their itselfness, which was made up of pale chintz, Aunt Vi's scones, the grandfather clock in the hall, *Dombey and Son,* and walks over the dead leaves, and sometimes tea at the vicarage, or at other houses; and at the vicarage, and the other houses, and at the one dance, Liza had found herself wondering, I might be going to meet him; and he wasn't Walter, he was never any one, but he waited in the Future; and she would meet one man, and another, and think, it might be you; and it isn't you. That was because, living on the morning's post, and dreams of a week-end, it would be surprising if she hadn't thought like that.

But the six weeks had gone. This time in three days she would have met Walter outside Swindon station, and they would be driving away to have lunch somewhere, and then on through the smoky winter afternoon to the hotel they had chosen from the A.A. book; it had three stars and dinner was 5s. 6d., and a double room, without breakfast, 15s., and it was in a village with a pop. of 579; a very good hotel in a very small village with, on Uncle George's map, a slope of 500 feet curving round behind it and a thin blue river trickling across the main street.

Liza listened carefully, and, pulling the chair back from the fire, mounted its fraying cane seat. In this distorting mirror she was a little fatter; well, she knew she was, because Uncle George's family ate so much that any one would be. But she wasn't fat. And if she had got thinner Walter might have thought she had missed him. Liza jumped off the chair and pulled it over to the typewriter, and began typing very fast, with a lot of jerks at the handle by the roller. She took the paper back to the fire.

> Hiefers
> Grey suit

Grey swagger coat with pink overcheck
Pink jersey
Blue jersey

and down the page, ending with

Buy tooth paste
Black dinner-dress, just in case (remember hem at back)
N. Nickleby, Vol. I

Liza saw the clock. She folded the paper away in her handbag and sat down to Mr. Duffey's Assessment of Acreage and Percentage (in Tons) of Production. You had to judge what space to leave between each column, and then get one figure under the other by pushing the typewriter along, as there was no tabulator; in the acreage columns the commas between the thousands had to match, in the percentage columns the decimal places; and to make a decimal you had to turn the full stop up to just the right height. Mr. Duffey was very keen on all this. Mr. Duffey was a tyrant. Liza was hot and sticky, and the floor was littered with thrown-out paper. Liza was a working girl struggling for no money at all, ground underfoot by a man who said 'Ha!' and had a disgusting moustache. It was ten to one, and Liza was only half-way through the second copy. She hated Mr. Duffey as she had never hated Mr. Hollis. In a panic that some one would see the paper she had wasted, Liza crammed it in a drawer which didn't lock. It was one, it was twenty-past; and suddenly Mr. Duffey was a kind of godfather who had blessed this afternoon, this evening, the next two days and the week-end.

Liza draped the typewriter in its tarpaulin and went downstairs. Darling Walter, he never wore porridge-coloured pants or striped pyjamas; when she next saw this shop, next Wednesday because she had been given Friday off, the weekend would be over. But she wouldn't see it again.

Liza thought, I don't know; the week-end is rather frighteningly near. Perhaps not quite the Future. All I know, and I think all that matters, is that I'm seeing Walter. She crossed the empty street to the Olde Spinning

Wheel and had her usual lunch—scrambled eggs, coffee, a cigarette and a *Tatler* for last June from the chair opposite; and the feeling, never so strong as to-day, that this was a lovely world, and she had earned it. She caught the two o'clock bus back, and, seeing the brown papery drifts on the grey roads, a naked beech lifting its silver-grey branches to a leaden sky, thought of fires and crumpets and, later, a red sun over snow.

Liza and Betty were going out to tea with the people who lived in the big house farther up the road. Liza changed into an old blue jersey and a blue and brown checked skirt; the jersey had shrunk and felt a bit scratchy, but it looked all right under a brown jacket. She stood before the mirror and told herself that palish blue and sandy brown were very nice together; yes, she really did look all right, but she felt rather guilty. She was saving all her nice clothes for the week-end. She had tried on the pink and grey swagger coat over the flannel suit and thought she had never looked so well dressed in her life, nor had any one else; and the coat was hanging up, unworn, next to the suit, which had been cleaned, and she didn't mind now that she hadn't bought a new tweed suit; and the rest of her clothes had been cleaned or washed, and her shoes soled and heeled, brushed and polished. She put on a pair of brown brogues she didn't want for the week-end. Yes, she looked all right; or good enough for tea with the nice but dull Carrolls, and she wasn't taking the edge off the week-end by looking smart. She said, as she walked along the road with Betty, who was wearing her tweed suit, 'I feel awful, but you know how it is with everything clean.' She wanted to talk about the week-end.

'I know,' said Betty. 'You can have my suit-case, if you like. The rawhide one.'

'Oh, I say, that's awfully nice of you. But I might spoil it.'

'No,' said Betty. 'You have it.'

'Well, that's awfully sweet of you. My only decent one is brown and dull.' Yes, grey and pink and a rawhide case; lovely world. Walter would know it wasn't hers, but she could be casual and say hers had bust at the last minute. 'Betty, has it got initials?'

'Yes. At the top, quite small.'

'Oh.' The lovely world fell to pieces.

'Well, you can stick a label on. When Edward and I stayed at that hotel in Dover I had a case with initials on. Big ones, in the middle.'

'That was a bit dangerous,' said Liza, who wouldn't have thought it of Betty. And she hadn't heard this episode yet.

'Oh, the people at Calais put a label over.' Betty patted the roll of hair above her forehead, tucking her chin in as she strode along. 'And we hadn't had any tea, and it was six when we got there, and the first thing that silly Edward did was to insist on tea-cakes because they were English.' The tale wandered on; Liza had heard this part. She followed the little glow in her mind back to the rawhide suit-case, and Christmas. Walter would ask her if she'd like one, and a hat-box to match; yes, being lent Betty's was a sort of omen. By the time they reached the Carrolls' house it didn't matter in the least how smart or unsmart she looked. The outside world was the outside world.

The Carrolls had moved to Uncle George's village early in September, and the house was still too newly painted for the architecture or the furniture. They were a nice family; Mrs. Carroll, stout and smoothly handsome; Mr. Carroll, a little man who wore loose tweeds and went shooting with Uncle George and, Liza suspected, shot everything Uncle George missed; and Miss Prince, Mr. Carroll's sister, tall and thin, and as obviously as unredeemably a virgin. Liza and Betty had been to tea several times before, and had never met any one else there; but this afternoon Mrs. Carroll, sailing to meet them, said, 'I'm so glad to see you, my dears. I've got a nephew upstairs. Percy, go and tell David.'

Liza was faintly excited, because David was that sort of name. But this David, when he appeared, turned out to be a pleasant young man, but not exciting; no, not so young, about thirty-something; tall, with very long legs, and no voice, which his aunt explained was the end of laryngitis, following a very bad cold.

'How do you do?' said David, in a croaking whisper. Liza had heard that his other name was Graham, because, with Walter so near, she was feeling detached and not at all shy. 'I am so sorry,' he went on, pointing at his tie, which matched his collar. Liza was reminded of Walter, who never wore a tie, and smiled; and David smiled back, and she did feel rather shy and think he was nice, and wish she had put her flannel suit on; one afternoon wouldn't have spoilt it.

'I don't think he's infectious,' said Mrs. Carroll, looking fondly at David as if he couldn't hear, either. 'Or do you catch colds?'

Betty and Liza said they never caught colds, and Miss Prince told every one *she* never caught a cold, and then tea came in, and they sat down round the fire and talked about the weather.

'I think it's about what we always have at this time of year, don't you?' said Mrs. Carroll from behind the teapot.

'Yes, isn't it?' said Betty.

'Chilly though,' said Mr. Carroll. 'Definite nip in the air.'

'I can't say I like the *eve*nings,' said Miss Prince, who had laid her crochet in her lap to drink her tea with a refined manner of not really enjoying it. 'It always *saddens* me to see them getting darker. And *dar*ker.' Miss Prince's voice ran to sudden heights and accentuations; it would have something to do with being a virgin.

David, who was next to Liza, whispered, 'I can't say anything. Every one would listen. Have to be important. Like singing opera.'

'Or talking to some one deaf,' said Liza, and found that she was whispering too; and they both laughed, in a whisper. Every one else was talking now, so Liza raised her voice to nearly its ordinary level, and said, 'Now I think I'm shouting.' She thought, he's got a nice smile, but it isn't exactly a smile, it's more sudden; a sort of grin.

'Sorry,' said David, raising his voice to a croak. 'No. No good. I shall subside. Have to keep my sentences short. Like writing notes in prep. Good for the style. Do you live here?'

'Not really,' said Liza. 'London.' She found she was keeping her sentences short too.

'Which part?' said David.

'Chelsea.'

'So do I.'

They worked out that they were only four streets apart, and then Liza said, 'I keep forgetting. I don't live there now. I'm going to get a new flat.

– 199 –

In Chelsea too, I expect.' And she was rather frightened to think that she was talking as if Walter had never existed. She said quickly, 'Well, perhaps not.'

'Oh, I hope so,' said David politely. 'Do you work?'

'Well, I did. I suppose I shall again.' Well, after all, she might, for a little.

'I infer that you're a secretary,' said David.

'Why?'

'They all loathe it. I'm in advertising.'

'Do you loathe it?'

'Loathe it.' He coughed. 'Sense of values. Grow them in my spare time.'

Liza thought, I do like you. She had found herself imagining David in London, and herself in her flat only four streets away; but it wasn't her flat now; then in another flat, and having dinner with David, talking to him as they were talking now, only he would have his ordinary voice, and she wondered what it was like; knowing him very well, as she did now. Then she thought of Walter, and the outside world was swept away on a wave of happiness.

But it was lovely to have some one to talk to. She said, 'Don't you think everything's frightful about sort of modern life?' But Mrs. Carroll had called across to David, who got up, giving Liza his grin, to go over and make his whisper heard; and the chance of saying something to some one who understood, without the obscuring cross-purposes of love, had gone. Liza took a rock-cake and turned to Mr. Carroll, and told him how much she liked working for Uncle George's committee, and how nice and kind every one was, particularly Mr. Duffey.

Later she had another chance to talk to David. But when she thought about him afterwards, she found herself pushing him aside, and was rather worried to think why. It was for the reason that she hadn't worn her flannel suit; she didn't want to take the edge off her happiness. She wanted life to be dark and dull till Saturday, when the sun would shine out all the brighter.

She thought, that's wrong; because it isn't Walter's attitude. Walter doesn't save his happiness for when he sees me. And Walter will spend five minutes on Saturday morning throwing his underclothes and an extra shirt into his suit-case; and he'll forget his comb and borrow mine.

On Friday evening Betty looked through Liza's bedroom door and said, 'David's on the telephone. He wants to drive us over to the pictures after dinner.'

'Oh, Betty,' said Liza, 'I can't. Not possibly, with all this sewing. You'll go, won't you?'

'Oh, do come.'

'I really can't. Tell him I'd have loved to. Make it sound that I can't. I can't, but *you* know, make it sound all right.'

So Betty went to the pictures with David, and came back and told Liza that Robert Taylor had his hair different; and while she was away Liza went on sewing new shoulder-straps on everything. She was angry with herself. She thought, Walter would have gone; but then Walter doesn't have clothes that need new shoulder-straps.

❀

On Saturday morning, while Uncle George got the car out to take her to the nearest station—she had explained that she was spending the week-end with some friends of the friends she'd spent the summer with—Liza stood in the hall with Betty's suit-case and considered the hall table. A clothes brush, a silver salver covered with Uncle George's ex-colleague's signatures; an ABC, a bowl of dried rose-leaves, a shoe-horn, a little ivory god; all arranged neatly on the shining mahogany. On Monday evening she would be in this hall again, and this table would be there to meet her; but it wouldn't look the same because she wouldn't be the same; a new Liza in a Future starting from now.

Uncle George put the case on the back seat and Liza got in beside him, and they drove off, Uncle George humming wheezily as soon as he had reached the top gear. Liza put her hand up to the back of her neck; her petticoat was twisted, one shoulder-strap cut into her armpit; and one bit of hair at the back hung down almost straight. She must remember to cut it off in the train. Well, then, not starting from exactly now; from when she got out of the car at the station.

❧

'Hullo,' said Betty from the stairs. 'Did you have a good time?'

'Yes, lovely, thank you,' said Liza, and saw the hall table, and ached because it reminded her of Saturday morning. They went up to Liza's room.

'Well,' said Betty, settling herself by the gas-fire and unscrewing the bottle of polish-remover, 'tell me about it. I've got to do my nails.'

Liza was nearly happy again. 'Lovely,' she said, and opened her suitcase. All just as she had packed it in a hurry after breakfast: haddock, and pink china, and very pale marmalade. She took out the black dinner-dress, crushed from three days and two nights in the case, and said, 'Well. First we got in the car. Oh, I never said how nice your case was, Betty. Walter was awfully impressed. And the label kept on.' She pulled it off.

'Where did you have lunch?' said Betty.

'At a teeny pub on the way.' She thought, *teeny*, you're the people you talk to. 'We just had bread and cheese, and it was all dark and beer-rings, you know, and there were two farm men and we all talked about the world, and they were so *nice* it sort of made you feel good.'

Betty said, 'Have you got any cotton-wool?'

Liza took some from the washstand, and Betty wrapped a piece round her orange-stick.

'Well,' said Liza, 'and then we got in the car and we had a Mars Bar, and it was the sort *not* in two, so it must have been years old, and it tasted it too, but we broke it in half and looked at the map and drove off, and we talked about Life with a capital L.'

Betty dug round her nail with the orange-stick. 'What a solemn sort of a day.'

'Well, you know how you do. And it was a lovely, cold windy day, and it was lovely and warm in the car—'

'I know,' said Betty. 'Edward and I were always talking about life. Once

– 202 –

we walked up one of those winding paths with a blick at the end, and we had such an argument that we never noticed we'd got to the top. It was the week-end we went to Freiburg, and the argument began all because my silly Edward went and bought one of those green straw hats with a cord round and a shaving-brush—'

'I know,' said Liza. 'They do begin from the silliest things, don't they? Though I don't think ours began from any reason except that we just wanted to talk. Well, we got to the hotel long before tea, and honestly it was *just* what I told you it would be. Only it was grey, not white, with a slate roof, but weather-beaten and *very* nice inside. And a hill, and quite a river.'

'Nice,' said Betty absently.

'I don't know,' said Liza. 'It's difficult to explain, but you know how sometimes everything has such a terrific atmosphere, even at the time—'

'Oh, I know,' said Betty. 'When we—' Betty's rather dreamy, full-throated voice stopped suddenly. 'Did you hear a bell?'

'I think I did,' said Liza untruthfully. 'It sounded like the back door. Shall I go?'

'No,' said Betty. 'Mummy's away for the day—did you know? and if it's the boy with the brussels sprouts I want to tell him off.' She ran downstairs.

Liza listened. Yes, there really was some one there. She heard voices, and the clatter of saucepans. Betty was safe. Liza thought, one day I really will let her talk and talk about her Edward; I'm a beast. I'll let her tell me everything so that she'll never be able to talk about him again because she'll know she's said it all before. Well, but she has, most of it.

Liza shut her door and knelt by the gas-fire.

She thought, I can't tell any one about it; I couldn't say it right, and anyhow no one would listen. But it was perfect. Then she thought, yes, it's perfect now, because it was being with Walter; but that's all. Nothing happened to change anything; but I didn't think it would.

Liza pulled the suit-case towards her and went on unpacking. Her walking shoes, wrapped in yesterday's *Observer*. She had worn them for the last time on Sunday evening. Most of the mud had come from that little lane; and some of it she had left in the Ye Olde, where the only other tea-eaters had been the two bachelor girls, so weather-beaten, so bravely cheerful. Here was the scarf she had tied over her ears when the wind sang through them, and the gap in the fringe where she had shut it in the car door. Perhaps Walter would find the bits of fringe still in the car; perhaps he would ache for the week-end, as she did now.

And here, on the crossword page of the *Observer*, was a design like a slice of Swiss roll, with a black and white striped filling; she had done it with Walter's pencil after dinner last night, only last night, sitting in the lounge, and a little later Walter had looked up from the *New Statesman* and said:

'Gor! I'd forgotten how I loathe Christmas.'

And Liza had looked up from *Vogue* and said, 'So do I.' And that was all they had said about Christmas. And Liza had gone on reading, thinking, I might as well be at the hairdresser's.

Liza put the scarf away. She saw the hotel, grey and foursquare, with yellow moss in its crevices, the wintry street emptied by Sunday and dinner-time; the tin can blowing along the gutter, Walter's hair lifting in the wind as he cried, 'Lunch! lunch!' and, as they ran in, she had said, 'You aren't suffering from convict's hair after all,' and Walter had run his hand through his hair and said, 'I know. I've got to get it cut on Tuesday, or else.' No, it almost hurt to think of Walter, already. She could still say, I saw him to-day; and to-morrow, I saw him yesterday, and it would hurt more.

Behind the chintz curtains the rain slashed the rattling window. The gas-fire hissed; Liza could hear the wireless, thumping distantly, only the bass part; it reminded her of the man in the flat above. She might be in her own flat now, listening to the gas-fire, shut from the world by the curtains. Alone. Wherever you went you took yourself. But you were only half yourself when the other half drove away into the darkness of Swindon, with a little red light shining on the only number-plate in the world.

Liza knelt up and thought, I am myself. Whatever happens is important to me, to be gathered up inside me and used to make me better and more interesting than I am. And a warm and comfortable thought pushed itself to the front of her mind. Now it was a hope, and the world was not quite a desolate vacuum.

Liza ran downstairs and found Betty in the kitchen. 'Can I do anything?'

'It's all done.'

'I say, I'm frightfully sorry.'

'It's all right. You can do all the washing up.'

'Oh, I'd love to,' said Liza. She stood by the Ideal boiler, and said casually, hooking up its lid:

'By the way, is David still here? I mean, did you see him this week-end?'

Betty said, from the gas-oven, 'He came round yesterday to say good-bye.'

'Oh,' said Liza. 'I'm just going up to get tidy.'

Liza combed her hair and thought, I only wanted to see David because I'm away from Walter. That's what's so miserable, the more you want to be with the person you love, and can't, the more you want to be with some one else. That's not independence; you're still a lean-to shed, moving to another house.

Liza sat at the dressing-table and stared at Hope, poor, despairing Hope, over the mantelpiece. Then she went down to the kitchen, where Betty was dishing up the dinner.

'I say, Betty, I've been thinking lately that I ought to go back to London. You know, start working again. I mean, do you sort of need me?'

'Oh, no,' said Betty. 'Well, that is, we *like* to have you. Mummy will be awfully sorry. So shall I, of course.'

'That's awfully nice of you, Betty.' Liza imagined another argument with Aunt Vi, and, on the last day, another orgy of thanks and good-bye. She thought, this isn't my real life, all these family cross-currents. I am living out of my atmosphere.

She sat down to dinner. The willow-patterned china was so familiar that she couldn't see it as it was; the wall-paper couldn't have been anything but itself, beige with a faint cream line. The log on the fire, kicked by Uncle George as he went past, fell and shot out its sparks. The world outside was cold and dark, and this settled room was bright and warm, and negative; it was home, and it stopped you being yourself.

Uncle George said, dabbing the soup from his moustache, 'Salt-spoons will always go green unless you put them *across* the salt cellar so that they don't touch the salt.'

Betty said nothing. Liza dutifully balanced a salt-spoon. 'Why, Uncle George?'

'Something to do with the salt.'

There was a silence. Liza had told Uncle George all she had to about the week-end, in the car; she was glad. And it didn't matter here if no one talked, because no one ever said anything to listen to.

Uncle George carved the lamb. 'Saw the Major this afternoon, Betty. He said he might have a puppy for you.'

'Is it a bitch?' said Betty. Liza nearly blushed, and told herself that in the country bitch didn't mean what it meant in London.

'Can't be helped,' said Uncle George. 'Why don't you have that Labrador?'

'Labradors are great lumping things,' said Betty. 'Daddy, I definitely do want a Pekinese bitch.'

'Peke!' said Uncle George. 'Little horrors.' Liza had been going to say, aren't they sweet? She was glad she hadn't; and anyway she hated them.

'Well, then a cocker spaniel might not be bad,' said Betty. 'But, Daddy, if the Major's puppies are all dogs, then *no*. Bitches are much easier to train.'

Liza listened absently, from across the frontiers. She was back in her own life.

'Well, but the Major *trains* 'em. For gun dogs. And old Jim Wyatt—'

Uncle George's committee would have to go back to notices typed with one finger and no space after the full stop. Oh, I'm not *me* here; oh, darling London, oh, darling Walter, hurry, hurry, hurry.

Part Four

Winter

XIV

Liza bumped her suit-case up the steps. A dusty green box stood on each side, holding a dusty shrub. It was a dusty day, with no colour in the sky or the street, or the faces of the people or their clothes. It was London on any November day when it wasn't raining. Liza passed through the swing-doors and said to the woman at the desk, 'Have you got a room, please?'

'A single room,' said the woman. Liza saw the date on the desk calendar. November the fifteenth. Soon she would know the date every day. She was a bachelor girl again. She had felt it coming on in the taxi from Waterloo. But the image of Walter was by her side, even if the woman didn't see it; and the real Walter was across the width of only two London parks, instead of a hundred miles away. She paid the taxi-man, who had dumped her trunk and the other case in the hall, and signed her name in a book, saying she would stay a week, she thought, and she didn't think longer.

A porter went up in the lift with Liza, and hauled the trunk along to her room. 'Thank you,' said Liza. He looked resigned and yet expectant; or was it just his face? Liza thought wildly; she would tip him when she left, she didn't have to now. She said, 'Thank you' again, willing him to understand that when she left he would get a colossal tip. The man said, 'Thank you, madam,' and went to the door. He would have six children and an invalid wife. Liza said, 'Wait just a moment,' and took a shilling from her bag. She wondered if it should have been sixpence. The man said

'Thank you, madam,' again, and, still looking resigned and expectant, went out. Liza felt young and silly.

It was cold. There was a gas-fire with a slot meter, but she had given the porter her only shilling. It was a quarter-past two; she would wait till four to ring Walter up. She could measure him in hours now, not weeks. She opened the window, looking down at the Cromwell Road, following it to its smoky horizon. No wonder there were all those jokes about it. She was four floors up, and the height was having its usual effect on the backs of her knees; she pulled her head in, shut the cold winter out and in, and thought that it was a dreadful parody of the hotels she and Walter had stayed in. Not so much because it was ugly, because hotel rooms often were, as because it had against its sombre wall a narrow bed built for one person, a bachelor girl, a poor soul, a Russell; for one life denied the richness of living, finding its small pleasures in a new shillingsworth of gas-fire or something nice for lunch.

Liza thought, if I stay here this room will seep into me; I'm more depressed already than I've ever been before. But it's only thirty-five shillings a week with breakfast; it's not for long; the world's mine oyster, all sorts of things are going to happen; and I shall ring up Walter, now. And she was happy again.

Liza found a telephone box in the hall and rang up Walter's school.

'Hullo?' said a slow, aproned voice.

'I can't speak to Mr. Latimer, I suppose?' said Liza.

'Mr. *who*?' said the voice.

'Mr. Latimer.'

'Mr. Latimer?'

'Yes, Mr. *Latimer*,' said Liza crossly. 'There *is* a Mr. Latimer there, isn't there?' And she hoped she hadn't sounded too cross; it might be the headmaster's wife, and she might tell the headmaster, and he might give Walter the sack.

'Yes, there's a Mr. *Latimer*,' said the maddening voice, 'but if you want to speak to *him*'—it paused—'you'll have to try the other number.' It gave the other number and rang off. Liza dialled it and the bell rang to the unknown for two minutes. Somehow even this counted as Walter.

Liza went out shopping. The wind blew her hat off at the street corners, and its dust in her eyes. She came back at six and dialled Walter's number again.

'Hullo?' said a nice voice. For one sickening moment she thought it was Walter. 'Hullo. Can I speak to Mr. Latimer?' It still might be him.

'I'm afraid he's gone out,' said the voice. But it was an extremely nice voice. She said, 'Oh. Do you know where? I mean, how long for?'

'I'm afraid I don't,' said the voice. 'Can I ask him to ring you when he gets back?'

'Please, if you would.' So the nice voice fetched a paper and pencil and wrote down the number, and read it out to make sure, and, when it finally said, 'Good-bye,' sounded quite sorry. While she unpacked in her room, Liza imagined a meeting between Walter and her and the nice voice.

Walter would ask her to call for him at the school before they went off to his flat for the evening and the night. He would invite her into the Common Room, or whatever you called it. Liza would be sitting on the table, from which he would have chivalrously cleared the exercise books, wearing a black coat with a little round black fur collar, over a plain black wool dress with pleats—she had seen them both to-day in Harrods—and what sort of hat? Black? Red, for a touch of colour? Say black for the moment; she would have a nice bright lipstick and wedgy black shoes. And into the Common Room would come the nice voice; tall, fair, very elegant, with a tweed coat and a pipe; Leslie Howard. His name would be Julian. He would be introduced to Liza; he would give her a glance of frank admiration, to which Liza would reply with a smile, gay but enigmatical, and, looking towards Walter, would see that he had been watching. Julian would be worried because he was correcting exam. papers—no, too early in the term; just prep. then—and he would be stuck over something and would ask Walter, who wouldn't know either; but Liza would, throwing it off casually. (What would it be? For the moment she fell back on botany, the only thing she could beat Walter on. Though it would be funny if some one teaching botany couldn't answer his own questions. Oh, well; it would do for the moment.) Julian would give a glance of even franker admiration, saying, 'I say, you've got a brain.' Walter, putting down the

New Statesman, would say, 'We're just off for the evening.' Julian would drop his exercise books and light Liza's cigarette with a lighter which worked first time, saying, 'We must meet again. Perhaps we can have dinner together next Wednesday?'

'I should love to,' Liza would say, with great simplicity. And in the taxi—why not Walter's car? no, a taxi—Walter would burst out:

'Oh, damn. Any one can ask you out to dinner.'

'Not any one,' Liza would say lightly. 'Julian's very nice. But I *am* free to go out with any one I like. You have no claims on me.'

'The hell I haven't,' Walter would say, and take her in his arms; and, as the taxi swung round the last corner before his flat, he would clear his throat and, in that voice she had sometimes heard, that funny shy voice—

Liza shut the dream into the empty suit-case and pushed it under the wash-basin. She looked round the room. The light in its fringed shade shone dismally down, the room shone dismally back. A yellow oak chest of drawers, with a white mat. A dressing-table, with another white mat. A linoleum-covered floor with a small blue carpet. A Notice to Residents. A bedside cupboard. Blue casement cloth curtains. An olive-green mantelpiece to match the tiles. Liza's bottles and jars, books, work-box and odds and ends had made the room a little better, and at the same time a little worse, because they linked her with it.

And Walter hadn't rung up, and it was after seven, and he knew she was back in London; so he was having dinner with a beautiful woman. Liza went down to the hotel dining-room.

The dining-room didn't look so bad; it had grey walls and pale green curtains. Liza told the waiter she was expecting a telephone call, and drank her soup and watched the other diners. Some of them wore jumpers and sat-out skirts. Some wore dark, long-skirted dresses with V-necks filled in with lace. She decided that they were playing bridge after dinner, and had dressed up in competition. There were a few men, none of them under about fifty, except for the two pale students who had balanced text-books against the water-jug on the corner table.

Liza said to the waiter, 'When the telephone call comes now I'll be in my room, but I'll tell them at the desk,' and went upstairs, stopping to read the envelopes stuck in the notice-board. She hesitated on the stairs. She could ring up John; or Funny; or Pauline; but she had said she would be in her room. Walking up all the stairs, because it took longer, Liza suddenly hated Walter. If it hadn't been for him she would still be in her flat, or in another even better; and at the office, or in another even better. She thought, because of you I am hanging in mid-air, I'm a ghost.

It was a quarter to nine. Liza had plugged her electric iron in the wall, telling herself that if the lights fused they fused, and it would do the hotel good; they didn't, but ironing on a newspaper on the floor had been impossible. Liza pinned a note on the door, Gone to Nearest Bathroom, and had a bath. The bathroom was sage green, and there was a rusty patch in the bath round the plug-hole. She thought, if this hotel was in some sociable part of London, just one hotel in a row of houses, it wouldn't be so bad. It's knowing that the whole Cromwell Road is the same; well, anyway the water's hot.

Liza got into bed and did half a crossword and a little problem about X and Y overtaking each other in express trains. Then she lay and thought of Uncle George's house, warm, flooded with electric light, blessedly safe, familiar and negative; and her stomach sank with homesickness. She drew back the curtains and opened the window. There, a distant traffic-noise, was the other world, where people worked and played, talked, laughed, lived. She stepped across the cold linoleum, turned out the light and got back into bed, thinking, I shall never go to sleep; and went to sleep. She woke to hear a strange clock striking three. It was the end of the world.

But the next morning, when Walter rang up, the world had already begun again, with coffee, an egg boiled just right, and somewhere in London a new flat and a new job.

🌀

Finding a job sounded large and easy and important till you got right up to it, when, like most things, it niggled. Liza called at the place which had taught her shorthand and typing a hundred years ago, and after waiting an hour by a radiator was given a bunch of typed forms, each with particulars of a firm which wanted a secretary. She read them on the bus to Regent Street, and thought, something must be dreadfully wrong with me. Because I believe that every other business girl wants to be a business girl; no, David said they loathed it. David had given her his telephone number; but she was seeing Walter this evening, and David was faint and far away.

Liza got off the bus and stood in the entrance of a block of offices; a black and white tiled hall, with black and white name-plates stretching up the high walls. She picked out the name she was looking for; and under it was *Furs, Wholesale.*

Liza thought, no. She got on another bus and went off to Cornhill, where she found a smaller and dirtier entrance, and, on the second floor, the office she was looking for. She sat in a small room with frosted glass panels and read a mining magazine till the door creaked open, and an egg-shaped face with little tight glasses said, 'Will you come this way, please?' Liza followed it down the passage to another room, with a worn Turkey carpet and a burst wicker waste-paper basket. The man with the egg-shaped face, whose name was Mr. Martin, slid himself behind his desk and crossed his hands on his stomach and said, peering at the paper before him:

'You are Miss Brett, eh?'

'Yes,' said Liza, and despised him, and herself for wishing so passionately to make a good impression on such a man.

'Well, Miss Brett,' said Mr. Martin, 'tell us your qualifications, now. Have a cigarette though, won't you?' and he pushed the box across. Liza felt extraordinarily humble and singled out. When Mr. Martin held out his lighter, she might have been shaking hands with the King.

'Well now,' said Mr. Martin, leaning back in his chair.

Liza blushed. 'Well, I've been a secretary for four years. No, five really. And I can type and write shorthand. Awfully fast.'

'Awfully fast, eh?' said Mr. Martin, with a smile which turned his silly mouth up but did nothing to his small pale eyes.

'Well, quite fast,' said Liza, blushing more. 'I should think about a hundred and thirty shorthand and, oh, I don't know, about ninety typing.'

It might be true, and you had to impress people. Mr. Martin didn't look specially impressed. He tapped his pencil on his false teeth.

'Well, now, Miss Brett, if you came here—' he launched into all the things she would have to do. They sounded exactly what you did in any job for three pounds ten a week.

'Mind you,' said Mr. Martin, 'it's a job for some one with initiative. I want a girl who can think for herself.'

'Oh, of course,' said Liza eagerly, hoping she showed the initiative she was bursting with. And while she wondered if her nose hadn't got shiny since she powdered it over the mining magazine, and if she had on enough lipstick and if at the same time she would have looked more suitable without any, she was thinking, you ghastly, mean-faced, horrible man. Oh, this can't be me. I wonder what Kate would say if she saw me now. Oh, darling Walter, I'm seeing you to-night. And then the summer crowded on her; that; and now this. No, she was being a White Russian; it wouldn't do.

'Well,' said Mr. Martin, 'anything you want to ask?'

'I—I don't think so. I mean, it all sounds awfully interesting. And just the kind of work I like.' And she thought, you must, you must choose *me*. I'm better than any one else.

They shook hands, and Mr. Martin promised he would write and tell her in a couple of days. 'Oh, thank you,' said Liza, with her nicest smile, and went out. Her cigarette was nearly burning her fingers. She trod on it, and went down in the dusty lift.

Liza walked to the bus-stop. The world was grey and ugly; life was a nightmare of drudgery among and for repulsive strangers. On the bus Liza suddenly saw herself as she used to be; settled in a dear, dusty, funny office, where every one was a friend, and Mr. Hollis made bad jokes out of the kindness of his heart, and Partridge ran little errands, and Miss Derry handed round acid drops; a place of sweetness and light, sunshine and happy laughter.

Liza got off the bus at Chancery Lane and walked down to the doorway. The old man in the baize apron was standing by the lift and didn't recognize her before he disappeared into the shadows. But he was still there; he was a sort of omen. She opened the door of Enquiries, and, feeling terribly shy, put her head round.

There was Miss Derry; blessed Miss Derry, just as she had left her. No, not quite; she wore a strange dark brown jumper with a polo collar; and she sat at right angles to the switchboard, at a separate table, with a different typewriter. But it was Miss Derry.

Miss Derry looked round, and her mouth fell open. '*Well*!' she cried. 'I never! Look who's here!'

Liza thought, I've come home.

She shook hands with Miss Derry, and Partridge, who had come in to see, and with Miss Netley and Miss Vane, who had heard her voice and wondered if it could be true; and Mr. Chiddock, who was at his desk, darker and scraggier than ever, and said, 'Why, hullo!' and went quite pink. And now for Mr. Hollis. She went through her old room and saw a tall, limp girl, picking away at a new typewriter, and through the door with the frosted glass top, and there was Mr. Hollis; not quite so pale as she had remembered, but drinking his glass of milk.

Mr. Hollis said he was delighted to see her, and it was a miserable day, though only what they could expect in November. But he looked faintly embarrassed, and Liza felt shy. She thought, if I ever met Mr. Hollis outside the office I would be his secretary and behave like one; even now, when I'm not.

Mr. Hollis finished his milk and wiped a drop from his chin with a mauve silk handkerchief. 'We've had four young women here since you left.'

Liza stopped feeling shy. She laughed, and said, 'Were they frightful?' with that unworthy but comforting sensation of being on the right side of the fence.

'Ghastly,' said Mr. Hollis. 'One wasn't bad, but she got married.' He looked as if he didn't know if he ought to ask Liza if she had too; then he jerked his thumb to the door. '*She's* going next month.'

'Oh, is she?' There was a silence. He seemed to be waiting for her to speak. She said, 'I wonder—' and found she had swallowed her voice. She got it back. 'Would you—I mean, you did say—would you like me to—'

'Would I not?' said Mr. Hollis. 'I say, though, would you want to?'

Liza thought, oh, darling Mr. Hollis, you *are* nice. And your suit fits. She said, almost with emotion, 'Why?'

'Why what?'

'I mean, you said it as if you thought I wouldn't. Oh, I *was* happy here, Mr. Hollis. It was only that I was in a tramline. I don't mean being here was a tram-line, but any office was just then.'

'So now you want to get back to the tram-lines?' said Mr. Hollis, and this was quite a good joke, for him. They laughed.

'Yes, I do,' said Liza. 'I think these are very nice tram-lines.'

'Well, we're all trams,' said Mr. Hollis, rather in the voice of a thwarted Marco Polo.

'Oh, I know. It's one of the things you learn from Life, isn't it?' And their eyes and their souls met, and Liza thought, he'll never be just Mr. Hollis again.

There was a dignified tap at the door, and Partridge's head appeared. 'Mr. Haines to see you, sir,' he said over his collar.

'Show him in,' said Mr. Hollis briskly. He was back to just Mr. Hollis. 'Well, Miss Brett, that's that. I wish you could come here before the month is up, but I've just fixed it with her, and I don't want to—'

'Oh, *no.* That will be quite all right. It will give me time to find somewhere to live and everything. Good-bye, Mr. Hollis. Thank you most *frightfully.*'

'December the twentieth, then. Good-bye, Miss Brett.' They shook hands again. Liza, his secretary again, stood at the door while Mr. Haines walked in, shut it and went back to Enquiries.

Miss Derry, Partridge, Miss Vane and Miss Netley were all having their tea round the gas-fire; usually Miss Vane and Miss Netley had theirs in their room, so perhaps this was a party for Liza. They gave her a cup and two Thin Rich Tea biscuits, and, when they heard her news, said, 'My!' and 'Fancy!' and 'I say!' and, from Miss Derry, '*Well!* Back again, like a bad penny!'

Every one had a cold except Miss Vane, who said that she had been inoculated and after one frightful cold all September she hadn't had any more. 'Bet I do soon,' she said darkly, taking another biscuit. Liza saw that she had filed her nails more into points, and the varnish was now just pinker than life; and she wondered if Miss Vane had a Man,

'Miss Derry's going to Burma to marry Ted,' said Miss Netley. Liza hated Miss Derry.

'Go *on!*' said Miss Derry, leaping to the switchboard and winding the handle boisterously. Her voice rose. 'No, not there. *I'*ll tell them. *Righty*-ho. Go on, dear. I'm doing nothing of the sort.'

'Oh, you will,' said Miss Vane.

'Catch me,' said Miss Derry, blowing her nose. 'Nasty place, Burma. You wouldn't get me near it.'

Liza loved Miss Derry.

Liza left the office at five, feeling as if she had done a day's work there. It was heavenly to walk down Chancery Lane and along to the Strand; all the evening now, and Walter. A fat old woman shouting 'Starnews*sten*dard!' in a raucous boy's voice; taxis squelching past, street-lamps, shop windows, cheap jewellery, shoes, fun-fairs, buses; a blare, a glitter, a jumble; London; Walter.

🌀

Walter said, 'Well, I don't suppose this room has had this happen to it before.'

'I don't suppose so,' said Liza. She thought, yesterday this room looked like this; but it will never be the same again. It's come alive. The same olive-green mantelpiece, the same sickly yellow furniture, and their ugliness was exciting now for the secret it held.

'Actually, though, I don't not suppose so at all,' said Walter. 'It's the sort of thing that's always happening everywhere, Dame Nature being what she is. Cor, if you took a longitudinal section of any block of flats in Chelsea on a Sunday afternoon.'

That was all it was now. Something that happened everywhere.

'Any minute I may get up,' said Walter. 'Ducky, I do love your Notice to Residents. It's got everything. How would you define the pattern on this ceiling?'

– 216 –

'I thought roses yesterday.'

'I think buttercups.'

'Yes, perhaps.' There was a silence. Liza was wanting to ask him about the school. She shouldn't feel so shy of mentioning his work; he was lying in her arms, he was hers; but that made him a stranger in the world she couldn't share. She said, 'Is the school still nice, darling?'

'Nice you may call it. Yes. Nice.' Her heart ached. 'It really is, ducky. It's that heavenly atmosphere of stamp-albums and Autocars. And the little perishers are gorgeous. They're all like Hapgood Two. You know, ducky, I think I'm rather a good schoolmaster. I'm getting a sort of manner.'

'Darling, you are clever,' said Liza. She didn't feel shy any more. 'What will you do next term?'

Walter yawned. 'I think I shall go back to the law and the kippers. I rather see myself making impassioned speeches on behalf of small Galsworthian clerks. I don't know. There aren't enough small clerks to go round. Too many crooks are crooks.'

'Yes, I suppose they are.'

'And the trouble about the law is that you have to twist the truth up to suit your own mercenary ends. I suppose—'

'Yes?'

'Well, I suppose you're part of what they call a vast machine which acts for the best, but you don't feel like it when you're only a very small cog. End.' He kissed her neck. Liza thought, I wish we could stay like this for ever.

Walter yawned again, and said, 'I shall now get up,' and didn't. Liza said, 'Darling, which of your colleagues has a nice voice?'

'Don't tell me why you want to know. Let me work it out. Oh, yes, the telephone. That would be Harry.'

'What does he look like?'

'Squat. Short legs. A square face surmounted with red hair and a forehead villainous low.'

'Oh. Well, darling, he sounded awfully nice on the telephone.'

'The old devil,' said Walter. 'Well, he's all right. He's got quite a soul.' Liza wondered how easy it would be to make Walter jealous.

'I want my dinner,' said Walter, and got up. 'Where are we going, do you think, ducky?'

'Not down to this restaurant. I don't know, though. The food's all right, and it's frightfully funny.'

'Then we will. I want a good laugh. Has any one seen a pair of pants? Here we are.'

Liza sat up and put on her stockings. Lovely world. 'Darling, I wish you could have met that dreadful Mr. Martin.'

'I feel I have. Dozens of him. There's a whole mining department at the Science Museum. Once I hurled myself at a glass case and broke it, and my father had to pay. I was only about five, so I could hardly have made it on my pocket-money. And, ducky, I've never told you this, but when I was four I had a pinafore embroidered with gnomes, of all things.'

Liza was speechless with love. She kissed the top of his head as he knelt down to get his shoes from under the bed.

'There's something about lino,' said Walter. 'Darling, till you get a flat, would you like mine?'

There was such a thing as perfect happiness, and this was it.

XV

So Liza moved her luggage to Walter's flat, and worked out that, paying no rent but, say, seven and six a week for the electric light and gas, she would be able to live in luxury for four weeks on the fourteen pounds left in the bank; and on December the twentieth she would start work at the office, and the next day she would have another twenty-five pounds in the bank. She was rich; for the first time in her life she was living in London without working; and in Walter's flat. It was nearly as good as the summer.

On the eighth day there, Liza woke at eight to the alarm clock she had brought with her, and jumped out of bed to fetch the post. She hadn't really expected a letter from Walter, but there wasn't one; and he could ring up whenever he wanted to, and he had, five days out of the eight. There was one letter for her, typed, with an E.C.3 postmark. It was from Mr. Martin, to say that the position of secretary had been filled, and thanking her. Liza sat on the bed and thought, I wonder why I mind so much. It's only because it's like failing in an exam. Then she got back into bed and went to sleep, and woke at half-past nine with a headache. Outside the day had begun, people were sitting down at their office desks, or hurrying along, making up excuses for being late. Lucky people to be able to be late. She shut her eyes and thought, I've fetched the post. Walter can't ring up before six. Well, he can, but he won't. Then she remembered Mr. Martin, and found she didn't mind any more about failing in the exam.

Liza wanted to get up. The clock ticked to twenty to ten, and she wanted to get up more than anything in the world. At five to she got up. She boiled an egg and heated some coffee, and ate her breakfast in the kitchen, standing up, with the paper propped against the coffee percolator and sliding every few seconds over Walter's enamel-top kitchen table.

Then she laid the fire, dirtying the sleeves of her pink chenille dressing-gown. Then she re-varnished her nails and had to wait ten minutes while they dried before she could wash up; and when she washed up some of the varnish flaked off.

At twelve Liza had her bath, and dressed, and then it was a quarter to one. She thought, I've only got three weeks more. This time in three weeks I shall be working again. Then she stepped out into the winter sunshine, and the world was real again. She walked down Hampstead High Street, and stopped to look in an estate agent's window. She had several lists of flats already; she would have to begin looking round soon. She had said, I won't bother till I've been here a week, I'll have a week doing all I want. And she had done nothing; day after day had gone behind her; all she had achieved was just that, putting it behind her. And she had seen Walter once, for an hour last Saturday; when they had sat on the floor and drunk sherry, and then Walter had said, ducky, I must get; and kissed her, and stayed perhaps five minutes more, and then gone. And she had thought, if we were at the beginning, an hour together would have been lovely; we had too much too soon.

Liza walked on down Hampstead High Street. It was crowded with young married women, with or without prams. Wherever she looked Liza saw them; well-dressed, sometimes not so well-dressed, but always giving you the illusion that they were; because they wore wedding-rings, and hurried happily along, and bought cakes and joints and pound tins of coffee for their husbands, and carried little flat paper bags holding bits of lace and stockings to make themselves smart for their husbands, and packets of cigarettes to put in the cigarette-boxes their husbands expected to find cigarettes in.

Liza thought, once I was a young married woman. I don't know what I am now.

Then she went into a delicatessen shop and bought a jar of prawns. She had meant to have lunch out, but it seemed silly to pay one and sixpence to sit at a rickety table by a radiator when for one and fourpence you could sit on the floor by an electric fire. Liza went back to Walter's flat and, turning on the electric fire in his bedroom, sat down with the plate of prawns and a book. She speared the prawns with an orange stick and read. She had taken a novel at random from Walter's bookshelves; it was about Spain, all hot sun and crickets, languorous passion and sun-blinds. She hated reading it because it took her from her surroundings and put her down in a strange world, and that meant an effort of imagination. She read till five-past two, and then, seeing the clock in the sitting-room, knew that Walter couldn't possibly ring up till six now.

Liza turned the electric fire off and put the book back. She thought, in four hours he'll ring up. Perhaps in four hours he'll be here. And I haven't cleaned the flat up. I ought to care for Walter's flat better than I should care for mine; and I don't. That's terrible.

So Liza put on her overall and carpet-swept the flat, and dusted it and polished it, and the harder she worked the harder she wanted to work; and by half-past five, stopping at four for a cup of tea, she had made the flat beautiful, and she was happy, and life was real. She had a bath and put on her black cocktail-party dress, and put the two sherry glasses and the decanter on the table. Then she lit the fire, and drew it up to a blaze with a newspaper which nearly caught fire twice; and it was a quarter-past six. The fire shone on the glasses and the polished furniture, and twice she had been back to the bedroom to see if her lipstick looked all right.

And then, at twenty-five past six, the telephone rang louder than any telephone had ever rung before. Liza gave it three and a half rings.

'Hullo, ducky,' said Walter's voice. 'How's things?'

'Lovely, thank you, darling.' She thought, if I don't ask him if he's coming round he'll be more likely to. She said, 'Darling, are you coming round to-night?'

'No, ducky, can't be done.'

'Oh. Why?'

'The little perishers want to practise their carols. I've got to play for them. They're all teed up about their damned concert. God knows who they're giving it to, because they all seem to be in it. They are, Harry. Harry says they're not. Harry!' Walter's voice had gone far away. 'Get some for me!' There was a clatter, followed by a distant slam. Harry would have gone out. Walter's voice sounded very slightly different. 'Hullo again, ducky. We're alone.'

'Hullo, darling. So am I. I didn't mean that to sound pathetic.'

'Oh, ducky. Well, it did. It wrung my ear-drum. Now, what are you going to do this evening?'

'I don't know. Sorry, darling. I honestly can't help my voice.'

'Oh, ducky. Well, I'll cheer you up. I'm feeling terribly sad.'

'Are you, darling? Why?'

'I thought it would. Nothing like other people's troubles, is there? Well, I'm sad because I was gazing at Hapgood Two to-day and I suddenly had a Thought with a capital T. I thought, once *my* hair stuck up like that on top, and once *my* braces gave me no real confidence. And where am I now, twenty years on? I don't feel any different. Ah, life, life!'

'Oh, darling.' Liza was deeply touched. 'I think you're lovely.'

'Do you, precious? I don't know what I should do without you.' He sounded absent. 'Talking about being old, it's your birthday next week. Only ten more days.'

'Oh, is it? Oh, yes, so it is. I do hate birthdays, don't you?'

'My own, yes. I adore other people's. Wodger want, ducky?'

'I don't know, darling. Nothing.'

'Oh, now. Think.'

'Honestly I can't. I don't know of anything.'

'Well, you'll have to, ducky, or I shall buy you something frightful, on purpose. Hullo, Harry. Thank you, my man. There's a half-crown, and I want most of it back. Oh, and you've got me those. My God, they're created to promote sore throats. Didn't you know?'

Liza heard Harry's voice, and then Walter's. He seemed to have put the telephone down. Then he said, 'Hullo, ducky. Sorry. Look, I must go.'

Liza heard herself saying, 'Darling, tell me when you're next coming round. Or I may be out.'

'Ducky, I don't know.'

'Well, are you to-morrow? Yes or no.'

'If that's an ultimatum, it won't be took up. Ultimatums never are. I shall have to say no, and perhaps after all it may be yes. I don't know, ducky, honestly.'

'Is Harry still there?'

'No. Why?'

'I just wondered.'

'I'm dimly insulted.'

'Oh, darling, I'm sorry.'

'It's all right, ducky. And I really will say no, because I'm pretty sure I can't. Look, darling, I'll be round on Friday. And on the tenth we'll have a birthday party. And there's the week-end in between, and we'll arrange something on Friday.'

'Darling, I'm sorry. I didn't mean to sound all silly.'

'Never mind, ducky. You didn't. Now I must get. Goodbye, darling.'

'Good-bye, darling.' The receiver clicked and rattled, and Liza rang off. She poured out some sherry and thought, there's all the evening; but evenings aren't so bad. But tomorrow I'll find a flat, and now, this minute, I'll ring up every one I know. Beginning with David.

❦

Two days later David called to take Liza out to dinner. He fingered his tie—it didn't match his collar now, and he looked Londonish, and a little older, but still pleasant—and said, 'This is all very nice.'

Liza had heard his voice on the telephone; but now it was different again. She said, 'You've got yet another voice'; you always ran a joke to death with a person you didn't know very well.

David grinned. 'All I've got.' He still kept his sentences short. He drank his sherry and looked at the bookshelves. 'Litry.'

'Yes, he is,' said Liza, and thought how she would like Walter to be here too. Three was a good number, only of course two of them had to be men. She glanced at David, who had pushed himself back in his chair to study the book titles; he looked rather tired and somehow serious and responsible. She said, 'Did you work very hard at the office to-day?'

'Didn't do a thing,' said David, turning towards her and putting his glass on the floor. 'Much more tiring.'

'Oh, it is. I haven't done any work since I moved into this flat, except housework, and not much of that, and it's more than a week, and sometimes I think I'm going crazy and nothing's real. It didn't matter in the country. But here—I don't know. And I'm not really going crazy, I mean at the moment things are real. So I'm only telling you what I think sometimes, not what I think now, if you see what I mean.'

'I do,' said David, with his grin. 'I was about like that at lunch-time to-day. It's beastly, isn't it?'

'Yes, but it makes a difference if you know it's only for a certain time. It sort of keeps you sane.'

'It's all very comparative,' said David, picking up his glass. 'And I think sometimes you don't want to do anything, and if you've got the chance you should take it. Too much badgering in the world. Do you think people are divided into the badgered and the badgerers, or do the badgerers badger themselves as well?'

Liza was thinking, we're in tune, just as we were the first time we met. I haven't got to find his wave-length. She said, 'Yes and no.'

'It deserved no better answer.'

'I wasn't dismissing it,' said Liza. 'Lots of things are yes and no. I must think it out.'

'It wouldn't take it.'

'Do you know,' said Liza, 'I've never seen a badger. Isn't that awful?'

'Don't worry,' said David. 'I've never been inside the Albert Hall.'

Liza thought, it is fun getting to know some one.

They went out to dinner, and at the front door Liza said, 'Please, how old are you?'

David said, with his grin in his voice, 'Thirty-five. Now I can ask you.'

'Twenty-four,' said Liza, and remembered her birthday next week.

'Like it?'

'Yes. I think I like it better every year.'

'Yes. So do I.' They went along the street to Liza's and Walter's restaurant; she thought, funny, I'd felt sort of guilty about bringing us here. Now I don't; it's not like that.

They went back to the flat and played Mozart on Walter's gramophone. David lay back in his chair and shut his eyes. Liza, from her chair, tried to imagine David taking off his tie and his shoes and spreading himself over the floor, as Walter did when he listened to music. No, David wasn't like Walter.

At ten, when they had had some tea, David went home. He stood at the front door, buttoning his grey overcoat, and said, 'Then I'll ring you up.'

'That will be lovely.'

David put on his black hat, and looked older and paler. 'God bless you. Good night.'

'Good night,' said Liza. She went back to the warmth and cigarette-smoke and thought, I wonder if it's only because of Walter that I should simply hate David to kiss me. I don't think so, because I think he feels the same. You can always tell. And then she realized that she hadn't really thought about Walter for four hours, and he swept back into her mind on a tide of happiness. Not thinking of him for so long made it all the better now. She thought, oh, darling, I love you more than I ever have before; and it was desperately important that he should know, because she had suddenly had an idea that to-night he loved her more than ever; as much as she loved him; and that was something to be put right at once.

🌀

On Liza's birthday Walter brought her three pounds of chocolates and a copy of the *Rainbow*, and Liza promised to think of a real present, although she said she didn't want anything else. They went to their restaurant for dinner, and Liza thought, now it reminds me of David; but it doesn't really. Walter read the *Rainbow* till their grape-fruit arrived, when he dropped it and said, 'Ducky, tell me everything.' Liza had seen him on Friday, and told him about David; and on Saturday for an hour. She said, 'I haven't seen any one or done anything. I did have lunch with Funny. I've been looking for flats. But I haven't found anything. Darling, everything's such a mess. I must live somewhere. I feel all despairing. If I hadn't got a job I'd go crazy. Oh, I don't know. I wish I didn't worry so.'

'Don't worry, ducky,' said Walter. 'Worry floods your stomach with acid and burns the most ghastly holes in carpets. Otherwise it doesn't do a thing.'

Liza thought, that may be true, but you haven't helped much. She said, 'It's all very well for you to talk.'

'Don't spoil my dinner, darling. I mean, don't spoil yours. Take your elbow off the programme and I'll be an awful dog and order us some champagne, if they have any.'

'Oh, darling, that would be lovely. You shouldn't, but it would be lovely.' She thought, I wish I could tell Walter things. He always slides away.

Liza had seen a lot of flats in Hampstead, with big windows, high ceilings, folding doors, partitions, unfamiliar views; all strange and rather frightening. She had tried round Baker Street, and nearly taken one she didn't really like at all, but it was after her lunch with Funny, when anything would have looked nice. But on the day after her birthday she told herself that she was being very silly; Walter would be leaving his flat next year and might go anywhere. So she went down to Chelsea and called on the house-agent who had provided her last flat.

'You helped me last time,' she said graciously, an old and valued client.

'Oh, yes,' said the large young man, blank but polite. He was a different young man. Liza saw through the window a dyeing and cleaning shop which used to be a tobacconist's, and felt like Rip Van Winkle.

The large young man said that as it was Saturday and they were shutting down he'd run her round a few places in his car. No, he didn't want his lunch yet. He took an auctioneer's catalogue off the front seat and wrapped a rug over her knees, and Liza felt dreadfully coy. Then he ran her round a few places.

The first was in the middle of a big and fairly new block. Liza had been to parties here and remembered how some one else's gramophone was always playing as it was now. She said, 'I *like* it, but then I always like everything at first. But—do you think walls *ought* to crack the way these have?'

'Between you and me,' said the large young man, 'they all do. They won't fall down, mind you. But that's about all.' He offered her a cigarette, and Liza was shaking hands with the King again. They went on to a little flat in a mews. 'Georgian,' said the large young man. 'Tell by the doors and the windows.' It had a fair-sized bedroom and a sitting-room, and looked over a little wintry garden. It was thick with dust, and wanted painting, but the young man said that that would be all right, adding, 'They paid for it.'

'I *like* it, of course,' said Liza. She looked in the discoloured bath. 'There are some sort of dead insects here.'

'Ah,' said the young man, looking too. 'Silver fish.'

'Are they all right?' said Liza, trying to keep her eyes off the lavatory seat, which seemed to be everywhere.

'*They* are. But between you and me some of the things you get in this district aren't. See here.' He pointed across the wintry garden to the backs of a row of big houses. 'A year ago I was in the insecticide business. Look at those houses. Huge rents. Left to right: red ants, common or garden bugs, red ants, mice, mice again, bugs again, earwigs.'

Liza said, storing him up delightedly to tell Walter, 'You aren't awfully encouraging.'

The large young man smiled, shrugged his shoulders, said, 'Pshp!' and trod his cigarette end into the dusty floor. 'I won't put you off the right one. Might as well be honest.'

Liza decided that he had a soul; the sort that set you against any job you were in at the time.

'Now there's this one,' said the large young man, swinging the car round a familiar corner.

'Oh!' said Liza. 'It's *my* street. Oh, and it's *my* house. I had a flat here once. Which floor is it?'

'First.'

'*Oh*. Oh, it *is*.' They walked upstairs, and into Liza's flat.

There it was. Dusty from two and a half months; silent, patient, with unhealed gashes on the wall where the men had unscrewed the bookcase; and the newspapers still crumpled in one corner. She saw a date on one, September the fifth; and across the room, where the pale dusty boards once under the carpet became dark dusty boards, was a strip of black, and the footprint. But she couldn't see it from here, for dust.

'Well,' said the large young man, 'you seem to know it.'

Liza looked round. 'I ought to. I was thinking how much shabbier the walls are than I'd remembered.'

'Give 'em a coat of paint. I should say distemper. Washable. You paid for it.'

'I think,' said Liza, 'I *think*; yes, I *must* have it again.'

'Suppose it's home.'

'I must think, though.' She thought. 'Yes. I will.'

'No hurry,' said the large young man. 'But between you and me you might do worse.'

That settled it. Liza said she would call round on Monday morning, and they got back in the car. 'But you will remember I've got it definitely, won't you? As definitely as if I'd signed something?'

'That's all right.' He put the rug over her knees. 'Care for a spot of lunch?'

'Oh, it's awfully sweet of you. But I have to meet some one. If you could just drop me at Sloane Square station—'

And in the train, going back to Walter's empty flat, she thought, I'm a coward. I miss lots of bits of life by automatically shying off. And then for the rest of the way she thought about the flat, and the smallness of the world that had led her back to it.

❦

Two men, two step-ladders, a plank, some tins and brushes moved into Liza's flat and began on the walls and the paint work. Liza was there to meet them on the first day, explaining she wanted everything off-white, with no yellow in it, and the paint had gone yellow only because it was old. She chose what she wanted from the paint and distemper shade-cards, with about as much faith as she would choose stockings that way, and came back next day to find a yellowish strip down the recess where the bookshelves would go again. The men said they could make it all right. She watched over the new mixture and came back in the afternoon, and said she thought it would do. 'I'm sorry to fuss. But it does sort of make a difference.'

'That's all right, missy,' said the older man, mounting the plank and slapping his brush on the wall. 'It's all in the day's work.'

Liza thought, that's the trouble. I'm just another flat. She said anxiously, 'And the same shade everywhere,' and left them to it; and when it had had two coats it looked lovely.

Liza was still living in Walter's flat, and she hadn't started at the office; but because of her flat life was real again. She found that she was too busy walking round Peter Jones's, wondering what she could afford and choosing patterns for possible new curtains, to think so much about Walter; and that rather worried her. But she was happy, and Walter rang up every night at ten, and, if she was out, at half-past eight next morning.

On the night that the paint was really dry, Liza said, when he rang up, 'Darling, can you come round to the flat tomorrow, I mean *my* flat? I'm moving in.'

'I'm not sure, ducky. That's Sunday. Wait till I think about the little perishers and their end of term junketing. Term ends on Monday in a riot of sardines and cocoa, and Harry and I are having a dormy spread all of our own. Yes, ducky. I can manage a few minutes some time between six and half-past. Not counting the odd hour to get there and the other to get back. But Service is our motto.'

'You are a darling. I've got some curtain patterns.' Walter was good at colours, for a man.

'Well, ducky, the light will be wrong.'

'I'll put a very strong bulb in and tie something blue over.'

'Lovely. Well, ducky, I shall now go to bed.'

'Oh, darling. We haven't begun.'

'I can't think of a thing to say. I'm seeing you to-morrow. Precious. Are you on the floor?'

'Yes, darling. On the rug. The fire's going out, on purpose. I'm eating a peppermint. Can you smell it?'

There was a sniff. 'Just. I've undone my tie. I hope the Beak won't come in.'

'Is the room empty?'

'As the grave. Not much bigger, either.'

'I wish I could see it.'

'I don't think they let the fair sex in.'

There was a silence. Nothing else to say.

'Good night, ducky.'

'Good night, darling.' She heard the click and rattle, and rang off.

She thought, nothing to say because he's seeing me tomorrow. Once eight hours was a separation. To-morrow I shall really ask him about Christmas. He must have thought about it, it's only five days to Christmas Eve. And then I can answer Aunt Vi's letter. It will be all right, I know it. I haven't got any clothes ready, so it will be all right; that's a sort of omen.

And then she thought, I've stopped imagining Christmas quite the way I did; oh, but it *will* be almost the same, even if we don't get married first. We shall get engaged. Things happen at Christmas, because it's Christmas.

❀

Liza and Walter sat on the packing-case of books. The gas was working, but not the electricity; the furniture had arrived just after tea, and been dumped about in the dark. They sat by the light of two candles and the gas-fire.

Liza blew the candles out. 'Oh, sorry, darling. If you're reading.'

Walter had found an old magazine sticking out of somewhere. He grunted and got up to sit on the floor by the gas-fire. Liza lit the candles again, put them down near him and with an effort went back to the packing-case; and then back to Walter. She said, kneeling down, 'Darling, what about Christmas?'

Walter put his hand on her neck and turned a page. 'Well, ducky, I've got to go home. The old folks are rather keen.'

Liza stared at the gas-fire. Then she said, 'You said once you liked them better when you didn't see them, and so did they.'

'All very true. But this is a special occasion, like.'

'You said once that you loathed Christmas.'

'So I do. I mean, making a fuss because it's Christmas. The actual mafficking I rather enjoy. And for God's sake, ducky, if you tell me anything else I said once, I shall give a tiny scream.'

'All right. I won't tell you anything else.'

Walter dropped his magazine, and she felt frightened. He said, 'What do you expect me to say to that?'

'Nothing.'

Walter put his arms round her. 'Beloved, don't look at me.'

The gas-fire blurred suddenly. She said, 'I can't help my face. No, that was stupid. I'm stupid.' She wouldn't cry.

'Oh, sweetheart,' said Walter. 'Ducky, it's only for a few days. And we hadn't fixed anything. I didn't know what you were doing. And, precious, *you* said you loathed Christmas too. In the hotel.'

Liza blew her nose. She thought, I can never believe that any one remembers anything I say. 'I'm sorry, darling.'

'So am I. Dreadfully. Ducky, don't let's go back to that horrible stage. We were just getting it right. We were being ourselves, and seeing each other when we wanted to.'

So that was getting it right. Liza looked away and round the flat. She was glad of the candlelight, and the furniture dumped anywhere, because it wasn't her flat yet. She thought, I loom at you, like your wardrobe; when I want you you don't want me. And when you don't want me I want you. Just now I was six feet away from you, and that was six feet too far, and I couldn't stay there.

Then she thought, if we had had Christmas together, it would have been like the half-term week-end, when we sat in the pub after dinner on Saturday and I put my hand on yours on the bench, and you drew it away. *Leave me alone:* I won't leave you alone, because you want me to; I can't

– 231 –

leave you alone, because when you go away from me you pull the chain. No, Christmas wouldn't have been like the half-term weekend, because I should have been desperate and we should have had a scene. And then—I don't know.

Walter put a cigarette in her mouth, and lit it from the candle. They sat there, with his arm round her and his coat-sleeve against her face. Nothing to say; they knew it all.

Walter stirred. 'I must get.' He stood up. Liza stood up too. 'Can't you stay to supper?'

'I can't, darling.'

Liza heard herself saying, 'Please, please do. I've got masses of food and it will only take five minutes to cook something.'

'Darling, I can't. I told you.'

'I believe you're going to the pub with Harry.'

'And if I was going to the pub with Harry,' said Walter, 'or if I was going to a brothel, neither of which I am, and both of which I'm damned if I have to be checked up on—I've lost the beginning of that sentence, but you see its drift.'

Liza thought, he's angry. She was frightened; but she wasn't going to be sorry.

Walter pinched her nose, and put his arms round her. 'Ducky. Come off it. You're not being you.'

'Yes, I am. This is the real me.' She thought, it isn't, you've never seen it; I've had to stay as I was when you first knew me, because I've been too much of a coward to go my own way.

Walter pulled her hair over her eyes. 'Ducky, please smile. You would if you could see yourself as a Skye terrier. Highly laughable.'

'Well, you laugh then.'

'I don't think I can,' said Walter. 'Not straight off like that. I'll tell you something funny. I saw an aged man in Baker Street ticking off a carthorse. He tied its nose-bag on and said, shut up grumbling and get on wiv yer ruddy lunch. And once there was a man who came home drunk and met a policeman and said, I'll prove I'm not drunk and he took the policeman upstairs and there was a man in bed asleep with his wife, and he said there I am you see in bed asleep. And why is a chicken? And how much string from here to Edinburgh? Ducky, stop me before I get any unfunnier.'

Liza smiled. It had been very difficult not to. Walter put her hair back and kissed her. She said, 'I'm sorry, darling. And thank you for nearly choosing the curtains. I'm sorry about the light.'

'Bless you, precious. Now I shall go back to the lentil soup and what is whimsically known as shape because it has none, and think how much I love you.'

'Darling, I do love you.' He loved her too, and he was going because he had to. They were on the same side.

'Ducky,' said Walter, squeezing her, 'What about you? I mean, for Christmas?'

'I shall stay here.'

'Oh, darling.'

'No, I want to. I've got so much to do. Aunt Vi's invited me down there, but I'd rather be here.'

Walter flipped her neck and kissed her. 'I break up tomorrow, hooroo. We'll have a party on Wednesday.' And he ran downstairs.

When the sound of his car had gone, Liza took a candle into the kitchen and opened a tin of baked beans. She thought, Kate would tell you all the things I could. She'd tell you you were selfish, and an egoist, and a coward, and that you get your own way and then turn your bloody charm on so that the other person won't make you change your mind.

Then she thought about Christmas, telling herself that it was really a good thing, because there was so much to do in the flat; and, tipping the baked beans into the saucepan, she leant her head against the stove's plate-rack and felt sick with misery.

Then she thought, and David said he'd ring up, and that was seventeen days ago; more than anything in the world I want to see David. And she felt even sicker.

The next evening David opened the door of his flat and said, 'I'm awfully glad you could come. I thought you might not have got my message. Till I got yours.' He grinned. 'I do like your switchboard girl.'

'That was our Miss Derry,' said Liza. 'Isn't she heavenly? I do like your flat.' David had told her that it was a furnished service flat, and very dull. It wasn't, it was rather modern; and it was pleasantly impersonal, like him.

'Thank you,' said David. Liza sat down in a square armchair by the electric fire. 'Were you very busy all day?'

'I got back from Scotland this morning. That's why I didn't ring up. You must have thought me very rude. I tried, but you were out. I went the day after I saw you. They sent me all of a sudden.'

'What fun. Do they often?'

'It was New York last time. Nearly as sudden. The advertising world is a bit like that. They do it to impress themselves.' He took a decanter from a cupboard. 'How do you like working again?'

'It's fun. I've only had one day, so it won't be for long. But it's sort of cosy.' She added, 'And I've gone back to my old flat too.'

David held the decanter up, looking at it as if he found it rather amusing. 'Square one.'

'I know. Do you think it's a good thing?'

'Well, I think it rather depends why.'

Liza blushed; but David didn't know about her and Walter. 'I know. I suppose I wanted to go back to a phase I liked. But that might not be cowardice, might it?'

'No,' said David, handing her a glass. 'It might be the opposite.'

'Do you like backgrounds?'

'I'm not an addict.'

'No. I don't think I am, really.'

They drank their sherry. David put his glass down and lay back and crossed his ankles, looking very tired again. He said, with his hand over his eyes, 'Christmas is upon us. I suppose you aren't going to stay with your aunt?'

Liza was suddenly very happy. She said, 'I hadn't answered the letter yet. I didn't know what was happening till yesterday.'

David grinned and picked up his glass. 'Isn't it?'

'No.'

'Then we'll catch the six o'clock train together, if you're going on Thursday.'

'Oh, I am. Oh, how lovely.'

'And I don't think I said dinner, but will you stay and have some? There's a not bad restaurant downstairs. And then we might go to a flick.'

'Oh, that would be lovely. But'—she wanted to say, you've been travelling all night and you ought to go to bed, and felt rather embarrassed—'but I ought to go back and see about the flat. It's a terrible mess and the electric man only got the light going to-day.'

'Well, then,' said David, 'we'll have dinner, anyway.'

'I can't think of anything nicer.' And she couldn't; except, of course, Christmas.

XVI

The office was always the same on the day before Christmas Eve. In theory no one was allowed to go before five; but there was a general feeling that it would be silly to do any work after lunch-time, when the pay came round, so no one did. Miss Netley and Miss Vane went off at three to catch trains. The Happy Christmases began. Miss Derry and Partridge, who were supposed to have no home life that mattered, stuck to their switchboard and rubber stamp. Mr. Chiddock came back very late from lunch, flushed and almost mellow, and shut himself in his room, where he probably went to sleep. Mr. Hollis came back at four and left with Mr. Chiddock, when they had had tea, to more Happy Christmases. Liza had been to the hairdresser's at lunch-time and there was nothing to do but her nails. She sat in her room, under the light and by the gas-fire, and, seeing the holly on the calendar, had a sudden rush of excitement. Through the open door came the voices of Miss Derry and Partridge. She heard that Partridge was to be a Rover next month, and that Miss Derry's family were having a party on Christmas Day, and had asked all their relations.

'Dozens and dozens,' said Miss Derry's disillusioned voice. 'Uncle Hal and Aunt Effie and Uncle Fred and Cousin Molly and dozens of kids. Oh, the whole boiling. Eat their heads off and hate each other by the end of the day. What're you going to do, Partridge?'

'Church Parade,' said Partridge's voice. 'And then eat.' His rubber stamp banged.

At five, when all the others had gone, the office was very quiet indeed. Liza was ready to go; she went into Enquiries and sat down at Miss Derry's table to count the money in her bag. Three pounds ten and the two pounds extra for Christmas were five pounds ten, or they had been

– 236 –

at lunch-time; now she had four pounds nine and twopence. She couldn't have spent all that at the hairdresser's. She did a little sum on Miss Derry's carbon-paper box, and as soon as she knew where the money had gone, in bus-fares, lunch, gloves and odds and ends, she was happy again. Four pounds nine and twopence; she was rich.

The telephone rang very loudly, and the baize-aproned old man's voice said, 'Gentleman in a taxi, miss.'

Christmas had begun. No more work for four days, and David was waiting downstairs.

Paddington was the usual Christmas pandemonium. David bought the tickets and joined her in the queue at the barrier, and while they waited Liza gave him her sixteen shillings and threepence. David carried the suit-cases up to the front of the train and opened the door of a first-class compartment.

'Oh, I say,' said Liza, blushing. 'How silly of me. How much more do I owe you?'

'Oh, no, please,' said David. 'It was only because of the crowds. I acted on instinct. Self-preservation.'

'Oh, but I must.' She took out one of the pound notes and thought, it can't be more than twice the third-class fare.

'No, no. Call it a Christmas present. A spur of the moment one, because I must confess you weren't going to get anything. I'm very bad at choosing presents.'

'Oh, so am I,' said Liza, who had been thinking she would have to get him one now; but that had made it all right. 'You are a dear. And it's a lovely present. And we have it to ourselves.'

'A bit of luck. Hang out and cough while I go to the bookstall.'

While he was gone Liza stood at the window, gazing desperately up and down the platform, thinking, I'm expecting ten friends who will fill this compartment to the brim, and go away, you horrid fat man. The fat man stood at the door and met Liza's eyes. They stared at each other for perhaps fifteen seconds, and then the fat man's eyes dropped and he moved away. Liza stepped aside while David opened the door. She saw his grin, and thought, David makes me feel—I can't exactly describe it; sensible, and resourceful. The train moved off; they still had the compartment to themselves; sometimes everything went right, even when you expected it to, and perhaps Christmas was going to be one of such times.

David switched on the lights behind them, and Liza spread a newspaper on the opposite seat for them to put their feet on. Her legs weren't really long enough; she put her feet on the floor, thinking, Walter would have nearly called me a little woman.

They did the crossword in David's *Times*. 'Well,' said David, 'I suppose that word's chariot. But I can't say I've ever read *Titus Andronicus*.'

'I don't remember that bit, but I *have* read it. All through, too.'

'What was it like?'

'Well, I could have told you the plot when I'd finished, or, rather as I went along; but not now. All I remember is that it was all blood and thunder and ravishment, with one nice bit about a lute.'

'I'm impressed,' said David, giving her a cigarette; and Liza thought, and you make me feel intelligent too. And I don't have to tell you I read it to show off to Walter.

A sour-faced woman slid the door open, saw them and disappeared, slamming it. Liza thought, I suppose we look A Couple; and felt self-conscious. She glanced up and saw David's grin, and felt happy again; and thought, now we really know each other.

They did half the crossword. 'I think that's enough of that,' said David. 'Will you think me very dull if I do some work?'

'No, please do,' said Liza. David opened his brief-case and took out a bundle of typed papers, and Liza, anything typed making her feel shy and a secretary, opened the *New Statesman* David had bought, and sat back. Walter was perhaps reading it in Lincolnshire; and she was rather worried to find that thinking about him didn't hurt so much this evening. The darkness, rattling past this little bright world, was carrying her away from the muddle of the flat, the ache of listening for the telephone, the flying hours they had spent together this week. Sometimes, when Liza had been typing too hard all the morning, she felt, when she sat down to lunch at the Bygone Days Tea Shop, as she did now; that life was more exciting and splendid than it had ever been before, calling her to share its richness. She opened the *New Statesman*, and, skipping the political pages, began to read. The train rattled on and on. The rain slashed at the windows, making the little bright world brighter. Liza was aware that David was watching her, and looked up, and got his grin, and an 'All right?'

'Yes, thank you.' She went on reading, and the little bright world rattled on.

A steward came down the corridor, shouting. He put his head in at the door and said, with the respect proper to a first-class carriage, 'Is any one taking the first dinner?'

'Two,' said David. He put his papers back in his brief-case. 'Well, that's enough of that. I hope you've had a nice read.'

'Lovely. I know nearly everything, even about tin-plate shares.'

'Splendid,' said David, with his grin; 'you shall tell me all about them at dinner.' They went off down the rattling corridor, Liza thinking, oh, David, I do like you.

When they were drinking their coffee, Liza said, 'Please, while you have the bill there, what's exactly half of it, including everything?'

'Well, you know.' He turned the menu for the wine list. 'It takes a bit of working out. You had sherry and I had whisky. And half the tip. Seven and a penny.'

Liza thought, you are a dear.

※

On the next night, which was Christmas Eve, Betty pinned a very long pink silk stocking, with embroidered clocks, to Liza's bed-rail. Liza remembered it from past Christmases; Aunt Vi had half a dozen, all different colours, saved from her trousseau and brought out every year for this purpose. Liza had sometimes spent Christmas here when she was a child, and gone to sleep behind an empty stocking and woken to a full one. Now every one in the house knew about Santa Claus, and the stocking was bulging already. That lump in the toe meant a tangerine in silver paper.

''Night,' said Betty, wrapping her purple dressing-gown closer. 'Do you like Christmas?'

'I like this one.'

'I can't stand it ever. 'Night.'

''Night, Betty.' She fell asleep listening to the rain and thinking of the party at the Carrolls' house to-morrow evening.

Christmas Day was grey and hung with heavy clouds, but the rain had stopped. Every one but Liza and Margaret went to church before breakfast, and every one but Aunt Vi, who thought she was starting a cold, went at eleven. Uncle George, being a sidesman, showed them up the holly-decked aisle. He wore a different face and looked as if he recognized them, but only just. Liza wanted to giggle.

David's dark head showed a few rows up and to the right, among an apparently large house-party, with what at first seemed several gaps in the rows, but turned out to be children. Fun; Christmas was fun. Uncle George, trundling up the aisle with a holly berry he didn't know about on his shoulder, was fun. Liza's eyes went back to David; she hadn't seen him since their journey down; she had heard yesterday that they had all gone off somewhere in cars, and it had made the day suddenly empty. She thought she could pick out his father and mother, Mrs. Carroll's brother and sister-in-law; they were tall and thin and nice, and his mother, when she turned round to whisper, reminded Liza of David's face behind the decanter, because she looked as if she found life rather amusing.

Except for weddings, which didn't count, Liza hadn't been to church since her last Christmas Day here, three years ago. She could never persuade herself that a religion should be followed if it talked about life after death; she counted herself an unbeliever, but found in her attitude a defying 'You're not there!' to something there to hear it. She thought that on the whole religion was good for the world, so perhaps not wanting to go to church was mostly laziness. She wondered what David thought; Walter, she knew, considered being dragged to church every Sunday with his little perishers a mortal insult; she had said, 'What do you think of to pass the time?' and he had said, 'Pneumatic trousers, like Theodore Gumbril in *Antic Hay*.' That was in the hotel at half term. Liza was suddenly deeply miserable.

The vicar processed up the aisle, and David half turned; he seemed to be looking for Liza. They smiled at each other, and Liza saw that poor James, next to her, was watching sadly. James had given her the Oxford Book of English Prose and a revolving spider, which had decided Liza that he was an angel. She smiled and whispered, 'I wish I had my spider here.' James went red with delight; one of the silk handkerchiefs she had given him sprouted from his breast pocket. He pulled at it and blew his nose so loudly that Betty frowned and Margaret giggled. Everything was fun.

Liza found that church and the cinema had the same effect on her. She wanted to cry, especially at any music. But not during the sermon, when she played the A B C game which had got her through so many at school. You listened for a word beginning with A, and so on in order to Z, which was easier than it sounded because of Zacharias and zeal. Words like excellent counted for X. Liza didn't play very hard, sticking at K, waiting hopefully for the vicar to talk about kindness, knowledge or kingdoms, and wondering if David knew the game and was playing it. The back of his head looked serious, and Liza felt shy again, and a secretary.

Every one met and talked in the church porch. Liza and David walked to the lych-gate, and David said, 'Let's go on up to the big field.' They climbed the stile, and took the path round what had once been a cornfield and was now damp stubble, showing the dark earth. David stopped. 'I am so sorry; I forgot about mud.'

'No, let's go on.' They walked slowly along, and Liza asked David what he thought about church.

'Well, you know,' said David, 'I like it. It gives you time to think. And I can't say I ever feel any the worse for it. And seeing the clergyman looking so keen on it all, and for about sixpence a year—well, it sort of sets you a standard of unworldliness.'

'Yes. I hadn't exactly thought of it like that, but I do agree. Do you think that's why they pay them so little?'

'It's an idea.'

The church clock banged out three-quarters, and Liza said, 'I must go.'

'Zero hour?'

'Yes. I wish I felt hungry.'

'So do I.'

At the Carrolls' gate David said, 'I shall see you at seven. The house is a riot of paper-chains and holly and mistletoe.'

Liza's stomach fluttered with excitement.

Uncle George's household began to eat seriously at one o'clock. It ate turkey and stuffing and sausages, bread sauce and brussels sprouts and roast potatoes, Christmas pudding with brandy-butter and cream, nuts, raisins, dates, chocolates and Turkish delight. Then it went on to tangerines and the sweets it had had as presents. It switched over at four to paste sandwiches and Christmas cake, and drank a lot of tea. Then it went back to the sweets. Liza ate the least possible of everything, and thought that it would have lasted her a week in London. At half-past five she went up to dress, beginning with a bath, and heard Betty's voice through the door. Liza got out and unbolted it, and Betty whisked in, waved her hands, swallowed a sweet, and said, 'My boy friend's going to be at the party.'

For a dreadful moment Liza thought she meant Edward, who had died down lately. 'You don't know about him, Liza. I met him after you'd gone, only once, though, and I'd almost forgotten. But he's awfully attractive, and he's called Dobbie. I mean, that's his nickname.' Betty's eyes shone, and she had stopped being bossy.

'Will there be a lot of people there, Betty?'

'About twenty-five. Won't it be fun? I've got Dobbie and you've got David. Isn't Christmas fun? You do like David, don't you? You seem as if you do.'

'Yes. I like him very much indeed.'

Betty thrust her chin at the mirror, stared at it and whisked out. Liza got out and bolted the door again. She thought, as she dried, I like David as much as I can like any one. Liking people *is* fun; and I'm glad Betty's taped for the evening.

✿

At five to seven Aunt Vi, who had been wondering out loud about her cold all day, said she really didn't think she'd go to the party. Betty said, 'Oh, what a pity, Mummy. Won't you really?' and looked pleased. It was raining, and at a quarter-past seven Uncle George got the car to start, and the five of them squeezed in and drove to the Carrolls'. Liza wore her black dinner-dress. She had always liked it better than any other evening dress she had ever had, because it had cost too much and made her so thin. It had a straight skirt and little tucked sleeves, and showed up well against Betty's puffs and flares. Betty's dress was a bright blue taffeta, while Margaret wore apricot crêpe de Chine and hitched desperately at her stockings as they went up to the bedroom, through the wide hall and past a glittering Christmas tree.

'Don't *do* it, Margaret,' said Betty. 'It's getting a habit, and do remember those are silk.' They were, flesh-coloured and making Margaret's legs squarer than ever.

Liza wore the turquoise and gold stud ear-rings which Walter had given her for Christmas and her birthday together, Liza having seen them in a pawn-shop and saying he could give them to her on that condition only; and she had given him a pair of driving-gloves. Betty, who knew about the ear-rings, said, 'He's got awfully good taste,' and Liza said gratefully, 'You do look pretty.' It was true; Betty shone with happiness; and for some one called Dobbie. Margaret hitched once more, and they went down to the drawing-room, past the mistletoe hanging from the Chinese lantern.

The drawing-room was a riot of paper-chains, and a huge fire blazed so fiercely that no one stood very near it, and there were a lot of chairs no one sat on yet. It seemed as if every one else had arrived already, but then people were more punctual in the country. Liza knew some of them, and dismissed them all as nice and dull, and, as they were of all ages, from Margaret up to a retired General, as not the sort of party to play Sardines, which was rather disappointing. She looked round for David and saw him, unfamiliar in a dinner-jacket, talking to Uncle George; and Liza felt shy again, and glad he hadn't seen her yet.

The radiogram was playing dance music, and a tune came out to meet her; and suddenly Liza was swept with an unbearable desire to burst into tears. This tune had, in the autumn, linked itself with her dream of Christmas; it had woven itself into the clothes she had planned, the red evening dress, the firelight on the wealth of old oak, the antlers and the pewter mugs downstairs, upstairs the firelight again, and Walter's head on her lap; and here was the tune, playing for her at Christmas, and she was wearing a black dress she had had for a year, in a house Walter had never seen, among people he didn't know; and Walter was the other side of England.

I won't cry, thought Liza, turning towards the door, and anyway I can't here; and I'm *not* sorry for myself. The door blurred. She heard David's 'Hullo!' behind her, and slipped out into the hall, luckily empty; and, shutting her eyes and clenching her hands, said, nothing in the world matters, and I don't mind if it does. Then she half turned and saw David's soft white shirt, and had an almost as unbearable desire to cry into it; and then she felt very silly, and the desire passed, and she said, turning towards him, hoping her eyes weren't pink and not liking to raise them above his long fingers on his black tie:

'I'm awfully sorry. It's that tune.' The tune was a Sousa march now. 'I mean the last one; it reminded me of something'; and she wanted to cry again, but now, she thought, for self-pity.

'They are the devil, aren't they?' said David. 'I bet this one doesn't remind you of anything.' Finally put right by his agreeable impersonality, Liza said, 'It reminds me of marching out of prayers at school,' and blew her nose, and powdered it, and they went back to the drawing-room, where every one was arranging chairs for Turn the Trencher.

Turn the Trencher didn't go very well, but it wasn't expected to, any more than the not very funny man who comes on first at a music-hall.

But Mrs. Carroll sailed through with it, looking so handsome that Liza thought, I shall get fat when I'm older; only of course, with poor Miss Prince, it's something to do with being a virgin. Mrs. Carroll said, 'One more game before supper,' and every one cheered up, and Animal, Vegetable and Mineral went very well indeed.

A rash of paper hats and funny noses broke out at supper. Uncle George wore a tiny Donald Duck cap held on by elastic. Mr. Carroll lurked under a vast yellow crown. Miss Prince wore a sort of Admiral's hat and looked extraordinarily happy, for a virgin. Dobbie, which would be short for Dobbin, wore a pink sun-bonnet, and you expected to see holes for his ears. Liza had swopped a mauve pillow-case for David's little blue glengarry, which matched her ear-rings, and they stood together at the groaning table—it was a stand-up supper—and Liza took a glass from the tray a maid held out. It was a mild brown drink on which rode a strip of cucumber peel. She sipped at it.

'Give that to me,' said David, and came back with two glasses of gin and lime.

'How did you know I didn't want it?'

David grinned. 'Instinct.' He looked at his glass. 'What's the most ear-assaulting toast you can call to mind?'

'Bung ho,' said Liza.

'Bung ho, then,' and he lifted his glass. 'Bung ho.' She lifted hers.

A schoolboy in an Eton suit ate a plateful of éclairs and whispered to his mother, who hurried him out. Liza glanced up and saw David watching her.

'I'm awfully sorry for him, of course,' she said, 'but it was heavenly, wasn't it?'

'Oscar Wilde said something about nature imitating art and doing it badly,' said David. 'I don't think that was done so badly, do you?' He added, 'Finish it up and I'll get you another.' Liza gave him her glass and thought, I do like to be taken care of. She gazed round the room. Betty was eating an ice under the shadow of Dobbie's sun-bonnet, and giggling dotingly. David's mother and father stood with the retired General, all three hatless but gay. Every one was gay. James put on a pair of spectacles fitted with tin pop-eyes, and when he blew at the rubber tube his eyes whirled round and sent a straw-haired schoolgirl in yellow muslin into happy shrieks. A paper-chain came unhitched and flattened Mr. Carroll's crown. He perked it up with dignity, and Liza thought, I believe that because he's wearing a paper crown he's a king. Everything is heavenly.

After supper they played Subject and Object. The retired General and the schoolboy's mother went out of the room, came back and were guessed by Mrs. Carroll as George Washington and his axe. 'David darling,' she said, 'you come out with me.' David's hand went up to his tie. Liza thought, oh, poor David. He came back as King Arthur's sword Excalibur; and when it was all over, and he sat down next to her again, she thought, oh, I am glad to be near you again. She said, 'I don't think you had any say in that.'

David grinned. 'You wait.' Liza thought, David and I are the only sophisticated people in this room; that is, the only people from London. It was a nice cosy feeling.

The younger ones wanted General Post, and, every one still being very gay, the chairs were pulled into a closer half-circle round the fire. The schoolboy, all right again, pipped on a little whistle. James threw a streamer at Liza and blew, and his tin eyes raced horribly.

And then the lights went out.

There was a murmur, a scuffling of chairs. The fire shone on a half-circle of excited faces. The fact that the room was not in the least dark made it no less exciting that something had Happened. The lights had fused.

❧

Liza still sat in her chair. Most of the half-circle had scattered round the room, and James and the straw-haired schoolgirl were by the radiogram. Betty and Dobbie had disappeared. David had gone out with Mr. Carroll and Uncle George. So Liza sat in the firelight, and the radiogram played a dance tune which she had heard once before but which now came to life for her. The voices behind her rose and fell and laughed; they were somewhere outside the world. Only James and the straw-haired schoolgirl shared it, leaning on the radiogram, silent, dreaming, the girl's sharp nose and long narrow eyes lit by the fire, James staring at her hair as his foot jogged to the music.

Liza heard some one behind her chair; it was David. He stood there in the firelight, and said:

'I don't think we can be any use. Your Uncle George is having the time of his life with the fuse-box. My Uncle Percy is just watching, and saying there's no spare wire.'

Liza said, 'If Uncle George mends anything he always seems to make it worse.'

'Splendid. Shall we go and sit down somewhere?'

There were two candles in the hall. David took one, and their shadows spilt and shifted, moving before and behind them as he led the way across to the dining-room, where he put the candle on the sideboard and poured out two glasses of gin and lime, giving one to Liza, with his grin. They lifted their glasses, and said nothing.

The lights round the walls and on the Christmas tree on the table flashed, wobbled, held for a second and went off again.

'Oh dear,' said Liza, 'this is a lovely world.' Lovely, lovely world.

'Lovely,' said David; and they finished their laugh and their drink, and went up the passage to an open door. David handed her the candle; Liza thought, he's wondering too about Betty and Dobbie. She said, 'No, no one,' and they went in to a sort of study, with empty glasses on a table and a precisely ticking clock. Liza put the candle in the dead hearth and sat down in a leather armchair; David, shutting the door, came round behind her and sat on the leather-padded rail of the fender.

'Please,' said Liza. 'I wish you'd have this chair.'

'No, no,' said David. 'This is all right when you find where your head fits,' and he settled it into a recess. Liza thought, there's another armchair opposite; I don't think he remembered either.

David licked his finger and thumb and pinched the candle out. Liza said, into the sudden darkness, 'Clever.'

David's voice, with his grin in it, came back. 'Showing off.'

It was very dark, and very quiet. Liza heard a faint click. 'Cigarette,' said

David's voice. There was another click, and by the flame of the cigarette-lighter she saw his face and thought, just now, just this evening, yours is the only face in the world. They lit their cigarettes, and in the darkness she still seemed to see his face. It was very dark again, and very quiet. The clock's precise ticking made it all the quieter, the little red points of their cigarettes, glowing and fading, made it all the darker. Liza said:

'I am so happy.'

'Yes,' said David's voice. 'So am I.'

Liza thought, anything else we say will spoil it.

And then the lights went up.

Liza said, 'Some one must have left the switch on.'

David said, 'You know, I don't think your Uncle George was trying.'

They crossed the hall, where Betty and Dobbie were scurrying away from the mistletoe. Liza saw David's hand go up to his tie; and as they reached the Chinese lantern he took her elbow. She stopped; and, looking up, saw his grin as he stooped and kissed her, half on her mouth and half on her cheek.

Then they went into the drawing-room, where Uncle George was being a hero, with a modest smile on his flat face and still wearing his Donald Duck cap, now somewhere down by his ear.

❀

Liza lay in bed and thought.

She thought, when I am with David I'm different; the opposite of what I am with Walter. Oh, Walter, darling; she turned to the middle of the bed and imagined Walter beside her; he was almost there, but he wasn't. *Time passes, time passes, and I lie alone.* She heard herself whispering, darling, if we could go back and begin again I would be different. I know how to be now, and I will be, next time. Then she thought of David again; his black silk ankle hanging an inch from her skirt as they sat in the half-circle; his face by the light of the cigarette-lighter, his voice in the dark; his 'God bless you. Good night,' at the car door. She thought, when we go for our walk to-morrow perhaps I ought to tell him about me and Walter. But

I don't feel I have to; I think it would falsify us. *He* may have a mistress. And I mustn't spoil the way we are now. It's all so *itself* as it is. And it's funny, I don't want him and Walter to meet now.

Then she thought, I shall tell him if and when I think it's right. I shall know. Now I shall go to sleep. And she went to sleep, thinking about David and the long walk to-morrow.

XVII

It was New Year's Eve.

Liza had collected a few vague invitations to some not very exciting parties, and told Walter. Walter had said, 'Well, I've been asked to a few places too. I don't know that I want to go anywhere much. Let's see what we feel like.' The *we* was really all that mattered. Finally, that morning, he had said, 'I know. Let's go to the Savoy and pipe in the boar's head. Would that be nice?'

'Oh, *darling*. Oh, it would be lovely.'

So this evening, at half-past seven, Liza put on her black tulle dress, which had taken an hour to iron, and wasn't very happy about it. She thought it needed something underneath, but the shoulder-straps were very narrow and any others would show. But it was her dressiest dress. She tried on her green velvet coatee, but it looked wrong, hanging loose over that very full skirt. She stood at the mirror, wondering; now it was perhaps all right, now it was certainly all wrong. She looked round the flat, which had sheets for curtains, and a bare floor, because she had sent the curtains and the carpet to be cleaned, and thought, everything is unreal again. Then she heard Walter's key in the door. He wore his ordinary clothes and carried his much-labelled suit-case.

'Hullo, ducky.' He kissed her. 'Guess who I met in Victoria Street.'

'I can't, darling.' But she thought she could, from his voice.

'Kate. And, ducky, she wants us to go to their party. She told me, while Hasty wound his lead round my legs and a lamp-post, that she didn't know how to get hold of us or she'd have asked us weeks ago.'

'I should have thought she could have looked you up in the book.' She thought, or me; and wished Walter didn't seem so pleased about it. She had almost forgotten Kate.

'Now, ducky,' said Walter, pinching her shoulder. 'Come off it. You know the poor girl can't read. You do want to go, don't you? Because I took it on myself to say yes, and then I had lots of qualms, so tell me I done right, ducky.'

Liza was thinking, I can wear my dinner-dress now. She said, 'Of course you did, darling. It will be lovely. But you'll have to ring up and unbook the table.'

'Well, actually, darling, I forgot to ring up and book it. So all is for the best in the best of all possible worlds, don't you think? Though I've still got to wear my white tie.' He opened his suit-case and took out his tail-coat. 'Sweetie, would you like to iron this? And my trousies?'

Liza's heart sank. She ironed his suit, very conscientiously and struggling to keep the coat from slipping off the ironing-board; and, as she had expected, there wasn't time to do her dinner-dress properly. It didn't look so bad. But she thought of the last time she had worn it, and her heart held an island of happiness, and ached for it.

In the taxi Walter said, 'You look lovely, ducky.' Liza thought, he can hardly see me in this dark. But she said, 'Thank you, darling. So do you.'

Walter flapped down the seat and put his feet up. He took her hand. 'Sound happy, precious.'

'I am happy. I can't help my voice.'

Walter's finger-nail flipped her neck; and the taxi rattled on through the glitter to a little house which looked just as Liza had imagined it

There were a lot of people in the long white drawing-room. The men looked mostly rather raddled, and the women wore dresses with narrow shoulder-straps and all had the same voice. Kate wore a gold dress. She cried, 'Darlings! How lovely!' She was a different Kate.

Liza took a cocktail. She had lost Walter. She stood next to the man she had just been introduced to; a woman on his other side spoke, and he turned away. Liza thought, I don't belong, I don't belong. But I'm here, and I've got to last out the evening inside myself.

The party got better. Parties always did. They danced to the radiogram, and Liza danced with some quite nice men, and some very dull ones, and drank champagne down in the dining-room, where people wandered in and out for supper. She danced once with Walter, and they were strangers again. Walter was in the highest spirits, and had danced, and went on dancing after, with a succession of beautiful girls.

Liza danced with Maurice, looking floridly Grecian, and could think of nothing to say except, 'Where's Hasty?'

'Oh, he's in bed,' said Maurice.

'What a pity. He is an angel, isn't he?'

'Not a bad little beggar. Yaps a bit.'

'Oh, but he's awfully devoted,' said Liza. They went on talking about Hasty because there was nothing else to talk about. A swarthy young man switched off the radiogram and began to play the piano, going from one dance tune to another. People sat round the drawing-room, and gradually stopped talking. That was the best part of the evening. Liza sat next to Walter and thought about David; wondering where he was, what he was doing for New Year's Eve; and about Christmas. Then she thought that when the party was all over she and Walter would go to bed in his flat; then she thought of her new, clean flat, and had a little thrill of excitement, thinking that it was the Future, and that, by the light of the gas-fire, with Walter's head in her lap, anything might happen; the wireless would play the *Hassan* music, and Walter would say, ducky, we've been so happy together all this year, we've sort of tried it out and it's worked, and Fate had brought you back here, and there am I back in my flat and going to be a real barrister; sweetheart, would you be frightfully angry if, after all the bother of moving the furniture in, I asked you to leave your flat and marry me? And she would kiss his hair, and take him in her arms and say, no, darling, not frightfully angry.

The swarthy young man scattered a few chords over the piano and broke into the dance tune which had belonged to the dream of Christmas, and the firelight on the wealth of old oak. It was a sort of omen. Liza sat there in another dream, her eyes full of happy tears.

The music stopped, and most of the people stood up and drifted away. Walter disappeared; Liza sat there, wondering what she ought to do. The swarthy young man played some twiddly bits and a half-tune which he seemed to be improvising. Liza listened, as if academically interested. Her face felt set in plaster. It ought to be easy just to sit alone in a strange room; other people were, a few chairs away, talking and laughing. She sat, taut and miserable, now trying to look as if lost in thought; and the clock said a quarter to twelve. The party would never be over.

❦

And then it was nearly twelve. Kate drew the curtains back a little way and opened a window at the bottom, and Big Ben boomed the quarters, with a clamour of bells. The swarthy young man stood at the door, to some scattered cheering. There was a lump of coal on the parquet. People were standing round the room in couples, and holding champagne glasses, and as the first stroke of twelve struck there was a general burst of voices, laughter and kissing. Liza looked round for Walter. There he was across the room, kissing Kate; or, to be fair, Kate had stopped him and kissed him. Liza stood back against the wall, waiting for Walter to come over and kiss her, and thought all the thoughts every one thinks when an old year dies and a new one is born.

❦

Walter flapped the taxi seat down and put his feet up, saying, through a yawn, 'You didn't look to be enjoying the party, ducky.'

'I wasn't.'

'Come off it, ducky,' and he took her hand. 'Why didn't you?'

Liza wanted to cry. 'I don't know. I just don't like that sort of party.'

'Well, nor do I much. I thought every one was ghastly. But I hid my suffering beneath a brave front of gaiety, dammit.'

'I hate you,' said Liza suddenly, and was very frightened indeed.

Walter said, 'Say that again. In words of one syllable.'

'I don't hate you,' said Liza miserably. 'You know I don't. Only sometimes I wish I did.'

Walter put his arm round her, and the taxi rattled on. 'Sweetheart, I wasn't bullying you not to hate me.'

Liza thought, you were, or you wouldn't have said you weren't. Or perhaps you were bullying me to go on hating you. She put her head on his shoulder. 'I know, darling. It's only that with Kate I feel all wrong.' She thought, yes, I feel I'm not married.

'You're lovely,' said Walter, kissing her. There was nothing else to say. The taxi rattled them nearer and nearer to his flat; she thought, we shall go to bed, and I shall love him more than ever; and hate him more than ever; and be unhappier than ever. This is New Year's Day. To-morrow is January the second, and we shall have been lovers for a year. I can't go on like this any longer.

❦

New Year's Day was a Saturday, and Liza's Saturday off. Liza and Walter had a silent breakfast in dressing-gowns. Walter said he had a hangover, and Liza would have thought that she had, if you could have one without having felt in the least drunk the night before.

Walter drove her to her flat. 'I'll be round at about seven, ducky, and we'll go out somewhere to-morrow. Do you know we've never been to Kent together? Let's go.'

It was like last spring again. Liza said, 'Do you know, darling, it's a year to-morrow night that we first went to bed together?'

'Cor,' said Walter. 'Makes you think. Good-bye, precious.' He made his face and drove off.

There were two parcels in the hall: the carpet, rolled up, and the curtains. Mr. North was there too, reading his post. He smiled toothily.

'Let me help you up with them.' They carried them up in silence; officially they knew each other, but Liza could think of nothing to say except, I'm sorry about your girl friend. Because she had read a postcard saying, *No. Hannah*, and hadn't seen or heard Hannah. Hannah was all over; oh, poor, poor Mr. North.

Liza had eight hours to get the flat ready; the books were out of order and upside down, the curtains had to be hung, the carpet laid, the china arranged in the kitchen, the tablecloth washed and ironed for dinner to-night, everything swept and dusted. She shook out the curtains, which had been re-glazed and looked as new as the paint, and put them on the bed. She would have to make the bed with two clean sheets and pillow-cases. There was an awful lot to do; she must have her hair set, and iron and mend her black cocktail-party dress. Everything about her, the flat and the dinner must be exactly right; because to-night Walter would ask her to marry him.

Liza knelt by the gas-fire and thought, I shall *make* him ask me. You can make any one say anything, if you try.

Then Liza thought about David. She thought, perhaps he knows about Walter and me; at least, that there's some one. Why I am so happy with David, and unhappy with Walter, is because I am in love with Walter. I don't hold on to David, because I don't want to. When I see him, it's lovely; and that's all.

Then she imagined David asking her to marry him; and herself saying to Walter, David wants to marry me and if you say so I will; and Walter took her in his arms, saying, my God, say that again, in words of one syllable. Do you think I'm going to let any one else marry you? Oh, darling, and to think I nearly lost you.

Liza was suddenly terribly excited. But that couldn't happen without the preliminaries, without leading David up to it; and that meant a hard heart, and a mind which arranged things for its own benefit and didn't mind if it hurt every one else. And she wouldn't see David before she saw Walter this evening.

Then Liza imagined herself actually married to David, and in bed with him. She thought, all the time I should be pretending he was Walter.

Liza stared at the gas-fire, feeling its heat round her eyes, and saw more clearly and frighteningly than she ever had before, what happened to you when you lived for some one else.

❀

At a quarter to six Liza came in from shopping and the hairdresser's, to hear the telephone ringing. She ran upstairs, but before she could reach it it had stopped, and the receiver only rattled when she picked it up. She thought, Walter can't come to-night. She turned the oven on; at six she would put the guinea-fowl in. She thought, it's no good, he won't come. She shut the lid of the baking-tin on the guinea-fowl, and felt sick with misery. She took the shopping from the divan, putting the new tin of black paint on the table. She had seen it in the shop, the man had said it was the last they had; that was a sort of omen, after to-night she would be able to paint the footmark out, to say good-bye to the Past and face a new and lovely Future; and if she found herself moving out of the flat after however long it took to buy a special licence, well, buying the paint was just the kind of thing to make that happen.

At a minute to six the telephone rang again.

'Hullo,' said a pleasant voice which, in the relief of knowing it wasn't Walter, she couldn't place at once. 'A Happy New Year to you.' Then she could.

'A Happy New Year to you, David,' she said,

'I hope the office didn't think you were late,' said David; she hadn't seen him or heard his voice since Tuesday morning, when she got out of his taxi in Chancery Lane. She said, 'Not really. I hope yours didn't.'

'Mine is sending me to New York again. For two months. Can I come round now and say good-bye?'

'Please, yes.'

'In two minutes, then. Good-bye.'

❀

David fingered his tie and said, looking round, 'This is all very nice.'

'Well, it's clean. It will be better when I've got the carpet down.' The carpet was still rolled up, with its string and label.

'Can I help?'

'No, let's leave it,' said Liza, and rubbed her hands on her overall, remembering that she still wore a hair-net. She had put two glasses and the decanter ready for Walter. She poured out the sherry, and moved the paint-tin to the mantelpiece.

'Thank you,' said David, and looked at his wrist-watch. 'I've got ten minutes. I left the taxi outside.' He lifted his glass. 'Another Happy New Year.'

Liza lifted hers. 'Please sit in that chair. I never do.'

David grinned. 'Thank you'; and he sat down and unbuttoned his overcoat.

'Your office is being very sudden,' said Liza.

'Not quite so bad as it sounds. I've got to go to my parents' to collect some things. I sail to-morrow night. I rang you up last night, and several times to-day. I think I got all the wrong times.'

'I went to a party.'

'A good one?'

'No.'

David grinned, and picked his glass up from the floor. He was sitting forward in the armchair, and Liza thought he looked very tired again. There was a silence.

Liza said, 'New York must be lovely.'

'Yes,' said David. 'I think you'd like it.'

There was another silence. David finished his sherry and stood up and put the glass back on the tray. 'Thank you.'

Liza stood up too. She thought, I must tell him. I must.

David felt in his pocket and brought out an envelope. 'I suppose you haven't got a stamp?'

Liza looked in her handbag. 'I think I have, for once.' There was a strip of three halfpenny stamps and some stamp-paper in the white kid partition, with the bus-ticket and the hairpin. She put the stamps in his hand. She said, 'Look at the bit out of the mantelpiece. It would be because my tenants had either a quarrel or a party.'

David grinned and felt in another pocket. 'I infer that they had plenty of both.' He brought out twopence.

Liza handed him a halfpenny. 'Well, they used to sort of live together.'

David tore the first stamp off and licked it. 'Don't they any more?'

'Intermittently,' said Liza. 'I think they've reached a deadlock.' Her heart was thumping. 'I suppose it's because there's no outside reason why they shouldn't get married.'

David tore off the second stamp. He said, 'Well, you know,' and stopped, and gave his grin. 'Speaking in initial capitals, I suppose that One of the Things Life Teaches Us—' he stopped again.

'Yes?'

David licked the third stamp and stuck it on before he said, 'I suppose I mean that that sort of thing rather tends to defeat its purpose.'

'Yes.'

David turned the letter over, and back again.

'You do know about Walter and me, don't you?'

'Sort of.' He put the letter in his pocket.

'I don't want you to say anything,' said Liza. 'I only wanted to know that you knew.'

David grinned, and buttoned his overcoat.

Liza's tinny church clock, which she hadn't heard since she moved back to the flat, clanged a *ding-dong*. David looked at his wrist-watch. There was a spitting crackle from the kitchen, and Liza could smell the roasting guinea-fowl.

They stood in silence for a moment; and then they both began to speak at once, and both stopped and laughed.

'You first,' said David.

'Well,' said Liza, 'it sounds rather silly now.'

'Not so silly as mine.'

'I was only going to say, please take care of yourself.'

'Well, you know,' said David. 'So was I.' He picked up his hat, and they stood in silence again. Then, with his grin, he stooped and kissed her, half on her mouth and half on her cheek; and put on his black hat and looked older and paler, and said, 'God bless you. Good-bye,' and ran downstairs.

Liza stood there until the sound of the taxi had whirred into the faint traffic-hum in the distance. Then she looked at the clock. Walter would be here at seven, and she had to have a bath, and dress, and varnish her nails. She knelt down and began to struggle with the knots in the string round the carpet.

❁

Liza said to the gas-fire, 'We—we're defeating our purpose.' She was sitting on the floor, with Walter in the armchair behind her; she felt his knees move as he put his beer-glass down. They had finished dinner, and piled the washing-up round the kitchen; and it was ten o'clock.

Walter said nothing. He didn't move, he didn't speak. Liza was frightened. She ran a finger along the carpet; it was like the plush on Major Hobie's sofa; smooth with you, sharp against you. She thought, everything I think now, and see, and hear, and say, reminds me of Walter. And here I am putting it all into a gamble; win everything or lose everything; and I can't go back.

Walter stood up; she moved aside, and he walked soundlessly across the carpet, and banged the kitchen door shut. She was looking at his shoes by the table, thinking, those were the ones I cleaned when Mr. Thorne told me his life-story. The bang slapped against her ear-drums. Walter came back to the armchair, and said, sitting on its arm, with one knee against her shoulder, 'It depends on what you call our purpose.'

Liza thought, yes, your purpose and mine have never been the same; no, they were that first evening. She said, 'I don't know. I do know. I know that at first all I wanted was—I don't know. Something beautiful.'

She felt Walter's hand on her neck. She thought, don't, don't; we're not friends now, or lovers. We're enemies, fighting. We've always been enemies. All lovers are. Walter said, taking his hand away:

'And what do you think I wanted?'

'The same as I did.' She was swept with a wave of anger. 'And some one to cook your dinners, and iron your suits. Yes, I know that's a lie. I know all about unselfishness being selfishness. Everything I say comes back on me. It always does.'

'No, not everything,' said Walter. 'But that does. My God.' He got up again, and walked round the room. Liza thought, he's angry; and I'm not now, I'm frightened; and I can't look at his face. Walter went back to the arm of the chair, and said:

'Ducky, don't let's lose our tempers. We will if you like, and you can tell me all the things you've thought about me and never said; and I know them all.'

Liza said nothing. There was nothing to say.

'You see what I mean, ducky. Let's be what they call reasonable.'

'Reasonable,' said Liza. 'Reasonable. You know you've got all the reason on your side. I've only got what's right and what's wrong and what's true and—oh, I don't know.'

'Such as?'

'*You* know. You know everything's upside down. You know we began where we should have ended. I don't mean ended, I mean gone on to the next stage. How *could* we, when I've never known from one minute to another where we are? Every second of a whole year I've had to think, if I do this you'll love me, if I do that you won't. Oh, I don't *know*.' She thought, it's no good, it's no good. There must be a right way of saying it; oh, if I could only make my words go like my thoughts.

'Well, ducky,' said Walter's voice behind her, serious, but maddeningly normal, 'there's no answer to that. If you've felt like that all along, well, you should have said so a long time ago. No, that's an insult to both of us. *I* know how you felt. And I was always stopping and checking up on you, wasn't I?'

'Yes,' said Liza miserably.

'And you always said, all right, let's go on as we are. And I thought, or was justified in thinking, you've weighed up the for and against, and the for was worth it all. And I think I've been perfectly bloody, and I won't say, well, I'm a man; and that's a cowardly way of saying it.'

'But it's true,' said Liza. 'And you don't have to tell me about men wanting one thing and women another. I know it all. I want security. Why shouldn't I?'

'We both know a hell of a lot to-night,' said Walter. 'That's the trouble. Darling, I shall now get down to some very brass tacks.' Liza was frightened. She waited for Walter's voice.

'Ducky. You want us to get married.'

Liza thought, that's the first time we've ever said so, straight out. Her heart thumped wildly, hoping, hoping; and a voice inside her said, it's no good, how could it be?

'Darling,' said Walter, 'what would happen if we did?'

Liza thought, I can't bear it, I can't. This is the moment to say the right thing in the right way. She said:

'It would be the same as it is now.'

'Yes,' said Walter. And at that one small word her heart seemed to stop, and race on. But it didn't mean that, *yes* was just a word. She said:

'We're the same people as we always were. We've always loved each other. And it's a year now, and we've—we've built something up. We can't unlive that.'

'No,' said Walter. *No* was just a word too. 'Ducky, what we've built up is a ghastly and complicated structure for getting at each other.'

'You don't get at me. If I get at you—'

'Yes, I do, ducky. Don't pretend to be stupid. I'm horrible to you because I know exactly how to hurt you, and how to have my own way. And if you get at me, it's because you love me, and it's my fault, but you *do* get at me. You get at my freedom. God help us, what a silly word.'

'Of course, I get at it,' said Liza. 'You throw it at me. Sometimes I think you invented it to make me unhappy. *I* don't stop you from being free. No; I do now. I know that. If we were married I shouldn't because I shouldn't want to. I should be myself, and you'd have all the freedom you ever had, and more. Because I should be free too. Oh, don't you *see*?' She thought, I've never seen it so clearly. Oh, he *must* see.

'If we were married,' said Walter, still in that maddeningly sensible voice, 'I can foresee only one thing. I should have given my first hostage to fortune. And I don't want to. Yet.'

Liza had a wild surge of hope. One day he would want to, and he would still be the same person. The right words, now, would make him want to, now. She said:

'Why don't you?'

'Why does your hair curl?'

Liza thought, that was a year ago to-morrow. In this flat, almost at this time in the evening, with all the furniture in the same places. Square one. She thought suddenly of David, and said:

'Some people are wise and don't mind growing up. You're not wise. You're—you're nothing but an escapist.' And she was very frightened indeed. She had said something he didn't want to know about himself.

Walter moved; she heard him stand up, and waited, with a sinking misery, for his voice. It came.

'All right. Now we're throwing the china.'

'Oh, darling.' She turned round, for the first time. 'I didn't mean it. I don't want you to be anything you aren't. Only I can't bear this any longer. Say yes or no, and we'll get married, or we'll never see each other again.'

Walter knelt down and put his arms round her. 'Darling, I'm terribly sorry. And I do love you so much.'

The gas-fire still hissed, the electric clock still whirred faintly, and the carpet still felt like Major Hobie's sofa. But nothing meant anything any more. It was all over. She said:

'All right.'

'I can't say anything more. I don't know why it's happened. Yes, I do, and I suppose it had to. Oh, darling, and it was all so lovely.'

It was the Past. The gas-fire blurred, and Liza burst into the most dreadful tears. She saw the flat, white, bright, coloured with the books and the curtains. 'I've got to go on living here. Alone.'

'Please, sweetheart,' said Walter; and she thought he was crying too, but she didn't like to look.

❦

Liza got up and fetched her biggest handkerchief and blew her nose for what she hoped was the last time. Walter blew his nose too, and then he said:

'And now I suppose we go to bed.'

Liza sat down beside him. 'Yes. It's rather sort of frightening.' Walter took her hand, and she thought, we're on the same side again. We can't get at each other any more.

She said, 'I'll make some tea.' She put the tray on the floor and plugged the kettle into the wall. When the steam became a jet she said, 'Is it boiling now?'

Walter put his hand on her neck. 'No, ducky. Three and a half seconds more.'

'You always know. How do you know, darling?'

'I know everything. Your hair does look nice.' He kissed it. Liza poured out his tea; a very little milk, very weak tea, and one lump of sugar; and they sat on the floor, side by side.

Liza said, 'Did you have a nice lunch with your uncle?'

'Marvellous. The old boy will kill himself one day. But, ducky, I must tell you what happened on the Underground on the way back.'

'Why the Underground, darling?'

'The car had a very small mouse in the works.'

'Oh, poor car. What happened in the Underground, darling? Something awful?'

'No,' said Walter, kissing her hair again, 'just a small human drama.' He settled himself against the armchair. 'I was sitting by the door, all smug because it was a nice new train, and wondering what my friends would say if I got my hair polished up like the brilliantine ads, and opposite me were two middle-aged spinsters who seemed not to know about their hats, if you see what I mean.'

'Oh, I do, darling,' said Liza.

'I knew you would.' He threw his coat across the floor. 'Well, the hats aren't really the point. The point is that they were next to the door, and an awfully militant man, a bit like Major Hobie only angrier, was standing with his back to them sideways, I mean against the glass and at right angles to the door. Well, between him and them was his suit-case, straining fearfully at its one lock. It had two, but the other one was open. Well, now the drama begins. Only I must have some more tea first.'

Liza took his cup.

'The spotlight is trained on the woman nearest the door,' said Walter, 'and she is going through the most enchanting gamut of no doubt the nearest she's been to emotions in a wasted life. Glance at suit-case. First call of duty. Repulse of call. Thank you, ducky. Call persisting. Woman looking at suit-case and at angry man's back and then up at advertisements above me, call horning in again, woman pursing lips and glaring at suit-case lock as if that might keep it shut. Now the other woman takes it up. Roughly the same gamut, but with less range, making about two expressions do for everything.'

'Do the women know each other?'

'Not yet. Well, now it gets exciting. Something snaps inside the first woman. She leans over and digs the angry man very gently in the back. The angry man takes no notice. She digs quite hard, and the angry man takes no notice again, but this time on purpose, as if to say, women! women! always digging you in the back and knitting pullovers you can't wear. Well, now, darling, this is where I come in.'

'Oh, darling,' said Liza, 'how exciting. How?'

'Well, a combined speechless message flashes from the two stricken women. You're a man. So's he. You do it. Save us from ever being certain about men's underclothes.'

'Oh, darling. And do you save them?'

'Certainly I do. Remember that I've had about three kinds of drink at lunch. I flash back a message of cheer, and, tacking round the angry man to sort of warn him, I am just about to say, excuse me, sir, but I think your suit-case is about to burst open with an appalling explosion.'

'Oh, darling,' said Liza. 'You are brave. Why don't you?'

'Because, ducky, I remember that no word has yet been spoken. I mustn't spoil it. So I point, dropping my lower jaw and bringing it to with a snap.'

'Oh, darling. You are clever. And does *he* spoil it?'

'Surprisingly, no. He's suitably thunderstruck. He lunges at the case and squeezes it roughly into shape, and shuts the open lock and opens the shut lock, catches the women's eye and dives at the open lock, gives me a sort of hail and farewell look and goes back to his angry thoughts.' Walter pulled off his socks and reached for his coat. 'I've just remembered, ducky. I got this in a cracker. A triumph of matter over mind.'

Liza took it. It was a little pink celluloid animal, she couldn't tell what sort; it was all ridge, where the two halves joined.

She thought, when Walter pulled this cracker he didn't know. Nor did I. 'Darling, it's heavenly. What about the two women?'

'Well,' said Walter, 'drawn together by this cataclysm of events, their gazes meet. They nod, as if to say, it would have burst open. Yes. Burst open. Then they both stare at the ads above me, and we all spend the rest of the journey not catching any one's eye. End.' He stood up. 'I'll race you into bed.'

Liza stood up too, and thought, this is having only so many more hours to live.

※

The back page of the *Observer* said *Sunday, January 2nd*. Walter dropped it and got up from the armchair. 'Ducky, I must get.'

'Yes,' said Liza, and looked automatically at the clock, which said twenty-past eleven. It could have said anything.

Walter shut his suit-case. 'Have I left anything, do you think?'

Liza went into the bathroom and took the spare shaving-brush from the cupboard over the basin. She said, 'I can't think of anything else.'

'I'd forgotten I had it,' said Walter. He opened the case and put the brush in. Liza said, 'Your pyjamas.'

Walter put the pyjamas in and shut the case. 'I'm sure there must be something else.'

'I don't think so. I cleared things out last September.'

Walter shut the case again, and they stood there in silence. Liza said, 'I think last night was better than it's ever been before.'

'Yes,' said Walter. 'So do I.'

They stood in silence again. Liza looked at him. She looked at his hair, and his forehead, and his eyebrows, and his eyes, and his nose, and his mouth, and his chin, and the whole of his face together. It was here, in front of her, now.

Walter took her in his arms. 'Oh, darling, darling.'

Liza didn't speak. There were a few seconds left to say all she hadn't said in a year. She put her face up against his chin. Walter bent his head and they kissed; a long and empty kiss which could add nothing to the Past and gave nothing to the Future.

Walter drew back and stood for a moment looking at her. She thought he was going to say something. Then he smiled, and flipped her neck, and, snatching up his suit-case, ran downstairs. Liza didn't move till she heard the car start. Then she went over to the window, and watched it as far as she could see up the road; a dark blue car with the only number-plate in the world; and to-day they had been going to Kent because they'd never been there together. She thought, and now we never will.

She began to put the breakfast-things in the kitchen. It was still piled up with dinner-things; she would wash up later. Walter had left half a piece of toast, and there were two cigarette-ends in the pink marbled ash-tray. She emptied it, thinking, I was always going to buy another. When she had put everything in the kitchen, she folded the cloth away in the cupboard, and saw the new paint-brush. She took the new tin of black paint from the mantelpiece, thinking, I'd meant to put it away when I tidied the flat yesterday.

Liza stood there, holding the paint-tin, her eyes on the gas-fire. She thought, no, he won't ring up. There are two people in the world who can never see each other again, and they are Walter and me.

She looked at the tin, and thought, I must do something; and she spread the *Observer* on the floor, and knelt down, and saw the date, and thought, and I'm wearing my pink dressing-gown. She smiled. It hurt to smile.

She thought, one day we shall see each other again, and it will be worse than if we didn't. We shall be friends. There are two people in the world who can never be lovers again. I suppose one day I may be saying to some one, oh, I think Walter's running round with some girl or other. And that's all I shall know. Because it's all I shall care.

Liza stirred the brush in the tin and looked round the flat. The Stevenson, with the essay about children; the little pink animal on the middle bookshelf; the armchair, still with the dent in the cushion. Everything in the flat. She thought, it won't get better, it will get worse, because to-day I can think that I saw Walter to-day, and to-morrow it will be yesterday, and next Sunday a week ago.

Then she thought, more than anything in the world I want to see David; only because of Walter. And I can't, for two months; and perhaps not then. I don't know. No one knows about the Future.

Then she turned the carpet back, and, starting at the footmark, began to paint the floor.

Afterword

There is something curiously modern about the chief preoccupations of Angela Milne's only published novel, *One Year's Time*. If you were to pick any page at random, there is a high likelihood that you would find hint, mention or even a lengthy discussion of one of the two main themes that recur: sex and money.

The novel was published in 1942, and is set in a slightly indeterminate time in the late 30s – they are still at the stage of talking about 'the probable date of the war', without seeming to think it will be in the immediate future. As such, it may have surprised some readers that Walter so casually says that the thing he likes best in the world is sex, or to find how quickly Liza and Walter go from meeting each other to 'me in bed with nothing on, and him kneeling there with only his socks'. Liza and Walter have no qualms about discussing their past sexual history with each other, and Walter even casually mentions having had an affair with a married woman. Not, of course, that anybody should think that such encounters were invented in a later decade – rather, Milne writes about them with a candidness that doesn't seem to match most other novels about middle-class life from the period.

In their circle it is clearly not uncommon to live together before marriage: Liza muses to herself about friends,

Chloe and William Driffield, who had got married after living together for two years. Liza wondered, as she walked up the four flights of stairs, what had decided them. It wouldn't be anything as obvious as a baby.

The 'obvious' nature of the baby (the reader never learns if s/he exists or not, or, indeed, anything else about the Driffields) shows that unconventionality only goes so far. An impending child was still considered, even among the modern set, as a just cause for marriage – and Liza and Walter are not unorthodox enough to flaunt their unmarried state in front of hotel staff and hotel acquaintances. Walter, as a man, doesn't need to adopt any disguise or even lie about his name; Liza, meanwhile, puzzles over how best to write 'Mrs Latimer' in the guest book and goes to Woolworths to buy a cheap wedding ring. She is the one who has to worry that it might be identified as a fake.

The idea of it as 'fake' is quite subjective, and a sign of Liza's middle-classness. The ring certainly wasn't gold – most likely it was made with recently popularised Bakelite – but plenty of working-class young women would have chosen their ring at Woolworths for genuine weddings. As a popular 1920s song, 'A Woolworth Wedding' by R. P. Weston and Bert Lee, says:

> We'll have a Woolworth wedding, Sweetheart you and I.
> Everything except the grand piano, down at Woolworths we can buy.
> We'll buy the wedding ring there, it won't be gold it's true
> But our love is eighteen carat, so any kind of ring will do

It is only Liza's fears about the visible disparity between her ring and her class that would identify the ring as fraudulent. Somebody who looks, behaves, speaks like her would not be expected to wear a ring like that.

These are sops to appearances: Liza feels no inward moral anxiety about pre-marital sex (a term which, in the period, largely referred to an engaged couple having a sexual relationship before marriage – if there

☸ ☸ ☸

was no promise of marriage in place, it would be called fornication). She feels rather more shame about the idea of being, or being seen as, perpetually single.

A term Liza often returns to is 'Bachelor Girl', with those capitals making it clear that the Bachelor Girl is an archetype, rather than denoting an individual with their own characteristics. It appears in the first paragraph of the novel, as Liza looks around her flat – a bedsit or studio apartment:

> There was a scrubby patch on the carpet where she had washed the ink out; and two cushions hardly counted as heaping a divan, and chintz curtains weren't necessarily chintzy, and they weren't gay, they were just curtains hanging up. She thought, oh, all these things the newspaper say about what they call Bachelor Girls.

What *do* the newspapers say about Bachelor Girls? The term had originated in the US in 1895, according to the *Oxford English Dictionary*, before making its way across the Atlantic. As *Queen* magazine noted in 1906, 'The term "old maid" is now seldom or never heard; the expression "bachelor girl" has taken its place.' Initially it was a way to lose the negative connotations of 'old maid' or 'spinster', and to detach female singleness from a host of stereotypes about unattractiveness, desperation and melancholy. For instance, in Marjorie Hillis's cheerful 1936 non-fiction book for single women, *Live Alone and Like It*, she suggests that the label 'spinster' is 'rapidly becoming extinct – or, at least, being relegated to another period, like the bustle and reticule', while Mary Scharlieb chose the title of her 1929 book *The Bachelor Woman and Her Problems* because 'one or two ladies were very unwilling to accept the old-world appellation of "spinster"'.

Despite this optimistic origin of the term, Liza's reflections suggest that it is held in less high regard. She sees the chintz curtains as being vulnerable to being synecdochically interpreted for her whole lifestyle

– either 'chintzy', a term used to mean 'suburban, unfashionable, petit-bourgeois', or 'gay', in the sense of showy and bright. The latter might seem innocuous enough, but there is a theme throughout the novel of 'bachelor girls' using flimsy brightness as a way to cover up their own lack. 'Denied the richness of living, finding its small pleasures in a new shillingworth of gas-fire or something nice for lunch' or, as Liza reflects about herself at one point, 'under-sexed, cheerful to make up for it'.

But it isn't just the newspapers who disparage the bachelor girl. Despite initially seeming to stand against its use as an insult, once Liza is no longer single she also starts looking down on unmarried women. When she sees two women across a room at a hostel, she thinks:

> I suppose they lived in another hostel just like this, and waited for each other in the wrong rooms, and got all excited about it, and even more excited over meals; and nothing has happened to either of them, ever.

Liza, notably, often determines which strangers she thinks must be unmarried women based on very little actual evidence. In an earlier conversation with Walter, she is similarly dismissive of an archetype of the Bachelor Girl:

> "You have to wear a collar and tie and have square legs to be a bachelor girl."
> "It's awfully unfair that they don't call men spinster boys. I mean men who aren't married. Why do you think they don't?"
> "I suppose they aren't a new enough invention," said Walter.

Unmarried men and women had both, of course, existed for as long as the institution of marriage – the idea of the bachelor girl being a 'new invention' is only a reflection on the range of attributes and characteristics commonly associated with unmarried women by the popular press and in the popular consciousness at the time. While the peak of mockery against the 'two million surplus women' had come a couple of decades earlier – there were 1.75 million more women than men in the aftermath of the First World War, and consequently many who couldn't marry – clearly the censor persisted.

While independence might be considered a virtue of the self-sufficient, unmarried woman, it is another quality that is warped into an anxiety about how Liza is perceived, specifically about budgeting:

> "I can't *help* feeling like that about money," said Liza, as they walked up the lane to the car. "You would if you'd always had to earn your own living. I mean all of it, till a year and a half ago." She thought, that sounds like getting at Walter for not really earning his. And it makes me a Bachelor Girl; that's awful."

Liza's preoccupation with money is the other major thread throughout *One Year's Time*. She is not avaricious for it, nor has the miserable pride of characters like Gordon Comstock in George Orwell's *Keep the Aspidistra Flying* (1936) or the genuine poverty of the Hardcastle family *Love on the Dole* (1933) by Walter Greenwood. There is never any particular sense of precariousness that she might become destitute – like the Woolworths wedding ring, she is seemingly buoyed away from poverty by her class – but pounds, shillings and pence are still a continuous undercurrent in her mind.

Liza is paid £3 10s. a week for her work as a secretary – £182 a year, assuming she gets the paid holiday which had been legislated by the Holidays with Pay Act 1938. Additionally, 'for the last eighteen months she had had a little money of her own – twenty-five pounds a quarter from a dead great-uncle'. With a total of £282 a year, Liza has an income of about £23,000 in today's money. She certainly isn't rich, but nor is she destitute. When she checks her bank account and finds (on a slip of paper handed to her by a discreet young clerk) that she has 15s.

1od., she 'gave the man a smile which meant that she only had a bank account for fun'. It's also the impression that the reader is likely to get. Money is always on her mind, but without the prospect of real danger. There are times when she has to remind herself not to be angry about a small quantity of money – as in the quote below – but she still considers impulsively buying a 'lovely suit in Jaeger's window; my grey suit isn't new any more'.

> They went to the pay-desk and Liza said, "I'll get change." She gave the girl a ten-shilling note. She waited for Pauline to squeak and say, "How much do I owe you?" But Pauline was staring into the street, looking quite surprisingly thoughtful. Liza told herself that it was only one and twopence extra, and nothing to be so angry about.

Liza's judgements about others are often based on how they treat money. She notices when Pauline's order at a restaurant 'cost sixpence more than anything else', and one of the things against Carl is that he borrows half-crowns from his girlfriend Pauline (and presumably doesn't repay them). Liza acts nonchalantly but is determined in her negotiations over subletting him her flat – for which she pays 35s. a week, and manages to sublet at two and a half guineas (a guinea being 21s.). She reflects on the profit that 'seventeen and six a week added to her income made her rich'. The term recurs in her head with some dryness – 'she was rich' is also her reflection when a meal costs 8d. and she'd anticipated 1od. But on the other hand, when a cheque for rent of her flat is delayed, it is an annoyance rather than a disaster. She is able to leave her job without huge concern.

This security comes, of course, with some financial dependence on Walter. One of the first things she wonders about him is 'exactly how much money Walter had in a year', though 'she found that she would hate to know exactly how much'. Liza is from a class where exactitude about income is not classy and financial security is both a blessing and unspoken. It's not the only safety that she looks ahead to. Despite her modernity about sexual ethics, she believes that marriage is the only way she can be herself – free of the taint of the 'bachelor girl', but also free of the possibility of rejection. In a period where divorce was still very uncommon, a (genuine) wedding ring came with all sorts of guarantees:

> She could never be herself till she was married. When they were married she could be nasty to Walter when it was necessary, because she wouldn't be afraid of losing him. She could tell him he was lazy, she could make him a proper barrister and bully him to write his book. And all she did now was stop him working; not by saying anything, by saying nothing; because he was afraid, because at the heart of their relationship, instead of the courage to take each other for life, was a blank, a fear on her side, on his – she sat down again and thought, trying to put herself in Walter's place. Yes, he was being perfectly reasonable; he had always told her what he wanted, she had always said she wanted it too, because she was afraid.

Liza might be modern in many ways, but *One Year's Time* is a novel poised between two periods. The couple live lives that are very distant from their parents' generation – but are not willing to detach themselves wholly from the appearances of those mores and morals. And, for the most part, it is the women of the 1940s who bore the brunt of managing the balance between progressiveness and appearances – and, at least in Liza's mind, still needed the security of marriage.

Simon Thomas

Series consultant **Simon Thomas** created the middlebrow blog Stuck in a Book in 2007. He is also the co-host of the popular podcast Tea or Books? Simon has a PhD from Oxford University in Interwar Literature.